TOEIC®
NEW

金色證書一擊必殺
—聽力全真模擬試題

學習有捷徑
夢想最接近

使用說明之 *1*

多益的聽力部分有哪些題型？

　　多益的聽力部分分為四個大題，分別為「照片描述」、「應答問題」、「簡短對話」、「簡短獨白」，各大題的詳細內容介紹及作答方式請看以下：

▶ Part 1：「照片描述」

　　在 Part 1 的題目中，考生只會看到一張張的照片，題本上不會有文字。錄音會朗誦出四個選項，考生必須選擇出與本圖片最為符合的選項做為此題答案，選項只會朗誦一遍。

例題：

(A)They are in a conference room.

(B)The kids are raising their hands.

(C)The kids are having an exam.

(D)They are eating breakfast.

正確答案為 (B)

解題小撇步：

・有時會聽見一些「不確定是對或錯」的選項，可能是因為考生認為在圖片中看不清楚或被物品擋住而猶豫不決、模稜兩可、不敢下決定，通常這樣的選項就可以排除了，因為考題設計成正確的選項就一定能從圖片中看出來。

・請注意，出現在圖片較為中間、較大或較明顯的人或物不一定就是正確答案，建議考生還是要詳細觀察整張圖片。

▶ Part 2：「應答問題」

在 Part 2 的題目中，考生在考題本上只會看到一整排文字寫道：「Mark your answer on your answer sheet.」這是因為這個部份的題目及選項皆從音檔出題，錄音中首先會念出一句話，考生必須從接下來念出的三個選項中選出最適合的答案，題目及選項只會朗誦一遍。

例題：

你會先聽見：Did you have dinner at the restaurant yesterday?

然後再聽見：(A) Yes, it lasted all day.

(B) No, I went to the movie with my girlfriend.

(C) Yes, the client was nice.

正確答案為 (B)

· 這部分沒有印製題目及選項於題目本上，因此請考生務必仔細聆聽，否則一晃神就不知道該如何解答了。

· 若話者提出問句，請注意問句的類型為「Wh 問句」還是「Yes-No」問句，若為前者，回答為「Yes」或「No」的選項可以首先排除。

▶ Part 3：「簡短對話」

　　Part 3 的部分考生會在題目本上看到問題及選項或有部分甚至有圖表出現，並且會在音檔中聽見兩人或兩人以上的對話，考生必須在聽完對話之後從下列選項中一題題選出正確答案，對話只會朗誦一遍。

例題：

Questions 32-34 refer to the following conversation.

Woman   Hello, sir. Would you please put down your tray table?

Man   Oh, sure. Sorry.

Woman   No problem. Would you like pork or beef ?

Boy   What about my kid's meal?

Man   Quiet, Bob. It will come later. I'll have pork, please.

Boy   I'm so hungry now! I can't wait!

Woman   The kid's meal is on the way. You just need to have a bit more patience, because it's gonna come with a surprise.

Boy   A surprise? Yeah!

Woman   Your pork chop with rice, sir. Please enjoy.

32. Where most likely is the conversation taking place?

    (A) In a buffet restaurant.

    (B) On an airplane.

    (C) At the food court.

    (D) In a fast food restaurant.

    正確答案為 (B)

33. According to the conversation, what is true about the man?

    (A) He is the captain of the flight.

    (B) He is a flight attendant.

    (C) He is the boy's father.

    (D) He likes pork better than beef.

    正確答案為 (D)

34. What do we know about the boy's meal?

    (A) It's meat-free.

    (B) It comes with a gift.

    (C) It's complimentary.

    (D) It's undercooked.

    正確答案為 (B)

解題小撇步

· 考生除了要十分清楚哪句話是誰說的之外，有時題目所問到的內容在對話裡不一定有明說，可能是隱含的語意，如以上例題中，只說了「come with a surprise.」卻沒有明說是什麼樣的驚喜，考生必須充分瞭解對話情境才能選出正確選項。

· 在多益改制後新增了圖表題，考生要能一心多用，聽著對話的同時也要對照圖表，並要充分理解圖表內容。

▶ Part 4：「簡短獨白」

　　Part 4 也是題目和選項會印製在題目本上，但這部分的音檔為一個人的獨白，例如：會議報告內容、電話留言…等，考生需在聆聽完獨白之後選出各題的正確答案，並填寫於答案卷上，每題獨白只會朗誦一遍。

例題：

Questions 77-79 refer to the following announcement.

W Before we wrap up the meeting, I have an announcement to make. As most of you may have known, I am transferring to Tokyo headquarters next month. Jessica will succeed me as the Director of IT Department. I hope you can give her the same support and assistance. I have been working in this branch since I graduated from university, so it's really not easy for me to say goodbye. It's been a great experience working with you all. I hope we can stay in touch.

77. What is this announcement mainly about?

(A) A notice of relocation

(B) A change of business hours

(C) A notice of temporary closure

(D) A change of personnel

正確答案為 (D)

78. What information is not given in this announcement?

    (A) The speaker's replacement

    (B) The speaker's contact number

    (C) The speaker's current position

    (D) The speaker's future work place

正確答案為 (B)

79. What most likely is the reason the speaker's leaving her current position?

    (A) She got laid off.

    (B) She is retiring.

    (C) She is job-hopping to another company.

    (D) She has been promoted.

正確答案為 (D)

解題小撇步

· 獨白的主題通常是會議報告內容、電話留言…等，通常這類內容的重點會在獨自一開始就提到，請考生萬分注意。

· 常會有考生在獨白聽到一半就開始恍神了，惡魔就藏在細節中，通常內容常會有關於話者的相關細節，以及在最後常會包含話者之後要做的動作或發生的事，請一定要專心聆聽到最後。

· 這部分同樣也有圖表題，考生是否能在聽獨白同時邊對照圖表，並看懂圖表為一大解題重點。

使用說明之 *2*

新制多益改了哪些部份？

　　接下來就是大家最關心的：「新制多益到底是什麼？到底改了什麼？」最新多益改制除了改變題型之外，題目量的分配也有調整，以下為各位考生簡單整理出了新制多益聽力部分所做的更改！

▶ Part 1：「照片描述」

	目前題型	新制題型
題數	10 題	6 題
題目類型	從選項中選出符合圖片的描述。	題目類型不變。

▶ Part 2：「應答問題」

	目前題型	新制題型
題數	30 題	25 題
題目類型	從音檔出應答問題及選項。	題目類型不變。

▶ **Part 3：「簡短對話」**

	目前題型	新制題型
題數	30 題（3*10）	39 題（3*13）
題目類型	• 10 組對話，每組 3 個問題	• 13 組對話，每組 3 個問題 • 頻繁地來回交談 • 部分對話會有兩名以上的對話者 • 對話中包含口語化表達（例如：going to → gonna） • 測驗對話背景或隱含語意 • 新增圖表問題

▶ **Part 4：「簡短獨白」**

	目前題型	新制題型
題數	30 題（3*10）	30 題（3*10）
題目類型	• 10 則獨白，每則 3 個問題	• 10 則獨白，每則 3 個問題 • 測驗獨白內容的背景或隱含語意 • 新增圖表問題

Preface 作者序－李宇凡

「什麼！多益又要改制了！」、「天啊！
改制多益要怎麼應考啊！」這兩個問題大概是從
ETS 官方今年七月宣布將在 2018 年 3 月於台灣
正式實施新制多益考試的新聞稿出來之後學生
最常跟我說的話。可以看出這次多益大動作改
制，已經有許多考生開始尋求對應措施，我想這
正是我該出馬的時候了！

　　新制多益，新的考試不只對學生，對我們這些老師來說也是一種
考驗，要怎麼去幫助學生應考、要從什麼角度去剖析考試，一個個都
在測試老師們的專業度，以我個人來說，我最建議的就是從模擬試題
做起了。充分的練習除了訓練自己在指定時間內完成試題，培養在聽
力部分的注意力，同時也是認識新式題型的好機會。

　　為什麼必須要先透過模擬題來認識新題型呢？那是因為，考生必
須要先借由自己實際的操作、練習才可以得知自己不擅長新制題型的
部分，從而才能進一步想辦法去解決它、克服它。

另外，在練習模擬試題後的參閱解析動作也極其重要，解析中包含了詳細的題目內容、題型分析、單字補充以及解題說明，反覆的琢磨其中內容，一定能夠有效地獲取優良學習成果。特別是聽力部分這次增加了不少口語化的表現，除了在聆聽音檔時要更加注意之外，經由解析反覆確認口語化用法更是極其重要。

　　　模擬試題看起來普通，卻是對付新制多益考試的第一道防線，希望考生們務必在正式上場之前先小試身手一番，並期盼能藉由這些試題給予各位應考新制多益的信心，成功獲取理想佳績。

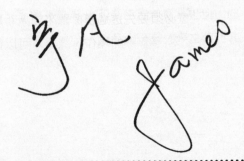

Preface 作者序－蔡文宜

TOEIC 多益考試是現今主流的英語能力測驗之一，不只時常被用來測試自我英語能力，甚至是許多學校機關的畢業門檻以及求職的利器。其主要針對的是在英語社會求職的需要，因此出題方向也著重於商業實用性質，有著如此信效度的多益考試據上次於 2006 年改制以來，時隔 10 年以上再度改制，臺灣也即將在明年 2018 年的 3 月開始實施，許多考生開始侷促不安，到底多益改制要怎麼因應才好？

多益的聽力考試一直以來都是以「國際英語」而知名，測驗中包含了較為主流的美國、英國、加拿大、澳洲四種口音，且題型越發與時俱進，不只會增加話者來回交談以更貼近日常生活，部分對話增加至兩名以上的說話者，甚至對話有更加口語化的趨勢，反映出日常生活之中社交及職場英語的使用習慣，這對學習實用英文絕對是有效的，但也就意味著考生不能再讀死書了，而是要靈活運用，這無疑對某些考生來說是一大考驗。

考生除了能在自己的日常生活中運用各項資訊媒體增進「聽」的能力之外，更可藉由以我們多年教學經驗出題的本書，搭配精心繪製改制多益將出題的表格類問題，詳解更是除了中譯、單字之外更添加了出題類型說明及分析，讓考生能「懂」，有「聽」有「懂」，考生才能百「考」百勝。

　　這次多益官方睽違已久的改制，相信許多人已經很有感了，尤其是望一眼市面上的多益參考書籍無一不與考生心情「神同步」，紛紛推出了本次改制多益的解題方法、新題目解析等書籍，要我們來說，這當然也是對應改制的一種方式，但練習模擬題也不枉是另一種有效備考的好招式。

　　透過系列模擬題的考驗並進行解題練習，相信考生定能獲得不小的學習成效，更重要的是能加以理解改制新題目的內容，即使明年將迎來新考驗也可以輕鬆面對，將新改制的多益考試迎刃而解、一擊必殺！

Wenny Tsai

Contents目錄

PART 1

金色證書一擊必殺
──聽力全真模擬試題

PART 2

金色證書一擊必殺
──聽力關鍵解題分析

聽力全真模擬試題

新多益聽力全真模擬試題 — 第1~6回

 請聆聽 Track 1~6 作答。

金色證書一擊必殺 Part 1

New TOEIC Listening Test 1

新多益**聽力**全真模擬**試題第1回**

▶ **LISTENING TEST**

In the Listening test, you will be asked to demonstrate how well you understand spoken English. The entire Listening test will last approximately 45 minutes. There are four parts, and directions are given for each part. You must mark your answers on the separate answer sheet.

▶ **PART 1**

Directions: For each question in this part, you will hear four statements about a picture in your test book. When you hear the statements, you must select the one statement that best describes what you see in the picture. Then find the number of the question on your answer sheet and mark your answer. The statements will not be printed in your test book and will be spoken only one time.

01

02

03

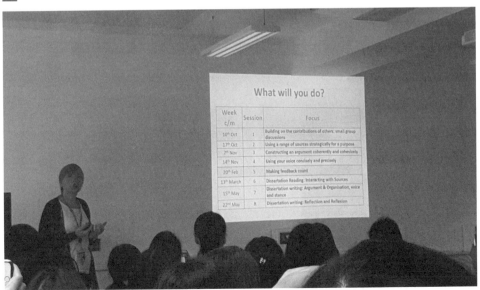

▶ PART 2

Directions: You will hear a question or statement and three responses spoken in English. They will not be printed in your test book and will be spoken only one time. Select the best response to the question or statement and mark the letter (A), (B) or (C) on your answer sheet.

Example

You will hear: Did you have dinner at the restaurant yesterday?

You will also hear: (A) Yes, it lasted all day.

(B) No, I went to a movie with my girlfriend.

(C) Yes, the client was nice.

The best response to the question "Did you have dinner at the restaurant yesterday?" is choice (B), "No, I went to a movie with my girlfriend," so (B) is the best answer. You should mark answer (B) on your answer sheet.

07 Mark your answer on your answer sheet.

08 Mark your answer on your answer sheet.

09 Mark your answer on your answer sheet.

10 Mark your answer on your answer sheet.

11 Mark your answer on your answer sheet.

12 Mark your answer on your answer sheet.

13 Mark your answer on your answer sheet.

14 Mark your answer on your answer sheet.

15 Mark your answer on your answer sheet.

16 Mark your answer on your answer sheet.

17 Mark your answer on your answer sheet.

18 Mark your answer on your answer sheet.

19 Mark your answer on your answer sheet.

20 Mark your answer on your answer sheet.

21 Mark your answer on your answer sheet.

22 Mark your answer on your answer sheet.

23 Mark your answer on your answer sheet.

24 Mark your answer on your answer sheet.

25 Mark your answer on your answer sheet.

26 Mark your answer on your answer sheet.

27 Mark your answer on your answer sheet.

28 Mark your answer on your answer sheet.

29 Mark your answer on your answer sheet.

30 Mark your answer on your answer sheet.

31 Mark your answer on your answer sheet.

PART 3

Directions: You will hear some conversations between two people. You will be asked to answer three questions about what the speakers say in each conversation. Select the best response to each question and mark the letter (A), (B), (C) or (D) on your answer sheet. The conversations will not be printed in your test book and will be spoken only one time.

32 Where is the man most likely to work?

(A) In a restaurant.
(B) In a bank.
(C) In a hotel.
(D) In a library.

33 What can the woman get by booking online?

(A) A complimentary drink.
(B) A discount of 25% off the room rate.
(C) A 25% off coupon.
(D) A free shipping code.

34 What will the woman do later?

(A) Find her way to the hotel.
(B) Book a hotel room online.
(C) Talk to the hotel manager.
(D) Order room service.

35 How does the woman feel about the invitation?

(A) She's indifferent.
(B) She's interested.
(C) She's disappointed.
(D) She's frustrated.

36 What is Tim trying do?

(A) Sell the concert tickets.
(B) Ask the woman out.
(C) Give a concert.
(D) Go to the concert.

37 What keeps the woman from buying the tickets?

(A) She can't afford them.
(B) She has to work.
(C) She doesn't like the singer.
(D) She's not interested.

	Monday	Tuesday	Wednesday
9:00-11:00	CMA Company Printers Repair		Day Off
13:00-15:00	Meeting	HDX Company digital copiers Repair	

38 Why is the man calling?

(A) To schedule a meeting.

(B) To cancel an appointment.

(C) To request for after-sales service.

(D) To postpone a dinner party.

39 What does the man want?

(A) To refund the damaged items.

(B) To return the defective items.

(C) To have some items checked.

(D) To retrieve the defective goods.

40 According to the graph, when will the engineer go to Exeter Company?

(A) Wednesday morning.

(B) Tuesday morning.

(C) Monday afternoon.

(D) Tuesday afternoon.

41 Where is the woman most likely to be?

(A) In a police station.

(B) On the highway.

(C) At the airport.

(D) In her office.

42 According to the speaker, what has caused the traffic jam?

(A) A traffic accident.

(B) The road construction.

(C) A damaged traffic light.

(D) The stormy weather.

43 What will the man do next?

(A) To host the meeting.

(B) To book a flight ticket.

(C) To book a meeting room.

(D) To cancel the meeting.

★**Questions 44-46 refer to the following graph.**

Types of flooring tiles	Quotations
Belem Ceramic	NT$90 Sq Ft
Toronto Grey Ceramic	NT$75 Sq Ft
Andes Tronador Ceramic	NT$120 Sq Ft
Recife Ceramic	NT$95 Sq Ft

44 What are the speakers talking about?

(A) An office expansion proposal.
(B) A house renovation plan.
(C) The meeting agenda.
(D) The design of a new product.

45 According to the man, what can be modified?

(A) The maintenance cost.
(B) The renovation time.
(C) The construction cost.
(D) The staffing arrangement.

46 Look at the graph. Which type of tiles will be used in this proposal?

(A) Belem Ceramic
(B) Toronto Grey Ceramic
(C) Andes Tronador Ceramic
(D) Recife Ceramic

★**Questions 47-49 refer to the following inventory.**

Inventory for the shirts	XS	S	M	L
white	3	1	2	0
black	3	3	1	4
grey	1	1	0	0
blue	1	0	0	2

47 Where does the conversation most likely take place?

(A) In a restaurant.
(B) In a bookstore.
(C) In an alteration shop.
(D) In a clothing store.

48 Why does the skirt need alteration?

(A) It's too short for the man.
(B) It's too long for the woman.
(C) It's too big for the woman.
(D) It's too small for the man.

49 Look at the inventory. Which shirt is the woman likely to buy?

(A) The white one
(B) The blue one
(C) The grey one
(D) The black one

50 What are the speakers discussing?

(A) A business offer.
(B) Orientation programs.
(C) A promotion event.
(D) A new production presentation.

51 What did Mr. Harrison request?

(A) Free delivery.
(B) Prompt payment.
(C) Reduced prices.
(D) 20 free iPhone chargers.

52 What does the woman think of Mr. Harrison's request?

(A) Acceptable.
(B) Offensive.
(C) Unreasonable.
(D) Disagreeable.

53 Where are the speakers?

(A) On a coach.
(B) In a library.
(C) In a bank.
(D) In a cafeteria.

54 What does the man offer to the woman?

(A) Some money.
(B) A coupon.
(C) His seat.
(D) His assistance.

55 Who is the woman traveling with?

(A) Her husband.
(B) Her daughter.
(C) Her son.
(C) Her mother.

56 Where are the speakers?

(A) At the reception.
(B) At the ticket machine.
(C) At the checkout.
(D) At a taxi station.

57 What does the man need?

(A) A train ticket.
(B) His electricity bill.
(C) His receipt.
(D) A reservation number.

58 What does the woman suggest the man do?

(A) Go to the service counter.
(B) Get some coins.
(C) Lend her some coins.
(D) Get on the train.

59 What are the speakers doing?

(A) Having a party.
(B) Having a meeting.
(C) Having lunch.
(D) Having a quarrel.

60 What is the woman in charge of?

(A) Meeting minutes.
(B) Seat arrangement.
(C) Equipment control.
(D) Product presentation.

61 What does the woman want to price the product?

(A) Make it $ 10,000.
(B) Make it lower than their competitors'.
(C) Keep it affordable.
(D) Make it 15,000 and give discounts later.

62 Which part of the contract needs to be revised?

(A) Production procedure.
(B) Delivery deadline.
(C) Payment terms.
(D) Defect guarantee.

63 According to the speakers, when should the payment be made?

(A) Within 2 weeks after receipt of order.
(B) As soon as the contract is signed.
(C) Before the order is put into production.
(D) Within 14 days after the order is placed.

64 What is the woman supposed to do next?

(A) Phone Mr. Donald.
(B) Sign the contract.
(C) Talk to Mr. Donald in person.
(D) Modify the contract.

★Questions 65-67 refer to the following graph.

Quantity of order	Discount
500 units or above	5% discount
700 units or above	10% discount
1000 units or above	15% discount
1500 units or above	20% discount

65 What are the speakers negotiating for?

(A) Dealership.
(B) A lower price.
(C) Copyright.
(D) Manufacturing rights.

66 What does the woman wish the man could offer?

(A) A lower quotation.
(B) Same-day delivery.
(C) A larger order.
(D) Free maintenance service.

67 Look at the graph. How many units should the man order for a discount of 15%?

(A) 500 units.
(B) 700 units.
(C) 1000 units
(D) 1500 units.

68 Where does the conversation take place?

(A) A medical clinic.
(B) A dentist clinic.
(C) A foot massage parlor.
(D) A pharmacy.

69 What is most likely to be the man's problem?

(A) Bird flu.
(B) Dengue fever.
(C) Influenza.
(D) Indigestion.

70 According to the woman, what should the man do next?

(A) Take the medicine.
(B) Take a vacation.
(C) Get enough sleep.
(D) Ask for a sick leave.

PART 4

Directions: You will hear some talks given by a single speaker. You will be asked to answer three questions about what the speaker says in each talk. Select the best response to each question and mark the letter (A), (B), (C) or (D) on your answer sheet. The talks will not be printed in your test book and will be spoken only one time.

★Questions 71-73 refer to the following agenda.

Meeting Agenda

Time	Agenda
9:30-10:00	Brochure Design/ Product Specification Sheet
10:00-11:00	Product Presentation Ideas
11:00-11:45	Marketing Plan
11:45-12:00	Feedback about 2016 Hong Kong Trade Show

71 What type of occasion is this?
(A) A wedding ceremony.
(B) A symphony concert.
(C) A special meeting.
(D) A welcoming party.

72 Where will 2017 Trade Show be held?
(A) Taipei.
(B) Hong Kong.
(C) Bangkok.
(D) London.

73 Look at the agenda. When is the meeting supposed to end?
(A) 9:00.
(B) 10:00.
(C) 11:45.
(D) 12:00

★Questions 74-76 refer to the following talk and graph.

Sales Performance in Quarter 3

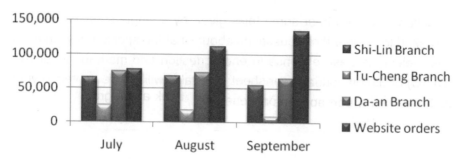

74 What is the man doing?

(A) Giving a sales report.
(B) Negotiating with his clients.
(C) Presenting a new product.
(D) Hosting a press conference.

75 What did the man suggest?

(A) A celebration party.
(B) A review conference.
(C) A promotion campaign.
(D) A clearance sale.

76 According to the graph, which branch store did the man refer to at the end of his speech?

(A) Shi-Lin Branch.
(B) Tu-Cheng Branch.
(C) Da-An Branch.
(D) None of the above.

77 Who is the woman talking to?

(A) Her students.
(B) Her patients.
(C) Passengers.
(D) Audience.

78 According to this announcement, the alcoholic drinks are:

(A) prohibited.
(B) affordable.
(C) unavailable.
(D) free of charge.

79 Where is the in-flight menu?

(A) Under the seat.
(B) Behind the seat.
(C) In the overhead compartment.
(D) By the window.

★Questions 80-82 refer to the following program.

List of nominees

1	Emily Johnson
2	Roy Simpson
3	Gabriel Larson
4	Frank Chessman

80 What is the purpose of the meeting?

(A) Select a Staff Welfare Commissioner.

(B) Establish a Staff Welfare Committee.

(C) Raise funds for the Staff Welfare Committee.

(D) Nominate someone as the representative.

81 How will the representative be decided?

(A) By secret ballot.

(B) By a show of hands.

(C) By anonymous vote.

(D) By open vote.

82 Look at the graph. Who is going to speak next?

(A) Emily Johnson.

(B) Roy Simpson.

(C) Gabriel Larson.

(D) Frank Chessman.

★**Questions 83-85 refer to the following program.**
Promotion Deals

Dates	Locations	Deals
Dec 11	GOSO Department Store	Buy 250 ml, get 100 ml free
Dec 12	Sea Breeze Shopping Mall	10% off on all Silky Skin products
Dec 13	Mitsukoshi Outlet Mall	FREE beauty bag with any $1000 purchase
Dec 14	Daisy's Department Store	Buy 500 ml, get 175 ml free
Dec 15	Luisa's Shopping Center	Free cosmetic case with any $2500 purchase

83 What type of occasion is this?

(A) New employee orientation.

(B) An antiques auction.

(C) New product launch.

(D) Branch office opening ceremony.

84 How long will the promotional campaign be?

(A) 24 hours.

(B) Three days.

(C) Five days.

(D) Two weeks.

85 Look at the graph. When do they offer 10% off on their new product?

(A) December 11
(B) December 12
(C) December 13
(D) December 14

★**Questions 86-88 refer to the following form.**
Company Outing Registration Form

Department	Name	Accompanying family members		
Planning	Jon	0 ☑	1 ☐	2 ☐
R&D	Steven	0 ☐	1 ☐	2 ☑
R&D	Vincent	0 ☐	1 ☑	2 ☐
Finance	Rachel	0 ☐	1 ☐	2 ☑

86 What is this announcement about?

(A) An employee-training course.
(B) A one-day company trip.
(C) A meeting cancellation.
(D) An office relocation notice.

87 Who can the employees bring with them to the outing?

(A) Their supervisors.
(B) Their children.
(C) Their neighbors.
(D) Their friends.

88 Look at the form. Who is going to the outing without companions?

(A) Jon
(B) Vincent
(C) Steven
(D) Rachel

★Questions 89-91 refer to the following email.

Subject: Interview Invitation
To: Derrick Kristanik
From: HR Prime Start

Hi, Mr. Kristanik,

Interview information

Date	January 12th, 2018
Time	9 a.m. – 11 a.m.
Room	Room 131
Address	Manor Hall, Lower Clifton Hill Road, BS8 1BU

Best wishes,
Paula Ashley
Secretary of HR Prime Start

89 What is this message about?

(A) An interview notice.
(B) A modification request.
(C) An change of order request.
(D) A status of payment inquiry.

90 What is the position that Mr. Kristanik applied for?

(A) HR Manager
(B) Chief editor
(C) Computer programmer
(D) Technique engineer

91 Look at the email. When will the interview start?

(A) At 9 a.m.
(B) On Wednesday.
(C) In two days.
(D) In October.

92 Who is the speaker?

(A) One of the guests.
(B) Linda's best friend.
(C) The host.
(D) Kevin's daughter.

93 What most likely is this occasion?

(A) Graduation ceremony
(B) Wedding anniversary
(C) House warming party
(D) College reunion

94 What are the guests going to watch?

(A) A short play.
(B) A talk show.
(C) An animation.
(D) An edited film.

★Questions 95-97 refer to the following program.

Name	Leave of Absence	Substitute
Jennifer Lin	Jan 12th-Jan 15th	Diana Chou
Benjamin Chang	Jan 18th-Jan 24th	Joseph Wang
Samantha Chen	Jan 22nd- Jan 25th	Peter Yang
Diana Chou	Jan 24th-Jan 29th	Jennifer Lin

95 What is the talk most related to?

(A) Leave policy.
(B) Overtime rule.
(C) Data analysis.
(D) Product design.

96 What does the speaker ask the listeners to do?

(A) Join an after-work club.
(B) Identify a substitute during vacation.
(C) Improve their sales performance.
(D) Come up with creative marketing ideas.

97 Look at the form. Who is taking the longest leave next month?

(A) Jennifer
(B) Benjamin
(C) Samantha
(D) Diana

★Questions 98-100 refer to the following program.

5-Day Forecast

	FRI	SAT	SUN	MON	TUE
HIGH	17℃	19℃	18℃	16℃	18℃
LOW	12℃	15℃	13℃	11℃	12℃

98 Who most likely is the speaker?

(A) A fortuneteller.
(B) A physics professor.
(C) A weather forecaster.
(D) A newspaper journalist.

99 According to the speaker, what is going to affect the weather in next five days?

(A) A warm front.
(B) A cold front.
(C) A storm.
(D) A mild typhoon.

100 Look at the graph. When will it rain within next five days?

(A) Friday
(B) Saturday
(C) Sunday
(D) Monday

New TOEIC Listening $\boxed{\text{Test 2}}$

新多益聽力全真模擬試題第2回

> ### ▶ LISTENING TEST
>
> In the Listening test, you will be asked to demonstrate how well you understand spoken English. The entire Listening test will last approximately 45 minutes. There are four parts, and directions are given for each part. You must mark your answers on the separate answer sheet.
>
> ### ▶ PART 1
>
> **Directions:** For each question in this part, you will hear four statements about a picture in your test book. When you hear the statements, you must select the one statement that best describes what you see in the picture. Then find the number of the question on your answer sheet and mark your answer. The statements will not be printed in your test book and will be spoken only one time.

01

02

03

▶ PART 2

Directions: You will hear a question or statement and three responses spoken in English. They will not be printed in your test book and will be spoken only one time. Select the best response to the question or statement and mark the letter (A), (B) or (C) on your answer sheet.

Example

You will hear:　　　　　Did you have dinner at the restaurant yesterday?
You will also hear:　　　(A) Yes, it lasted all day.
　　　　　　　　　　　　(B) No, I went to a movie with my girlfriend.
　　　　　　　　　　　　(C) Yes, the client was nice.

The best response to the question "Did you have dinner at the restaurant yesterday?" is choice (B), "No, I went to a movie with my girlfriend," so (B) is the best answer. You should mark answer (B) on your answer sheet.

07 Mark your answer on your answer sheet.

08 Mark your answer on your answer sheet.

09 Mark your answer on your answer sheet.

10 Mark your answer on your answer sheet.

11 Mark your answer on your answer sheet.

12 Mark your answer on your answer sheet.

13 Mark your answer on your answer sheet.

14 Mark your answer on your answer sheet.

15 Mark your answer on your answer sheet.

16 Mark your answer on your answer sheet.

17 Mark your answer on your answer sheet.

18 Mark your answer on your answer sheet.

19 Mark your answer on your answer sheet.

20 Mark your answer on your answer sheet.

21 Mark your answer on your answer sheet.

22 Mark your answer on your answer sheet.

23 Mark your answer on your answer sheet.

24 Mark your answer on your answer sheet.

25 Mark your answer on your answer sheet.

26 Mark your answer on your answer sheet.

27 Mark your answer on your answer sheet.

28 Mark your answer on your answer sheet.

29 Mark your answer on your answer sheet.

30 Mark your answer on your answer sheet.

31 Mark your answer on your answer sheet.

▶ PART 3

Directions: You will hear some conversations between two people. You will be asked to answer three questions about what the speakers say in each conversation. Select the best response to each question and mark the letter (A), (B), (C) or (D) on your answer sheet. The conversations will not be printed in your test book and will be spoken only one time.

★**Questions 32-34 refer to the following invitation.**

> *You are invited to*
> *Amy's BBQ Party!*
>
> Date: December 16 Saturday
> Time: 3 p.m. – 9 p.m.
> Location: 20, Park Street, North
>   District BS8
>
> *Bring Your Own Beer!*

32 What did the man just receive?

(A) An invitation.
(B) A traffic ticket.
(C) A shopping receipt.
(D) An emergency call.

33 What is the woman planning?

(A) A wedding banquet.
(B) An outdoor party.
(C) An opening ceremony.
(D) A company outing.

34 Look at the invitation. When will the party start?

(A) 15:00
(B) 16:00
(C) 18:00
(D) 21:00

35 What did the couple ask for?

(A) A table in the outdoor dining area.
(B) A table that is reserved.
(C) A table away from the restroom.
(D) The bill for their meals.

36 What did the woman complain about?

(A) The quality of their food.
(B) The location of their table.
(C) The waiter's attitude.
(D) The price of the food.

37 What did the man decide to do at last?

(A) Remain at the same table.
(B) to outdoor dining area.
(C) Talk to the restaurant manager.
(D) Pack the food and leave.

★**Questions 38-40 refer to the following table.**
Foreign Currency Exchange Rates Table

US Dollar	1.00 USD
Euro	0.846564
British Pound	0.756687
Canadian Dollar	1.245736
Japanese Yen	112.897602

38 Where most likely are the speakers?

(A) In the bank.
(B) In the hospital.
(C) At the gas station.
(D) In a police office.

39 What does the man need?

(A) Some US dollars.
(B) Some Canadian dollars.
(C) Some British pounds.
(D) Some Japanese yens.

40 Look at the table. What is the exchange rate of US dollars to British pounds?

(A) 0.84   (B) 0.75
(C) 1.24   (D) 112.89

★Questions 41-43 refer to the following chart.

Mail receiver	Parcel receiver	Collecting Date	Collector signature
	A. Goofy	2017/12/20	Angela Goofy
S. Goofy			
L. Fisherman		2017/12/22	Layla Fisherman
	M. Dickson		
	A. Goofy	2017/12/20	Angela Goofy
L. Fisherman		2017/12/22	Layla Fisherman
L. Fisherman		2017/12/22	Layla Fisherman

41 What was the woman waiting for?

(A) Her order.
(B) Her salary.
(C) Her bill.
(D) Her food.

42 According to the woman, when should the parcel arrive?

(A) Yesterday.
(B) This morning.
(C) Tomorrow.
(D) In 24 hours.

43 Look at the graph. What did the woman sign for?

(A) One mail and one parcel.
(B) Two mails and one parcel.
(C) Three mails.
(D) Two parcels.

44 What are the speakers discussing?

(A) What to order.
(B) What to eat.
(C) When to meet.
(D) Whom to invite.

45 When does the speakers' lunchtime end?

(A) At 12:30.
(B) At 1:00.
(C) At 1:30.
(D) At 3:00.

46 Where will the speakers go for lunch?

(A) A nice and cozy hotel.
(B) A fancy Chinese restaurant.
(C) A nearby Italian bistro.
(D) A food truck on the street.

47 What will the speakers attend this evening?

(A) A negotiation conference.
(B) A celebration party.
(C) A business dinner.
(D) A class reunion.

48 What did the woman just do?

(A) Called the police.
(B) Reserved a table.
(C) Cancelled a meeting.
(D) Confirmed her flight.

49 According to the woman, what will she do within a month?

(A) File for reimbursement.
(B) Resign her position.
(C) Reserve a restaurant table.
(D) Cancel a reservation.

★**Questions 50-52 refer to the following list.**

Things to buy from S-Mart
1. toilet paper
2. toothpaste
3. hand wash
4. shampoo
5. paper towels
6. laundry detergent

50 Where do the speakers plan to go?

(A) The library.
(B) The convenience store.
(C) The supermarket.
(D) The grocery store.

51 Why doesn't the man want to wait?

(A) He has to see his dentist.
(B) He wants to watch a football game.
(C) He needs to catch a flight.
(D) He is tired of waiting.

52 Look at the list. Which supermarket section should the man go to?

(A) Furniture & Appliances
(B) Household essentials.
(C) Electronics & Office
(D) Health & Beauty

53 Who is the woman?

(A) The hotel porter.
(B) The hotel guest.
(C) The hotel receptionist.
(D) The hotel manager.

54 Why did the woman call?

(A) To extend her stay.
(B) To request a morning call.
(C) To complain about her room.
(D) To order room service.

55 How did the woman feel about the manager's solution?

(A) Satisfied.
(B) Reluctant.
(C) Doubtful.
(D) Uncertain.

★**Questions 56-58 refer to the following form.**

Office Supplies Request Form		
Name: David Wallick	Date: 2017/12/15	
Items	Quantity	stock status
staples	3 (boxes)	☑ in stock ☐ out of stock
thumbtacks	1 (box)	☑ in stock ☐ out of stock
filing box	1	☐ in stock ☑ out of stock
file folder	5	☑ in stock ☐ out of stock
Handled by: Murphy Byron		

56 What did the woman request for?

(A) Some stationery items.
(B) Some application forms.
(C) Some financial support.
(D) Some office equipment.

57 What is Murphy responsible for?

(A) Recruitment.
(B) Product inventory.
(C) Equipment maintenance.
(D) Office supplies.

58 Look at the form. Which item won't the woman get right away?

(A) Filing box.
(B) Staples.
(C) Staplers.
(D) Thumbtacks.

★Questions 59-61 refer to the following form.

Compensatory Leave Form			
Name:	Date:	Time:	Total hours
Diana Jones	2017/11/30	13:00-18:00	5
Substitute's signature		Tim Leonard	

59 What is the woman applying for?

(A) Maternity leave.
(B) Compensatory leave.
(C) Annual leave.
(D) Marriage leave.

60 What's the relationship between the speakers?

(A) Coworkers.
(B) Teacher and student.
(C) Classmates.
(D) Doctor and patient.

61 Look at the form. How long will the woman be absent from work?

(A) Five hours.
(B) Two days.
(C) One week.
(D) A whole morning.

62 Who is Mr. Williams?

(A) A client.
(B) A writer.
(C) A bus driver.
(D) A relative.

63 Why is the man eager to meet with Mr. Williams?

(A) To ask for a raise.
(B) To get the contract signed.
(C) To cancel his order.
(D) To postpone an appointment.

64 When will the man meet Mr. Williams next week?

(A) During lunchtime.
(B) After work.
(C) Before work.
(D) During the weekend.

★Questions 65-67 refer to the following form.

	original	rearranged
Meeting time	Feb 12 10 a.m -12 p.m.	Feb 12 2 p.m.- 4 p.m.
Meeting location	Meeting Room	Room 3113

65 What do we know about the meeting?

(A) It's been postponed.
(B) It's been cancelled.
(C) It's been advanced.
(D) It's been interrupted.

66 What did the woman ask the man to do?

(A) Forward her the notice letter.
(B) Tell her when the meeting is held.
(C) Help her find the meeting room.
(D) Modify the meeting agenda.

67 Look at the form. When will the meeting start?
(A) At 10 a.m.
(B) At 12 p.m.
(C) At 2 p.m.
(D) At 4 p.m.

68 What role is the woman playing in the meeting?

(A) The moderator.
(B) The note-taker.
(C) The timekeeper.
(D) The convener.

69 What did the two men disagree on?

(A) The marketing strategy.
(B) The prices of the products.
(C) The promotion campaign.
(D) The sales target.

70 What does the woman think matters most?

(A) After-sales service.
(B) Sales pitch.
(C) Sales performance.
(D) Work attitude.

Directions: You will hear some talks given by a single speaker. You will be asked to answer three questions about what the speaker says in each talk. Select the best response to each question and mark the letter (A), (B), (C) or (D) on your answer sheet. The talks will not be printed in your test book and will be spoken only one time.

71 What most likely is this occasion?

(A) A welcoming party.
(B) A farewell party.
(C) A funeral ceremony.
(D) A ground-breaking ceremony.

72 Why is Mr. Schmidt leaving?

(A) He was promoted.
(B) He was fired.
(C) He resigned.
(D) He's been headhunted.

73 How long has Mr. Schmidt been working for this company?

(A) Five years.
(B) Ten years.
(C) Fifteen years.
(D) Twenty years.

★Questions 74-76 refer to the following program.

New Employee Orientation Program

	Wednesday	Thursday	Friday
9:00 – 12:00	HR-Employment Issues Introduction	HR- Leave policy	HR- Employee performance evaluation
12:00 – 1:30	Lunch Time		
1:30 – 5:00	Your Department – Overall work of the department	Your Department – Department policies, procedures and job expectations	New Employee Welcoming Party

74 Who most likely are the listeners?

(A) New employees.
(B) Job interviewers.
(C) Job applicants.
(D) New college students.

75 How long is the new-hire orientation?

(A) One day.
(B) Two days.
(C) Three days.
(D) Five days.

76 Look at the program. When will the welcoming party take place?

(A) Tuesday
(B) Wednesday
(C) Thursday
(D) Friday

77 How did the listeners answer the speaker's question?

(A) By sign language.
(B) By text messages.
(C) By e-mails.
(D) By show of hands.

78 What was the woman's point?

(A) The new-hire training was insufficient.
(B) The company is understaffed.
(C) The comment was unconstructive.
(D) The punishment was unfair.

79 What's the purpose of the meeting?

(A) Improve new employee training.
(B) Assign meeting roles.
(C) Select a party organizer.
(D) Design a questionnaire.

❧ J&P's Cosmetics Inc. ❧

Sales Representative

Michelle Chang

    Office/ 02-9876-5432 (9 a.m. – 6 p.m.)

    Mobile/ 0912345678

    Email/ Michelle.Miller@jpcosmetics.com

---

80 Who most likely is the woman talking to?

(A) Her neighbor.

(B) A potential customer.

(C) Her boss.

(D) A police officer.

81 What's the purpose of the woman's talk?

(A) Make a new friend.

(B) Find a new client.

(C) Explore investment opportunities.

(D) Job-hop to another company.

82 Look at the business card. When does the woman's working day start?

(A) 6:00 a.m.

(B) 8:00 a.m.

(C) 9:00 a.m.

(D) 10:00 a.m.

★Questions 83-85 refer to the following checklist.

Checklist
1. passport validity ☐
2. increase credit card spending limit ☐
3. exchange NT dollars for US dollars ☐
4. get international phone service ☐
5. get an outlet converter ☐

83 What most likely is this occasion?

(A) A pre-departure orientation.
(B) A new staff orientation.
(C) A new student orientation.
(D) A parent-teacher conference.

84 What industry does the speaker work in?

(A) Logistics
(B) Semiconductor
(C) Financial
(D) Tourism

85 Look at the checklist. Which country are the listeners most likely to visit?

(A) Thailand.
(B) Japan.
(C) South Korea.
(D) Guam.

86 What's the purpose of this voice message?

(A) To offer a job.
(B) To reply to an inquiry.
(C) To schedule a meeting.
(D) To give an invitation.

87 What type of business is Leicester Fads?

(A) Travel agency
(B) Interior design
(C) Logo design
(D) Book publisher

88 How does the speaker wish the listener to contact her?

(A) By e-mail.
(B) By telephone.
(C) By text.
(D) By voice message.

Program	
19:00 – 19:10	Opening
19:10 – 19:40	Mayday
19:40 – 19:50	First Lucky Draw
19:50 – 20:10	Jolin
20:10 – 20:30	JJ
20:30 – 20:40	Second Lucky Draw
20:40 – 20:50	Closing

89 What are the listeners encouraged to do?

(A) To work harder in the next year.
(B) To drink a toast to the boss.
(C) To perform on the stage.
(D) To participate in the lucky draw.

90 Who is going to perform at the festivities?

(A) Some employees.
(B) A magician.
(C) Popular singers.
(D) A circus.

91 Look at the program. How many times will the lucky draw take place?

(A) Only once
(B) Twice
(C) Three times
(D) Four times

Presentation order	
A001	Jenny Liu
A002	Sophia Tsai
A003	Doris Yang
A004	James Wang
A005	Peter Song

92 Where is this talk taking place?

(A) In a gas station.
(B) In a restaurant.
(C) In a classroom.
(D) In a bakery.

93 What is the length of each presentation?

(A) An hour.
(B) Half an hour.
(C) A quarter.
(D) Ten minutes.

94 Look at the list. Who will be the last one to present?

(A) Jenny   (B) Peter
(C) Sophia   (D) Doris

★Questions 95-97 refer to the following floor guide.

Floor Guide	
3F	Executive office
2F	Staff office
1F	Information-processing center
GF	Entrance/Reception
B1	Staff Cafeteria
B2	Parking lot

95 Who are the listeners?

(A) Visitors from Tokyo.

(B) New employees.

(C) New interns.

(D) Family members of the staff.

96 Which section will the speaker introduce first?

(A) Research and development center.

(B) Information-processing center.

(C) Main conference hall.

(D) Staff lounge.

97 Look at the floor guide. What is on the first basement floor?

(A) The executive office.

(B) The staff office.

(C) The parking lot.

(D) The staff cafeteria.

98 What's the purpose of the talk?

(A) To launch a new product.

(B) To introduce an intern engineer.

(C) To welcome a new manager.

(D) To commend an employee.

99 What's the intern's professional specialty?

(A) Computer software design.

(B) Machinery maintenance.

(C) Marketing and advertising.

(D) Graphic design.

100 What are the listeners encouraged to do after the meeting?

(A) Teach the intern a lesson.

(B) Take the intern to lunch.

(C) Make the intern feel welcome.

(D) Show the intern around.

New TOEIC Listening Test 3

新多益**聽力**全真模擬**試題第3回**

▶ **LISTENING TEST**

In the Listening test, you will be asked to demonstrate how well you understand spoken English. The entire Listening test will last approximately 45 minutes. There are four parts, and directions are given for each part. You must mark your answers on the separate answer sheet.

▶ **PART 1**

Directions: For each question in this part, you will hear four statements about a picture in your test book. When you hear the statements, you must select the one statement that best describes what you see in the picture. Then find the number of the question on your answer sheet and mark your answer. The statements will not be printed in your test book and will be spoken only one time.

`01`

Test
3

02

03

04

05

06

▶ PART 2

Directions: You will hear a question or statement and three responses spoken in English. They will not be printed in your test book and will be spoken only one time. Select the best response to the question or statement and mark the letter (A), (B) or (C) on your answer sheet.

Example

You will hear: Did you have dinner at the restaurant yesterday?
You will also hear: (A) Yes, it lasted all day.
                       (B) No, I went to a movie with my girlfriend.
                       (C) Yes, the client was nice.

The best response to the question "Did you have dinner at the restaurant yesterday?" is choice (B), "No, I went to a movie with my girlfriend," so (B) is the best answer. You should mark answer (B) on your answer sheet.

07 Mark your answer on your answer sheet.

08 Mark your answer on your answer sheet.

09 Mark your answer on your answer sheet.

10 Mark your answer on your answer sheet.

11 Mark your answer on your answer sheet.

12 Mark your answer on your answer sheet.

13 Mark your answer on your answer sheet.

14 Mark your answer on your answer sheet.

15 Mark your answer on your answer sheet.

16 Mark your answer on your answer sheet.

17 Mark your answer on your answer sheet.

18 Mark your answer on your answer sheet.

19 Mark your answer on your answer sheet.

20 Mark your answer on your answer sheet.

21 Mark your answer on your answer sheet.

22 Mark your answer on your answer sheet.

23 Mark your answer on your answer sheet.

24 Mark your answer on your answer sheet.

25 Mark your answer on your answer sheet.

26 Mark your answer on your answer sheet.

27 Mark your answer on your answer sheet.

28 Mark your answer on your answer sheet.

29 Mark your answer on your answer sheet.

30 Mark your answer on your answer sheet.

31 Mark your answer on your answer sheet.

▶ PART 3

Directions: You will hear some conversations between two people. You will be asked to answer three questions about what the speakers say in each conversation. Select the best response to each question and mark the letter (A), (B), (C) or (D) on your answer sheet. The conversations will not be printed in your test book and will be spoken only one time.

32 What are the speakers talking about?

(A) An investment project.
(B) Marketing strategy.
(C) Product quality.
(D) Cost reduction.

33 Who's going to help with the promotions?

(A) Part-time sales personnel.
(B) Colleagues from other departments.
(C) College students.
(D) The makeup artist.

34 When will the speakers have a meeting again?

(A) The day after tomorrow.
(B) Next Monday.
(C) Tuesday morning.
(D) Two weeks later.

Jasmine Second-hand Bookstore

Open Monday-Saturday

10 a.m. – 7:00 p.m.

Lunch break 12:30 p.m. – 3:30 p.m.

35 Where are the speakers?

(A) At the flower store.
(B) On the bus.
(C) In front of the bookstore.
(D) In a convenience store.

36 According to the conversation, why is the bookstore closed?

(A) It's time for the lunch break.
(B) The staff is on annual leave.
(C) It's currently undergoing renovation.
(D) It has been relocated.

37 Look at the sign. What time is this conversation most likely to take place?

(A) 11:30 a.m.
(B) 12:45 p.m.
(C) 4:00 p.m.
(D) 6:15 p.m.

38 What most likely is taking place?

(A) A video conference.
(B) An acting audition.
(C) A charity sale.
(D) A boutique auction.

39 What is the woman trying to do?

(A) Organize an exhibition.
(B) Give a presentation.
(C) Schedule an appointment.
(D) Book a flight ticket.

40 What did the speakers decide to do?

(A) Cancel the appointment.
(B) Proceed with the meeting later.
(C) Discuss in private.
(D) Give up trying.

41 Why is the man calling?

(A) To call in sick.
(B) To cancel an appointment.
(C) To invite a friend.
(D) To reserve a table.

42 What will the woman do?

(A) Pay a visit to the man.
(B) Cover the man's work.
(C) Go to the doctor.
(D) Take care of the man.

43 When will the man's visitor come?

(A) At 9.

(B) At 10.

(C) Around noon.

(D) By five.

★**Questions 44-46 refer to the following coupon.**

ะ๛๛ **Thai Thai** ๛๛

Buy 1 Entree

Get 1 Entree **Free**

Valid until Jan 31, 2018

44 What does the man suggest for dinner?

(A) Fast food.

(B) His signature dish.

(C) Thai cuisine.

(D) Street food.

45 Where did the man get the coupon?

(A) From the restaurant.

(B) From a magazine.

(C) From the website.

(D) From his colleague.

46 Look at the coupon. When will the coupon expire?

(A) January the first.

(B) In two weeks.

(C) The end of January.

(D) The last Sunday of January.

47 Who most likely is Mr. Selfridge?

(A) The boss of the speakers.

(B) A supplier that the speakers work with.

(C) The father of the woman.

(D) The guard of the office building.

48 What can we know about the contract?

(A) It's urgent.

(B) It needs modification.

(C) It's been signed.

(D) It's already been sent to Mr. Selfridge.

49 What does the woman imply at the end of the conversation?

(A) They will have to work late.
(B) They can take their time.
(C) She can take care of this by herself.
(D) Mr. Selfridge is too demanding.

★Questions 50-52 refer to the following receipt.

| **Looking Sharp** |
| **Men's Clothing, Co. Ltd.** |

Cashier: Joanne   26-May-2017 3:55:43P

1 Black Suit Trousers	$2,599
Total	$ 2,599
Cash Sale	$ 2,599

Thank you!

50 Where most likely does the woman work?

(A) At the post office.
(B) On the flight.
(C) In a local school.
(D) In a clothing store.

51 What can we know about the man?

(A) He works with the woman.
(B) He bought a watch at the store.
(C) He wants to return an item he bought.
(D) He is looking for a shirt to go with his trousers.

52 Look at the receipt. What most likely is the date when this conversation takes place?

(A) 28-May-2017.
(B) 30-May-2017.
(C) 1-June-2017.
(D) 3-June-2017.

★Questions 53-55 refer to the following timetable.

Monday through Friday	
Leave	Back
8:00	9:05
9:30	10:35
10:45	11:50
11:15	12:20

53 Where did the conversation take place?

(A) In their car.
(B) At the train station.
(C) On the flight.
(D) On a ferry.

54 What will the woman do next?

(A) Buy the ferry tickets.
(B) Give Larry a call.
(C) Check out the ferry schedule.
(D) Park the car.

55 Look at the schedule. Which ferry should the speakers take?

(A) The one that leaves at 8:00.
(B) The one that leaves at 9:30.
(C) The one that leaves at 10:45
(D) The one that leaves at 11:15.

56 What is mainly discussed in this conversation?

(A) Which movie to watch.
(B) Getting a booth at the fair.

(C) Where the book fair will be held.
(D) How to get to the exhibition hall.

57 Which information is NOT provided in the conversation?

(A) The name of the fair.
(B) The duration of the fair.
(C) The price of the booth.
(D) The location of the fair.

58 What did the woman imply at the end of the conversation?

(A) They need the set up the exhibition within the budget.
(B) They can have a booth as big as they wish.
(C) There's no need to worry about the budget.
(D) She can negotiate with the sponsor for a better price.

Date	Flight	From/To	Departure Time
July 22	FA1330	TPE/YVR	9:35
August 3	FA1331	YVR/TPE	13:40

59 What type of transportation will the man use to get to Vancouver?

(A) Train
(B) Coach
(C) Plane
(D) Subway

60 What job does the woman probably do?

(A) Travel agent
(B) Aircraft mechanic.
(C) Mail carrier
(D) Flight attendant

61 Look at the table. What time will the man's flight leave the airport on July 22?

(A) At 7:35.
(B) At 9:35.
(C) At 11:40.
(D) At 13:40.

62 Where did this conversation take place?

(A) At the ticket booth.
(B) In the cinema.
(C) In a library.
(D) On the platform.

63 What can we learn from this conversation?

(A) Admission is free for children under 16.
(B) All children should be accompanied by an adult.
(C) Admission is free to all visitors on Fridays.
(D) The museum does not open on the weekends.

64 What did the woman get for free?

(A) An adult ticket.
(B) A family ticket.
(C) A map of the museum.
(D) A ticket for the temporary exhibition.

65 What is the purpose of the woman's visit?

(A) To sell a new product.
(B) To give a new product presentation.
(C) To place an order.
(D) To interview for a job.

66 Why does the woman want to order the same products again?

(A) The previous ones are broken.
(B) She wants to buy them as gifts.
(C) They're flying off the shelves.
(D) They're on sale now.

67 What request did the woman make?

(A) Bring down the price.
(B) Offer her the position.
(C) Compensate for her loss.
(D) Grant her leave for two days.

68 How did the woman feel about her food?

(A) Satisfied.
(B) Grateful.
(C) Dissatisfied.
(D) Doubtful.

69 What did the restaurant chef offer the woman?

(A) A free dinner.
(B) Some coupons.
(C) A part-time job.
(D) A 10 percent discount.

70 What is the woman going to do next?

(A) Leave the restaurant.
(B) Wait for ten more minutes.
(C) Go to the restroom.
(D) Pack the leftovers.

Directions: You will hear some talks given by a single speaker. You will be asked to answer three questions about what the speaker says in each talk. Select the best response to each question and mark the letter (A), (B), (C) or (D) on your answer sheet. The talks will not be printed in your test book and will be spoken only one time.

★**Questions 71-73 refer to the following chart.**

Price per month	Data	Minutes	Texts
NT$299	100 MB	150	300
NT$499	1 GB	250	500
NT$899	3 GB	500	Unlimited
NT$1,299	Unlimited	Unlimited	Unlimited

71 What industry is the speaker most likely to work in?

(A) Telecom industry.
(B) Clothing industry.
(C) Food processing industry.
(D) Renovation industry

72 According to the speaker, what is true about their plans?

(A) They are 2-year contracted plans.
(B) They don't include data.
(C) They can be cancelled anytime.
(D) They are unchangeable.

73 Look at the table. Which plan includes unlimited data, minutes and texts?

(A) The $299 plan
(B) The $499 plan
(C) The $899 plan
(D) The $1299 plan

74 Why is the speaker making this announcement?

(A) The year-end sale is about to start.

(B) Two passengers are late for boarding.

(C) The store is about to close soon.

(D) The birthday party will begin soon.

75 According to the announcement, what's going to happen in five minutes?

(A) The airplane will start to land.

(B) The airplane will take off.

(C) The door of the airplane will be closed.

(D) The inflight entertainment will be available.

76 Where are we most likely to hear this announcement?

(A) On the airplane.

(B) On the train station.

(C) In the department store.

(D) At the airport lounge.

★**Questions 77-79 refer to the following agenda.**

Meeting Agenda	
9:00-9:20	Review last meeting's minutes
9:20-9:40	Ruby's project presentation
9:40-10:00	Vote on proposed budget
.	
.	
.	
12:00	Adjournment

77 What type of assembly is this?

(A) A college reunion.

(B) A press conference.

(C) A department meeting.

(D) A dinner gathering.

78 What would Robbie be in charge of if he were able to attend the meeting?

(A) Taking the minutes.

(B) Hosting the meeting.

(C) Reserving the meeting room.

(D) Making copies of the agenda.

79 Look at the agenda. What will be decided in the meeting?

(A) Where to hold the department dinner.
(B) The proposed budget.
(C) The chairman of the next meeting.
(D) The date of new product launch.

80 Where most likely is the speaker working?

(A) In a seafood restaurant.
(B) In a seafood processing plant.
(C) In a local supermarket.
(D) In a tourist night market.

81 What's the purpose of this talk?

(A) To announce an employee's retirement.
(B) To convene an impromptu meeting.
(C) To announce a flash sale.
(D) To cancel an appointment.

82 Which of the following can be bought at half price during the sale?

(A) Salmons and squids
(B) Beef and pork
(C) Cheese and milk
(D) Tissue and toothpaste

83 What most likely is the woman doing?

(A) Selling spatulas.
(B) Promoting a new butter.
(C) Filming for a cooking video.
(D) Helping her mom in the kitchen.

84 What is the woman demonstrating?

(A) How to cook English scrambled eggs.
(B) How to cook scrambled eggs in different ways.
(C) How to choose perfect eggs for scrambled eggs.
(D) How to fried eggs without oil or butter.

85 What did the woman imply at the end?

(A) Cream is the key to scrambled eggs.
(B) Cream and milk are not really necessary.
(C) Most people like creamy scrambled eggs.
(D) Her scrambled eggs recipe is the best.

★Questions 86-88 refer to the following table.

	Days	Package price	
India	5 days	NT$ 56,000	
Thailand	4 days	was NT$ 25,000	now NT$ 18,000
Maldives	12 days	NT$ 120,000	
Italy & Greece	14 days	NT$ 180,000	

86 Who most likely is the man speaking to?

(A) A newlywed couple.
(B) A group of elementary school students.
(C) His wife.
(D) His dentist.

87 According to the man, what's the distinguishing feature of their packages?

(A) They are private tour packages.
(B) They can be cancelled anytime.
(C) The prices include tips for local guides.
(D) They can be customized.

88 Look at the table. Which package is this travel agency promoting?

(A) The package to Thailand.
(B) The package to Italy and Greece.
(C) The package to India.
(D) The package to the Maldives.

★Questions 89-91 refer to the following table.

	accommodates	rates (meal/drinks/equipment)
Dragon Hall	30 people	NT$ 30,000/ 4 hours
Phoenix Hall	50 people	NT$ 55,000/ 4 hours
Kylin Hall	100 people	NT$ 120,000/ 4 hours
Crystal Hall	250 people	NT$ 280,000/ 4 hours

89 What is the purpose of this talk?

(A) To advertise a restaurant.

(B) To promote a new product.

(C) To congratulate a couple on their wedding.

(D) To express gratitude.

90 What do we know about the restaurant according to the talk?

(A) It provides authentic Italian food.

(B) It provides modern audiovisual equipment.

(C) It is a great place to enjoy a quiet breakfast.

(D) It is a one-star Michelin restaurant.

91 Look at the table. Which of the following has the greatest capacity?

(A) Dragon Hall

(B) Phoenix Hall

(C) Kylin Hall

(D) Crystal Hall

92 What is the woman doing?

(A) She is making a reservation.

(B) She is taking a message.

(C) She is leaving a voice message.

(D) She is cancelling an appointment.

93 What can we learn from the message?

(A) The woman is having a party.

(B) The woman is going on a vacation.

(C) The woman is looking for a job.

(D) The woman will attend a party.

94 Which of the following information is provided in the message?

(A) The purpose of the party.

(B) The time of the party.

(C) The location of the party.

(D) The dress code of the party.

★**Questions 95-97 refer to the following list.**

Don't wear these to work—
1. shorts
2. tank tops
3. sandals
4. sports shoes

95 What is this talk mainly about?

(A) The company's dress code policy.

(B) The clothing store's return policy.

(C) The website's privacy policy.

(D) The company's leave policy.

96 How does the speaker expect the listeners to look at workplace?

(A) Neat

(B) Casual

(C) Friendly

(D) Professional

97 Look at the list. Which of the following is unacceptable in this company?

(A) Trousers

(B) Ties

(C) Sleeveless shirts

(D) Necklaces

98 Why will the office be closed?

(A) There's a blackout.

(B) A typhoon is coming.

(C) It's flooded.

(D) An earthquake just occurred.

99 What are the listeners asked to do?

(A) Assemble in the meeting room.

(B) Hand in their reports immediately.

(C) Leave the office in thirty minutes.

(D) Work overtime tonight.

100 How will the listeners reach the ground floor?

(A) Take the elevators

(B) Take the escalators

(C) Use the emergency ladder

(D) Take the stairs

New TOEIC Listening Test4

新多益聽力全真模擬試題第4回

▶ LISTENING TEST

In the Listening test, you will be asked to demonstrate how well you understand spoken English. The entire Listening test will last approximately 45 minutes. There are four parts, and directions are given for each part. You must mark your answers on the separate answer sheet.

▶ PART 1

Directions: For each question in this part, you will hear four statements about a picture in your test book. When you hear the statements, you must select the one statement that best describes what you see in the picture. Then find the number of the question on your answer sheet and mark your answer. The statements will not be printed in your test book and will be spoken only one time.

01

02

03

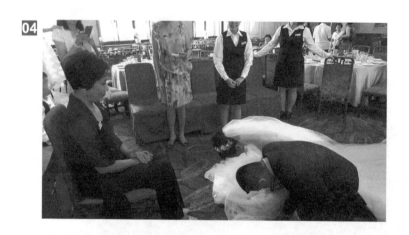

▶ PART 2

Directions: You will hear a question or statement and three responses spoken in English. They will not be printed in your test book and will be spoken only one time. Select the best response to the question or statement and mark the letter (A), (B) or (C) on your answer sheet.

Example

You will hear: Did you have dinner at the restaurant yesterday?

You will also hear: (A) Yes, it lasted all day.

(B) No, I went to a movie with my girlfriend.

(C) Yes, the client was nice.

The best response to the question "Did you have dinner at the restaurant yesterday?" is choice (B), "No, I went to a movie with my girlfriend," so (B) is the best answer. You should mark answer (B) on your answer sheet.

07 Mark your answer on your answer sheet.

08 Mark your answer on your answer sheet.

09 Mark your answer on your answer sheet.

10 Mark your answer on your answer sheet.

11 Mark your answer on your answer sheet.

12 Mark your answer on your answer sheet.

13 Mark your answer on your answer sheet.

14 Mark your answer on your answer sheet.

15 Mark your answer on your answer sheet.

16 Mark your answer on your answer sheet.

17 Mark your answer on your answer sheet.

18 Mark your answer on your answer sheet.

19 Mark your answer on your answer sheet.

20 Mark your answer on your answer sheet.

21 Mark your answer on your answer sheet.

22 Mark your answer on your answer sheet.

23 Mark your answer on your answer sheet.

24 Mark your answer on your answer sheet.

25 Mark your answer on your answer sheet.

26 Mark your answer on your answer sheet.

27 Mark your answer on your answer sheet.

28 Mark your answer on your answer sheet.

29 Mark your answer on your answer sheet.

30 Mark your answer on your answer sheet.

31 Mark your answer on your answer sheet.

PART 3

Directions: You will hear some conversations between two people. You will be asked to answer three questions about what the speakers say in each conversation. Select the best response to each question and mark the letter (A), (B), (C) or (D) on your answer sheet. The conversations will not be printed in your test book and will be spoken only one time.

32 Who most likely is the woman?

(A) A flight attendant.
(B) A taxi driver.
(C) A stay-at-home mother.
(D) A receptionist.

33 What is the man's purpose of his visit?

(A) To interview for a job.
(B) To attend a conference.
(C) To meet his client.
(D) To collect his parcel.

34 What is the man going to do next?

(A) Fill in some forms.
(B) Take the written test.
(C) Talk to Mr. Chen.
(D) Interview some applicants.

35 What kind of occasion is this?

(A) A negotiation conference
(B) A job interview
(C) A project presentation
(D) An academic seminar.

36 Which of the following position is the man applying for?

(A) The headwaiter
(B) The manager
(C) The chef
(D) The accountant

37 What does the man mean at the end of the conversation?

(A) The applicant has been offered the job.
(B) The applicant should wait a week for the result.
(C) They are interviewing more applicants later.
(D) The applicant doesn't meet their requirements.

38 How does the woman feel?

(A) Upset
(B) Confused
(C) Appreciated
(D) Reluctant

39 Which most likely is the woman's job?

(A) An insurance sales agent
(B) An R&D engineer
(C) A librarian
(D) An interior designer

40 What does the man suggest the woman do?

(A) Resign her position.
(B) Find a decent job.
(C) Speak with her boss.
(D) Revise the contract.

★Questions 41-43 refer to the following table.

Meeting Rooms Reservation Table

08-Feb	Room G011 (6 people)	Room 1011 (10 people)	Room 2011 (18 people)	Room 3011 (25 people)
12:00-14:00		Marketing Dep.	R&D Dep.	HR Dep.
14:00- 16:00	Planning Dep.			Finance Dep.

41 What is the woman planning to do?

(A) To convene a meeting.
(B) To postpone a meeting.
(C) To advance a meeting.
(D) To cancel a meeting.

42 How long will the meeting last?

(A) Approximately one hour.
(B) At least two hours.
(C) Only ten minutes.
(D) No more than three hours.

43 Look at the table. Which room will the man probably book for the meeting?

(A) Room G011
(B) Room 1011
(C) Room 2011
(D) Room 3011

★Questions 44-46 refer to the following table.

Rosemont Manor	30 guests	Indoor/ Outdoor Pool
California Hotel	10-50 guests	Indoor/ Outdoor Beach
West Lynn Farm	80 guests	Outdoor Garden
Whitehall Estate	60- 200 guests	Indoor

44 According to the conversation, what are the speakers planning for?

(A) Their honeymoon trip.
(B) An annual family reunion.
(C) A department dinner.
(D) Their wedding reception.

45 What does the man urge the woman to do?

(A) Decide on the venue.
(B) Send the invitations.
(C) Return Nikki's call.
(D) Pick a wedding dress.

46 Look at the table. Which location will the couple most likely choose?

(A) Rosemont Manor
(B) West Lynn Farm
(C) California Hotel
(D) Whitehall Estate

47 Why is Tracy planning to take a long leave from work?

(A) She's going abroad for further study.
(B) She's going to have a baby.
(C) She's going on a vacation abroad.
(D) She's going to have a surgery.

48 According to the conversation, which statement is true?

(A) Tracy is going to have her first baby.
(B) Tracy is on her annual leave at the moment.
(C) Tracy hasn't applied for her leave yet.
(D) Tracy will give birth to her baby in about six weeks.

49 What does the man mean?

(A) Tracy's leave application will be approved.
(B) Tracy shouldn't take her annual leave now.
(C) He didn't receive Tracy's leave application.
(D) Tracy's boss won't grant her leave.

50 Why is the woman calling?

(A) To urge the man to make the payment.
(B) To request the man to advance the delivery.
(C) To cancel an order she made earlier.
(D) To tell the man they have shipped his order.

51 According to the conversation, which statement is true?

(A) The man has received his purchase.
(B) The woman hasn't received the payment.
(C) The delivery will be delayed for 24 hours.
(D) The man's order has been delivered.

52 When can the man expect to get his aero bike?

(A) No later than 5 o'clock tomorrow.
(B) By 5 p.m. today.
(C) In two weeks.
(D) Within 7 days.

★Questions 53-55 refer to the following table.

Ordinary Postage Rates/ Surface Parcel

Weight	Rate
Up to 5 kg	70
Up to 10 kg	90
Up to 15 kg	110
Up to 20 kg	135

53 Where most likely is this conversation taking place?

(A) In a post office.
(B) At the stadium.
(C) In a bank.
(D) At a TV station.

54 How did the man decide the postage rate of the parcel?

(A) According to its superficial measurements.

(B) According to its weight.

(C) According to the items inside.

(D) According to the distance to the delivery destination.

55 Look at the table. How much does the parcel probably weigh?

(A) 3.8 kg

(B) 8.5 kg

(C) 13.6 kg

(D) 18.7 kg

56 Where most likely is the conversation taking place?

(A) In a buffet restaurant.

(B) On an airplane.

(C) At the food court.

(D) In a fast food restaurant.

57 According to the conversation, what is true about the man?

(A) He is the captain of the flight.

(B) He is a flight attendant.

(C) He is the boy's father.

(D) He likes pork better than chicken.

58 What do we know about the boy's meal?

(A) It's meat-free.

(B) It comes with a gift.

(C) It's complimentary.

(D) It's undercooked.

59 What is taking place in this conversation?

(A) The speakers are deciding what to order.

(B) The speakers are discussing where to eat.

(C) The speakers are complaining about the food.

(D) Two of the speakers want to pack their food.

60 Which statement about the restaurant is true?

(A) It doesn't provide takeout service.

(B) It provides home delivery service.

(C) It doesn't provide free takeout boxes.

(D) It encourages customers to bring leftovers home.

61 How does the woman see the restaurant's takeout policy?

(A) Advantageous

(B) Irrational

(C) Embarrassing

(D) Appropriate

Page	Item No.	Product Name	error	correction
4	EM10023	Eyeliner Marker	$1,299	$1,099
8	FD20139	Foundation	5 shades	3 shades
15	CC50288	Cushion Compact	SPF 15	SPF 50

62 Why is the woman calling?

(A) To announce a new product launch.

(B) To apologize for the errors in the catalogue.

(C) To reconfirm her hotel reservation.

(D) To remind the man of his unsettled payment.

63 By what means did the woman send the corrections to the man?

(A) By a courier

(B) By freight

(C) By fax

(D) By email

64 Look at the list. Which item has been mispriced?

(A) Eyeliner marker

(B) Foundation

(C) Cushion compact

(D) None of the above.

★Questions 65-67 refer to the following table.

Rates for Dome Tents

Brands	Rates/per night
The North Face	800
Marmot	1200
MSR	900
Big Agnes	650

65 Where are the speakers?

(A) At a tent rental shop
(B) At the hotel lobby
(C) At the campsite
(D) At a holiday resort

66 According to the conversation, which statement is true?

(A) The woman can't afford a teepee.
(B) The woman's budget for the tent rent is limited.
(C) The woman prefers a tunnel tent.
(D) The woman will buy a family tent.

67 Look at the table. Which tent will the woman probably rent?

(A) The North Face one
(B) The Marmot one
(C) The MSR one
(D) The Big Agnes one

68 What are the speakers doing?

(A) Asking directions.
(B) Rescheduling their meeting.
(C) Arguing with each other.
(D) Complaining about their work.

69 Why can't the woman make it to the appointment with the man?

(A) She has to attend a more important meeting.
(B) She is not feeling very well today.
(C) She got trapped in the traffic jam.
(D) She hasn't had the contract ready.

70 When will the speakers meet up?

(A) Sometime next week.
(B) At lunchtime tomorrow.
(C) At two o'clock this afternoon.
(D) This Friday evening.

► PART 4

Directions: You will hear some talks given by a single speaker. You will be asked to answer three questions about what the speaker says in each talk. Select the best response to each question and mark the letter (A), (B), (C) or (D) on your answer sheet. The talks will not be printed in your test book and will be spoken only one time.

71 Why is the woman leaving this message?

(A) To complain about the defective product.

(B) To explain for the late delivery.

(C) To apologize for the unsatisfactory product.

(D) To request for a replacement.

72 How does the woman deal with the complaint about faulty products?

(A) Send a replacement immediately.

(B) Accept returns unconditionally.

(C) Refund the money to customers.

(D) Compensate customers for their loss.

73 According to this message, which statement is incorrect?

(A) The replacement will arrive today.

(B) The courier will withdraw the faulty item.

(C) The shop is responsible for their products.

(D) Mrs. Tung was pleased with the rice cooker.

74 What most likely is this store selling?

(A) Household appliances

(B) Women's clothes and accessories

(C) Men's sportswear

(D) Children's books and toys

75 According to this talk, what is going to take place?

(A) A beauty contest

(B) A job fair

(C) An annual clearance sale

(D) An opening ceremony

76 Why should the listeners try on everything before they buy it?

(A) No returns on clearance items

(B) There are plenty of fitting rooms.

(C) In case they don't know their sizes.

(D) Not all items are in stock.

★Questions 77-79 refer to the following schedule.

Regular Entertainments

Magical Trip with Hoody	10:00 a.m./13:00 p.m.
Laughter Maker Company	11:00 a.m./15:00 p.m.
Animals' Fantasy Parade	3:00 p.m.
Fireworks Show	8:30 p.m.

77 According to the talk, what takes place every other hour?

(A) Magical Trip with Hoody

(B) Animals' Fantasy Parade

(C) Cowboy Rappers' show

(D) Laughter Maker Company

78 Where can the event schedule be found?

(A) At the entrance of the park

(B) On the map of the park

(C) Behind the ticket

(D) On the cover of the manual

79 Look at the schedule. When does the park give a fireworks display?

(A) 10:00 a.m.

(B) 11:00 a.m.

(C) 3:00 p.m.

(D) 8:30 p.m.

80 What kind of occasion is this?

(A) An induction ceremony

(B) A scientific symposium

(C) An award ceremony

(D) A university commencement

81 Who most likely is the speaker?

(A) The host of the symposium

(B) The supervisor of the presentation

(C) The winner of the poster competition

(D) The director of the Ecology Research Center

82 What is Jason Molly going to do?

(A) To announce the winner of the poster competition.

(B) To give a presentation about his ecology research.

(C) To give his comments on the presentation.

(D) To answer the questions from the audience.

83 What is the speaker doing?

(A) Promoting an eye cream

(B) Advertising for her book

(C) Demonstrating a bread machine

(D) Introducing a new friend

84 Where most likely is the speaker giving a talk like this?

(A) In a tourist information center

(B) At the airport check-in counter

(C) At the ticket booth of a museum

(D) At a department store skin care product counter

85 What special offer can the listeners get?

(A) 20 percent off

(B) Free delivery service

(C) Buy two, get one free

(D) Buy one, get one half price

★Questions 86-88 refer to the following post.

Spring Semester 2018

Mar 5-7 11am-4pm	Engineering/Technology
Mar 8-9 11am-4pm	Investment Banking
Mar 12-13 11am-4pm	Law & Accounting
Mar 14-16 11am-4pm	Media/journalism

86 Who most likely is the speaker talking to?

(A) College freshers
(B) College sophomores
(C) College juniors
(D) College seniors

87 What will take place in school from next Monday?

(A) A series of job fairs
(B) An educational exhibition
(C) An International travel fair
(D) An auto show

88 Look at the post. When should those who are interested in working in journalism attend the fair?

(A) March 6
(B) March 10
(C) March 12
(D) March 15

★Questions 89-91 refer to the following note.

The Old John's Restaurant	Tel: 20233035
	Quantity
Rice with stewed pork	3
Rice with fried chicken leg	5
Rice with pork chop	8
Vegetarian lunch box	6

89 What is the purpose of this voice message?

(A) To ask the listener to run an errand.
(B) To order lunch takeout.
(C) To convey gratitude.
(D) To notify the listener of the meeting.

90 Why does the listener need to ask for a receipt?

(A) To return the purchase later.
(B) To apply for reimbursement.
(C) To file a tax return.
(D) To keep track of her business expenses.

91 Look at the note. How many people will attend the luncheon?

(A) 8 people   (B) 14 people
(C) 22 people   (D) 30 people

★**Questions 92-94 refer to the following table.**

Ceremony Team		Party Team	
Leader:	Jason	Leader:	Kyle
Members:	Heidi	Members:	Larson
	Steven		Wendy
	Billy		Amelia
	Daniel		Max
	Rosie		Sam

92 Who are the participants of this meeting?

(A) The R&D Department staff
(B) The Planning Department staff
(C) The Marketing staff
(D) The HR Department staff

93 Who will be commended in the awarding ceremony?

(A) Outstanding staff
(B) Senior staff
(C) The winner of the competition
(D) Employees with perfect attendance

94 Look at the table. Who will be in charge of the year-end party?

(A) Mike
(B) Jason
(C) Max
(D) Kyle

95 What is the purpose of this message?

(A) To change the delivery address
(B) To change the delivery date
(C) To confirm the order
(D) To request an invoice

96 Where does the speaker want his order to be delivered?

(A) His office
(B) The hotel he is staying in
(C) His parents' place
(D) Directly to the airport

97 By what means will the speaker pay for the additional fee?

(A) By cash
(B) By credit card
(C) Through direct debit
(D) By his stored value card

98 Who most likely is the speaker talking to?

(A) Job applicants
(B) Potential business partners
(C) Travel agents
(D) Target customers

99 What is the speaker doing?

(A) Promoting a new product
(B) Introducing a new friend
(C) Recommending a restaurant
(D) Seeking a sales agent

100 According to the talk, where does the company plan to market their products?

(A) South Korea
(B) India
(C) Singapore
(D) The Philippines

New TOEIC Listening Test 5

新多益**聽力**全真模擬**試題第5回**

> ### ▶ LISTENING TEST
>
> In the Listening test, you will be asked to demonstrate how well you understand spoken English. The entire Listening test will last approximately 45 minutes. There are four parts, and directions are given for each part. You must mark your answers on the separate answer sheet.
>
> ### ▶ PART 1
>
> **Directions:** For each question in this part, you will hear four statements about a picture in your test book. When you hear the statements, you must select the one statement that best describes what you see in the picture. Then find the number of the question on your answer sheet and mark your answer. The statements will not be printed in your test book and will be spoken only one time.

01

02

03

▶ PART 2

Directions: You will hear a question or statement and three responses spoken in English. They will not be printed in your test book and will be spoken only one time. Select the best response to the question or statement and mark the letter (A), (B) or (C) on your answer sheet.

Example

You will hear: Did you have dinner at the restaurant yesterday?
You will also hear: (A) Yes, it lasted all day.
                       (B) No, I went to a movie with my girlfriend.
                       (C) Yes, the client was nice.

The best response to the question "Did you have dinner at the restaurant yesterday?" is choice (B), "No, I went to a movie with my girlfriend," so (B) is the best answer. You should mark answer (B) on your answer sheet.

07 Mark your answer on your answer sheet.

08 Mark your answer on your answer sheet.

09 Mark your answer on your answer sheet.

10 Mark your answer on your answer sheet.

11 Mark your answer on your answer sheet.

12 Mark your answer on your answer sheet.

13 Mark your answer on your answer sheet.

14 Mark your answer on your answer sheet.

15 Mark your answer on your answer sheet.

16 Mark your answer on your answer sheet.

17 Mark your answer on your answer sheet.

18 Mark your answer on your answer sheet.

19 Mark your answer on your answer sheet.

20 Mark your answer on your answer sheet.

21 Mark your answer on your answer sheet.

22 Mark your answer on your answer sheet.

23 Mark your answer on your answer sheet.

24 Mark your answer on your answer sheet.

25 Mark your answer on your answer sheet.

26 Mark your answer on your answer sheet.

27 Mark your answer on your answer sheet.

28 Mark your answer on your answer sheet.

29 Mark your answer on your answer sheet.

30 Mark your answer on your answer sheet.

31 Mark your answer on your answer sheet.

▶ **PART 3**

Directions: You will hear some conversations between two people. You will be asked to answer three questions about what the speakers say in each conversation. Select the best response to each question and mark the letter (A), (B), (C) or (D) on your answer sheet. The conversations will not be printed in your test book and will be spoken only one time.

★**Questions 32-34 refer to the following quotation.**

Quotation

Qty	Item/Description	Unit List Price (NT$)	Discount	Unit Net Price (NT$)
5,000	CT-S20BH8 sports bluetooth headphones	2,500.00	40%	1,500
Total				7,500,000

32 What did the woman give the man?

(A) The quotation
(B) The signed contract
(C) The purchase order
(D) The invoice

33 What are the speakers doing?

(A) Negotiating the order
(B) Wrapping up a deal
(C) Confirming the delivery date
(D) Inquiring about prices

34 Look at the quotation. How much discount has the man got?

(A) 20%
(B) 30%
(C) 40%
(D) 50%

35 What's the relationship between the speakers?

(A) High school classmates
(B) Colleagues at work
(C) Business partners
(D) Next-door neighbors

36 Why can't the man get off work on time?

(A) He wants to get his job done on schedule.
(B) He has to run errands for his boss.
(C) He is covering for the woman.
(D) He has an appointment with a client.

37 What will the man do next?

(A) Talk to his boss.
(B) Leave work early.
(C) Proceed with his work.
(D) Have dinner with the woman.

38 Which of the following do the speakers probably work for?

(A) A kitchen appliance manufacturer
(B) A cosmetics company
(C) An auto parts manufacturer
(D) A book publisher

39 How did the speakers achieve the monthly sales targets so fast?

(A) They were all professional salespeople.
(B) They adopted a new sales strategy.
(C) They set realistic sales goals.
(D) They received a huge order.

40 What is the woman expecting?

(A) The sales incentive
(B) A long-planned vacation
(C) A raise in her salary
(D) A promotion at work

41 What are the speakers talking about?

(A) The annual bonus
(B) The staff trip
(C) The year-end banquet
(D) The department meeting

42 According to the conversation, which statement is true?

(A) The company never gives away annual bonus.
(B) The company's profit fell this year.
(C) The company's business grew this year.
(D) The company doesn't give cash bonus.

43 When will the annual bonus be announced?

(A) It remains uncertain
(B) No later than December 23
(C) Next Monday at the earliest
(D) This Friday at the latest

★Questions 44-46 refer to the following graph.

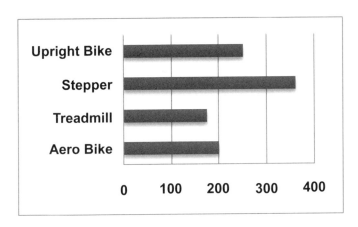

44 What do we know about the speakers?

(A) They are preparing for a trade show.
(B) They plan to go to a show together.
(C) They sell gym equipment.
(D) They are not happy with their booth.

45 What is the selling point of their products?

(A) Better quality
(B) Lower price
(C) Multiple functions
(D) Longer warranty

46 Look at the graph. Which is the best-selling product at the show?

(A) Upright bike
(B) Stepper
(C) Treadmill
(D) Aero bike

47 Where is this conversation taking place?

(A) At a dental clinic
(B) At the Health Insurance Bureau
(C) In a pharmacy
(D) In the Counselors' Office

48 Who most likely is the man?

(A) A surgeon
(B) A physician
(C) A nurse
(D) A dentist

49 What will the woman undergo next?

(A) A heart surgery
(B) A plastic surgery
(C) A teeth cleaning
(D) A tooth extraction

★Questions 50-52 refer to the following table.

	Max Capacity	Daily Rates (NT$)
GMC Acadia	7	2,500
Honda Pilot	8	3,000
Mazda CX9	7	2,750
Volkswagen Atlas	7	2,800

50 What does the man need?

(A) An SUV for eight people
(B) A sports car
(C) A convertible car
(D) A camper

51 According to the conversation, which statement is true?

(A) The man wants a full-sized car.
(B) The cars are insured.
(C) The man reserved a car three days ago.
(D) All mid size cars are reserved.

52 Look at the table. Which one meets the man's requirements?

(A) GMC Acadia
(B) Honda Pilot
(C) Mazda CX9
(D) Volkswagen Atlas

53 What is the man going to do?

(A) Pack for a trip
(B) Go shopping with the woman
(C) Buy some warm clothes
(D) Book a flight

54 According to the conversation, which statement is true?

(A) The man is going on a business trip.

(B) The woman is helping the man pack.

(C) The man is visiting London in the winter.

(D) The man will spend a long time in London.

55 What does the woman mean?

(A) The man should take a shower.

(B) There's a good chance it will rain in London.

(C) It's a bad idea to visit London in the winter.

(D) She prefers outdoor activities.

56 What is taking place in this conversation?

(A) Two people are waiting for a table.

(B) A woman is calling to get a reservation.

(C) A man is inviting his friends for dinner.

(D) A man is seeing his friends off at the airport.

57 According to the conversation, what do we know about the restaurant?

(A) It doesn't take reservations.

(B) It has a table time limit.

(C) It's not open for business yet.

(D) It doesn't serve alcohol.

58 How long do the speakers have to wait for a free table?

(A) At least an hour.

(B) Probably 90 minutes.

(C) About half an hour.

(D) It depends.

★Questions 59-61 refer to the following table.

Student Membership	Discount
12-month	20%
6-month	15%
3-month	10%
Monthly rolling	5%

59 What does the woman want to join?

(A) A gym
(B) A drama club
(C) A band
(D) The army

60 Which membership package is the woman interested in?

(A) A no contract monthly membership
(B) A day pass
(C) A fixed-term membership
(D) A student membership

61 Look at the table. Which package offers the biggest discount?

(A) The monthly rolling membership
(B) The three-month membership
(C) The six-month membership
(D) The 12-moth membership

62 Where are the speakers?

(A) At the currency exchange counter
(B) At the airport check-in counter
(C) At the luggage claim area
(D) In the duty free shop

63 What do we know about the woman?

(A) She missed her connecting flight.
(B) She couldn't find her luggage.
(C) She was forced to give up her seat.
(D) She was charged for her overweight luggage.

64 What happened to the woman's luggage?

(A) It was put on a wrong flight.

(B) It didn't make the flight.

(C) It wasn't put on the right carousel.

(D) Someone else took it by mistake.

65 Where did the couple try to buy a drink?

(A) In a convenience store

(B) From a vending machine

(C) From a street vendor

(D) In a supermarket

66 What's wrong with the machine?

(A) It gives wrong change.

(B) It won't take debit cards.

(C) It won't take cash.

(D) It is out of order.

67 What does the woman mean?

(A) The machine needs an out-of-order sign.

(B) The machine needs to be discarded.

(C) She can fix the machine by herself.

(D) She will compensate the man for his loss.

68 What are the speakers planning?

(A) A scholarly presentation

(B) A birthday celebration

(C) A funeral ceremony

(D) A farewell party

69 How will the going away party be?

(A) Sad

(B) Joyful

(C) Awkward

(D) Emotional

70 What will the woman do in preparation for the party?

(A) Send the invitation

(B) Bake a cake

(C) Reserve a venue

(D) Buy a gift

Directions: You will hear some talks given by a single speaker. You will be asked to answer three questions about what the speaker says in each talk. Select the best response to each question and mark the letter (A), (B), (C) or (D) on your answer sheet. The talks will not be printed in your test book and will be spoken only one time.

★**Questions 71-73 refer to the following table.**

Result of the vote

Place	Votes
Kenting	22
Yilan	34
Alishan	18
Tainan	12

71 Which event will take place at the end of October?

(A) Re-election of directors
(B) Opening anniversary celebration
(C) Annual company trip
(D) Company sports fest

72 What will the speakers vote for?

(A) The destination of the trip
(B) The dates of the trip
(C) The leader of the preparatory group
(D) The location of the staff dinner

73 Look at the table. Which place is selected as the trip destination?

(A) Kenting
(B) Yilan
(C) Alishan
(D) Tainan

74 What is the workshop mainly about?

(A) How to strengthen customer service skills
(B) How to motivate employees to work harder
(C) How to enhance work efficiency
(D) How to improve time management skills

75 Which of the following will not be included in the workshop?

(A) Telephone skills
(B) Complaint resolution
(C) Building customer loyalty
(D) Interpersonal skills

76 Which statement about the workshop is NOT true?

(A) It's a two-hour training program.
(B) It's optional.
(C) It will take place next Wednesday morning.
(D) The registration ends today.

★Questions 77-79 refer to the following picture.

> Attachments (4)
>
> 1. Last meeting's minutes
>
> 2. Meeting agenda
>
> 3. Team monthly sales report
>
> 4. budget proposal

77 What is the speaker doing?

(A) Taking a message
(B) Leaving a message
(C) Reserving a meeting room
(D) Inviting the man for the meeting

78 According to the message, which is not Daniel responsible for?

(A) Reserving a meeting room
(B) Making seat arrangements
(C) Getting the video equipment ready
(D) Sending invitation notices

79 Look at the picture. Which is not included in the attachments?

(A) The last meeting's minutes
(B) Meeting agenda
(C) Presentation outline
(D) Budget proposal

	Time	Prices
Weekdays	17:30-21:00	$580 (per adult) $290 (per child)
Weekend & Holiday	17:00-22:00	$650 (per adult) $320 (per child)

80 What is the speaker doing?

(A) Booking a table
(B) Making a reservation
(C) Canceling a reservation
(D) Taking a reservation

81 What type of restaurant is this?

(A) A fast food restaurant
(B) A barbecue restaurant
(C) A buffet restaurant
(D) A bistro

82 Look at the table. What's the price for dinner buffet per adult during the weekdays?

(A) $580
(B) $290
(C) $650
(D) $320

83 What do we know about the speaker?

(A) She got pregnant.
(B) She got her first job offer.
(C) She nailed the job interview.
(D) She has been proposed.

84 What is the purpose of this message?

(A) To share happy news
(B) To announce pregnancy
(C) To express gratitude
(D) To give a warning

85 According to the message, what will take place in the coming August?

(A) An engagement party
(B) A wedding banquet
(C) A graduation ceremony
(D) An opening tea party

86 What is the man doing?

(A) Asking his secretary to run his errands

(B) Providing feedback to an employee

(C) Interviewing a job candidate

(D) Showing his boss a workable plan

87 What does the speaker ask the listener to do?

(A) Estimate the cost of developing the product

(B) Work on the launch plan

(C) Rewrite her proposal

(D) Integrate her ideas into the market

88 When is the listener expected to turn in a revision?

(A) In two weeks

(B) By the end of this week

(C) By next meeting

(D) By the end of this month

89 How does the speaker sound?

(A) Excited

(B) Furious

(C) Regretful

(D) Embarrassed

90 What is the purpose of this call?

(A) To announce a promotion

(B) To offer an apology

(C) To make a complaint

(D) To claim a insurance

91 When is the listener supposed to make a response?

(A) Within 12 hours

(B) Within 24 hours

(C) Within 48 hours

(D) Within 72 hours

★Questions 41-43 refer to the

Spring Concert

Sonata No. 3 in D minor, Op. 108

Johannes Brahms (1833-1897)

=== Intermission (20 minutes) ===

Sonata in A Major, FWV 8

Cêser Franck (1822-1890)

---

92 What will start in twenty minutes?

(A) A music concert
(B) A football match
(C) A carnival parade
(D) A religious festival

93 What are the listeners advised to do?

(A) Silence their phones
(B) Get a concert program
(C) Go to the restroom
(D) Buy souvenirs at the gift shop

94 Look at the program. How long is the intermission?

(A) Five minutes
(B) Ten minutes
(C) Fifteen minutes
(D) Twenty minutes

95 What is this announcement mainly about?

(A) A notice of relocation
(B) A change of business hours
(C) A notice of temporary closure
(D) A change of personnel

96 What information is not given in this announcement?

(A) The speaker's replacement
(B) The speaker's contact number
(C) The speaker's current position
(D) The speaker's future work place

97 What most likely is the reason the speaker's leaving her current position?

(A) She got laid off.

(B) She is retiring.

(C) She is job-hopping to another company.

(D) She has been promoted.

98 Why is the man calling?

(A) To turn down an invitation

(B) To request a product sample

(C) To reschedule a meeting

(D) To cancel a purchase order

99 Why can't the man join the celebration?

(A) He is hospitalized.

(B) He is on a vacation.

(C) He has a prior arrangement.

(D) He has to work overtime.

100 What does the man offer at the end of his message?

(A) A special discount

(B) A dinner invitation

(C) A business proposal

(D) An apprenticeship

New TOEIC Listening Test 6
新多益**聽力**全真模擬**試題第6回**

▶ **LISTENING TEST**

In the Listening test, you will be asked to demonstrate how well you understand spoken English. The entire Listening test will last approximately 45 minutes. There are four parts, and directions are given for each part. You must mark your answers on the separate answer sheet.

▶ **PART 1**

Directions: For each question in this part, you will hear four statements about a picture in your test book. When you hear the statements, you must select the one statement that best describes what you see in the picture. Then find the number of the question on your answer sheet and mark your answer. The statements will not be printed in your test book and will be spoken only one time.

01

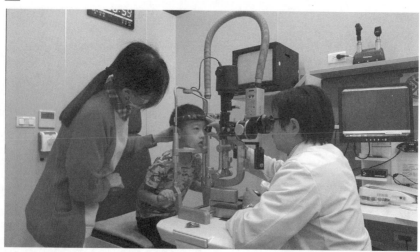

02

03

▶ **PART 2**

Directions: You will hear a question or statement and three responses spoken in English. They will not be printed in your test book and will be spoken only one time. Select the best response to the question or statement and mark the letter (A), (B) or (C) on your answer sheet.

Example

You will hear: Did you have dinner at the restaurant yesterday?
You will also hear: (A) Yes, it lasted all day.
                      (B) No, I went to a movie with my girlfriend.
                      (C) Yes, the client was nice.

The best response to the question "Did you have dinner at the restaurant yesterday?" is choice (B), "No, I went to a movie with my girlfriend," so (B) is the best answer. You should mark answer (B) on your answer sheet.

07 Mark your answer on your answer sheet.

08 Mark your answer on your answer sheet.

09 Mark your answer on your answer sheet.

10 Mark your answer on your answer sheet.

11 Mark your answer on your answer sheet.

12 Mark your answer on your answer sheet.

13 Mark your answer on your answer sheet.

14 Mark your answer on your answer sheet.

15 Mark your answer on your answer sheet.

16 Mark your answer on your answer sheet.

17 Mark your answer on your answer sheet.

18 Mark your answer on your answer sheet.

19 Mark your answer on your answer sheet.

20 Mark your answer on your answer sheet.

21 Mark your answer on your answer sheet.

22 Mark your answer on your answer sheet.

23 Mark your answer on your answer sheet.

24 Mark your answer on your answer sheet.

25 Mark your answer on your answer sheet.

26 Mark your answer on your answer sheet.

27 Mark your answer on your answer sheet.

28 Mark your answer on your answer sheet.

29 Mark your answer on your answer sheet.

30 Mark your answer on your answer sheet.

31 Mark your answer on your answer sheet.

▶ PART 3

Directions: You will hear some conversations between two people. You will be asked to answer three questions about what the speakers say in each conversation. Select the best response to each question and mark the letter (A), (B), (C) or (D) on your answer sheet. The conversations will not be printed in your test book and will be spoken only one time.

32 What are the speakers talking about?

(A) A celebrity's marriage life

(B) A party held last weekend

(C) A colleague absent from work

(D) A new product launched last month

33 According to the conversation, what do you know about Alice?

(A) She is in the meeting.

(B) She is under the weather.

(C) She is the speakers' supervisor.

(D) She's on business trip.

34 What's Alice's role in the meeting tomorrow?

(A) The chairperson

(B) The minute taker

(C) The interpreter

(D) The photographer

35 What are the speakers doing?

(A) Debating on the marketing plan

(B) Setting up a time to meet

(C) Gossiping about their boss

(D) Planning for their weekend

36 Why doesn't Wednesday work for the woman?

(A) She will fly to Tokyo for a meeting.

(B) She's going to take a day off.

(C) She has a prior arrangement.

(D) She is going grocery shopping.

37 What does the woman volunteer to do?

(A) Send the meeting invitation

(B) Make document copies

(C) Book the meeting room

(D) Prepare related documents

★**Questions 38-40 refer to the following table.**

Mother's Day Deals		
Deal 1	Shampoo + Haircut + Treatment	$1,200
Deal 2	Shampoo + Haircut + Perm	$3,200
Deal 3	Shampoo + Haircut + Highlights	$3,500
Deal 4	Shampoo + Perm + Highlights	$5,000

38 Where are the speakers?

(A) The police station
(B) A beauty parlor
(C) The City Hall
(D) A hypermarket

39 Who's the woman talking to?

(A) Her personal assistant
(B) A convenience store clerk
(C) A hair stylist
(D) An interior designer

40 Look at the table. How much money is the woman going to spend on her hair?

(A) $1,200
(B) $3,200
(C) $3,500
(D) $5,000

41 Why is the woman making this call?

(A) To request for reimbursement
(B) To apologize for not making the payment
(C) To remind the man to settle their account
(D) To request for an invoice

42 Why didn't the man make the payment?

(A) He forgot to request for reimbursement.
(B) He didn't receive the invoice.
(C) His company has financial problems.
(D) There was an error on the invoice.

43 When will the woman receive the payment at the earliest?

(A) Within seven days
(B) Within this month
(C) The tenth of the next month
(D) Ten days later

44 What are the speakers discussing?

(A) The budget of the project

(B) A client's request

(C) The company's dress code

(D) The meeting agenda

45 What request did they receive?

(A) To advance the delivery date

(B) To work overtime on the weekend

(C) To make a further discount

(D) To issue an invoice

46 What is the speakers' conclusion?

(A) To hasten the production

(B) To breach the contract

(C) To turn down the request

(D) To follow the instruction

★**Questions 47-49 refer to the following table.**

Region	Oversize Luggage Fees
U.S. & Canada	$ 4,800
Europe	$ 4,500
Asia	$ 4,200
Australia & New Zealand	$ 4,000

47 Where is this conversation taking place?

(A) At the boarding gate

(B) At the hotel check-in counter

(C) At the airport check-in counter

(D) At the supermarket check-out counter

48 What does the man need to pay for?

(A) His overweight luggage

(B) His oversize luggage

(B) His extra luggage

(D) His carry-on luggage

加★部分為多益新題型以及相關小提醒，考生要特別注意喔！ 115

49 Look at the table. Where most likely is the man traveling to?

(A) New Zealand
(B) South Korea
(C) Canada
(D) Germany

50 What are the speakers mainly discussing?

(A) Whether to give out free samples
(B) How to promote their new product
(C) Whether to purchase a Smart Board
(D) The shortcomings of a dry erase board

51 What is the woman's main concern about a Smart Board?

(A) The size
(B) The brand
(C) The price
(D) The warranty

52 What will the speakers do next?

(A) Place a purchase order
(B) Get a sample to try out
(C) Discard the dry erase board
(D) Have a Smart Board installed

53 What are the speakers doing?

(A) Scheduling a meeting
(B) Discussing a construction project
(C) Negotiating a discount
(D) Getting ready for the presentation

54 What is the woman busy doing?

(A) She is dressing up for a party.
(B) She has a meeting to attend.
(C) She is looking for a new apartment.
(D) She is looking for a job.

55 When will the speakers meet up for the construction project?

(A) Later today
(B) Sometime next week
(C) This weekend
(D) Before the seminar

★Questions 56-58 refer to the following table.

Charter Rates 2018	
Vehicle type	one-day local trip
55-seat coach	$ 10,000
32-seat coach	$ 7,500
12-seat van	$ 4,800
9-seat van	$ 4,000

56 What is the woman reserving?

(A) Home delivery service

(B) Car and driver service

(C) Airport pickup service

(D) Catering service

57 According to the conversation, which statement is true?

(A) Charter service is a type of delivery service.

(B) The woman needs a van without a driver.

(C) The woman is traveling alone.

(D) The woman wants to charter a van.

58 Look at the table. How much will the woman spend on charter service?

(A) $4,000

(B) $4,800

(C) $7,500

(D) $10,000

59 What are the speakers discussing?

(A) Last meeting's minutes

(B) Exhibition layout

(C) An upcoming event

(D) Orientation program

60 Which event will take place following the opening ceremony?

(A) A two-hour orientation course

(B) A tea party

(C) A press conference

(D) A charity bazaar

61 What have the speakers reserved in preparation for the tea party?

(A) Catering service

(B) A whole restaurant

(C) A shuttle bus

(D) A conference room

62 What are the speakers doing?

(A) Trying to come up with marketing ideas

(B) Working on their marketing proposal

(C) Dealing with a difficult customer

(D) Demonstrating their new products

63 What do the speakers think may boost the sales?

(A) Letting customers try out products for free.

(B) Giving out free samples on the streets.

(C) Using celebrities in advertising.

(D) Offering early payment discounts

64 What is the woman's attitude toward the marketing idea?

(A) Opposing

(B) Doubtful

(C) Hesitant

(D) Supportive

★Questions 65-67 refer to the following table.

Commercial Legal size	Price (NT$)
metal filing cabinet	$ 4,500
wood filing cabinet	$ 4,250
plastic filing cabinet	$ 2,980
mobile filing cabinet	$ 3,550

65 What are the speakers doing?

(A) Contacting the office furniture manufacturer

(B) Discussing whether to buy a filing cabinet

(C) Determining which filing cabinet to buy

(D) Requesting quotation from their supplier

66 What kind of filing cabinet are the speakers looking for?

(A) A commercial legal size one

(B) A two-drawer one

(C) A three-drawer one

(D) A customized one

67 Look at the table. Which cabinet will the speakers probably buy?

(A) Metal filing cabinet
(B) Wood filing cabinet
(C) Plastic filing cabinet
(D) Mobile filing cabinet

68 What's the speakers' attitude toward the woman's project?

(A) Concerned
(B) Uninterested
(C) Impatient
(D) indifferent

69 Which statement is true about the woman's project?

(A) It will be completed early.
(B) It has been put on hold.
(C) It's progressing slowly.
(D) It is short of funds.

70 What does the woman request?

(A) Financial assistance
(B) Technical assistance
(C) A multifunction printer
(D) Additional manpower

Directions: You will hear some talks given by a single speaker. You will be asked to answer three questions about what the speaker says in each talk. Select the best response to each question and mark the letter (A), (B), (C) or (D) on your answer sheet. The talks will not be printed in your test book and will be spoken only one time.

71 How does the speaker feel about the sales for Q3?

(A) Dissatisfied
(B) Hopeful
(C) Content
(D) Apathetic

72 According to the speaker, which is the least possible reason for the drop in sales?

(A) Out-of-date selling techniques
(B) Incompetent marketing alignment
(C) Inadequate training
(D) Weak economy

73 What does the speaker expect to get by this week?

(A) A review report
(B) A budget proposal
(C) A draft contract
(D) A quotation

74 What is the purpose of this call?

(A) To request for a fast delivery
(B) To request for additional manpower
(C) To call an emergency meeting
(D) To work out new quality control procedures

75 According to the talk, what is true about the hot air stylers?

(A) They can be bought online.
(B) They are unsalable.
(C) They are selling like hot cakes.
(D) They haven't been launched yet.

76 What will the woman do if the store is out of stock of the hot air stylers?

(A) Purchase from the supermarket
(B) Complain to customer service
(C) Transfer inventory to head office
(D) Issue rain checks to customers

★**Questions 77-79 refer to the following table.**

Additional order for Dinner Boxes

Michael	3
Jeremy	2
Lauren	2
Benjamin	1

77 What is this announcement mainly about?

(A) The company's anniversary celebration
(B) The company's sports day
(C) The annual company trip
(D) The department's monthly meeting

78 Which statement about the sports day events is correct?

(A) It's a morning event.
(B) It can continue to the evening.
(C) It's a staff-only activity.
(D) It's a quarterly event.

79 Look at the table. Who will bring most people to the Sports Day?

(A) Michael
(B) Jeremy
(C) Lauren
(D) Benjamin

80 Why is the speaker calling?

(A) To notify a buyer of his order status
(B) To request a product catalogue
(C) To postpone a scheduled meeting
(D) To invite a client for dinner

81 Who most likely is the speaker?

(A) A bank clerk
(B) A restaurant manager
(C) A food wholesaler
(D) A school teacher

82 What will Mr. Carter get before the delivery arrives?

(A) A visit from the speaker
(B) A call from the delivery driver
(C) A letter from customer service
(D) An invitation to a tea party

83 What's the purpose of this message?

(A) To put off a meeting
(B) To order takeout
(C) To ask for a day off
(D) To pass on a message

84 Why is the office closed today?

(A) Due to water shortage
(B) Due to a power failure
(C) Due to a typhoon
(D) Due to office renovation

85 What does the speaker remind the listener to do?

(A) Fill out the leave request form
(B) Put off the meeting with his client
(C) Ask someone to cover his position
(D) Take the laundry to the cleaners

★**Questions 86-88 refer to the following form.**

Order Form

Customer	Phone	Item	Qty
Ann Jordan	2123-4567	Ceiling light ZR24566-GB	20

86 Why is the speaker calling?

(A) To confirm a purchase order
(B) To request a product catalogue
(C) To turn down a purchase order
(D) To cancel a meeting with a client

87 What does the speaker wish to offer?

(A) A special discount
(B) The product catalogue
(C) A helping hand
(D) Free home delivery

88 Look at the form. What item is the store running short of?

(A) Wall lights
(B) Ceiling lights
(C) floor lamps
(D) Table lamps

89 Why is the speaker calling?

(A) She forgot to lock the door.
(B) She left the bills at home.
(C) Her car won't start.
(D) She feels under the weather.

90 What does the speaker ask the listener to do?

(A) Pay the bill
(B) Call the landlord
(C) Call the police
(D) Flush the toilet

91 What does the speaker plan on doing?

(A) Getting an alarm system
(B) Setting up automatic payments
(C) Installing anti-theft security alarm
(D) Applying for leave without pay

★**Questions 92-94 refer to the following schedule.**

Recycling collection for White Pine Street	
Monday	19:30 p.m.
Tuesday	NA
Wednesday	16:00 p.m.
Thursday	NA
Friday	19:30 p.m.
Saturday & Sunday	NA

*NA=Not Available

92 According to the message, which statement is true?

(A) The speaker will bring dinner home.
(B) The speaker won't come home for dinner.
(C) The speaker will cook dinner by herself.
(D) The speaker is having a day off today.

93 What is the listener asked to do?

(A) Drive the speaker home
(B) Pick up the kids at school
(C) Take out the garbage
(D) Do the dishes

94 Look at the schedule. How often does the recycling truck come?

(A) Once a week
(B) Twice a week
(C) Thrice a week
(D) Every other day

★Questions 95-97 refer to the following table.

Audio guide	fees (per person per day)
Regular	$150
Children under 12	$100
Groups of 20 or more	$60
Seniors over 65	Free

95 What is the purpose of this talk?

(A) To introduce different tours at the gallery
(B) To request the listeners to make a donation
(C) To make an introduction of the gallery
(D) To ask the listeners to follow the rules

96 According to the talk, which statement is true?

(A) The highlights tour is free.
(B) The spotlight tour is only 20 minutes.
(C) The audio guide is designed for adults only.
(D) The audio guide is not for rent.

97 Look at the table. Who can use the audio guide for free?

(A) Regular visitors
(B) Children under 12
(C) Groups of 25
(D) Seniors aged 70

★Questions 98-100 refer to the following form.

Vegetables	Current price (per kilo)	previous price (per kilo)
Cabbage	$140-$150	$70
Carrots	$180	$100
Celery	$180	$70
Cucumber	$50	$20

98 What is this news report about?

(A) Petrol price hike
(B) Vegetables price hike
(C) House price crash
(D) Stock market crash

99 According to the report, what is the main cause of the price hike?

(A) The typhoon
(B) The flood
(C) The blizzard
(D) The impassable roads

100 Look at the table. Which vegetable is twice as expensive?

(A) Cabbage
(B) Carrots
(C) Celery
(D) Cucumbers

NOTE

NEW TOEIC® 新多益考試
金色證書一擊必殺

6回聽力共600題
字字精細翻譯，
幫助快速消化理解

學習有捷徑
夢想最接近

聽力關鍵解題分析

新多益聽力全真模擬試題解析 — 第1~6回

金色證書一擊必殺 Part 2

New TOEIC Listening Analysis 1
新多益聽力全真模擬試題解析第1回

(A) 這些人正在等他們的火車。
(B) 這些人正在等他們的行李。
(C) 這些人正在聽演講。
(D) 這些人正在享用他們的晚餐。

【類型】多人照片題型

【詞彙】
wait for 等候／luggage 行李／
speech 演説

【正解】(B)

01 (A) These people are waiting for their train.
   (B) These people are waiting for their luggage.
   (C) These people are listening to the speech.
   (D) These people are enjoying their dinners.

【解析】當題目出現的是多人照片時，便要注意照片中人們的舉動與四周環境的關係。由照片中人們彼此沒有交談，且站在行李提領處等候，便能判斷(B) 正確地描述出照片中「人們正在等他們的行李」的正確答案。(A)中雖然提到「等候」，但是照片中並未出現火車月台或其他與火車相關的事物；照片中沒有人在發表演説，因此(C)的描述也不正確；(D)表示人們在享用晚餐，更是與圖片內容不符。

(A) 這間自助餐廳即將打烊。
(B) 桌上陳列著一些蛋糕。
(C) 一位女服務生正帶這對夫妻入座。
(D) 這間自助餐廳滿滿都是饑餓的人們。

【類型】兩人以上照片題型

【詞彙】
cafeteria 自助餐館／
close 打烊／display 展示／
waitress 女服務生／
couple 一對（夫妻）

【正解】(B)

02 (A) The cafeteria is about to close.
   (B) Some cakes are displayed on the table.
   (C) A waitress is taking the couple to their table.
   (D) This cafeteria is filled with hungry people.

【解析】當題目出現兩人以上的照片時，除了注意照片中人們的舉動與四周環境的關係之外，有關照片中事物的客觀描述也是重點。由照片中我們看到一對夫妻正在餐點展售區，而照片後方的櫃檯人員正在幫其他客人結帳，無法看出自助餐廳正要打烊的跡象，而且店內也看不出有客滿的樣子，因此(A)與(D)皆非正確描述；再來這對夫妻旁邊並無服務生做帶位動作，因此(C)亦非正解。照片中除了這對夫妻客人之外，我們可以看到展售中上擺放了各式蛋糕，因此判斷(B)為最適當的描述。

03 (A) A new student orientation is going on.
　(B) A year-end clearance sale is going on.
　(C) A traffic accident is being taken care of.
　(D) A symphony concert is about to start.

(A) 現在正在舉行一場新生入學說明會。
(B) 現在正在舉行一場年終清倉特賣。
(C) 現在有一場交通事故正在處理中。
(D) 一場交響音樂會即將開始。

【類型】情境照片題型

【詞彙】
new student orientation
新生說明會／go on 發生／
clearance sale 清倉特賣／
traffic accident 交通事故／
take care of 處理／
symphony concert 交響音樂會

【正解】(A)

【解析】當題目照片中的情境很簡單明確時，要能立刻判斷照片中的情境是何種狀況。由照片中我們可以看到一名女子正利用白板上的投影表格對一群人作說明，可判斷(A)為正確描述。(B)中提到的年終清倉特賣、(C)中提到的交通事故以及(D)中提到的交響音樂會，都與照片內容不符，因此都可以排除在可能的選擇之外。

04 (A) The passengers are getting off a train.
　(B) The passengers are exchanging their seats.
　(C) The passengers are waiting to be seated.
　(D) The passengers are boarding a train.

(A) 乘客們正在下火車。
(B) 乘客們正在交換座位。
(C) 乘客們正在等著入座。
(D) 乘客們正在上火車。

【類型】情境照片題型

【詞彙】
passenger 乘客／
get off 下（車）／
exchange seats 交換座位／
board the train 搭車

【正解】(D)

【解析】當題目為情境簡單明確的照片，照片中人們的舉動及四周環境的關係便是描述的重點。由照片中一列月台上的火車，以及排隊上車的乘客，可判斷(D)為正確的描述。(A)中描述乘客們正在下火車，是錯誤的；而(B)與(C)中所描述的交換座位或入座狀況，都是發生在火車車廂內的狀態，由照片中是看不出來的，因此皆非適當的選項。

(A) 女子正在考慮要點什麼。

(B) 女子正在為她的餐點付錢。

(C) 女子正在問路。

(D) 女子正在跟店員對話。

【類型】人物照片題型

【詞彙】

consider 考慮／pay for 付錢／
ask for directions 問路／
have a conversation with sb.
與某人對話

【正解】(A)

05 (A) The woman is considering what to order.

(B) The woman is paying for her meal.

(C) The woman is asking for direction.

(D) The woman is having a conversation with the clerk.

【解析】看到人物照片題時，要特別留意照片中主要人物在做什麼，以及其與四周環境及人物的互動關係。照片中的婦人並沒有與任何人對話，因此(C)與(D)都可先刪除不考慮。(B)提到的「付錢」舉動，也並未出現在照片中。由照片中婦人摸著下巴、看著餐點思考的模樣，可判斷(A)是最適合照片內容的描述。

(A) 顧問正在回答學生的問題。

(B) 醫生正在幫病人開處方籤。

(C) 他們正在馬路上彼此爭執。

(D) 女子正在打電話給她的朋友。

【類型】多人照片題型

【詞彙】

consultant 顧問／
prescription 處方籤／
make a phone call 撥打電話

【正解】(A)

06 (A) The consultant is answering the student's question.

(B) The doctor is writing a prescription for his patient.

(C) They are arguing with each other on the street.

(D) The woman is making a phone call to her friend.

【解析】看到多人照片題時，除了照片中人物的動作之外，也要觀察照片中的環境以及人物的服裝等，以判斷照片人物所在的場所及身份。由於照片並未透露出「醫院或診所」的相關訊息，因此可直接刪去(B)不考慮。此外，照片中的環境並非在馬路上，而且人物並沒有出現「打電話」的動作，因此(C)與(D)也是可以直接刪去不考慮的選項。(A)所陳述的「顧問回答學生問題」是最符合照片情境的句子，因此為正解。

▶ PART 2

Directions: You will hear a question or statement and three responses spoken in English. They will not be printed in your test book and will be spoken only one time. Select the best response to the question or statement and mark the letter (A), (B) or (C) on your answer sheet.

Example

You will hear:

Did you have dinner at the restaurant yesterday?

You will also hear:

(A) Yes, it lasted all day.

(B) No, I went to a movie with my girlfriend.

(C) Yes, the client was nice.

The best response to the question "Did you have dinner at the restaurant yesterday?" is choice (B), "No, I went to a movie with my girlfriend," so (B) is the best answer. You should mark answer (B) on your answer sheet.

07 Would you mind opening the window?
　(A) No problem.
　(B) In a minute.
　(C) That's right.

【解析】題目為 would you mind +v-ing 「你介不介意……」，為用來詢問對方意願的句型。聽到題目問「是否介意打開窗戶？」(A)以「沒問題」給予肯定回覆是最適當的回答。(B)與(C)都是答非所問，並非正解。

你介意打開窗戶嗎？
(A) 沒問題。
(B) 一會兒。
(C) 沒錯。

【類型】詢問意願題型

【詞彙】
　mind 介意／in a minute 一會兒

【正解】(A)

慶祝派對會在哪裡舉辦？
(A) 這個星期結束之前。
(B) 在帝國飯店。
(C) 一個新應徵者。

【類型】where疑問句題型

【詞彙】
celebration party 慶祝派對／
hold 舉辦

【正解】(B)

08 Where is the celebration party going to be held?
(A) By the end of this week.
(B) At Empire Hotel.
(C) A new applicant.

【解析】遇到where的疑問句題型，答案一定必須與「場所」
或「地點」有關。題目詢問派對舉行的地點，(B)針對問題，
說明派對舉辦的地點，是最適當的回答。(A)與時間有關，而
(C)與人物及對象有關，均非where疑問題型所需要的答案，
因此不需考慮。

你將會被調到哪一個部門？
(A) 人資部。
(B) 從下個月起。
(C) 我很樂意幫忙。

【類型】which疑問句題型

【詞彙】
department 部門／
transfer 轉調／
Human Resources 人力資源

【正解】(A)

09 Which department will you be transferred to?
(A) Human Resources.
(B) Starting from next month.
(C) I'd be glad to help.

【解析】題目為以which為句首的疑問句，目的是要詢問對方
將被轉調到「哪一個」部門，因此(A)針對問題明確回覆「人
資部門」是最適當的答案。(B)是用來回覆轉調的時間，並非
正解；(C)的回覆則答非所問，不需考慮。

你覺得羅賓森小姐的演說怎麼
樣？
(A) 我很期待。
(B) 很具啟發性。
(C) 會延遲幾分鐘。

【類型】詢問感想題型

【詞彙】
lecture 演說；講課／
look forward to 期待／
instructive 具啟發性的／
delay 延遲

【正解】(B)

10 How did you like Ms. Robinson's lecture?
(A) I'm looking forward to it.
(B) Very instructive.
(C) There will be a few minutes' delay.

【解析】How did you like ... 是用來「詢問意見或感想」的
疑問句型，有「你覺得……怎麼樣」之意。(B)認為這次演講
「很具啟發性」，是最適當的答案；(A)表示對此演講「很期
待」以及(C)表示這次演講將會延遲幾分鐘，都沒有針對問題
給予正面回覆，因此均非正解。

11 When is the meeting scheduled?
(A) 9 a.m. tomorrow.
(B) At the headquarters.
(C) By Mr. Anderson.

【解析】題目為以when為句首的疑問句，要問的是會議的時間。(A)回答明天上午九點，是最正確的答案。(B)為與地點有關的答案，而(C)回答由 Mr. Anderson來做，均答非所問，故不需考慮。

會議安排在什麼時候？
(A) 明天上午九點。
(B) 在總公司。
(C) 由安德森先生做。

【類型】when疑問句題型

【詞彙】
meeting 會議／
schedule 安排；預定／
headquarters 總公司；總處

【正解】(A)

---

12 Where would you like me to drop you off?
(A) That's exactly what I meant.
(B) At the post office, please.
(C) Tomorrow will be fine.

【解析】題目為以where為句首的疑問句題型，意在詢問對方希望下車的地點，因此答案必須與「地點」有關。(B)回答 At the post office意即「在郵局下車」，是最適當的答案。(A)的回答完全與問題無關，(C)的回答則是與時間有關，亦非正解。

你希望我讓你在哪裡下車？
(A) 我就是那個意思。
(B) 在郵局門口，麻煩你。
(C) 明天可以。

【類型】where疑問句題型

【詞彙】
drop sb. off 讓某人下車／
post office 郵局

【正解】(B)

---

13 It seems that the photocopier is out of order.
(A) No, I don't work on the weekend.
(B) He was late for the meeting today.
(C) Again? We definitely need a new one.

【解析】遇到陳述句的題型時，必須正確理解陳述句所表達的意思，並選出最適當的對應答覆。聽題目時，聽到題目的關鍵詞彙out of order便可以推測有東西故障了。選項(A)回答「週末不上班」與(B)提及「今天上班遲到」，均與「東西故障」無關，而(C)回答Again? 表示「又故障了？」並緊接著說「需要一個新的」，是針對此問題最適當的回覆，故為正解。

影印機好像不能用。
(A) 不，我週末不上班。
(B) 他今天開會遲到了。
(C) 又來了？我們絕對需要一個新的。

【類型】陳述句題型

【詞彙】
photocopier 影印機／
out of order 故障

【正解】(C)

加★部分為多益新題型以及相關小提醒，考生要特別注意喔！　135

請問我可以跟彼得森先生說話嗎？
(A) 請稍等。我幫您轉過去。
(B) 你已經好一陣子沒見過他了，
對不對？
(C) 讓我想一下。

【類型】May疑問句題型

【詞彙】
hold the line 稍等／
put sb. through 幫某人轉接／
for a while 一陣子

【正解】(A)

14 May I speak to Mr. Peterson, please?
   (A) Please hold the line. I'll put you through.
   (B) You haven't seen him for a while, have you?
   (C) Let me think about it.

【解析】May I speak to sb.? 是用來表示「欲找某人說話」的電話用語，因此(A)要對方「稍等」，並表示會為對方將電話轉過去，是最適當的回答，故為正解。(B)與(C)的反應皆不是聽到May I speak to sb.?這個問題時會出現的適當回覆。

我們明年將會在牙買加開一間分公司。
(A) 誰會是分公司經理？
(B) 這新產品相當受歡迎。
(C) 如果你需要改時間，請跟我說。

【類型】陳述句題型

【詞彙】
branch office 分公司／
branch manager 分公司經理／
popular 受歡迎的

【正解】(A)

15 We're going to open a branch office in Jamaica next year.
   (A) Who's going to be the branch manager?
   (B) The new product is quite popular.
   (C) Let me know if you need to change the time.

【解析】遇到陳述句的題型時，務必確實抓到陳述句的重點或關鍵字，以便掌握各種可能的適當回應。本題的關鍵字詞為open a branch office「開設分公司」，(A)回問「誰會是分公司經理」是與問題相關的適當反應，故為正解。(B)提到「新產品」以及(C)提到「改時間」，都是答非所問，故不考慮。

你見過我們的新人資部經理了嗎？
(A) 對，我剛剛才跟他一起開會。
(B) 我被告知會議取消了。
(C) 不，你不應該在這個地方。

【類型】yes／no疑問句題型

【詞彙】
meet 見到／
HR manager 人資部經理／
meeting 會議／cancel 取消／
be supposed to 應該

【正解】(A)

16 Have you met our new HR Manager yet?
   (A) Yes, I just had a meeting with him.
   (B) I was told that the meeting was cancelled.
   (C) No, you're not supposed to be here.

【解析】本題為以完成式助動詞have為句首的yes／no疑問句，要問對方「有沒有見過新的人資部經理」。(A)肯定回覆，並表示剛才跟他一起開會，是為正解。(B)表示收到會議取消的通知，以及(C)表示對方不應該出現在這裡，都不是此問題的適當回應。

17 How far is it from your apartment to the office?
(A) Well, I'm quite happy with it so far.
(B) It's only fifteen minutes' walk.
(C) I've never been there before.

【解析】本題為以How far 為句首的疑問句題型，要問「從住家到公司」距離多遠。這類的問題可以用「實際距離」或是「以某種交通方式到達的時間」等兩種方式來回答。因此(B)回答「走路只要十五分鐘」是最適當的答案。(A)提到對某事感到滿意以及(C)表示從未到那裡，均為答非所問的回覆，故不需考慮。

你家到公司有多遠？
(A) 嗯，我目前對它很滿意。
(B) 走路只要十五分鐘。
(C) 我以前從沒去過那裡。

【類型】How far疑問句題型

【詞彙】
apartment 公寓／
happy with sth./
sb. 對某事或某人感到滿意／
walk 步行

【正解】(B)

18 How long will the conference last?
(A) Three days.
(B) Maybe later.
(C) It was three days ago.

【解析】以how long為句首的疑問句，主要是要問「時間長短」。本題問的是「會議將會持續多久時間」，(A)回答三天，是最適當的答案。(B)表示「也許晚一點」，以及(C)回答「三天前」都是牛頭不對馬嘴的不適當回覆，故不需考慮。

會議將會持續多久？
(A) 三天。
(B) 也許晚一點。
(C) 那是三天前的事。

【類型】How long 疑問句題型

【詞彙】
conference 會議／last 持續

【正解】(A)

19 Why is the meeting cancelled?
(A) We will reschedule the meeting.
(B) Please meet me in my office.
(C) There's no meeting room available.

【解析】以why為句首的疑問句，主要是要問某事發生的「原因」。本題詢問會議取消的原因，(A)雖然也有提到meeting，但是回答的卻是「會重新安排會議時間」，答非所問。(B)的回答中提到meet，是故意在聽力上誤導應試者，需要留意。(C)表示沒有會議室可以用，是回答本題的最適當答案，故為正解。

會議為什麼取消了？
(A) 我們會重新安排會議時間。
(B) 請到我的辦公室見我。
(C) 沒有空的會議室可以用。

【類型】Why疑問句題型

【詞彙】
cancel 取消／
reschedule 重新安排時間／
meeting room 會議室／
available 可利用的

【正解】(C)

我們有可能將會議延遲到下週二嗎？

(A) 不，下週我休假。

(B) 聽起來很有意思。

(C) 當然，我會順路到郵局。

【類型】yes／no疑問句題型

【詞彙】

possible 有可能的／

postpone 延後／

be on leave 休假／

stop by 順道經過

【正解】(A)

你這個週末連假有什麼計劃嗎？

(A) 抱歉。我這個週末沒空。

(B) 不，你不能要求我週末上班。

(C) 有啊，我要跟家人一起去露營。

【類型】yes／no疑問句題型

【詞彙】

long weekend 週休連假／

available 有空的／

go camping 去露營

【正解】(C)

我想退這件兩天前在貴店買的襯衫。

(A) 沒問題。您有帶收據嗎？

(B) 應該兩小時後就會好了。

(C) 這項商品目前缺貨。

【類型】陳述句題型

【詞彙】

return 退還／receipt 收據／

out of stock 缺貨

【正解】(A)

---

20 Is it possible that we postpone our meeting till next Tuesday?

(A) No, I will be on leave next week.

(B) That sounds interesting.

(C) Yes, I will stop by the post office.

【解析】本題為以be動詞為句首的疑問句題型，Is it possible that...? 是用來詢問「某事可能性」的句型。題目問的是「將會議延後到下週二」的可能性，(A)回答不行，並說明原因為「下週我休假」是最適當的答案。(B)的回答比較適合用在附和某項提議，而(C)雖然答非所問，卻想利用post office這個字與問題中的postpone做聽力上的誤導，要注意不要上當了。

---

21 Do you have any plans for the coming long weekend?

(A) Sorry. I am not available this weekend.

(B) No, you can't ask me to work on the weekend.

(C) Yes. I'm going camping with my family.

【解析】本題為以助動詞do為首的yes／no疑問句，要問對方週末連假是否有計劃。(A)的回答通常用在婉拒某個邀約，(B)的回答則是用來拒絕加班要求，故皆非適當的選擇。(C)以yes回答問題，並接著說明計劃內容，是最適合本題的答案。

---

22 I'd like to return this shirt that I bought at your store two days ago.

(A) Sure. Do you have your receipt?

(B) It should be ready in two hours.

(C) This item is currently out of stock.

【解析】理解陳述句想要表達的重點，是能夠選出最適當回應的關鍵。本題的重點字詞在：return the shirt「退還襯衫」，抓到重點之後就不難判斷(A)表示可以退還，並索取退還手續中必要的收據，是正確的答案。(B)的回答與時間有關，而(C)的回答則與商品是否有存貨有關，皆與題目所表示的「退還襯衫」沒有直接關係，故不需考慮。

23 What's the purpose of your visit this time?
   (A) I'm going to stay for two weeks this time.
   (B) I will stay at Grand Palace Hotel.
   (C) I'm here for an academic symposium.

您這次來訪的目的是什麼？
(A) 這次我將會停留兩個星期。
(B) 我會住在皇宮飯店。
(C) 我是來參加學術研討會的。

【解析】聽到what為句首的疑問句時，要注意聽what後面接的名詞是什麼，以判斷問題想要問的重點。如本題what後面接著purpose，可知詢問重點在於「目的」。(A)是用來回答停留時間，(B)是用來回答住宿地點，因此都與問題中想知道的「目的」無關。(C)表示I'm here for ...「為了……來這裡」，即說明了來此地的目的，即使不知道academic symposium是什麼意思，也可以輕鬆選出正確答案。

【類型】what疑問句題型

【詞彙】
purpose 目的／visit 拜訪／
academic symposium
學術研討會

【正解】(C)

---

24 I would like to reserve a table for two at six p.m. tomorrow.
   (A) Sure. May I have your last name, please?
   (B) I'm sorry. All of our double rooms are booked.
   (C) It's impossible to reschedule your appointment.

我想預訂明天下午六點，一張兩個人的桌子。
(A) 當然。請您告訴我您貴姓？
(B) 很抱歉。我們所有的雙人房都被訂走了。
(C) 沒有辦法重新安排您預約的時間。

【解析】本題陳述句的重點在於reserve a table「預訂一張桌子」，抓到關鍵後就可以將答案鎖定在與「餐廳訂位」有關的內容上。(A)表示沒問題，並詢問對方貴姓，由此一正常訂位程序可判斷是適當的答案。(B)提到double room「雙人房」，是用在向飯店訂房的回覆，而(C)提到reschedule your appointment「重新安排會面時間」，更是與餐廳訂位無關，因此皆不是需要考慮的選項。

【類型】陳述句題型

【詞彙】
reserve 預訂／last name 姓／
double room 雙人房／
reschedule an appointment
重新安排會面時間

【正解】(A)

---

25 What would you like for dinner?
   (A) I haven't had anything today.
   (B) I prefer French cuisine.
   (C) Just give me my bill.

翻譯：你晚餐想吃什麼？
(A) 我今天什麼都還沒吃。
(B) 我比較想吃法國菜。
(C) 把我的帳單給我就好。

【解析】聽到以what疑問詞為首的疑問句，記得要聽清楚問句要問的重點名詞是什麼，本題問dinner，也就是想吃的晚餐是什麼，因此答案一定會跟食物有關。(A)回答「今天什麼都沒吃」，與(C)表示「給我帳單」，都與食物內容無關，因此皆非適當選項。(B)表示想吃法國菜，正是最適合的答案。

【類型】what疑問句題型

【詞彙】
French cuisine 法國菜

【正解】(B)

你有任何相關的工作經驗嗎？
(A) 其實我今天得加班。
(B) 去年我在一家出版公司實習。
(C) 我工作態度好，而且學得很快。

【類型】yes／no疑問句題型

【詞彙】
related 相關的／
work experience 工作經驗／
work late 加班／intern 實習生／
publishing company 出版公司／
work attitude 工作態度

【正解】(B)

26 Do you have any related work experience?
  (A) Actually, I have to work late today.
  (B) Last year I worked as an intern for a publishing company.
  (C) I have a good work attitude and I learn fast.

【解析】本題的關鍵字為work experience「工作經驗」，因此答案會跟資歷有關。(A)回答「今天必須加班」與(C)提到「工作態度」等，皆與問題無關。(B)表示「曾在出版公司實習」，是最適合本題的答案，因此為正解。

我們何時應該把這件案子做完？
(A) 期限是十二月十五日。
(B) 我們絕對需要一台新的投影機。
(C) 它還需要做修改。

【類型】when疑問句題型

【詞彙】
project 案子；計劃／
deadline 截止期限／
projector 投影機／revision 修改

【正解】(A)

27 When should we have this project done?
  (A) The deadline is December 15.
  (B) We definitely need a projector.
  (C) It still needs some revision.

【解析】聽到以when為句首的疑問句，便知道這題要問的是與「時間」相關的答案。題目問「何時」需要把案子完成，(A)表示最後期限是12月15日，是正確答案。(B)提到與問題中project這個字聽起來相似的projector，要小心別被誤導；(C)的答案則完全答非所問，不需考慮。

我跟史賓塞先生上午十點有約。
(A) 你需要醫生證明才能請病假。
(B) 我會通知史賓塞先生您到了。
(C) 下次請事先預訂。

【類型】陳述句題型

【詞彙】
doctor's note 醫生證明／
sick leave 病假／
notify sb. of sth. 通知某人某事／
make a reservation 預約／
beforehand 事先

【正解】(B)

28 I have an appointment with Mr. Spencer at 10 a.m.
  (A) You need a doctor's note for a sick leave.
  (B) I'll notify Mr. Spencer of your arrival.
  (C) Please make a reservation beforehand next time.

【解析】聽到陳述句題型，要確實抓到陳述句的重點。本題表示自己與某人約好十點見面。(A)提到「醫生證明」，是適合用來回答與「請病假」相關的問題；(C)則是適合用來回答與「餐廳或飯店等訂位」相關的問題，以上兩個選項皆非本題的適當答案。(B)表示將告知Mr. Spencer他已經到達，是最適合本陳述句的反應，故為正解。

29 Who should I contact for your new product catalogue?
　(A) Please call Jane at extension 123.
　(B) It won't be available until next week.
　(C) I have already lost contact with him.

【解析】以who為句首的疑問句，主要是要詢問「對象是誰」，因此答案多半會與「人」有關。(B)的回答並沒有呼應問題中的who，因此可刪去不選。(C)表示「跟某人失去聯繫」，雖然有提到「人」，但是卻與題目中的「型錄」無關。(A)表示要打分機給Jane，意指可以找Jane拿型錄，因此可判斷為最適當的答案。

要索取你們的新產品型錄，我應該跟誰聯繫呢？
(A) 請撥分機123找珍。
(B) 要下星期才有得拿喔。
(C) 我已經跟他失去聯繫了。

【類型】who疑問句題型

【詞彙】
contact 聯絡／
product catalogue 產品型錄／
extension 分機／lose contact
with sb. 與某人失去聯絡

【正解】(A)

---

30 I forgot to bring my wallet with me.
　(A) Well, check the lost and found.
　(B) Don't worry. The lunch is on me.
　(C) Promise me you'll never be late again.

【解析】此題的陳述句表示「忘記帶皮夾」，而非「弄丟皮夾」，因此可判斷(A)提到的「失物招領」是與之無關的回答。由於一般皮夾內容物經常與「證件」或「現金」有關，因此聽到(B)回答午餐費用將由其支付時，便能知道此乃回覆此陳述句的適當答案。(C)提到「遲到」，與本陳述句內容無關，因此可以刪去不選。因此可確定(B)為正解。

我忘了帶皮夾了。
(A) 噢，到失物招領處看一下。
(B) 別擔心。午餐我請客。
(C) 答應你不會再遲到。

【類型】陳述句題型

【詞彙】
wallet 皮夾／
lost and found 失物招領處

【正解】(B)

---

31 Why are we taking the stairs?
　(A) The printer is out of order.
　(B) Our client is waiting.
　(C) The elevator is under maintenance.

【解析】聽到以why為句首的疑問句，務必抓到問題中的關鍵詞彙，以便能根據關鍵字找出「原因」。本題要問的是「選擇爬樓梯的原因」，(A)提到印表機故障，以及(B)提到客戶在等，都與「爬樓梯」無關，因此可以直接刪去不考慮。(C)表示電梯在維修，可判斷「電梯目前不能使用」是爬樓梯的原因，是為正解。

我們為什麼要爬樓梯？
(A) 印表機故障了。
(B) 我們的客戶在等了。
(C) 電梯正在維修中。

【類型】why疑問句題型

【詞彙】
take the stairs 爬樓梯／
elevator 電梯／
under maintenance 維修中

【正解】(C)

女子：嗨，我試著在你們網站上訂一間雙人房，但是你們的訂房系統不接受我的預訂。

男子：非常抱歉，女士。我們的線上預約系統今天早上發生了一些問題，不過現在問題已經解決了。

女子：原來如此。那，既然我的訂房沒有成功，我直接在電話上訂房好了。你們飯店現在正提供房價七五折的特別優惠，對吧？

男子：您當然可以透過電話訂房，但是這個特別優惠只有透過線上訂房系統訂房才有效喔。

女子：了解。既然這樣，我就待會兒再試試。

【詞彙】
double room 雙人房／
website 網站／booking system
訂房（位）系統／
online reservation system
線上訂位系統／
special discount 特別折扣／
room rate 房價／
at the moment 現在、此刻

▶ PART 3

Directions: You will hear some conversations between two people. You will be asked to answer three questions about what the speakers say in each conversation. Select the best response to each question and mark the letter (A), (B), (C) or (D) on your answer sheet. The conversations will not be printed in your test book and will be spoken only one time.

Questions 32～34 refer to the following conversation.

W Hi, I was trying to book a double room from your website, but your booking system didn't accept my reservation.

M I'm very sorry, ma'am. There was a problem with our online reservation system this morning, but the problem has been fixed.

W I see. Well, since my reservation wasn't successful, I'll just make a reservation through the phone. You are providing a discount of 25% off the room rate at the moment, right?

M You certainly can reserve a room by phone, but I'm afraid the special discount is only available through our online reservation system.

W Understood. Well, if that's so, I'll try again later.

男子最可能在哪裡工作？
(A) 餐廳。　(B) 銀行。
(C) 飯店。　(D) 圖書館。

【類型】where題型

【詞彙】
restaurant 餐廳／library 圖書館

【正解】(C)

32 Where is the man most likely to work?
　(A) In a restaurant.　　(B) In a bank.
　(C) In a hotel.　　　　(D) In a library.

【解析】由女子在與男子的對話中提及她「在對方網站上試圖預訂一間雙人房」，從關鍵字「雙人房」可推測男子的工作最可能與「住宿」有關，選項中以(C)飯店最為可能的答案，其他選項內容不可能提供「雙人房」的預訂，因此答案選(C)。

33 What can the woman get by booking online?
(A) A complimentary drink.
(B) A discount of 25% off the room rate.
(C) A 25% off coupon.
(D) A free shipping code.

【解析】在對話中，女子先是向男子確認他們是否確實有提供a discount of 25% off the room rate（房價七五折的優惠），接著男子表示該優惠only available through our online reservation system（只有透過線上訂房系統才有效），因此可知女子透過線上訂房系統訂房，才可以得到房價七五折優惠，故答案選(B)。

女子透過網路訂房可以得到什麼？
(A) 一客免費晚餐。
(B) 房價七五折優惠。
(C) 一張七五折優惠券。
(D) 一組免運費密碼。

【類型】提問細節題型

【詞彙】
complimentary dinner 免費晚餐／
free shipping code 免運費密碼

【正解】(B)

34 What will the woman do later?
(A) Find her way to the hotel.
(B) Book a hotel room online.
(C) Talk to the hotel manager.
(D) Order room service.

【解析】在男子說明「優惠只能透過線上訂房使用」之後，女子以Understood.說明她已經「明白、了解」這一點，並接著表示will try again later（晚點會再試一次），由此可知女子稍晚將會再嘗試在線上訂房，故答案選(B)。★多益新制的聽力考題中，會較常出現類似Understood. 這種省略主詞 I 的口語用法。雖非正式用語，但是對於理解整篇對話相當重要，因此在聽力上也要特別留意。

女子稍晚會做什麼？
(A) 找路去飯店。
(B) 在線上預訂飯店房間。
(C) 跟飯店經理談話。
(D) 訂客房服務餐點。

【類型】提問細節題型

【詞彙】
hotel manager 飯店經理／
room service 客房服務

【正解】(B)

Questions 35～37 refer to the following conversation.

Man A　Hi, Josephine. I have two tickets to James Blunt's concert at Taipei Arena. Interested?

Woman　Absolutely! You know I am a big fan of James Blunt! When's the concert?

Man A　October 31. The concert will start at 7 p.m.

Woman　Oh, I'm not sure. I have to visit a few clients on that day. I don't know if I can make it on time to the concert.

男子A：嗨，約瑟芬。我有兩張詹姆士布朗特在台北巨蛋的演唱會門票。有興趣嗎？

女子：當然啊！你知道我可是詹姆士布朗特的超級歌迷！演唱會是什麼時候？

男子A：十月三十一日。演唱會晚上七點開始。

女子：噢，我不確定耶。我那天要去拜訪幾個客戶。不知道能不能準時趕上演唱會。

男子B：那個……我那天完全有
空。我可以跟你去喔，提
姆。

男子A：啊……不是啦。我沒有要
去。我是要賣她門票。如
果你有興趣的話，我可以
給你打個折噢。

【詞彙】
Taipei Arena 台北巨蛋／
make it on time 準時趕上

Man B　　Well... I'm totally free on that day. I can go with you, Tim.

Man A　　Ah...no, no. I am not going. I was trying to sell her the tickets. I can give you a discount if you are interested.

女子對此演唱會感覺如何？
(A) 漠不關心。
(B) 很有興趣。
(C) 大失所望。
(D) 灰心氣餒。

【類型】提問細節題型

【詞彙】
indifferent 不關心的／
interested 感興趣的／
disappointed 感到失望的／
frustrated 洩氣的

【正解】(B)

35 How does the woman feel about the invitation?
(A) She's indifferent.
(B) She's interested.
(C) She's disappointed.
(D) She's frustrated.

【解析】男子在對話中表示自己有演唱會的門票，並詢問女子★Interested?「有興趣嗎？」這個問句是Are you interested?省略了be動詞及主詞的口語化用法，在新制多益聽力考題中會經常出現。女子對此問句的回答為肯定的Absolutely「當然、絕對」，因此可知(B)為正解。

提姆是想要做什麼？
(A) 賣掉演唱會門票。
(B) 約女子出去。
(C) 開演唱會。
(D) 去演唱會。

【類型】提問細節題型

【詞彙】
ask sb. out 約某人出去／
give a concert 開演唱會

【正解】(A)

36 What is Tim trying do?
(A) Sell the concert tickets.
(B) Ask the woman out.
(C) Give a concert.
(D) Go to the concert.

【解析】聽對話前半段內容，可能會誤以為提姆是想要約女子去聽演唱會，但是對話最後，提姆才表示I am not going.（我沒有要去演唱會），可知(D)並非正解；提姆接著表示I was trying to sell her the tickets.（我是要賣她票），可知他詢問女子對演唱會是否有興趣的目的，並不是要約她一起去，故(B)亦非正解，而是要賣掉門票，故答案為(A)。

37 What keeps the woman from buying the tickets?
(A) She can't afford them.
(B) She has to work.
(C) She doesn't like the singer.
(D) She's not interested.

是什麼原因讓女子不能買票？
(A) 她買不起。
(B) 她必須工作。
(C) 她不喜歡歌手。
(D) 她沒興趣。

【解析】由女子的回答表示自己對演唱會有興趣，可知(D)的描述是錯誤的，可以刪除不考慮；女子接著表示I am a big fan of James Blunt!（我是詹姆士布朗特的超級歌迷），可知(C)亦可不考慮；對話中並未提及女子是否買得起門票，因此(A)亦非適當的答案。女子在對話中表示I have to visit a few clients on that day.（我那天要拜訪幾位客戶），可知這一天女子必須工作，故正解為(B)。

【類型】提問細節題型

【詞彙】
keep sb. from V-ing 阻止某人做某事／afford 負擔得起

【正解】(B)

Questions 38-40 refer to the following conversation.

M Hi, I am Justin Smith calling from Exeter Company. We purchased 10 colored laser printers from you last week, I found three of them not working.

W I'm sorry to hear that. Do you mind having our maintenance engineer go to your office and check the printers for possible problems?

M Not at all. When is the earliest time he can come? This afternoon?

W We're having a meeting this afternoon. Let me check his work schedule and get back to you on this in a minute.

★ Maintenance Engineer's work schedule

	Monday	Tuesday	Wednesday
9:00-11:00	CMA Company Printers Repair		Day Off
13:00-15:00	Meeting	HDX Company digital copiers Repair	

男子 嗨，我是艾克斯特公司的賈斯汀史密斯。我們上星期跟你們買了十台彩色雷射印表機，並發現有三台不能用。

女子 很抱歉聽到這件事。你介意讓我們的維修工程師到你們公司去檢查印表機可能的問題嗎？

男子 不介意啊。他最快什麼時候可以過來？今天下午嗎？

女子 今天下午我們有個會議要開。讓我查一下他的工作排程表，然後馬上回電給您。

★維修工程師的工作時程表

	週一	週二	週三
9:00-11:00	CMA 公司印表機修繕		休假
13:00-15:00	開會	HDX 公司數位影印機修繕	

【詞彙】
color laser printer 彩色雷射印表機／maintenance engineer 維修工程師／work schedule 工作排程表／get back to sb. 回覆某人／in a minute 馬上

加★部分為多益新題型以及相關小提醒，考生要特別注意喔！ 145

男子為何來電？
(A) 安排會議時間。
(B) 取消會面。
(C) 要求售後服務。
(D) 將晚宴延後。

【類型】提問原因題型

【詞彙】
after-sales service 售後服務／
dinner party 晚宴

【正解】(C)

38 Why is the man calling?
(A) To schedule a meeting.
(B) To cancel an appointment.
(C) To request for after-sales service.
(D) To postpone a dinner party.

【解析】由男子在對話一開始便表示We purchased 10 color laser printers from you last week，可知男子有向對方購買物品，接著由男子表示found three of them not working，並詢問對方的維修工程師最快何時可來檢查問題，可推測男子來電的目的應該是「請對方提供售後維修服務」，故以(C)為最適當的答案。

男子想要做什麼？
(A) 將受損物品退費。
(B) 退還瑕疵品。
(C) 讓部分商品接受檢查。
(D) 回收瑕疵品。

【類型】提問細節題型

【詞彙】
defective 有瑕疵的／
retrieve 收回

【正解】(C)

39 What does the man want?
(A) To refund the damaged items.
(B) To return the defective items.
(C) To have some items checked.
(D) To retrieve the defective goods.

【解析】男子在表示部分產品有問題之後，並未提出退貨或退費等要求，故(A)與(B)的答案皆不正確。男子所代表的公司乃為產品買方，而(D)所提到的「收回瑕疵品」應該是賣方會做的動作，故不需考慮。女子在對話中詢問「是否介意讓維修工程師前去檢查印表機可能的問題」，由男子回覆Not at all.（一點也不介意）可知男子希望有問題的印表機讓工程師檢查，故(C)為正解。

根據表格，工程師何時會去Exeter公司？
(A) 星期三上午。
(B) 星期二上午。
(C) 星期一下午。
(D) 星期二下午。

【類型】圖表對照題型

【正解】(B)

40 According to the graph, when will the engineer go to Exeter Company?
(A) Wednesday morning.
(B) Tuesday morning.
(C) Monday afternoon.
(D) Tuesday afternoon.

【解析】對話中男子在詢問「維修工程師最快何時會到」，並試探性地接著問 This afternoon?（今天下午嗎？）女子回覆「今天下午要開會」。★ 維修工程師的工作排程表，顯示週一13:00-15:00有排入meeting（會議），可知對話發生時間為星期一，而工程師最快有空檔的時間為週二9:00-11:00，因此推測女子會安排工程師在週二上午前往Exeter公司檢查印表機，故答案為(B)。新制聽力題型中，會在對話中加入圖表，應試者在專心聽對話內容時，必須將對話內容與圖表內容相對應，才能選出正確答案。

Questions 41~43 refer to the following conversation.

W Hi, this is Jessica. I am on my way to the office right now, but there's a car crash or something up ahead. Anyway, I'm stuck in traffic, and I think it's gonna take a while.

M So I guess you won't be able to make it to the meeting this morning. Do you want me to put it off till tomorrow?

W Yes, please. Oh, wait! I have an appointment with a client tomorrow. Just cancel the meeting first and we'll reschedule it.

M Got it!

女子 嗨，我是Jessica。我正在往公司的路上，但是前面有車禍還是什麼的。總之，我被塞在路上了，而且我覺得可能會要好一陣子。

男子 所以我想你沒辦法準時趕上今天早上的會議了吧。你希望我把它延到明天嗎？

女子 好啊，麻煩你。噢，等等！我明天有跟一個客戶約見面。直接把會議取消，我們在另外安排時間吧。

男子 明白了。

【詞彙】car crash 車禍

---

41 Where is the woman most likely to be?
(A) In a police station.　(B) On the highway.
(C) At the airport.　(D) In her office.

【解析】由對話中女子表示I am on my way to the office ... I'm stuck in traffic （我正在往公司路上……我被塞在路上了）可知女子說話的時候，人應該是在路上，因此選項中以(B)「公路上」為最適合的答案。

女子最有可能在哪裡？
(A) 警察局　(B) 公路上。
(C) 機場。　(D) 辦公室。

【類型】where題型

【詞彙】
police station 警察局／
highway 公路

【正解】(B)

---

42 According to the speaker, what has caused the traffic jam?
(A) A traffic accident.
(B) The road construction.
(C) A damaged traffic light.
(D) The stormy weather.

【解析】女子在對話中表示there's a car crash or something up ahead （前方有個車禍還是什麼的），接著表示it's gonna take a while （可能會耗上一陣子），暗示自己可能會塞在路上好一段時間。因此可推測造成交通堵塞的原因最有可能是「一起交通事故」，故選(A)。crash意指「相撞之事故」，car crash即「車禍事故」。★ be gonna 為be going to的口語用法，gonna是將going to兩個字快速合在一起說時而形成的口語字彙，在英文口語中經常使用。

根據對話內容，造成交通阻塞的原因為何？
(A) 交通事故。
(B) 道路施工。
(C) 交通號誌燈損毀。
(D) 暴風雨氣候。

【類型】提問細節題型

【詞彙】
traffic jam 交通堵塞／
traffic accident 交通事故／
road construction 道路施工／
traffic light 交通號誌燈

【正解】(A)

加★部分為多益新題型以及相關小提醒，考生要特別注意喔！　147

男子接下來會做什麼？
(A) 主持會議。
(B) 預訂飛機票。
(C) 訂會議室。
(D) 取消會議。

【類型】提問細節題型

【詞彙】
flight ticket 飛機票／
meeting room 會議室

【正解】(D)

43 What will the man do next?
(A) To host the meeting.
(B) To book a flight ticket.
(C) To book a meeting room.
(D) To cancel the meeting.

【解析】女子在對話中要求男子cancel the meeting first（先取消會議）and we'll reschedule it （然後我們再來重新安排會議時間），而男子回答Got it，表示「明白了」，可推測男子下一步動作應該是「取消會議」，故答案為(D)。★ get這個動詞有許多意思，在這裡做「理解」用，因此男子以省略主詞的口語表示Got it，意指他已經理解女子的指示。

女子 安德魯，我已經看過你的辦公室擴建提案，而且覺得很有可行性。

男子 謝謝，潘。很高興你喜歡。

女子 我只擔心一點。我想知道有沒有可能降低工程成本。

男子 這個嘛……我們可以改變地磚來降低地板工程成本。我會跟供應商聯絡，請他們提供不同地磚的報價。

女子 就是盡可能讓地磚成本低一點。期待你修改過的提案。

★

地磚種類	報價
貝倫磚	NT$90 平方呎
多倫多灰色磚	NT$75 平方呎
安地斯磚	NT$120 平方呎
里塞夫磚	NT$95 平方呎

【詞彙】
office expansion 辦公室擴建／
practicable 可行的／
construction cost 施工成本／
flooring tile 地磚

Questions 44-46 refer to the following conversation.

W Andrew, I have reviewed your office expansion proposal and found it practicable.

M Thanks, Pam. I am glad you like it.

W There is only one thing that I am concerned about. I'm wondering if it is possible to reduce the construction cost.

M Well, we can change the flooring tiles to lower the cost of flooring works. I'll contact the supplier to request for quotations of different flooring tiles.

W Just try to keep the cost of flooring tiles as low as possible. Looking forward to your revised proposal.

★

Types of flooring tiles	Quotations
Belem Ceramic	NT$90 Sq Ft
Toronto Grey Ceramic	NT$75 Sq Ft
Andes Tronador Ceramic	NT$120 Sq Ft
Recife Ceramic	NT$95 Sq Ft

44 What are the speakers talking about?
(A) An office expansion proposal.
(B) A house renovation plan.
(C) The meeting agenda.
(D) The design of a new product.

【解析】由女子在對話一開始提到office expansion proposal（辦公室擴建提案），隨後男子與女子便以此為對話主軸，可知他們所討論的就是這個擴建提案，故答案為(A)。

說話者在討論什麼？
(A) 辦公室擴建提案。
(B) 房屋翻新計劃。
(C) 會議議程。
(D) 新產品設計。

【類型】內容主題題型

【詞彙】
renovation 翻新／
meeting agenda 會議議程

【正解】(A)

45 According to the man, what can be modified?
(A) The maintenance cost.
(B) The renovation time.
(C) The construction cost.
(D) The staffing arrangement.

【解析】女子在對話中提到希望能reduce the construction cost（降低施工成本），而男子答覆可以change the flooring tiles to lower the cost of flooring works（以換地磚來降低地磚施工成本），可知此提案將修改的是(C)所表示的「施工成本」，是為正解。

根據男子所說，何者可以被修改？
(A) 維護成本　　(B) 翻新時間
(C) 施工成本　　(D) 人員配置

【類型】提問細節題型

【詞彙】
maintenance cost 維護成本／
staffing arrangement
人員安排配置

【正解】(C)

46 Look at the graph. Which type of tiles will be used in this proposal?
(A) Belem Ceramic
(B) Toronto Grey Ceramic
(C) Andes Tronador Ceramic
(D) Recife Ceramic

【解析】根據對話內容，女子表示希望能keep the cost of flooring tiles as low as possible（盡可能讓地磚成本越低越好），因此在對照圖表所示之地磚報價後，可推測男子在提案中將會把地磚改成價格最低的Toronto Grey Ceramic（多倫多灰磚），故答案選(B)。

請看圖表。哪一種瓷磚將會使用在本提案中？
(A) 貝倫磚　　(B) 多倫多灰磚
(C) 安地斯磚　　(D) 里塞夫磚

【類型】圖表對照題型

【正解】(B)

女子 我要買這件裙子，不過我希
望可以改短一點。你們有修
改服務嗎？

男子 很抱歉，沒有。不過三樓有
間修改店。他們以合理價格
提供很棒的修改服務。

女子 太好了。噢，我還需要一件
搭配這件裙子的襯衫，不過
我不太喜歡白襯衫。這件襯
衫還有出別的顏色嗎？

男子 有的。您穿什麼尺寸呢？

女子 中的。

男子 讓我幫您查一下庫存表。

★ 襯衫庫存表

	特小	小號	中號	大號
白	3	1	2	0
黑	3	3	1	4
灰	1	1	0	0
藍	1	0	0	2

【詞彙】

alteration service 修改服務／
fair price 合理價格／
inventory 庫存

這段對話最可能發生在哪裡？

(A) 餐廳
(B) 書店
(C) 修改店
(D) 服裝店

【類型】where題型

【詞彙】
gas station 加油站／
clothing store 服裝店

【正解】(D)

Questions 47-49 refer to the following conversation.

W I'll take this skirt, but I would like to have it shorter. Do you offer alteration services?

M Unfortunately, no. But there's an alteration shop on the third floor. They provide amazing alteration services at a fair price.

W That's great. Oh, I also need a shirt to go with this skirt, but I don't really like white shirts. Does this shirt come in other colors?

M Yes, it does. What size do you wear?

W Medium.

M Let me check our inventory for you.

★ Inventory for the shirts

	XS	S	M	L
white	3	1	2	0
black	3	3	1	4
grey	1	1	0	0
blue	1	0	0	2

47 Where does the conversation most likely take place?
(A) In a restaurant.
(B) In a bookstore.
(C) In an alteration shop.
(D) In a clothing store.

【解析】由對話中女子詢問男子是否有提供alteration service
（服裝修改服務），男子表示這裡不提供此服務，並推薦一
間alteration shop（服裝修改店）給女子，可知此處並非服裝
修改店，故(C)並非正確答案。我們聽到女子提到I'll take this
skirt（我要買這件裙子）以及I need a shirt to go with this
skirt（我需要一件可以搭這件裙子的襯衫），可推測這裡是
個有提供裙子及襯衫等服裝給消費者的地方，選項中以(D)的
服裝店為最有可能的答案。

48 Why does the skirt need alteration?
(A) It's too short for the man.
(B) It's too long for the woman.
(C) It's too big for the woman.
(D) It's too small for the man.

裙子為何需要修改？
(A) 對男子來說太短。
(B) 對女子來說太長。
(C) 對女子來說太大。
(D) 對男子來說太小。

【類型】詢問原因題型

【正解】(B)

【解析】由女子在對話中表示I would like to have it shorter.（我希望它短一點）可知這件裙子對女子而言太長了，故選(B)。想要購買裙子的是女子，因此跟對話中的男子無關，故(A)及(D)可刪除不考慮。short的反義詞為long，而不是big，故(C)亦非合適的答案。

49 Look at the inventory. Which shirt is the woman likely to buy?
(A) The white one   (B) The blue one
(C) The grey one   (D) The black one

請看庫存表。女子可能會買哪一件襯衫？
(A) 白色的   (B) 藍色的
(C) 灰色的   (D) 黑色的

【類型】圖表對照題型

【正解】(D)

【解析】女子在對話中表示其襯衫尺寸為Medium（中等尺碼），對照題目中所提供的庫存表所示各種顏色襯衫之庫存量，只有白色和黑色襯衫還有中等尺碼的庫存。而女子也在對話中明白表示I don't really like white shirts（我並不太喜歡白襯衫），因此可推測女子最可能買下的是黑色的襯衫，故選(D)。

Questions 50-52 refer to the following conversation.

Woman　Henry Harrison from ACME Industries called this morning. ACME wants to purchase 1,000 iPhone chargers from us if we can offer them a discount of 20% off.

Man A　It would be fantastic to accept such a bulk order. But 20% off is a little bit too much. Don't you think?

Man B　Totally. Our prices are already lower than our competitors'. Giving them 20% off will reduce our profit.

女子　ACME企業的亨利哈里森今天早上打電話來。如果我們能給他們八折優惠的話，ACME想要跟我們購買一千個蘋果手機充電器。

男子A　如果可以接下這麼大一筆訂單會很棒。不過八折有一點太多了。你們不覺得嗎？

男子B　對啊。我們的價格已經比競爭對手的低了。給他們八折，會降低我們的利潤。

女子　我不這麼認為。ACME經常下大筆訂單。他們是我們最重要的客戶之一，而且已經跟我們合作超過十年了。八折的優惠很合理啊。

Woman　I don't see it that way. ACME always makes bulk purchases. They are one of our most important clients and have been doing business with us for more than ten years. A discount of 20% is fairly reasonable.

【詞彙】
iPhone charger 蘋果手機充電器／fantastic 極棒的／
bulk order 大訂單／
competitor 競爭者／profit 利潤

說話者在討論什麼？
(A) 合作機會　　(B) 說明會節目
(C) 促銷活動　　(D) 新品簡報

【類型】對話主題題型

【詞彙】
business offer 合作機會／
orientation（新生／新進人員）
說明會／promotion 促銷／
presentation 簡報

【正解】(A)

50 What are the speakers discussing?
(A) A business offer.
(B) Orientation programs.
(C) A promotion event.
(D) A new production presentation.

【解析】對話一開始提到ACME公司希望購買iPhone充電器，條件是希望能提供八折優惠，而且整個對話的脈絡都以此為主題，可知說話者在討論一個涉及買賣的「合作機會」，故答案為(A)。

哈里森先生要求什麼？
(A) 免費運送。
(B) 快速付款。
(C) 降低價格。
(D) 二十個免費iPhone充電器。

【類型】提問細節題型

【詞彙】
delivery 運送

【正解】(C)

51 What did Mr. Harrison request?
(A) Free delivery.
(B) Prompt payment.
(C) Reduced prices.
(D) 20 free iPhone chargers.

【解析】對話一開始女子便說明哈里森先生的合作條件為a discount of 20% off（八折優惠），因此可知他的要求是希望能「降低價格」，故答案為(C)。

52 What does the woman think of Mr. Harrison's request?

(A) Acceptable.   (B) Offensive.

(C) Unreasonable.   (D) Disagreeable.

【解析】★ 在新制多益測驗中，聽力測驗的對話題型中常出現三人以上的對話，因此必須仔細聽對話中不同角色所說的話，尤其是說話者彼此意見不同的時候，要特別留意持有不同意見的人所說的話。對話中的兩名男子對於哈里森先生所提出的要求，一個認為「八折有點太多」，另一個認為「給他們八折會減少我們的收益」，但是女子卻表示A discount of 20% is fairly reasonable（八折很合理），因此可知女子認為對方的要求是可以接受的，故(A)是正確答案。

女子認為哈里森先生的要求如何？

(A) 可接受的。

(B) 很唐突的。

(C) 不合理的。

(D) 令人不快的。

【類型】提問細節題型

【詞彙】

acceptable 可接受的／

offensive 冒犯的、唐突的／

unreasonable 不合理的／

disagreeable 討厭的、令人不快的

【正解】(A)

Questions 53-55 refer to the following conversation.

W Excuse me. Is this seat taken?

M No. You can take it.

W David, come over and take this seat. There's another vacant seat in the back. I'll go sit there.

B Can't I sit with you, Mom?

W Sweetheart, it's just a two-hour journey...

M Uh... I can take the seat in the back so you and your boy can sit together.

W Oh, would you mind? Thank you so much!

女子 不好意思。這個位子有人坐嗎？

男子 沒有。妳可以坐在這裡。

女子 大衛，過來這裡，坐這個位子。後面有另一個位子，我去那兒坐。

男孩 我不能跟妳坐嗎，媽媽？

女子 親愛的，這只是個兩小時車程而已……

男子 呃……我可以坐後面的位子，這樣妳跟妳兒子就可坐在一起了。

女子 噢，你不介意嗎？真是太謝謝你了。

---

53 Where are the speakers?

(A) On a coach.   (B) In a library.

(C) In a bank.   (D) In a cafeteria.

【解析】聽前半部對話內容時，可知道整篇對話脈絡是繞著seat（座位）轉，但無法確定是哪裡的座位。但是聽到女子表示it's just a two-hour journey（這只是個兩小時的旅程），由其中的關鍵字journey（旅程），便可推測這篇對話裡的「座位」跟交通工具有關，因此選項中以「遊覽巴士」為最有可能的地點，故選(A)。

說話者在何處？

(A) 在巴士上。

(B) 在圖書館裡。

(C) 在銀行裡。

(D) 在自助餐館裡。

【類型】where題型

【詞彙】coach 遊覽車、巴士

【正解】(A)

男子向女子提供什麼？
(A) 一些金錢。
(B) 一張優惠券。
(C) 他的座位。
(D) 他的協助。

【類型】提問細節題型

【正解】(C)

女子跟誰一起旅行？
(A) 她的丈夫。　(B) 她的女兒。
(C) 她的兒子。　(D) 她的母親。

【類型】who題型

【正解】(C)

女子 需要幫忙嗎？
男子 噢，是的，麻煩妳。這是我第一次用這個機器。我該從哪兒開始？
女子 嗯，你必須先選擇車票種類。一日票嗎？
男子 呃，不。我只要一張到台北車站的單程票。
女子 那好。一個大人……單程票……台北車站……好了。螢幕顯示你的票價是30元。你現在可以投錢了。
男子 糟糕。我沒零錢耶。機器收一千元紙鈔嗎？
女子 那兒有台兌幣機。

【詞彙】
one day pass 一日通行票／
single ticket 單程票／
insert 投入／
coin change machine 兌幣機

54 What does the man offer to the woman?
(A) Some money.　(B) A coupon.
(C) His seat.　(D) His assistance.

【解析】對話一開始，女子詢問男子Is the seat taken?（這個位子有人坐嗎？）依常理，這個問題通常是問空位旁座位上的人。男子表示該座位沒人坐之後，女子趕緊喚男孩過來坐，可推測女子希望男孩來坐在男子旁邊的位子。接著男子向女子提出I can take the seat in the back so you and your boy can sit together（我可以去坐後面的位子，讓妳跟妳兒子坐在一起），可知男子應該是要讓出自己的座位給女子坐，因此答案以(C)最為適當。

55 Who is the woman traveling with?
(A) Her husband.　(B) Her daughter.
(C) Her son.　(C) Her mother.

【解析】在對話中，男孩問女子Can't I sit with you, Mom?（我不能跟妳坐嗎，媽媽？）由男孩稱呼女子為「媽媽」，可知女子與男孩之間的關係為「母子」，因此答案為(C)。

Questions 56-58 refer to the following conversation.

W Can I help you?

M Uh, yes, please. It's my first time using this machine. Where should I start?

W Well, you need to select a ticket type first. One day pass?

M Uh, no. I just need a single ticket to Taipei Main Station.

W Okay, then. One adult... single ticket... Taipei Main Station....OK. The screen says your ticket price is $30. You can insert the money now.

M Oops. I don't have any small change. Does the machine take $1,000 bills?

W There's a coin change machine over there.

56 Where are the speakers?
(A) At the reception.
(B) At the ticket machine.
(C) At the checkout.
(D) At a taxi station.

【解析】由對話中男子表示It's my first time using this machine.（這是我第一次用這機器），加上對話中提到ticket（票）、one day pass（一日通行票），以及Taipei Main Station（台北車站），可知男子正想利用售票機買車票，因此推斷說話者的所在地應該是售票機器前，故選(B)。

説話者位在何處？
(A) 接待處　　(B) 售票機前
(C) 結帳區　　(D) 計程車站

【類型】where題型

【詞彙】
reception 接待處／
taxi station 計程車站

【正解】(B)

---

57 What does the man need?
(A) A train ticket.
(B) His electricity bill.
(C) His receipt.
(D) A reservation number.

【解析】承56題，由女子協助男子利用售票機買票，且男子表示I just need a single ticket to Taipei Main Station（我只需要一張到台北車站的單程票），可知男子是要買車票。選項中只有(A)最可能是男子所需要的東西，故為正解。

男子需要什麼？
(A) 一張火車票。
(B) 他的電費帳單。
(C) 他的收據。
(D) 一個訂位號碼。

【類型】提問細節題型

【詞彙】
electricity bill 電費帳單／
reservation number 訂位號碼

【正解】(A)

---

58 What does the woman suggest the man do?
(A) Go to the service counter.
(B) Get some coins.
(C) Lend her some coins.
(D) Get on the train.

【解析】對話中男子表示自己沒有small change（零錢或面額小的紙鈔），並詢問女子機器是否接受千元紙鈔。由女子回答男子There's a coin change machine over there.（那裡有台兌幣機），可推測女子建議男子去兌幣機「換一些硬幣」來買票。選項中以(B)為最適當的答案，故為正解。

女子建議男子做什麼？
(A) 到服務台去。
(B) 取得一些硬幣。
(C) 借她一點硬幣。
(D) 上火車。

【類型】提問細節題型

【詞彙】
service counter 服務台

【正解】(B)

加★部分為多益新題型以及相關小提醒，考生要特別注意喔！　　155

男子A 現在我們的議程是要想 XP3003的行銷策略。我們從價格開始討論。艾蜜莉,妳可以做記錄嗎?

女子 好的。

男子A 好。考慮到我們的利潤百分比,我們必須將價格定在一萬元至一萬五千元這個範圍內。有什麼想法嗎?

男子B 既然我們有空間可以提供更具競爭力的價格,我認為可以訂個讓大部分人都負擔得起的價格。

男子C 我們何不將價格定在一萬五千元,然後再提供折扣作為促銷?

女子 我也這麼認為。提供具吸引力的優惠來刺激消費者購買產品,更能增加我們的利潤。

【詞彙】
marketing strategy 行銷策略／
take notes 做記錄／
profit margin 利潤百分比／
competitive 具競爭力的／
affordable 負擔得起的／
motivate 給予動機

Questions 59-61 refer to the following conversation.

Man A　Now our agenda is to figure out a marketing strategy for XP3003. Let's start with the price. Emily, could you take notes?

Woman　Will do.

Man A　OK. Considering our profit margin, we have to keep it in the $10,000 to $15,000 range. Any thoughts?

Man B　Since we have room to offer a more competitive price, I think it's good to keep it affordable.

Man C　Why don't we make it $15,000, and offer discounts later for promotion?

Woman　My thoughts exactly. Giving attractive discounts can motivate consumers to purchase our products and increase our profit even more.

說話者正在做什麼?
(A) 開派對。　　(B) 開會。
(C) 吃午餐。　　(D) 爭執。

【類型】提問細節題型

【詞彙】
quarrel 口角,爭執

【正解】(B)

---

59 What are the speakers doing?
(A) Having a party.
(B) Having a meeting.
(C) Having lunch.
(D) Having a quarrel.

【解析】由對話一開始男子便提到agenda(會議議程),並要大家figure out a marketing strategy(想出行銷策略),接下來的對話內容中,說話者紛紛提出自己的意見,可推測他們應該是正在開會,故(B)為正解。

60 What is the woman in charge of?
(A) Meeting minutes.
(B) Seat arrangement.
(C) Equipment control.
(D) Product presentation.

【解析】對話中男子A對女子提出要求Could you take notes?（你可以做記錄嗎？）女子以Will do.（好的）表示她會做記錄，可知女子在會議中將扮演「會議記錄」的角色，答案為(A)。★ 要正確選出本題答案，首先應試者必須知道take notes這個片語即「做記錄」之意；此外，女子回答Will do.是完整回答：I will take notes. 省略了主詞I，並且以do取代take notes這個動作的口語化表達方式；最後，minute這個名詞一般是指「分鐘」，但是也常以複數形態minutes做「會議記錄」解，因此選項(A)的meeting minutes即「會議記錄」的意思。

女子負責什麼事務？
(A) 會議記錄。
(B) 座位安排。
(C) 設備管理。
(D) 產品簡報。

【類型】提問細節題型

【詞彙】
meeting minutes 會議記錄／
equipment 設備

【正解】(A)

---

61 What does the woman want to price the product?
(A) Make it $ 10,000.
(B) Make it lower than their competitors'.
(C) Keep it affordable.
(D) Make it 15,000 and give discounts later.

【解析】在對話中，男子C提出「定價一萬五千元，之後再提供優惠折扣」的想法，隨後女子便說My thoughts exactly（我也是這麼想）予以附和，可知女子贊同男子C的產品定價方式，故選(D)。★ 新制聽力考題中會經常出現非正式用語的口語化說法，這裡的My thoughts exactly. 即為一例。這個句子的完整說法應為My thoughts are exactly the same as yours.（我的想法跟你的一模一樣。）應試者必須聽出並理解這個省略了be動詞及受詞的口語所要表達的意思，才能選出正確答案。

女子希望如何定價該產品？
(A) 定價在一萬元。
(B) 定價低於競爭對手的產品。
(C) 定個讓大家都買得起的價格。
(D) 定價在一萬五千元，再給折扣。

【類型】提問細節題型

【詞彙】
price 將……定價

【正解】(D)

Questions 62-64 refer to the following conversation.

M　Any feedback from Mr. McDonald?

W　Yes. He wants us to fine-tune the payment terms. They expect us to settle the payment within 14 days of receipt of our order.

M　Do they have problems with the delivery deadline?

男子　唐納先生有回覆什麼嗎？

女子　有。他希望我們稍微調整一下付費條款。他們希望我們能在收到貨的十四天內結清貨款。

男子　他們對交貨期限有意見嗎？

加★部分為多益新題型以及相關小提醒，考生要特別注意喔！　**157**

女子 很意外，沒有。看來他們對自己的生產效率十分有信心。

男子 好。我會打電話給唐納先生告訴他我們接受他的要求。請妳在今天之內將合約準備好。我們一定要在這週內把合約簽好，這樣他們才能立即將訂單交付生產。

女子 明白。

【詞彙】
feedback 反饋訊息／
fine-tune 微調／
payment terms 付費條款／
settle the payment 結清帳款／
delivery deadline 交貨期限／
production efficiency 生產效率／
put into production 交付生產

W Surprisingly, no. Looks like they're very confident in their production efficiency.

M Good. I'll phone Mr. McDonald and tell him that his request is accepted. Please have the contract ready by today. We must get it signed this week so they can put our order into production without delay.

W Understood.

合約的哪一個部分需要修改？
(A) 生產程序　　(B) 交貨期限
(C) 付費條款　　(D) 瑕疵保證

【類型】提問細節題型

【詞彙】
revise 修改／
production procedure 生產程序／
defect guarantee 瑕疵保證

【正解】(C)

62 Which part of the contract needs to be revised?
(A) Production procedure.
(B) Delivery deadline.
(C) Payment terms.
(D) Defect guarantee.

【解析】女子在對話中提到He wants us to fine-tune the payment terms.（他希望我們稍微調整付費條款），其中fine-tune指「微調」，即對某事物「做小幅度修改」之意，與題目中的revise（修改）可互相呼應，故可知答案為(C)。

根據對話內容，帳款何時該付？
(A) 收到貨兩週內。
(B) 合約一經簽署立即付款。
(C) 訂單交付生產之前。
(D) 下訂單兩週內。

63 According to the speakers, when should the payment be made?
(A) Within 2 weeks after receipt of order.
(B) As soon as the contract is signed.
(C) Before the order is put into production.
(D) Within 14 days after the order is placed.

【解析】對話中，女子提到唐納先生提出settle the payment within 14 days of receipt of our order（在貨到十四天內結清貨款）的要求，可知帳款必須在十四天，也就是兩週內付清，故答案為(A)。

【類型】提問細節題型

【正解】(A)

---

64 What is the woman supposed to do next?
(A) Phone Mr. Donald.
(B) Sign the contract.
(C) Talk to Mr. Donald in person.
(D) Modify the contract.

女子下一步應該要做什麼？
(A) 致電唐納先生。
(B) 簽署合約。
(C) 親自與唐納先生談。
(D) 修改合約。

【解析】對話中男子對女子提出Please have the contract ready by today.（請在今天之前準備好合約）的請求，而女子回答Understood.（明白了）表示已經收到並理解對方的指示。★ 女子回答的Understood，是省略了主詞I的口語化用法。對照對話前面提到「唐納先生希望能修改付費條款」的內容，可推測女子接下來應該會進行「修改合約內容」的動作，故選(D)。modify與revise一樣，都是表示「修改」的動詞。

【類型】提問細節題型

【詞彙】
be supposed to 應該／
in person 親自；本人／
modify 修改

【正解】(D)

Questions 65-67 refer to the following conversation.

M We are very interested in doing business with you, but your price is much higher than other suppliers. Could you bring it down a little more?

W It's the best we can do. I have already lowered the quotation. It's not profitable for us unless you can increase the quantity of your order.

M I thought an order of 500 units is already a bulk purchase.

W It is. That's why we offered you a discount of 5%.

M 5% off is not good enough. We hope to get a discount of 15%.

W In that case, you may need to increase your order a little more.

男子 我們很有興趣跟你們做生意，不過你們的價格比起其他供應商要高出許多。你能不能再把價格降低一點呢？

女子 這已經是我們能給的最好價格了。我已經降低了報價。除非你可以增加訂單數量，否則對我們來說沒有利潤可言。

男子 我以為訂五百個已經是大筆採購了。

女子 的確是。所以我們才會提供您九五折的優惠啊。

男子 九五折不夠優惠啦。我們希望能拿到八五折的優惠。

女子 那樣的話，您可能需要再多增加一點訂單數量喔。

訂購數量	優惠內容
500 個以上	九五折優惠
700 個以上	九折優惠
1000 個以上	八五折優惠
1500 個以上	八折優惠

【詞彙】
bring down 降低／
bulk purchase 大宗採購

★

Quantity of order	Discount
500 units or above	5% discount
700 units or above	10% discount
1000 units or above	15% discount
1500 units or above	20% discount

說話者在協商什麼？
(A) 代理權
(B) 較低的價格
(C) 著作權
(D) 製造權

【類型】對話內容主題題型

【詞彙】
dealership 代理權／
copyright 著作權／
manufacturing right 製造權

【正解】(B)

65 What are the speakers negotiating for?
(A) Dealership.
(B) A lower price.
(C) Copyright.
(D) Manufacturing rights.

【解析】對話中，男子提到女子提供的「價格高出其他供應商」，希望女子能提供更多discount（折扣），可知對話中的兩人正在針對「更低的價格」進行協商討論，故選(B)。

女子希望男子能提供什麼？
(A) 更低的報價
(B) 當天寄送服務
(C) 更大的訂單
(D) 免費維修服務

【類型】提問細節題型

【詞彙】
same-day 當日的／
maintenance service 維修服務

【正解】(C)

66 What does the woman wish the man could offer?
(A) A lower quotation.
(B) Same-day delivery.
(C) A larger order.
(D) Free maintenance service.

【解析】對話中男子希望女子能夠提供更優惠的折扣，而女子提出You may need to increase your order a little more.（您可能需要再多增加一點訂單），可知女子希望男子能給她「更大一筆訂單」，故答案為(C)。

67 Look at the graph. How many units should the man order for a discount of 15%?
(A) 500 units.
(B) 700 units.
(C) 1000 units
(D) 1500 units.

【解析】對話中男子明白表示We hope to get a discount of 15%. （我們想拿到八五折優惠），對照圖表中所示之訂購數量及對應優惠，可知訂購數量必須超過1000個才能享有八五折優惠，故答案為(C)。

請看圖表。男子應該訂購多少數量才能得到八五折優惠？
(A) 500個
(B) 700 個
(C) 1000 個
(D) 1500個

【類型】圖表對照題型

【正解】(C)

Questions 68-70 refer to the following conversation.

Man A	So, what brings you here today?
Woman	My stomach doesn't feel right.
Man B	She started to complain about abdominal pain after eating breakfast. We all had the same food for breakfast, but she's the only one that feels uncomfortable.
Man A	So it's nothing to do with the food. Do you have any other symptoms? Nausea? Diarrhea?
Woman	No. But I haven't defecated for a week.
Man A	Hmm…, I'll prescribe some medicine that helps digestion for you. If it doesn't get any better in three days, come again and I'll give you a thorough examination.

男子A 你今天怎麼啦？

女子 我的肚子不太對勁。

男子B 她今天早上吃過早餐後就一直抱怨肚子痛。我們所有人都吃一樣的早餐，但是只有她覺得不舒服。

男子A 所以應該不是食物的問題。你還有其他症狀嗎？想吐？拉肚子？

女子 沒有。但我已經一星期沒排便了。

男子A 嗯……，我先開些幫助消化的藥給你。如果三天內沒有好轉，你再過來，我會幫你做詳細檢查。

【詞彙】
abdominal 腹部的／
uncomfortable 不舒服的／
symptom 症狀／nausea 嘔吐／
diarrhea 腹瀉／defecate 排便／
prescribe 開處方籤／
digestion 消化／
examination 檢查

這段對話發生在何處？
(A) 內科診所　　(B) 牙科診所
(C) 足部按摩店　(D) 藥局

【類型】where題型

【詞彙】
medical 內科的／
clinic 診所／dentist 牙醫／
foot massage 腳底按摩／
pharmacy 藥局

【正解】(A)

68 Where does the conversation take place?
(A) A medical clinic.　　(B) A dentist clinic.
(C) A foot massage parlor.　(D) A pharmacy.

【解析】由對話中並未提到牙齒或足部的問題，因此可先不考慮(B)與(C)。由對話中男子表示I'll prescribe some medicine... for you（我幫你開點藥）可知女子並不是在藥局，故(D)亦可排除。(A)的medical clinic指的是「內科診所」，一般與內科有關的問題或疾病都應該是到內科診所求診，故答案以(A)為最有可能的答案。

何者最有可能是女子的問題？
(A) 禽流感
(B) 登革熱
(C) 流感
(D) 消化不良

【類型】提問細節題型

【詞彙】
Bird flu 禽流感／
Dengue fever 登革熱／
influenza 流感／
indigestion 消化不良

【正解】(D)

69 What is most likely to be the woman's problem?
(A) Bird flu.
(B) Dengue fever.
(C) Influenza.
(D) Indigestion.

【解析】由對話內容提到stomach（胃部）、abdominal pain（腹部疼痛）、nausea（嘔吐）等症狀，而且男子也表示要prescribe some medicine that helps digestion（開些幫助消化的藥物），可推測女子的不適應該是「與消化系統有關」的問題，選項中以(D)所表示的「消化不良」為最有可能的答案，故選(D)。

根據男子所說，女子接下來應該做什麼？
(A) 服藥
(B) 休假
(C) 充足睡眠
(D) 請病假

【類型】提問細節題型

【正解】(A)

70 According to the man, what should the woman do next?
(A) Take the medicine.
(B) Take a vacation.
(C) Get enough sleep.
(D) Ask for a sick leave.

【解析】由對話中男子提到要為女子開處方籤，並提醒女子If it doesn't get any better in three days, come again...（如果三天內沒有好轉，再來一次）可知男子囑咐女子應先服藥，故正解為(A)。

▶ PART 4

Directions: You will hear some talks given by a single speaker. You will be asked to answer three questions about what the speaker says in each talk. Select the best response to each question and mark the letter (A), (B), (C) or (D) on your answer sheet. The talks will not be printed in your test book and will be spoken only one time.

Questions 71-73 refer to the following talk and agenda.

Man   Good morning everyone. Thank you all for coming at such a short notice. I know you are all very busy, so I really appreciate your attendance. Today's meeting is mainly about the upcoming trade show held in Bangkok. Many of our competitors will also be participating, so we need to make our exhibit booth stand out from the rest. As you can see here on the agenda, we have a lot to cover. If time allows, I will request some feedback from you concerning last year's trade show in Hong Kong and where you think we can improve. Now let's get started.

★ **Meeting Agenda**

Time	Agenda
9:30-10:00	Brochure Design/ Product Specification Sheet
10:00-11:00	Product Presentation Ideas
11:00-11:45	Marketing Plan
11:45-12:00	Feedback about 2016 Hong Kong Trade Show

男子　各位早。謝謝各位在這麼短時間通知的情況下來參加。我知道你們都非常的忙，所以我真的很感謝你們能出席。今天的會議主要是關於即將在曼谷舉辦的貿易展覽會。我們許多競爭對手也都會參加，所以我們務必要讓我們的展覽攤位比其他的更突出。如你們在這兒的會議議程上所見，我們有很多東西要討論。如果時間允許的話，我會請你們提出有關去年香港商展的意見，以及各位認為我們可以改進的地方。現在讓我們開始開會吧。

★ 會議議程

時間	議程
9:30-10:00	手冊設計／產品規格說明單
10:00-11:00	產品展示構想
11:00-11:45	行銷計劃
11:45-12:00	2016 香港商展之意見及檢討

【詞彙】
trade show 商展；貿易展覽會／
participate 參加／
exhibit booth 參展攤位

加★部分為多益新題型以及相關小提醒，考生要特別注意喔！　163

這是個什麼樣的場合？
(A) 結婚典禮。
(B) 交響音樂會。
(C) 特別會議。
(D) 迎新派對。

【類型】what題型

【詞彙】
wedding ceremony 結婚典禮／
symphony 交響樂／
extraordinary 特別的／
welcoming party 歡迎派對

【正解】(C)

---

71 What type of occasion is this?
   (A) A wedding ceremony.
   (B) A symphony concert.
   (C) A special meeting.
   (D) A welcoming party.

【解析】本題要問的是說話者說話的「場合」是什麼。建議應試者可以用「刪去法」迅速且確實地回答此題。首先由說話者一開始便表示Thank you all for coming at such a short notice.（感謝各位在這麼短的通知時間內到來），可知這是並不是一個事先計劃中的聚會場合；接著從說話者提到Today's meeting is mainly about ...（今天的會議主要是有關於……），可知這是個「會議」，因此可很快速地判斷這個場合並不是選項(A)之「婚禮」、選項(B)之「音樂會」，亦非選項(D)之「派對」。由「臨時」和「會議」這兩個關鍵訊息，可判斷(C)之「特別會議」是最有可能的答案，故選(C)。

2017商展將在何處舉辦？
(A) 台北
(B) 香港
(C) 曼谷
(D) 倫敦

【類型】where題型

【正解】(C)

---

72 Where will 2017 Trade Show be held?
   (A) Taipei.　　　(B) Hong Kong.
   (C) Bangkok.　　(D) London.

【解析】本題問的是2017商展舉辦的「地點」。由說話者在這句話：Today's meeting is mainly about the upcoming trade show held in Bangkok.（今天的會議主要是即將在曼谷舉辦的商展），可知2017商展舉辦地點在「曼谷」，故答案為(C)。

請看會議議程。這個會議應會在何時結束？
(A) 9:00.
(B) 10:00.
(C) 11:45.
(D) 12:00

【類型】對照圖表題型

【正解】(D)

---

73 Look at the agenda. When is the meeting supposed to end?
   (A) 9: 00.　　　(B) 10:00.
   (C) 11:45.　　　(D) 12:00

【解析】★ 新制多益聽力測驗在簡短獨白這部分會加入「圖表」，應試者必須根據聽到的獨白內容，對照圖表所示內容，也就是邊聽邊看圖表，才能回答出正確答案。本題問的是會議將在何時結束。雖然說話者的獨白中並未提及會議結束時間，但是在會議中附上的會議議程中，可以清楚地看到會議最後一個安排的議程是在11:45~12:00的fee back，在此之後便沒有其他議程，可知此會議預計結束的時間應是在12:00 p.m.左右。故答案為(D)。

Questions 74-76 refer to the following talk and graph.

Man Now, according to this graph, our revenue has increased briskly in the third quarter, and as illustrated, our sales peaked at NT$200,000 in September. It is noticeable that there is a considerable increase in online orders, which means that our website marketing strategy works well; however, our sales performance in stores was relatively less satisfactory. Therefore I highly suggest that we should plan a promotion campaign to boost our retail sales in each branch store, especially the one whose sales had been literally too ghastly to look at in the past two months.

★ Sales Performance in Quarter 3

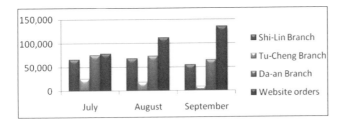

男子 現在,這張圖表說明了,我們的營收在第三季已經有大幅的增加,同時如圖所顯示,我們的營業額在九月份到達了二十萬元的高峰。值得注意的是線上訂購大量的增加,這表示我們的網站行銷策略很成功;但是我們在各店的業績表現就相對地不那麼令人滿意。因此我強力建議我們應該策劃一個促銷活動來促進各分店的零售額,尤其是過去兩個月內業績根本慘不忍睹的那間分店。

★ 第三季業績表

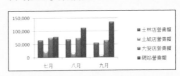

【詞彙】
revenue 營收／peak 達到高峰／
website marketing strategy
網站行銷策略／
sales performance 業績／
promotion campaign 促銷活動／
retail sales 零售額／
ghastly 糟透的

男子正在做什麼？
(A) 做業績報告。
(B) 與客戶協商。
(C) 介紹新產品。
(D) 主持記者會。

【類型】獨白主題題型

【詞彙】
sales report 業績報告／
negotiate 協商／
press conference 記者會

【正解】(A)

74 What is the man doing?
    (A) Giving a sales report.
    (B) Negotiating with his clients.
    (C) Presenting a new product.
    (D) Hosting a press conference.

【解析】要正確答出男子正在進行的事情，必須由男子發表獨白的內容來判斷。若能抓到獨白前幾句：our revenue... in the third quarter, ... our sales peaked at NT$200,000 in September. ...our sales performance in stores... 的關鍵字如「第三季／營收」、「九月份／營業額」以及「店面業績」等，可以判斷男子應該正在做「業績報告」，答案為(A)。由於獨白中並未出現針對價格或服務上的「協商內容」或提及有關「新產品」的事項，因此選項(B)與(C)皆可刪除不考慮。由獨白最後，男子提議策劃一起促銷活動以增加銷售，可知這應該是在公司內部所進行的獨白，因此也可直接不考慮選項(D)之「記者會」。

男子建議什麼？
(A) 一場慶功宴
(B) 一次檢討會
(C) 一次促銷活動
(D) 一次清倉特賣

【類型】提問細節題型

【詞彙】
celebration party 慶功宴／
review 檢討／
clearance sale 出清特賣

【正解】(C)

75 What did the man suggest?
    (A) A celebration party.
    (B) A review conference.
    (C) A promotion campaign.
    (D) A clearance sale.

【解析】說話者在做完過去六個月的業績說明之後，表示I highly suggest that we should plan a promotion campaign ...（我強烈建議我們應該策劃一次促銷活動……），可知本題答案為(C)。

根據圖表，男子發言最後指的是哪一間分店？
(A) 士林店　　　(B) 土城店
(C) 大安店　　　(D) 以上皆非

【類型】圖表對照題型

【正解】(B)

76 According to the graph, which branch store did the man refer to at the end of his speech?
    (A) Shi-Lin Branch.　　(B) Tu-Cheng Branch.
    (C) Da-An Branch.　　(D) None of the above.

【解析】這題要問的是男子在獨白最後一句...especially the one whose sales had been literally too ghastly to look at in the past two months中所指的那一間分店是哪一間？由「最後兩個月業績根本慘不忍睹」這句關鍵句，對照題目所提供之圖表，後兩個月（即八、九月）業績最低的是第二間分店「土城店」，因此可選出正確答案(B)。

Questions 77-79 refer to the following announcement.

Woman Ladies and gentlemen, the Captain has turned off the Fasten the Seat Belt sign, and you may now move around the cabin. However we always recommend that you keep your seat belt fastened while you're seated. The flight attendants will start offering you hot or cold drinks as well as dinner in a few minutes. Alcoholic drinks are also available with our compliments. You can find our menu and wine list in the seat-back pocket in front of you. Now, please sit back, relax, and enjoy the flight.

女子 女士先生們，機長已經將繫緊安全帶警示燈關閉，您現在可以在機艙內走動。但我們還是建議您在座位上要隨時繫著安全帶。空服員會在幾分鐘後開始為您提供冷熱飲料及晚餐。酒精類飲料也是由我們免費贈送讓您享用的。您可以在您座位前方的椅背口袋中找到我們的菜單及酒單。現在請您坐好，放輕鬆，並享受這趟飛行旅程。

---

77 Who is the woman talking to?
(A) Her students.　(B) Her patients.
(C) Passengers.　(D) Audience.

【解析】本題問的是這段廣播對象是「誰」。由女子廣播內容提到幾個關鍵字如Captain（機長）、Fasten the Seat Belt sign （安全帶燈號）、cabin（機艙）等，可判斷這應該是一則飛機機艙內的廣播，因此廣播對象以「乘客」是最有可能的答案，故選(C)。

女子在跟誰說話？
(A) 她的學生。　(B) 她的病人。
(C) 乘客。　(D) 聽眾。

【類型】提問廣播對象

【正解】(C)

---

78 According to this announcement, the alcoholic drinks are:
(A) prohibited.　(B) affordable.
(C) unavailable.　(D) free of charge.

【解析】看到題目中出現alcoholic drinks，在聽本段廣播內容時，就應該特別注意聽alcoholic drinks這個詞彙，因為答案通常就在這個字彙出現後的內容裡。由Alcoholic drinks are also available with our compliments.（酒精飲料也是免費由我們供應）這句話，可知酒精飲料是不用另外付費的。with sb.'s compliments為表示「由某人贈送」的片語用法。與free of charge「免費的」同義，故答案為(D)。

根據廣播內容，酒精類飲料是：
(A) 禁止的。　(B) 負擔得起的。
(C) 沒供應的。(D) 免費的。

【類型】提問細節題型

【詞彙】
prohibit 禁止／
affordable 可負擔的／
unavailable 沒供應的／
free of charge 免費的

【正解】(D)

機上菜單在哪裡？
(A) 在座位下方。
(B) 在座位後面。
(C) 在頭頂上方置物櫃。
(D) 在窗戶旁。

【類型】細節提問題型

【詞彙】
overhead 頭頂上方的／
compartment 隔間

【正解】(B)

---

79 Where is the in-flight menu?
(A) Under the seat.
(B) Behind the seat.
(C) In the overhead compartment.
(D) By the window.

【解析】本題問的是機上菜單的所在「位置」。由女子在廣播中表示 You can find our menu and wine list in the seat-back pocket in front of you.（您可以在您前方的椅背袋中找到菜單及酒單），可知菜單是被放在椅子背後的袋子內，故正解為(B)。

男子　好的，在今天的會議中，我們將選出我們在員工福利委員會的代表。我們必須清楚地知道，這個委員會的主要責任是要確保所有員工都能擁有合宜的工作環境。因此我們一定要選出一個會優先考慮一般員工之利益與福利的人。這裡是我們所有提名者的名單。他們每一個人都會有五分鐘的時間做簡單的自我介紹。然後，我們就會以舉手投票的方式作出決定。現在就讓我們歡迎第一位提名者。

★ 提名者名單

1	Emily Johnson
2	Roy Simpson
3	Gabriel Larson
4	Frank Chessman

Questions 80-82 refer to the following talk and program.

Man　Well, in our meeting today, we will be selecting our representative at the Staff Welfare Committee. We must be well aware that the main responsibility of the committee is to ensure a favorable working environment for all staff. Therefore we must choose a person who gives priority to the benefit and welfare of the general staff. Here is the list of all our nominees. Each of them will be given five minutes to make a brief self-introduction. Then, we shall make our decision by a show of hands. Now let's welcome our first nominee.

★ **List of nominees**

1	Emily Johnson
2	Roy Simpson
3	Gabriel Larson
4	Frank Chessman

80 What is the purpose of the meeting?
(A) Select a Staff Welfare Commissioner.
(B) Establish a Staff Welfare Committee.
(C) Raise funds for the Staff Welfare Committee.
(D) Nominate someone as the representative.

【解析】說話者一開始表示會議目的為：we will be selecting our representative at the Staff Welfare Committee，抓住關鍵字select（選出）／representative（代表）及committee（委員會），便可判斷會議目的應是要選出一個該部門在委員會的代表委員，故選(A)。

此會議的目的為何？
(A) 選出一名員工福利委員。
(B) 成立一個員工福利委員會。
(C) 為員工福利委員會募款。
(D) 提名某人為代表。

【類型】提問細節題型

【詞彙】
commissioner 委員／
establish 成立／fund 資金／
nominate 提名

【正解】(A)

---

81 How will the representative be decided?
(A) By secret ballot.　　(B) By a show of hands.
(C) By anonymous vote.　(D) By open vote.

【解析】本題要問的是決定推派哪一位提名者的「選舉方法」。由這段發言最後we shall make our decision by a show of hands這句話的關鍵字by a show of hands，可知他們將以「舉手」的方式選出代表，故答案為(B)。選項(D)的open vote表「記名投票」，也就是投票者會在投票過程中出示自己的名字。show of hands 雖然並非匿名投票，但是並不需要在過程中留下名字。

代表將會以何種方式決定？
(A) 秘密投票。
(B) 舉手投票。
(C) 匿名投票。
(D) 記名投票。

【類型】細節提問題型

【詞彙】
secret ballot 秘密投票／
anonymous 匿名的／
open vote 記名投票

【正解】(B)

---

82 Look at the graph. Who is going to speak next?
(A) Emily Johnson.　(B) Roy Simpson.
(C) Gabriel Larson.　(D) Frank Chessman.

【解析】說話者在最後表示「歡迎第一位提名者」上來自我介紹。對照本題附上的圖表內容，可看到提名名單上排在第一位的是Emily Johnson，可知她將是繼說話者之後下一個上來發言的人，故選(A)。

請看圖表。誰將是下一個發言者？
(A) Emily Johnson.
(B) Roy Simpson.
(C) Gabriel Larson.
(D) Frank Chessman.

【類型】圖表對照題型

【正解】(A)

女子 哈囉，大家好。我很興奮而且很驕傲地能夠為您介紹本公司歷經多月的研發所推出的最新臉部保養產品—Silky Skin。這是項特別針對亞洲婦女所設計的創新產品。在我做進一步介紹之前，我很高興宣布，未來五天我們將會在各大百貨設置促銷攤位，並且每天都會提供不同的驚喜優惠。相關資訊都在我們的海報上了。現在就讓我來向各位介紹這款超棒的臉部滋潤露……

★ 促銷優惠

日期	地點	優惠內容
12/11	GOSO 百貨	買250 ml，送100 ml
12/12	海風購物城	Silky Skin產品全面九折
12/13	三越暢貨購物城	購物滿$1000元送美妝包
12/14	黛西百貨	買500 ml，送175 ml
12/15	路易莎購物中心	購物滿$2500元送化妝箱

Questions 83-85 refer to the following talk and program.

Woman Hello, everyone. I'm very excited and proud to be able to reveal to you our very new face care product, Silky Skin, the result of many months of research and development. It is a revolutionary product designed especially for Asian women. Before I make a further introduction, I am very happy to announce that we will have a promo stall across major department stores for the coming five days and we're going to provide different amazing deals every day. Related information can be found on our posters. Now let me tell you more about this superb facial moisturizer ...

★ Promotion Deals

Dates	Locations	Deals
Dec 11	GOSO Department Store	Buy 250 ml, get 100 ml free
Dec 12	Sea Breeze Shopping Mall	10% off on all Silky Skin products
Dec 13	Mitsukoshi Outlet Mall	FREE beauty bag with any $1000 purchase
Dec 14	Daisy's Department Store	Buy 500 ml, get 175 ml free
Dec 15	Luisa's Shopping Center	Free cosmetic case with any $2500 purchase

83 What type of occasion is this?
(A) New employee orientation.
(B) An antiques auction.
(C) New product launch.
(D) Branch office opening ceremony.

【解析】★ 新制多益聽力測驗，會加入測試應試者是否能由談話內容推斷出談話背景的考題。如本題所問的即女子發表此段對話的場合。由女子在簡單的招呼語後，表示I'm very excited and proud to be able to reveal to you our very new face care product. 這句話的關鍵字為reveal（揭露、展示）、new（新的）及product（產品），抓到這幾個關鍵字，不難推斷出女子發表此段談話的目的是為了「介紹新產品」，可知這應該是個「新品發表會」的場合。故選(C)。

這是什麼種類的場合？
(A) 新進員工說明會
(B) 古董拍賣會
(C) 新品發表會
(D) 分公司開幕典禮

【類型】談話背景場合題型

【詞彙】
orientation 説明會／
antique 古董／auction 拍賣會

【正解】(C)

---

84 How long will the promotional campaign be?
(A) 24 hours.
(B) Three days.
(C) Five days.
(D) Two weeks.

【解析】本題以how long為句首，詢問這次的促銷活動將「為期多久時間」。女子在談話中表示we will have a promo stall across major department stores for the coming five days... 一旦能抓住關鍵字five days（五天），就能輕易選出本題的正確答案(C)。

促銷活動將會持續幾天？
(A) 24小時
(B) 三天
(C) 五天
(D) 兩週

【類型】how long疑問句題型

【詞彙】
promotional campaign
促銷活動

【正解】(C)

---

85 Look at the graph. When do they offer 10% off on their new product?
(A) December 11
(B) December 12
(C) December 13
(D) December 14

【解析】本題為需要參照圖表內容來回答的題型，要問的是「提供九折優惠是哪一天」。由圖表上，提供產品10% off（九折優惠）的時間只有一天，即Dec 12（十二月十二日），故答案為(B)。

請看圖表。他們何時提供新品九折優惠？
(A) 十二月十一日
(B) 十二月十二日
(C) 十二月十三日
(D) 十二月十四日

【類型】圖表對照題型

【正解】(B)

男子 好的。在我們結束會議之前，我很高興宣布，為了慶祝即將到來的聖誕季節，我們將會在本月底為所有員工及其家人舉行一次為期一天的公司郊遊。這次郊遊將會在陽明山國家公園舉辦，所有的費用將會由公司支付。歡迎每位員工都參與這次活動，而且我們鼓勵每個人都帶家人來共襄盛舉。為了確認出席，請在這週之前找Leslie登記。希望那天能看到你們每一位！

★ 公司旅遊登記表

部門	姓名	同行家人		
企劃	Jon	0 ☑	1 □	2 □
研發	Steven	0 □	1 □	2 ☑
研發	Vincent	0 □	1 ☑	2 □
財務	Rachel	0 □	1 □	2 ☑

【詞彙】
company outing 公司旅遊／
in celebration of 為了慶祝……／
expense 費用／
participate 參加／
encourage 鼓勵／
confirmation 確認／
attendance 出席／
approach 聯繫

Questions 86-88 refer to the following talk and form.

Man OK. Before we end the meeting, I am very happy to announce that we will be have a one-day company outing for all employees and their families by the end of this month in celebration of the coming Christmas season. The outing will be held at Yang Ming Shan National Park where all your expenses will be paid for by the company. Every employee is welcome to participate in this activity and everyone is encouraged to bring your family members. For the confirmation of your attendance, please approach Leslie by the end of this week. Hope to see all of you on that day!

★ **Company Outing Registration Form**

Department	Name	Accompanying family members		
Planning	Jon	0 ☑	1 □	2 □
R&D	Steven	0 □	1 □	2 ☑
R&D	Vincent	0 □	1 ☑	2 □
Finance	Rachel	0 □	1 □	2 ☑

86 What is this announcement about?
(A) An employee-training course.
(B) A one-day company trip.
(C) A meeting cancellation.
(D) An office relocation notice.

這篇通告是有關於什麼？
(A) 員工訓練課程
(B) 一日公司旅遊
(C) 會議取消
(D) 公司搬遷通知

【解析】本題要問的是本篇通告的「內容為何」，由男子在作此訊息佈達時表示I... announce that we will be have a one-day company outing...，抓到關鍵字one-day company outing即可知此通告所欲傳達的訊息內容與「一日公司旅遊」有關，故(B)為正解。

【類型】段落主題題型

【詞彙】
employee-training 員工訓練／
relocation notice 搬遷通知

【正解】(B)

87 Who can the employees bring with them to the outing?
(A) Their supervisors.
(B) Their children.
(C) Their neighbors.
(D) Their friends.

員工可以帶誰一起參加郊遊？
(A) 他們的上司
(B) 他們的孩子
(C) 他們的鄰居
(D) 他們的朋友

【解析】本題要問的是員工可以帶「誰」一起參加公司旅遊。男子在佈達時表示 ...everyone is encouraged to bring your family members，其中family members（家庭成員）為能夠正確回答本題的關鍵字。選項中只有(B)表示的「員工的孩子」為家庭成員，其他都不屬於家庭成員，故正解為(B)。

【類型】who疑問句題型

【詞彙】
supervisor 上司

【正解】(B)

88 Look at the form. Who is going to the outing without companions?
(A) Jon
(B) Vincent
(C) Steven
(D) Rachel

請看表格。誰將獨自參加郊遊？
(A) Jon　　　(B) Vincent
(C) Steven　(D) Rachel

【類型】圖表對照題型

【詞彙】
companion 陪伴

【解析】本題問的是「誰」將獨自參加郊遊。由表格內容看來，只有(A)的Jon在同行家人人數那一欄勾選了「0」這個格子，其他人都分別勾選「1」或「2」，可知只有Jon將不會帶任何家人，而是自己獨自參加公司旅遊，故答案為(A)。

【正解】(A)

女子 Kristanik先生，您早。我是 Prime Start人事部的Paula Ashley。我們收到您表達對本公司總編一職有興趣的簡歷。在看過您的應徵信後，我們認為您符合我們對此職務的所有要求條件，因此希望能邀請您來跟我們進行一場面試。我們會將您所需要的面試資訊以電子郵件寄給您。如果您有任何問題請儘管與我聯絡。

★

主旨: 面試邀請
收件人: Derrick Kristanik
寄件人: Prime Start人事部

嗨，Kristanik先生，

面試資訊

日期	2018年一月12日
時間	9 a.m. – 11 a.m.
面試地點	131室
地址	Manor Hall, Lower Clifton Hill Road, BS8 1BU

謹祝 安好
Paula Ashley
Prime Start人事部秘書

Questions 89-91 refer to the following telephone message and email.

Woman Good morning, Mr. Kristanik. This is Paula Ashley from Prime Start's Human Resources department. We received your resume and CV expressing your interest in our position of Chief Editor. After reviewing your application, we found that you meet all our requirements of this position; therefore we would like to invite you to have an interview with us. We will send you an email with all information you need for the interview. Please feel free to contact me if you have any questions.

★

Subject: Interview Invitation
To: Derrick Kristanik
From: HR Prime Start

Hi, Mr. Kristanik,

Interview information

Date	January 12th, 2018
Time	9 a.m. – 11 a.m.
Room	Room 131
Address	Manor Hall, Lower Clifton Hill Road, BS8 1BU

Best wishes,
Paula Ashley
Secretary of HR Prime Start

89 What is this message about?
(A) An interview notice.
(B) A modification request.
(C) An change of order request.
(D) A status of payment inquiry.

這通留言是有關什麼？
(A) 面試通知
(B) 請求修改
(C) 請求修改訂單
(D) 詢問款項進度

【解析】本題為一則通知留言訊息。由女子表示we would like to invite you to have an interview with us（我們想邀請您來跟我們做一次面試）可知這通留言訊息是有關「面試通知」，故答案為(A)。

【類型】訊息主題題型

【詞彙】
modification 修改／
request 請求／status 狀態／
inquiry 詢問

【正解】(A)

---

90 What is the position that Mr. Kristanik applied for?
(A) HR Manager
(B) Chief editor
(C) Computer programmer
(D) Technique engineer

Kristanik先生應徵的職務為何？
(A) 人資部經理
(B) 總編輯
(C) 電腦程式設計師
(D) 技術工程師

【解析】女子在訊息中提到：We received your resume and CV expressing your interest in our position of Chief Editor，若能抓到這句的關鍵字Chief Editor，即可得知Kristanik應徵的是「總編輯」一職，故答案為(B)。

【類型】細節提問題型

【詞彙】
computer programmer
電腦程式設計師／
technique engineer 技術工程師

【正解】(B)

---

91 Look at the email. When will the interview start?
(A) At 9 a.m.
(B) On Wednesday.
(C) In two days.
(D) In October.

請看郵件。面試何時開始？
(A) 上午九點。
(B) 星期三。
(C) 兩天後。
(D) 十月。

【解析】看到以when為句首的疑問句，即可知本題是要問面試的「時間」。因此對照本題附上的郵件內容時，只需要看有關時間方面的訊息：January 12th, 2018（2018年一月十二日）及9 a.m. – 11 a.m.（上午九點至十一點）。訊息中的月份顯示為「一月」，並非選項(D)的「十月」；此外，這份郵件並無透露任何有關「今天日期」及「星期」的資訊，因此選項(B)(C)(D)皆可直接刪除不考慮。訊息中顯示面試時間為上午九點至十一點，故(A)為正解。

【類型】圖表對照題型

【正解】(A)

女子 嗨，我是Linda與Kevin的孫女——Brenda。我想向各位說，謝謝你們來參加我最親愛的爺爺奶奶結婚五十年的慶祝會。我會是今晚派對的主持人，希望你們每一位在這兒都能有賓至如歸的感受。在為您端上晚餐前，我們想要與您分享一段我們特別為今晚所編製的影片。好吧，我的爺爺奶奶希望我低調一點，但是，五十年耶！要兩個人在一起五十年，可有多長啊！是他們的愛與奉獻，讓他們一起走了這麼久。這段影片包含了Linda與Kevin這五十年婚姻生活的照片與短片，我相信一定會觸動到各位的心！請欣賞！

【詞彙】
marriage 婚姻／host 主持人／
in good hands 受到妥善照顧／
keep it low 保持低調／
devotion 奉獻

Questions 92-94 refer to the following talk.

Woman Hi, I'm Brenda, granddaughter of Linda and Kevin. I just want to say thank you to everyone for coming to our celebration of 50 years of marriage between my dearest grandparents. I will be the host of tonight's party and I hope that you'll find yourselves in good hands. Before the dinner is served, we would like to share with you a film that we edited especially for tonight. Well, My grandma and grandpa wanted me to keep it low, but, 50 years! 50 years is a very long time for two people to be together. It is their love and devotion that enabled them to make it this far. The film contains a series of photos as well as videos of Linda and Kevin's 50-year married life and I'm sure it's gonna touch your heart. Enjoy!

說話者是誰？
(A) 賓客之一
(B) Linda最好的朋友
(C) 主持人
(D) Kevin的女兒

【類型】who疑問句題型

【正解】(C)

92 Who is the speaker?
(A) One of the guests.
(B) Linda's best friend.
(C) The host.
(D) Kevin's daughter.

【解析】根據演說者的自我介紹：I'm Brenda, granddaughter of Linda and Kevin.可知說話者為Linda及Kevin的孫女，因此選項(A)(B)(D)都可以直接刪除。剩下一個選項(C)，可以從I will be the host of tonight's party（我將是今晚派對的主持人）得到確認，故為正確答案。

93 What most likely is this occasion?
    (A) Graduation ceremony
    (B) Wedding anniversary
    (C) House warming party
    (D) College reunion

【解析】本題需要應試者根據演説內容，來判斷這是什麼場合。女子在演説中表示 ... thank you to everyone for coming to our celebration of 50 years of marriage between my dearest grandparents. 由這句話的關鍵字celebration of 50 years of marriage（結婚五十年慶祝）可知這是個慶祝結婚五十年的慶祝會，因此選項(B)為正確答案。

這最有可能是什麼樣的場合？
(A) 畢業典禮
(B) 結婚週年紀念
(C) 喬遷派對
(D) 大學同學會

【類型】演説場合題型

【詞彙】
graduation ceremony 畢業典禮／
anniversary 週年紀念／
house warming party 喬遷派對／
reunion 團聚

【正解】(B)

94 What are the guests going to watch?
    (A) A short play.
    (B) A talk show.
    (C) An animation.
    (D) An edited film.

【解析】由女子表示we would like to share with you a film that we edited ...（我們想跟各位分享一段我們編輯的影片）及最後對賓客們説Enjoy!（請觀賞），可知賓客們即將觀賞該影片，故答案為(D)。

賓客將要觀賞什麼？
(A) 一齣短劇
(B) 一齣脱口秀
(C) 一齣卡通片
(D) 一個編輯影片

【類型】細節提問題型

【詞彙】
short play 短劇／
talk show（電視）訪談節目／
animation 卡通動畫片

【正解】(D)

男子 據我所知，你們之中有些人已經申請下個月的休假。雖然我們鼓勵所有員工都利用年假好好放鬆休息，但是容我提醒各位，如果你們不希望在休假時受到不必要的打擾，一定要指定一個在你休假期間對所可能發生的各種狀況都能安然處理的同事來代理你的工作。因此，我會將這張表格張貼在佈告欄上。所有下個月要休假的同仁，請將你與你職務代理人的名字填上，如此一來我們才知道，你不在的期間，要讓業務繼續順利進行要找誰。

★

姓名	休假期間	代理人
Jennifer Lin	1/12 – 1/15	Diana Chou
Benjamin Chang	1/18 – 1/24	Joseph Wang
Samantha Chen	1/22 – 1/25	Peter Yang
Diana Chou	1/24 – 1/29	Jennifer Lin

【詞彙】

leave of absence 休假／
take advantage of 利用／
annual leave 年假／
interrupt 打擾／
identify 指認；認出／
colleague 同事／
come up 出現／
bulletin board 佈告欄／
backup 支援／
approach 與……聯繫／
substitute 代理人

Questions 95-97 refer to the following talk and program.

Man As far as I know, some of you have applied for leave of absence from work next month. While all employees are encouraged to take advantage of your annual leave for a relaxing vacation, allow me to remind you that if you don't want your vacation to be interrupted unnecessarily, you must identify a colleague who is able to cover for you and is comfortable with all kinds of situations that might come up while you are away from the office. So, I will post this form on the bulletin board. Anyone who is taking a leave next month, please fill in this form with you and your vacation backup buddy's name so that we will know who to approach to make business continue smoothly in your absence.

★

Name	Leave of Absence	Substitute
Jennifer Lin	Jan 12th-Jan 15th	Diana Chou
Benjamin Chang	Jan 18th-Jan 24th	Joseph Wang
Samantha Chen	Jan 22nd- Jan 25th	Peter Yang
Diana Chou	Jan 24th-Jan 29th	Jennifer Lin

95 What is the talk most related to?
    (A) Leave policy.   (B) Overtime rule.
    (C) Data analysis.   (D) Product design.

【解析】由説話者在這段談話中不斷提到leave（休假）、annual leave（年假）、vacation （假期）以及與職務代理相關的cover（代理）、vacation backup buddy（休假支援夥伴）等關鍵字，可判斷這片談話應該與選項(A)的「休假政策」最有關係，故選(A)。由於這段談話並未提及與「加班」相關的事情，故可不考慮(B)。

這篇談話與何者最有關係？
(A) 休假政策　　(B) 加班規定
(C) 資料分析　　(D) 產品設計

【類型】段落主題題型

【詞彙】
leave policy 休假政策／
overtime 加班／
data analysis 數據、資料分析

【正解】(A)

---

96 What does the speaker ask the listeners to do?
    (A) Join an after-work club.
    (B) Identify a substitute during vacation.
    (C) Improve their sales performance.
    (D) Come up with creative marketing ideas.

【解析】由本篇談話整體脈絡看來，説話者先以you must identify a colleague who is able to cover for you （你必須指定一名可以幫你代理職務的同事）來説明「職務代理人」的重要性，接著更直接要求fill in this form with you and your vacation backup buddy's names （在這張表格中填入你與你的休假支援夥伴的名字），可知説話者希望有休假需求的人「務必指定休假代理人」，故選(B)。

說話者要求聽者做什麼？
(A) 參加下班後社團。
(B) 指定休假代理人。
(C) 提升業績表現。
(D) 想出有創意的行銷點子。

【類型】細節提問題型

【詞彙】
come up with 想出

【正解】(B)

---

97 Look at the form. Who is taking the longest leave next month?
    (A) Jennifer
    (B) Benjamin
    (C) Samantha
    (D) Diana

【解析】根據表格中的休假時間長短來看，名單上的四位員工中以Benjamin從一月18日到一月24日共休七天，休假天數最多，故答案為(B)。

請看表格。誰下個月的休假最長？
(A) Jennifer
(B) Benjamin
(C) Samantha
(D) Diana

【類型】表格對照題型

【正解】(B)

男子 好的，沒太多意外地，這週我們將會有幾天十五度以上的高溫，然後每天入夜後氣溫會降個五度左右，所以現在還不算是游泳季節，不過就快了。現在讓我們來看一下島上天氣圖。我們看到從北部有一個小小的冷鋒面正朝我們移動。這道冷鋒面積有明顯變大，而且看起來持續在增強中。我們來看看這對五天的天氣預報有什麼影響……

★ 連續五日氣象預報

	五	六	日	一	二
最高溫	17℃	19℃	18℃	16℃	18℃
最低溫	12℃	15℃	13℃	11℃	12℃

【詞彙】
cold front 冷鋒／
expand 擴大／forecast 預報

Questions 98-100 refer to the following talk and program.

Man Well, not a lot of surprises, this week we're gonna have some highs in the mid to upper 10s, and things are gonna cool down about 5 degrees each night, so not quite swimming season just yet, but we're getting there. Now Let's take a look at the island. We've been tracking a small cold front that's been moving in from the north here. It appears that the cold has expanded in size and it looks like it continues to grow. Let's see how this will affect the five-day forecast ...

★ 5-Day Forecast

	FRI	SAT	SUN	MON	TUE
HIGH	17℃	19℃	18℃	16℃	18℃
LOW	12℃	15℃	13℃	11℃	12℃

說話者最有可能是什麼身份？
(A) 一名算命師
(B) 一名物理學教授
(C) 一名氣象預報員
(D) 一名報社記者

【類型】細節提問題型

【詞彙】
fortuneteller 算命師／
physics 物理／
forecaster 預報員／
journalist 記者

【正解】(C)

98 Who most likely is the speaker?
　　(A) A fortuneteller.
　　(B) A physics professor.
　　(C) A weather forecaster.
　　(D) A newspaper journalist.

【解析】本題要應試者根據聽到的內容判斷說話者最有可能是何種身份。這段談話相當生活口語化，不經常收看或收聽新聞氣象預報的應試者可能無法一下子知道這是篇關於什麼內容的演說，但是如果能夠抓到關鍵字degree（溫度），以及 cold front（冷鋒），大致就能推測出答案。談話最後還有一句非常清楚的關鍵字：five-day forecast（五日預報），由forecast（天氣預測）這個字加上前面的關鍵字，應該就能確定答案是(C)「氣象預報員」。雖然forecast這個字除了用在「預測」氣象之外，也可以用在「預測」未來可能發生之事，但是通常是對「有所徵兆」的事提出預測；像「命運」這種無徵兆可循的事，就不適合用forecast這個動詞，因此不太可能與(A)「算命師」有關。

99 According to the speaker, what is going to affect the weather in next five days?

(A) A warm front.

(B) A cold front.

(C) A storm.

(D) A mild typhoon.

【解析】由說話者表示先表示 ...a small cold front（一道小冷鋒）...moving in from the north here（由北向我們移動）...the cold has expanded（冷鋒已經擴大）...continues to grow（持續增強），接著並表示Let's see how this will affect the five-day forecast ...（讓我們看看這將對未來五日的天氣預測有何影響），可知未來五天的天氣可能會受前面提到的這道冷鋒影響，故選(B)。

根據說話者所說，何者將影響未來五天的天氣？

(A) 一道暖鋒。

(B) 一道冷鋒。

(C) 一場暴風雨。

(D) 一個輕度颱風。

【類型】細節提問題型

【詞彙】
front 鋒面／storm 暴風雨／
mild 輕度的／typhoon 颱風

【正解】(B)

---

100 Look at the graph. When will it rain within next five days?

(A) Friday

(B) Saturday

(C) Sunday

(D) Monday

【解析】根據本題圖表所示，未來五天只有Monday這一天有出現下雨的圖案，因此答案為(D)。

請看圖表。未來五天內何時會下雨？

(A) 星期五

(B) 星期六

(C) 星期天

(D) 星期一

【類型】圖表對照題型

【正解】(D)

(A) 這是個遊樂場。
(B) 這是個遊樂園。
(C) 這是個網球場。
(D) 這是個高爾夫球場。

【類型】景物描述題型

【詞彙】
playground 遊樂場／
amusement park 遊樂園／
tennis court 網球場／
golf course 高爾夫球場

【正解】(A)

01 (A) It's a playground.
(B) It's an amusement park.
(C) It's a tennis court.
(D) It's a golf course.

【解析】照片為一處有許多幼兒遊樂器材的場地，因此可知(A)為最符合照片內容的描述，故為正解。選項(B)的 amusement park指的是有「雲霄飛車」等大型遊樂設施的遊樂園；選項(C)與選項(D)指的分別是「網球場」及「高爾夫球場」，以上皆與圖片不符，故可直接刪除。

(A) 人們在此託運行李。
(B) 人們在此等接駁車。
(C) 人們在此採買雜貨。
(D) 人們在此試穿衣服。

【類型】場合題型

【詞彙】
check in 託運／luggage 行李／
shuttle bus 接駁車／
grocery shopping 雜貨採買／
try on 試穿、戴（衣飾）

【正解】(A)

02 (A) It is where people check in their baggage.
(B) It is where people wait for the shuttle bus.
(C) It is where people do grocery shopping.
(D) It is where people try on clothes.

【解析】由照片中出現的人物是站在櫃檯前，並且可以看到人物旁邊有堆放行李的推車，可推測這裡應該是機場的報到及託運行李櫃檯。選項中以(A)所描述的「這是人們託運行李的地方」最符合照片內容，故為正解。

03 (A) There's an ambulance.
(B) There's a fire engine.
(C) There's a police car.
(D) There's a tow truck.

【解析】照片中可看到一輛警車及兩名警察,因此可知正確描述為(C)。

(A) 有輛救護車。
(B) 有輛消防車。
(C) 有輛警車。
(D) 有輛拖吊車。

【類型】人物及景物題型

【詞彙】
ambulance 救護車／
fire engine 消防車／
police car 警車／
tow truck 拖吊車

【正解】(C)

04 (A) This room is messy.
(B) It is a double room.
(C) This room is empty.
(D) This room has a window.

【解析】出現無人物的照片時,應注意照片中出現的事物或景物之狀態。(B)提到的double room通常是指只有一張雙人床的雙人房,照片中為兩張床的房間,這樣的房間通常稱之為twin room(雙床房),故(B)非正確描述。由於照片中的房間並未呈現凌亂的模樣,故(A)亦非正確描述。照片中的房間內有兩張床及其他傢俱擺設,並非空無一物的狀態,故(C)亦非正解。在照片中可以看到窗簾後有一扇窗戶,可知(D)為最符合照片的描述,是為正解。

(A) 這個房間很凌亂。
(B) 這是個雙人房。
(C) 這個房間空無一物。
(D) 這個房間有扇窗。

【類型】單純景物題型

【詞彙】
messy 凌亂的／
double room 雙人房／
empty 空的

【正解】(D)

(A) 小販正忙著工作。
(B) 小販對顧客微笑。
(C) 有人在等著買了。
(D) 小販戴著黑手套。

【類型】單人照片題型

【詞彙】
vendor 小販

【正解】(A)

05 (A) The vendor is busy working.
(B) The vendor is smiling at the customers.
(C) There are people waiting to be served.
(D) The vendor wears black gloves.

【解析】題目為單人照片題時，要特別留意照片人物的表情、動作或裝扮。觀察照片中的人物，其臉上並無(B)所提到的「微笑」，手上戴的是白色手套，而非(D)提到的「黑手套」。照片中只能看到小販低頭處理食物，也就是(A)所述之「忙著工作」的模樣，並未看到有客人等著向他買東西，故可排除選項(C)，並選出最符合照片描述的選項(A)。

(A) 櫃檯前隊伍很長。
(B) 這地方擠滿了人。
(C) 警衛正站在門邊。
(D) 沒人盯著上方螢幕。

【類型】多人照片題

【詞彙】
queue 隊伍／
security guard 警衛／
overhead 頭頂上方的

【正解】(D)

06 (A) There are long queues at the counters.
(B) This place is filled with people.
(C) The security guard is standing at the door.
(D) No one is staring at the overhead screens.

【解析】在此照片中可到服務櫃檯前各只有一位顧客，並未看到(A)所述「很長的隊伍」；更遑論(B)所述的「擠滿了人」，此外，(C)所提到的「警衛」也沒有出現在照片中。故以上三個選項皆可刪除不考慮。在照片中出現的人物看起來都正專心在處理手上的事情，沒有人盯著頭頂上方的螢幕，故(D)為最符合照片內容之描述。

▶ **PART 2**

Directions: You will hear a question or statement and three responses spoken in English. They will not be printed in your test book and will be spoken only one time. Select the best response to the question or statement and mark the letter (A), (B) or (C) on your answer sheet.

Example

You will hear: Did you have dinner at the restaurant yesterday?

You will also hear:

(A) Yes, it lasted all day.

(B) No, I went to a movie with my girlfriend.

(C) Yes, the client was nice.

The best response to the question "Did you have dinner at the restaurant yesterday?" is choice (B), "No, I went to a movie with my girlfriend," so (B) is the best answer. You should mark answer (B) on your answer sheet.

07 Do you want me to join the meeting?

　(A) No, I wasn't invited.

　(B) If you have time.

　(C) Yes, he should.

【解析】本題疑問句旨在詢問對方「是否希望我參加會議」，選項(B)以if條件句表示「如果你有時間的話」，意即「如果你有時間，就來參加」，是為最適當的答案，故為正解。選項(A)與(C)皆答非所問，故不需考慮。

你希望我參加會議嗎？

(A) 不，我沒被邀請。

(B) 如果你有時間的話。

(C) 是，他應該要。

【類型】yes/no 疑問句題型

【正解】(B)

我要一張兩人的座位。
(A) 您要訂幾點的？
(B) 您有多少人會來？
(C) 抱歉。飯店房間都被預訂了。

【類型】陳述句題型

【正解】(A)

08 I need a table for two.
    (A) When do you need it?
    (B) How many of you are coming?
    (C) Sorry. All the hotel rooms are booked.

【解析】本題為表示「我需要一張兩人的桌子」之陳述句，是在跟餐廳人員表示要「訂位」所使用的句子。選項(A)詢問「請問幾點需要？」意思就是在問對方「要訂幾點的位子」，是最適當的答案，故為正解。由於題目已經表明需要「兩人」的座位，故選項(B)詢問「有幾個人會來」，便不適當。選項(C)提到「飯店房間已被訂光」，則與本題陳述句完全無關。

您想怎麼付帳？
(A) 三點前。
(B) 付現。
(C) 搭汽車。

【類型】how 疑問句題型

【正解】(B)

09 How would you like to pay?
    (A) By three o'clock.
    (B) By cash.
    (C) By car.

【解析】本題為以how為首的疑問句，要問付費的「方法」。選項(B)以by cash表示要「用現金付費」，是正確答案。選項(A)的回答通常用來回應「時間期限」，而(C)的回答通常用來回應「搭哪一種交通工具」，皆與問題無關。

我們最好現在走，不然會遲到。
(A) 我沒事。
(B) 現在還很早。
(C) 我不是故意的。

【類型】提出建議題型

【正解】(B)

10 We'd better go now or we'll be late.
    (A) I'm fine.
    (B) It's still early.
    (C) I didn't mean it.

【解析】had better為用來表示「建議」的句型用法，本題的We'd better... 即「我們最好……」之意。對於「我們最好現在出發，不然會遲到」的建議，選項(B)回答It's still early.（現在還早），暗示對方不要擔心會遲到，是最適當的回應，是為正解。選項(A)與(C)都答非所問，故不選。

11 What's the problem with this shirt?

(A) It's the wrong size.

(B) It's too dangerous.

(C) It was delayed.

【解析】本題疑問句是在問「這件襯衫有什麼問題？」選項 (B)表示「這太危險了」，似乎與襯衫無關；選項(C)表示「時間延遲」，亦非襯衫所會發生的問題，故以上兩個選項皆非答案。選項(A)表示「尺碼不對」，是當店員在顧客想退貨時，以「襯衫有什麼問題」詢問顧客退貨原因，最適當的回應，故選(A)。

這件襯衫有什麼問題嗎？

(A) 尺碼不對。

(B) 太危險了。

(C) 時間延遲了。

【類型】what 疑問句題型

【正解】(A)

---

12 Don't forget to exchange some money before our trip to Japan.

(A) My passport has expired.

(B) Thanks for reminding me.

(C) The flight is completely booked.

【解析】祈使句前面加了don't forget to...，則使之具有「提醒注意」的作用，故本題為提醒對方不要忘記做某件事的祈使句。選項(B)以Thanks for reminding me（謝謝你提醒我）表示感謝對方提醒，是最適當的回應，故為正解。(A)表示「護照到期」以及(C)表示「班機已被訂滿」皆與「兌換錢幣」無關，故不需考慮。

別忘了在我們去日本前換點錢。

(A) 我的護照已經到期。

(B) 謝謝你提醒我。

(C) 這班機已經全訂滿了。

【類型】提醒祈使句題型

【詞彙】

passport 護照／expire 到期

【正解】(B)

---

13 Doesn't this train go to Taipei?

(A) It's bound for Yilan.

(B) Yes, it's on schedule.

(C) No, it's not Friday.

【解析】本題以否定助動詞為句首的疑問句，主要是要問「這班火車是不是開往台北？」選項(B)回答「準點（出發）」以及選項(C)回答「不是星期五」皆答非所問。選項(A)雖未回答Yes或No，但是明確表示這班車「開往宜蘭」，確實回答了這個問題，故為最適當的答案。

這班火車不到台北嗎？

(A) 它開往宜蘭。

(B) 是，會準點。

(C) 不，不是星期五。

【類型】否定疑問句題型

【詞彙】

bound for（準備）前往／
on schedule 準點

【正解】(A)

你們何時會推出這個新產品？
(A) 明天就會安裝了。
(B) 我想我們會搭計程車去。
(C) 可能在兩星期後。

【類型】when疑問句題型

【詞彙】
launch 投放市場／install 安裝

【正解】(C)

14 When will you launch this new product?
   (A) It will be installed tomorrow.
   (B) I think we will go by taxi.
   (C) Probably in two weeks.

【解析】本題為以when為句首的疑問句，要問的是「何時」會推出新品。選項(A)雖然有提到時間，但是推出新品與install（安裝）這個動詞卻完全搭不上邊；選項(B)是用來答覆「搭哪一種交通工具」的回應，亦與問題無關。選項(C)回答「可能在兩星期後」推出新品，是合乎常理的回答，故為最適當的選擇。

我需要有人幫我把這箱子搬到樓下去。
(A) 那正是我需要的。
(B) 我可以幫你忙。
(C) 它在走廊盡頭。

【類型】陳述句題型

【詞彙】
downstairs 樓下／hallway 走廊

【正解】(B)

15 I need some help moving this box downstairs.
   (A) That's exactly what I need.
   (B) I can give you a hand.
   (C) It's down the hallway.

【解析】本題以陳述句I need some help...的方式做出「我需要幫忙」的請求。選項(B)的give sb. a hand為表示「幫某人忙」的片語用法，I can give you a hand（我可以幫你忙）呼應了陳述句的請求，故為正解。

電梯不能用。
(A) 那我們就走樓梯吧。
(B) 那是在二樓。
(C) 我已經付錢了。

【類型】陳述句題型

【詞彙】
elevator 電梯／
in service 服勤中的、可使用的

【正解】(A)

16 The elevator is not in service.
   (A) Let's take the stairs then.
   (B) It's on the second floor.
   (C) I have already paid for it.

【解析】本題陳述句表示「電梯不能用」，選項(A)於是回答「那就走樓梯」，是最適當的回應，故為正解。選項(B)與(C)所回答的內容皆與「電梯」無關，故不需考慮。

17 What's your special today?
(A) A tuna sandwich, please.
(B) The dinner is on me.
(C) Beef curry with rice.

你們今日特餐是什麼？
(A) 麻煩給我一份鮪魚三明治。
(B) 晚餐我請客。
(C) 牛肉咖哩飯。

【解析】本題疑問句中的special做名詞解，指的是餐廳或飯館的「特色菜；特餐」。選項(C)說出料理名稱，確實回答出「今日特餐為何」，是為正解。選項(A)沒有回答問題，反而點菜，不合常理；同樣地，選項(B)亦沒有回答特餐是什麼，反而表示「晚餐我請客」，也不是適當的回應，故不選。

【類型】what 疑問句題型

【詞彙】
special 特色菜，特餐

【正解】(C)

---

18 How old is your son?
(A) He's turning eighteen next week.
(B) You look younger than your age.
(C) I never celebrate my birthday.

你兒子年紀多大了？
(A) 他下星期就十八歲了。
(B) 你看起來比你年齡年輕。
(C) 我從來不慶祝生日。

【解析】本題疑問句問的是「你兒子年紀多大」，選項(B)回答「你看起來比你年齡年輕」以及(C)回答「我從不慶祝生日」，跟「你兒子的年紀」完全無關。選項(A) 中的turn為「成為」之意，He's turning eighteen即「他即將成為十八歲」，是最適當的回答，故為正解。

【類型】how 疑問句題型

【正解】(A)

---

19 The bus runs every ten minutes, doesn't it?
(A) Yes, the machine runs smoothly.
(B) Yes, during the rush hour.
(C) If you want to catch the bus.

公車每十分鐘一班，對不對？
(A) 對，每件事都進行得很順利。
(B) 對，在尖峰時間是如此。
(C) 如果你想要趕上公車的話。

【解析】本題為「向對方確認自己知道的事」之附加疑問句，目的在確認「公車是不是每十分鐘開一班」，動詞run在此問句中作「行駛」解。選項(A)的動詞run則是做「運作」解，「機器運作順利」與問題中的「公車行駛頻率」無關，故不需考慮。選項(C)以if條件句回答，完全答非所問。選項(B)肯定回答，並簡單表示「尖峰時間是每十分鐘一班車」沒錯，故為正解。

【類型】附加疑問句題型

【詞彙】
run 行駛；運作／
rush hour 尖峰時間

【正解】(B)

我可以知道您為什麼取消您的預訂嗎？
(A) 我以前從沒讀過這本書。
(B) 我改變了我的旅遊計劃。
(C) 我會再加訂一間房。

【類型】why 疑問句題型

【正解】(B)

20 May I know why you are cancelling your booking?
    (A) I've never read this book before.
    (B) I changed my travel plans.
    (C) I will book another room.

【解析】本題的疑問句前面加上了May I know...，使得這個why疑問句變成了間接問句。此疑問句想要知道cancel your booking（取消您的預訂）的「原因」，選項(A)雖然也提到book，但是這裡的book指的是「書」，與問句中的booking（預訂）無關，因此並非適合答案。選項(C)表示「會加訂另一個房間」，亦沒有直接回答「為何取消預訂」。選項(B)表示「旅遊計劃有所改變」，因為計劃有變而取消原來的預訂，符合常理，故為正解。

噢，我的牙齒快痛死了。
(A) 你得去看牙醫。
(B) 你車子得加油。
(C) 你得去報警。

【類型】陳述句題型

【詞彙】
refuel 為……補給燃料

【正解】(A)

21 Oh, my tooth is killing me.
    (A) You need to go to the dentist.
    (B) You need to refuel your car.
    (C) You need to report it to the police.

【解析】動詞kill在本題陳述句中為口語用法，做「使痛苦不堪；使極不舒服」解，而不是一般常用的「殺死」。因此My tooth is killing me. 意思是「我的牙齒使我痛到快死了」。選項(A)回應牙痛問題，表示「你應該去看牙醫」，是最適當的答案。選項(B)與(C)皆答非所問，故不考慮。

你看起來病得很重，我覺得你今天不應該去上班。
(A) 我想他是在學校傳染到感冒。
(B) 你說得對。我今天會請病假。
(C) 我目前在待業中。

【類型】陳述句題型

【詞彙】
pick up 感染／flu 感冒／
call in sick（臨時）請病假／
between jobs 待業中

【正解】(B)

22 You look so ill that I don't think you should go to work today.
    (A) I think he picked up the flu at school.
    (B) You're right. I'll call in sick today.
    (C) I am between jobs at the moment.

【解析】本題以陳述句的方式表示對方「看起來病得很嚴重」，並建議對方「不應該去上班」。選項(A)的主詞為與陳述句無關的第三人稱，故不考慮；選項(C)表示以between jobs表示「自己目前無業」，亦跟陳述句內容無關。選項(B)附和對方之後，表示自己會call in sick（打電話請病假），是本題陳述句最適當的回應。

23 This is the best chicken broth I've ever had.
(A) I'm glad you like it.
(B) About fifteen minutes.
(C) Thanks for having us.

【解析】本題為表示「這是我喝過最棒的雞肉濃湯」之陳述。選項(A)表示「很高興你喜歡」，為最適合這句陳述的回應，故為正解。選項(B)為用來回答「需要多少時間」的回應。選項(C)則通常是在參加活動後，對主辦人所表示的感謝用語。

這是我喝過最棒的雞肉濃湯。
(A) 很高興你喜歡。
(B) 大約要十五分鐘。
(C) 謝謝你邀請我們來。

【類型】陳述句題型

【詞彙】
broth 濃湯

【正解】(A)

---

24 Do you need some more time to read the menu?
(A) Please take your time.
(B) Sorry, I don't have the time.
(C) No. I can order now.

【解析】本題詢問「是否需要更多時間看菜單」，選項(C)以No簡答「不需要」，並接著表示「現在可以點餐了」，是最適當的回答。選項(A)中的take one's time為用來表示「不慌不忙、慢慢來」的片語用法；選項(B)的I don't have the time.是在沒有時鐘或手錶等報時工具的情況下，用以表示「我不知道時間」的用法。(A)與(B)皆答非所問，但因為都跟問句一樣有出現time這個字，要注意time的各種用法，以免被誤導而選錯答案。

你需要更多時間看菜單嗎？
(A) 請慢慢來。
(B) 抱歉，我不知道現在幾點。
(C) 不用。我可以點餐了。

【類型】yes/no 疑問句題型

【正解】(C)

---

25 I haven't talked to Nathan for weeks.
(A) What's going on between you two?
(B) He will be here tomorrow.
(C) Yes, we need to talk.

【解析】本題為表示「我與Nathan已經好幾週沒有講話」之陳述。選項(A)反問「你們兩個發生什麼事了？」為最自然的反應，故為最適當的答案。

我已經好幾個星期沒跟Nathan說話了。
(A) 你們兩個發生什麼事了？
(B) 他明天會來這裡。
(C) 對，我們得談談。

【類型】陳述句題型

【正解】(A)

印表機還是不能用，對嗎？
(A) 它今天早上已經被修好了。
(B) 對，那真的很刺激。
(C) 在影印機旁邊。

【類型】附加問句題型

【詞彙】
photocopier 影印機

【正解】(A)

26 The printer is still not working, is it?
(A) It was fixed this morning.
(B) Yes, it was really exciting.
(C) Next to the photocopier.

【解析】本題問句為「和對方確認自己已知事情」的附加問句題型。這句想要確認的事項是「印表機還不能用，對不對？」選項(B)與選項(C)的回答皆與「印表機能不能用」無關。而選項(A)回答「今天早上已經修好」，是最適合這個問句的回應，故為正解。

你介意跟我換位子嗎？
(A) 好，你可以。
(B) 一點也不。
(C) 當然，我會。

【類型】詢問意願題型

【正解】(B)

27 Do you mind changing seats with me?
(A) Yes, you can.
(B) Not at all.
(C) Sure, I will.

【解析】以Would/Do you mind 為首的問句，指在詢問對方意願。由於mind一字指「介意」，do you mind...問的是「你介不介意……」，而不是「你願不願意」，因此回答時，No, I don't. 表示接受對方提議，而Yes, I do. 則表示「介意對方提議」，也就是「不接受」。選項(A)與(C)的助動詞都與問句所使用的do不相符，故非適當的回答。選項(B)回答Not at all（一點也不），表示不介意跟對方換位子，是為正解。

你有需要超市的任何東西嗎？
(A) 有。我們的洗髮精快用完了。
(B) 不。你不覺得它太貴了嗎？
(C) 它離這裡只有三條街遠。

【類型】yes/no疑問句題型

【詞彙】
run out of 用完／
shampoo 洗髮精

【正解】(A)

28 Do you need anything from the supermarket?
(A) Yes. We're running out of shampoo.
(B) No. Don't you think it's too expensive?
(C) It's only three blocks away from here.

【解析】本題詢問「需不需要任何超級市場的東西」，選項(C)的描述是用來回答「某處距離多遠」，而(B)則在表示「某物太貴」，與問句毫不相關。選項(A)肯定回答本題問句，並以「洗髮精快用完」來暗示「需要洗髮精」，是為正解。

29 How long will you be on leave?
(A) I'll leave tomorrow.
(B) Seven days.
(C) At eight thirty.

你會休假多久？
(A) 我明天會離開。
(B) 七天。
(C) 八點三十分。

【解析】本題問句中出現的leave做名詞解，指「休假」，而be on leave則為表示「休假」的片語用法。以how long為句首的疑問句，主要是要問某事進行時間「多長」，因此以選項(B)的「七天」為最適當的回答。選項(A)中的leave做動詞解，指「離開」，要注意別被同字異義給誤導了。選項(C)回答「八點三十分」，根本答非所問，故不需考慮。

【類型】詢問時間長短題型

【詞彙】
on leave 休假

【正解】(B)

---

30 Are you going to use slides for the presentation?
(A) No, I'm going to use a flip chart.
(B) I'm a little nervous, but I'll be fine.
(C) I can't figure it out by myself.

你的簡報會用到幻燈片嗎？
(A) 不，我會用活動式掛圖。
(B) 我有點緊張，不過會沒事的。
(C) 我沒辦法自己想出來。

【解析】助動詞或be動詞為句首的疑問句，一般情況下會以yes或no來作答。本題詢問「簡報時會不會使用幻燈片」，選項(B)與(C)皆未正面回答問題，只有選項(A)先否定回答，接著表示「會使用其他設備」，故為正解。

【類型】yes/no 疑問句題型

【詞彙】
slides 幻燈片／
flip chart 活動式掛圖／
figure out 想出

【正解】(A)

---

31 Any comments about the new brochure?
(A) Yes, the shirt also comes in other colors.
(B) Yes. I think there should be more pictures.
(C) I don't think he will come today.

對新手冊有什麼看法嗎？
(A) 有，這襯衫也有出其他顏色。
(B) 有。我覺得應該要有多一點圖片。
(C) 我不認為他今天會來。

【解析】本題問句省略了Do you have，關鍵字 comment（意見、看法），意在詢問「對新手冊有沒有任何意見」。選項(A)與(C)的回答與新手冊完全無關，但是句子中皆出現come這個發音上與comment頗相似的這個字，要小心別被誤導。

【類型】詢問意見題型

【詞彙】
comment 意見／brochure 手冊

【正解】(B)

女子 嗨，Anthony。你在忙嗎？

男子 不，我不忙。怎麼啦？

女子 喔，我正在籌備星期六的烤肉派對。不知道你想不想來。

男子 當然想啊！謝謝妳邀請我。妳要在哪裡舉辦派對？

女子 在我家院子。這是邀請函，上面有所有你需要知道的資訊。你沒有任何飲食限制，對吧？

男子 完全沒有。我什麼都吃。

女子 太好了。回頭見囉！
★

```
邀請您參加
Amy的烤肉派對！
日期：十二月十六日星期六
時間：下午三點至下午九點
地點：20，派克街北區BS8

帶你自己的啤酒來！
```

【詞彙】
dietary restriction 飲食限制

Directions: You will hear some conversations between two people. You will be asked to answer three questions about what the speakers say in each conversation. Select the best response to each question and mark the letter (A), (B), (C) or (D) on your answer sheet. The conversations will not be printed in your test book and will be spoken only one time.

Questions 32-34 refer to the following conversation.

W Hi, Anthony. Are you in the middle of something?

M No, I'm not busy. What's up?

W Well, I'm planning a BBQ party for Saturday. I'm wondering if you would like to come.

M Of course! Thanks for inviting me. Where are you going to have the party?

W In my yard. Here's the invitation that includes all information you need to know. You don't have any dietary restrictions, do you?

M Not at all! I eat everything.

W Great! See you around!
★

```
You are invited to
Amy's BBQ Party!

Date: December 16 Saturday
Time: 3 p.m. – 9 p.m.
Location: 20, Park Street, North
          District BS8


Bring Your Own Beer!
```

32 What did the man just receive?
(A) An invitation.
(B) A traffic ticket.
(C) A shopping receipt.
(D) An emergency call.

男子剛剛收到什麼？
(A) 邀請
(B) 交通罰單
(C) 購物收據
(D) 緊急電話

【類型】提問細節題型

【解析】對話中，女子先以I'm wondering if you would like to come.（不知道你想不想來）詢問男子參加意願，接著拿出invitation，向男子提出正式邀請，可知男子剛剛收到一個活動邀請，故(A)為正解。

【詞彙】
traffic ticket 交通罰單／
emergency 緊急的

【正解】(A)

33 What is the woman planning?
(A) A wedding banquet.
(B) An outdoor party.
(C) An opening ceremony.
(D) A company outing.

女子正在籌備何事？
(A) 一場婚宴
(B) 一個戶外派對
(C) 一場開幕典禮
(D) 一次公司出遊

【類型】提問細節題型

【解析】在對話中，男子詢問「派對舉行地點」，女子回答In my yard（在我家院子），可知這個派對將會在院子舉行，並非在室內，因此是個戶外派對，故(B)為正解。

【詞彙】
banquet 宴會／outing 出遊

【正解】(B)

34 Look at the invitation. When will the party start?
(A) 15:00
(B) 16:00
(C) 18:00
(D) 21:00

請看邀請函。派對將何時開始？
(A) 15:00
(B) 16:00
(C) 18:00
(D) 21:00

【類型】圖片對照題型

【解析】由邀請函所示內容，可知這個派對的時間是安排在3 p.m.～9 p.m.，也就是下午三時開始，至下午九時結束，以24小時制時間表示法，即15:00～21:00，因此(A)為正解。

【正解】(A)

男子A 不好意思，你可以幫我們換到另一桌嗎？

女子 我們覺得這張桌子離廁所太近了，有點影響到我們的食慾。我們比較想要靠窗的桌子。

男子B 很抱歉讓您覺得不舒服，不過餐廳現在客滿。我們目前沒有其他空桌。

男子A 那角落的那張桌子呢？

男子B 那張桌子有人預約了。噢，如果您不介意移到我們的戶外用餐區的話，我們其實是有空桌的。

女子 不，謝了。外面太熱了。

男子A 這樣啊，我想我們只好把食物帶走了。

Questions 35-37 refer to the following conversation.

Man A Excuse me, can you move us to another table?

Woman We think this table is too close to the toilet, and it kind of affects our appetite. We prefer a table by the window.

Man B I'm sorry that it makes you uncomfortable, but the restaurant is currently full. We have no other tables available at the moment.

Man A What about that table in the corner?

Man B I'm afraid it's reserved. Oh, we actually have tables available if you don't mind moving to our outdoor dining area.

Woman No, thanks. It's too hot outside.

Man A Well, I think we'll just take away our food.

這對男女要求什麼？
(A) 一張在戶外用餐區的桌子。
(B) 一張預訂的桌子。
(C) 一張離廁所遠的桌子。
(D) 他們餐點的帳單。

【類型】主題提問題型

【正解】(C)

35 What did the couple ask for?
   (A) A table in the outdoor dining area.
   (B) A table that is reserved.
   (C) A table away from the restroom.
   (D) The bill for their meals.

【解析】由對話一開始，這對用餐的男女分別向服務生表示 can you move us to another table?（可以幫我們換到另一張桌子嗎？）以及 this table is too close to the toilet（這張桌子離廁所太近），可知他們希望換到一張離廁所遠一點的桌子。故答案為(C)。

36 What did the woman complain about?
(A) The quality of their food.
(B) The location of their table.
(C) The waiter's attitude.
(D) The price of the food.

【解析】由女子向服務生表示this table is too close to the toilet（這張桌子離廁所太近）以至於影響了他們的食慾，可知女子對於目前用餐的桌子的所在位置不滿意，故答案為(B)。

女子在抱怨什麼？
(A) 餐點的品質。
(B) 餐桌的位置。
(C) 服務生的態度。
(D) 餐點的價格。

【類型】細節提問題型

【詞彙】
quality 品質／location 位置／attitude 態度

【正解】(B)

37 What did the man decide to do at last?
(A) Remain at the same table.
(B) Move to outdoor dining area.
(C) Talk to the restaurant manager.
(D) Pack the food and leave.

【解析】這篇三人對話中，服務生表示只有戶外用餐區有空桌，而女子並不願意到戶外用餐區用餐，最後男子決定 we'll just take away our food（我們只好把食物帶走），可知他們將打包食物離開，故答案選(D)。

男子最後決定怎麼做？
(A) 留在原來的桌子。
(B) 移到戶外用餐區。
(C) 跟餐廳經理談話。
(D) 打包食物並離開。

【類型】細節提問題型

【正解】(D)

Questions 38-40 refer to the following conversation.

M Hi, I need to convert some US dollars into English pounds.

W No problem. What denominations would you like?

M Hmm... what denominations do you have?

W Let me see. Well, we have 5, 10, 20 and 50 sterling banknotes.

M What about coins?

W No. Only banknotes. Sorry.

男子 嗨，我需要把一些美金換成英鎊。

女子 沒問題。您想要什麼面額呢？

男子 嗯⋯⋯你們有什麼面額呢？

女子 我看看。噢，我們有五元、十元、二十元和五十元的英鈔。

男子 硬幣呢？

女子 沒有，只有紙鈔。抱歉。

男子 噢，沒關係。我可以知道目前英鎊的兌換匯率嗎？

女子 你可以在牆上的貨幣兌換表上看到喔。

M Oh, it's alright. May I know what the rate of exchange on pound sterling is at present?

W You can see it from the Currency Exchange Table on the wall.

★ 外幣兌換匯率

美金	1.00 美金
歐元	0.846564
英鎊	0.756687
加幣	1.245736
日幣	112.897602

★ Foreign Currency Exchange Rates Table

US Dollar	1.00 USD
Euro	0.846564
British Pound	0.756687
Canadian Dollar	1.245736
Japanese Yen	112.897602

【詞彙】
convert 轉換／US dollar 美金／
English pound 英鎊／
denomination 面額／
sterling 英鎊／banknote 紙鈔／
exchange 兌換／currency 貨幣

說話者最可能位在何處？

(A) 銀行

(B) 醫院

(C) 加油站

(D) 警局

【類型】where 疑問句題型

【詞彙】
gas station 加油站

【正解】(A)

38 Where most likely are the speakers?

　(A) In the bank.

　(B) In the hospital.

　(C) At the gas station.

　(D) In a police office.

【解析】本題詢問說話者最有可能的「地點」。由男子一開始便表示I need to convert some US dollars into English pounds（需要將美金換成英鎊），依常理判斷一般提供貨幣兌換的地方，選項中以(A)「銀行」為最有可能的地點，故答案為(A)。

男子需要什麼？

(A) 一些美金。　(B) 一些加幣。

(C) 一些英鎊。　(D) 一些日幣。

【類型】細節提問題型

【詞彙】
Canadian dollar 加拿大幣／
Japanese yen 日本幣

【正解】(C)

39 What does the man need?

　(A) Some US dollars.

　(B) Some Canadian dollars.

　(C) Some British pounds.

　(D) Some Japanese yens.

【解析】由男子表示自己需要convert some US dollars into English pounds（將美金換成英鎊），可知男子目前需要英鎊，故答案為(C)。

40 Look at the table. What is the exchange rate of US dollars to British pounds?

(A) 0.84
(B) 0.75
(C) 1.24
(D) 112.89

【解析】本題需對照題目後附上的匯率兌換表。匯率表上顯示美金兌換英鎊的匯率為0.756687，取小數點後兩位，可知正確答案為(B)。

請看圖表。美金兌英鎊的匯率是多少？

(A) 0.84
(B) 0.75
(C) 1.24
(D) 112.89

【類型】圖表對照題型

【詞彙】
exchange rate 兌換匯率

【正解】(B)

Questions 41-43 refer to the following conversation and chart.

W Hi, I am Layla Fisherman from Flat 5. I'm here to collect my mails and parcel.

M OK ... Fisherman... Alright. Here are your mails and ... uh ... no, no parcels for you today.

W Really? I received a text message yesterday, saying that my order had been dispatched. It is supposed to come today. Could the parcels be taken by someone else?

M That's not possible. All mails and parcels need to be signed for before they are collected. So don't worry about it. I'll let you know as soon as your parcel arrives okay? Here, ...please sign here for your mails.

W There you go. Thank you.

★

Mail receiver	Parcel receiver	Collecting Date	Collector signature
	A. Goofy	2017/12/20	Angela Goofy
S. Goofy			
L. Fisherman		2017/12/22	Layla Fisherman
	M. Dickson		
	A. Goofy	2017/12/20	Angela Goofy
L. Fisherman		2017/12/22	Layla Fisherman
L. Fisherman		2017/12/22	Layla Fisherman

女　嗨，我是五樓的Layla Fisherman。我是來拿我的信件跟包裹的。

男　好的……Fisherman……好的。這是妳的信件跟……呃……不，今天沒妳的包裹。

女　真的嗎？我昨天收到簡訊，說我的訂單已經被派送。今天應該就會到了。包裹有可能被別人拿了嗎？

男　那是不可能的。所有的信件跟包裹都要簽收才能拿。所以不用擔心這個問題。妳的包裹寄到我會立刻通知妳，好嗎？請在這裡簽收妳的信件。

女　好的。謝謝你。

★

信件收件人	包裹收件人	領取日期	領取人簽名
	A. Goofy	2017/12/20	Angela Goofy
S. Goofy			
L. Fisherman		2017/12/22	Layla Fisherman
	M. Dickson		
	A. Goofy	2017/12/20	Angela Goofy
L. Fisherman		2017/12/22	Layla Fisherman
L. Fisherman		2017/12/22	Layla Fisherman

【詞彙】
dispatch 派送／sign for 簽收

加★部分為多益新題型以及相關小提醒，考生要特別注意喔！　199

女子在等什麼？
(A) 她訂購的東西。
(B) 她的薪水。
(C) 她的帳單。
(D) 她的食物。

【類型】細節提問題型

【正解】(A)

41 What was the woman waiting for?
 (A) Her order.
 (B) Her salary.
 (C) Her bill.
 (D) Her food.

【解析】男子表示沒有收到包裹後，女子接著解釋「收到簡訊說我訂的東西已經寄出來了」，由關鍵字my order可知女子的包裹就是「她訂購的東西」，故答案為(A)。

根據女子所言，包裹應該何時抵達？
(A) 昨天
(B) 今天上午
(C) 明天
(D) 二十四小時內

【類型】提問時間題型

【正解】(B)

42 According to the woman, when should the parcel arrive?
 (A) Yesterday.
 (B) This morning.
 (C) Tomorrow.
 (D) In 24 hours.

【解析】女子表示It is supposed to come today（應該今天要到），可知女子認為包裹應該已經在今天的時間寄達了，選項中只有(B)「今天上午」符合女子的期待，故選(B)。選項(A)指的是過去的時間，而選項(C)(D)都是指未來的時間，故可直接刪除不考慮。

請看表格。女子簽收了什麼？
(A) 一封信及一個包裹。
(B) 兩封信及一個包裹。
(C) 三封信。
(D) 兩個包裹。

【類型】圖表對照題型

【正解】(C)

43 Look at the graph. What did the woman sign for?
 (A) One mail and one parcel.
 (B) Two mails and one parcel.
 (C) Three mails.
 (D) Two parcels.

【解析】對話最後男子請女子簽收信件。對照表格中，可看到女子簽收了三封信件，故可知答案為(C)。若在聽對話的過程中沒有聽清楚女子的名字也無妨，從表格中看到其他兩格為簽收包裹，而男子在對話中已經表示「沒有女子的包裹」，因此可判斷簽收包裹的簽名不屬於女子。

Questions 44-46 refer to the following conversation.

Man A   Time for lunch. I'm hungry.

Man B   Me too. What shall we eat today?

Man A   Any ideas, Amy?

Woman You guys wanna try the new Italian bistro down the back lane?

Man A   Sounds good to me, but should we check the guest comments and reviews before we go?

Man B   C'mon, guys. We need to be back for work by 1:30, so no time for a slow meal. Let's just grab a quick sandwich from the food truck down the street.

Woman Alright. I don't mind having a tuna sandwich with a cup of coffee.

Man A   Let's go.

男子A　午餐時間到了。我好餓。

男子B　我也是。今天要吃什麼？

男子A　Amy，有什麼想法嗎？

女子　　你們想試試後面巷子底的那間新開的義大利小酒館嗎？

男子A　我覺得可以喔，不過去之前是不是要先查一下顧客評價？

男子B　拜託啊，你們。我們得在一點半之前回來工作，沒時間慢慢吃。就到樓下街上的餐車買個三明治就行啦！

女子　　好啊！我不介意來份鮪魚三明治和一杯咖啡。

男子A　我們走吧。

【詞彙】
bistro 小酒館

44 What are the speakers discussing?
(A) What to order.
(B) What to eat.
(C) When to meet.
(D) Whom to invite.

【解析】由對話中的三個人針對其中一名男子提出的問題 What shall we eat today?（今天要吃什麼）輪流交換意見，可知他們正在討論「應該去吃什麼」，故答案為(B)。

說話者在討論什麼？
(A) 要點什麼餐。
(B) 要吃什麼。
(C) 要在哪裡碰面。
(D) 要邀請誰。

【類型】對話主題題型

【正解】(B)

說話者的午餐時間何時結束？
(A) 十二點半。
(B) 一點。
(C) 一點半。
(D) 三點。

【類型】時間相關題型

【詞彙】
lunchtime 午餐時間

【正解】(C)

45 When does the speakers' lunchtime end?
   (A) At 12:30.
   (B) At 1:00.
   (C) At 1:30.
   (D) At 3:00.

【解析】對話中其中一名男子說出了關鍵句We need to be back for work by 1:30（我們得在一點半前回來工作），可判斷說話者的午餐時間應該要在1:30前結束，故答案為(C)。

說話者將到何處午餐？
(A) 一間優雅舒服的飯店。
(B) 一間高級中國餐廳。
(C) 一間附近的義大利酒館。
(D) 一輛位在街上的餐車。

【類型】提問結果題型

【詞彙】
cozy 舒服的／fancy 高級的

【正解】(D)

46 Where will the speakers go for lunch?
   (A) A nice and cozy hotel.
   (B) A fancy Chinese restaurant.
   (C) A nearby Italian bistro.
   (D) A food truck on the street.

【解析】對話最後，其中一名男子提議Let's just grab a quick sandwich from the food truck down the street.（我們就到樓下街上餐車買份三明治吃就好了），並得到其他兩人的附議，可知他們討論結果是要「在餐車買三明治」，因此答案為(D)。

男子A 嘿，John。你知道今天晚上我們要跟Mark Mason先生一起用餐，對吧？

男子B 我知道啦。我們要帶他去哪兒吃？

女子 老橋餐廳。我已經訂了今晚七點八個人的座位。

男子A 八個？還有誰要去啊？

女子 業務行銷部的每個人都要去，包括Jefferson先生。

Questions 47-49 refer to the following conversation.

Man A Hey, John. You know we're having dinner with Mr. Mark Mason tonight, don't you?

Man B I know. Where are we taking him?

Woman Old Bridge. I've already reserved a table for eight at seven tonight.

Man A Eight? Who else is going?

Woman Everyone in the Sales & Marketing Department, including Mr. Jefferson.

Man B　Who's going to foot the bill? Mr. Jefferson?

Woman　It's all on the company's dime. I can pay with my credit card and file for reimbursement within a month.

男子 B 誰要買單啊？Jefferson先生嗎？

女子　全由公司買單。我會先刷卡，然後在一個月內報公帳。

【詞彙】

foot the bill 買單／

on the company's dime

由公司買單／

reimbursement 報銷；退款

---

47 What will the speakers attend this evening?
(A) A negotiation conference.
(B) A celebration party.
(C) A business dinner.
(D) A class reunion.

【解析】對話一開始，其中一名男子便點出主題：we're having dinner with Mr. Mark Mason（我們要跟Mark Mason先生吃晚餐）；接著女子不但表示「整個部門都要參加」，而且晚餐費用是on company's dime（由公司買單），可判斷這頓晚餐並非私人晚餐，而是與公事有關的business dinner（應酬）。故答案為(C)。

說話者今天晚上要參加什麼？
(A) 協商會議。
(B) 慶祝派對。
(C) 公司應酬。
(D) 同學會。

【類型】段落主題題型

【詞彙】

negotiation 協商／reunion 重聚

【正解】(C)

---

48 What did the woman just do?
(A) Called the police.
(B) Reserved a table.
(C) Cancelled a meeting.
(D) Confirmed her flight.

【解析】本題的問句時間為「過去式」，可知要問的是「已經發生的事情」。女子在對話中表示I've already reserved a table...（我已經訂了一張桌子），可知女子做了「訂位」這件事，故選(B)。

女子剛剛做了什麼事？
(A) 報警。
(B) 訂餐廳座位。
(C) 取消會議。
(D) 確認機位。

【類型】提問細節題型

【正解】(B)

加★部分為多益新題型以及相關小提醒，考生要特別注意喔！　203

根據女子所述，她將在一個月內做什麼？

(A) 申請公帳。

(B) 辭去職務。

(C) 預訂餐廳座位。

(D) 取消預訂。

【類型】提問細節題型

【詞彙】

resign 辭去／position 職位

【正解】(A)

---

49 According to the woman, what will she do within a month?

(A) File for reimbursement.

(B) Resign her position.

(C) Reserve a restaurant table.

(D) Cancel a reservation.

【解析】本題問句時間為「未來式」，問的是「尚未發生的事情」。由女子表示I can pay with my credit card and file for reimbursement within a month.（我可以先用我的信用卡付錢，並在一個月內報公帳），可知女子將在未來一個月內做「報公帳」這件事，故答案為(A)。

男　Alice，我認為我們需要去超市買些生活用品。

女　對，我們廁所衛生紙、牙膏和一些東西都快用完了。不過我現在有點事走不開。你介意等一下嗎？

男　要等很久嗎？我得在五點前趕回來，因為會有一場足球賽直播。

女　會要一下子喔。你可以自己去嗎？

男　當然啊。只要給我購物清單就行了。

女　喔，太好了。這是清單。

★

要在S-Mart買的東西
1. 廁所衛生紙
2. 牙膏
3. 洗手乳
4. 洗髮精
5. 廚房紙巾
6. 洗衣劑

【詞彙】

supplies 生活用品／

toilet paper 廁所衛生紙／

toothpaste 牙膏／

be tied up 被纏住／

live broadcast 直播／

match 比賽／

shopping list 購物清單

Questions 50-52 refer to the following conversation.

M　Alice, I think we need to go to the supermarket for some supplies.

W　Yeah, we're running out of toilet paper, toothpaste and some stuff. But I'm kind of tied up at the moment. Would you mind waiting?

M　Is it going to take a long time? I need to come back by five because there will be a live broadcast of the football match.

W　It's gonna take a while. Can you go by yourself?

M　Sure. Just make me a shopping list.

W　Oh, thank you so much. Here is the list.

★

Things to buy from S-Mart
1. toilet paper
2. toothpaste
3. hand wash
4. shampoo
5. paper towels
6. laundry detergent

50 Where do the speakers plan to go?
(A) The library.
(B) The convenience store.
(C) The supermarket.
(D) The grocery store.

【解析】男子在對話一開始便表示we need to go to the supermarket（我們需要去超市）並且得到女子的附議，可知他們計劃要去超市，故答案為(C)。

說話者計劃去何處？
(A) 圖書館。
(B) 便利商店。
(C) 超市。
(D) 雜貨店。

【類型】詢問細節題型

【詞彙】
grocery store 雜貨店

【正解】(C)

51 Why doesn't the man want to wait?
(A) He has to see his dentist.
(B) He wants to watch a football game.
(C) He needs to catch a flight.
(D) He is tired of waiting.

【解析】女子詢問男子「介不介意等她一下」，但男子表示I need to come back by five because there will be a live broadcast of the football match.（我得在五點前回來，因為有場足球賽現場直播），可知男子不想等的原因是「要趕回來看足球賽」，故答案為(B)。

男子為何不想等？
(A) 他還得去看牙。
(B) 他想看足球賽。
(C) 他需要趕飛機。
(D) 他厭倦等待。

【類型】詢問原因題型

【正解】(B)

52 Look at the list. Which supermarket section should the man go to?
(A) Furniture & Appliances
(B) Household essentials.
(C) Electronics & Office
(D) Health & Beauty

【解析】由本題所附購物清單內容為：toilet paper（廁所用紙）、toothpaste（牙膏）、hand wash（洗手乳）、shampoo（洗髮精）、paper towel（廚房紙巾）及laundry detergent（洗衣劑），都是屬於家庭平日的必需品，選項中只有(B)最有可能買到這些物品，故選(B)。

請看購物清單。男子應該至超市的哪一區？
(A) 傢俱及家電
(B) 家庭必需品
(C) 電子產品及辦公用品
(D) 健康美容用品

【類型】圖表對照題型

【詞彙】
furniture 傢俱／appliance 家電／household 家庭的；家用的／essential 必需品／electronics 電子產品

【正解】(B)

女　　嗨，我是1133號房的Wayne
　　　女士。我剛剛入住我的房
　　　間，發現浴室地板是濕的，
　　　而且浴缸裡還有毛髮。

男A　噢，我很抱歉。我會立刻
　　　讓我們的房務員把浴室打
　　　掃乾淨。

女　　房間應該要在我入住之前
　　　就清理好才對吧。這完全
　　　讓人無法接受。

男B　Wayne女士，我是飯店經
　　　理。我對這麼糟糕的事感
　　　到抱歉。如果您不介意的
　　　話，我們會幫您移到另一
　　　間房，並會提供您免費客
　　　房升等以作為補償。

女　　這還差不多。

【詞彙】
bathtub 浴缸／
housekeeper 房務員／
unacceptable 無法接受的／
upgrade 升級／
compensation 補償

Questions 53-55 refer to the following conversation.

Woman　Hi, this is Mrs. Wayne from Room 1133. I just checked into my room and found the bathroom floor wet. There's even hair left in the bathtub.

Man A　Oh, I am so sorry to hear that. I'll have our housekeeper clean up the bathroom immediately.

Woman　The room should have been cleaned when I checked in. This is totally unacceptable.

Man B　Mrs. Wayne, this is the hotel manager. I'm sorry for all this mess. If you don't mind, we'll move you to another room and offer you a free room upgrade as compensation.

Woman　That's more like it.

女子是誰？
(A) 飯店行李員。
(B) 飯店客人。
(C) 飯店櫃檯。
(D) 飯店經理。

【類型】詢問說話者身份題型

【詞彙】
porter 行李搬運工／
receptionist 櫃檯；接待人員

【正解】(B)

53 Who is the woman?
　　(A) The hotel porter.
　　(B) The hotel guest.
　　(C) The hotel receptionist.
　　(D) The hotel manager.

【解析】由對話一開始女子表示this is Mrs. Wayne from Room 1133. I just checked into my room，可知女子是剛剛入住1133號房的房客，因此其身份應為飯店的客人，故答案為(B)。

54 Why did the woman call?
(A) To extend her stay.
(B) To request a morning call.
(C) To complain about her room.
(D) To order room service.

【解析】由女子在對話中先對「客房浴室的狀態」進行說明，接著表示The room should have been cleaned when I checked in.（房間在我入住時就應該已經清理好）並且認為This is totally unacceptable.（這完全令人無法接受）可知女子並不是打電話來要求飯店服務，而是打電話來表達對客房的不滿，故答案選(C)。

女子為何要打這通電話？
(A) 為了延長住宿時間。
(B) 為了要求晨呼服務。
(C) 為了抱怨房間。
(D) 為了點客房服務。

【類型】詢問原因題型

【詞彙】
morning call 晨呼服務／
room service 客房（送餐）服務

【正解】(C)

---

55 How did the woman feel about the manager's solution?
(A) Satisfied.
(B) Reluctant.
(C) Doubtful.
(D) Uncertain.

【解析】對話中身為飯店經理的男子提出「換房間並且免費客房升等」作為解決方案。對此女子以That's more like it. 表示「這還差不多」。That's more like it.這句話通常是在「對先前的回答不甚滿意，現在這個回答還比較可以聽」的狀況下，用來表示「這才像話」的口語用法。由女子的回答可知女子對飯店經理的處理方式感到可以接受，故選(A)。

女子對經理的解決方式有什麼想法？
(A) 感到滿意。
(B) 感到不情願。
(C) 感到懷疑。
(D) 感到不確定。

【類型】詢問結果題型

【詞彙】
reluctant 不甘願的／
doubtful 懷疑的

【正解】(A)

女　Mike，我可以跟妳借訂書針嗎？

男A　我剛好用完了，抱歉。

女　沒關係。還是謝了。對了，妳知道如果我需要辦公室用品要找誰嗎？

男A　要找Murphy。他是負責消耗性辦公室用品的人。

男B　嘿，我剛剛聽到我的名字耶！你需要文具用品嗎？這是申請表。填好交給我。

女　噢，好。表格填好了。我什麼時候可以拿到申請的東西？

男B　如果有存貨的話馬上就能拿到了。

辦公室用品申請表		
姓名：大衛華力克		日期：2017/12/15
品項	數量	存貨狀況
釘書針	3 (盒)	☑有庫存 □無庫存
大頭釘	1 (盒)	☑有庫存 □無庫存
檔案盒	1	□有庫存 ☑無庫存
檔案夾	5	☑有庫存 □無庫存
經手人：　Murphy Byron		

【詞彙】

staple 釘書針／
office supplies 辦公用品／
in charge of 負責／
consumable 消耗性的／
stationery 文具

Questions 56-58 refer to the following conversation.

Woman　Mike, can I borrow some staples?

Man A　I just ran out of them. Sorry.

Woman　It's okay. Thanks anyway. By the way, do you know whom I should approach if I need any office supplies?

Man A　Murphy. He's in charge of consumable office supplies.

Man B　Hey, I just heard my name! Do you need any stationery items? Here's the request form. Fill it out and give it to me.

Woman　Oh, OK. Here's the form. When can I get the items I applied for?

Man B　You can get them right away if they're in stock.

★

Office Supplies Request Form		
Name: David Wallick		Date: 2017/12/15
Items	Quantity	stock status
staples	3 (boxes)	☑ in stock □ out of stock
thumbtacks	1 (box)	☑ in stock □ out of stock
filing box	1	□ in stock ☑ out of stock
file folder	5	☑ in stock □ out of stock
Handled by:　Murphy Byron		

56 What did the woman request for?
(A) Some stationery items.
(B) Some application forms.
(C) Some financial support.
(D) Some office equipment.

女子要求何物？
(A) 一些文具用品。
(B) 一些申請表格。
(C) 一些財務支援。
(D) 一些辦公設備。

【類型】提問細節題型

【正解】(A)

【解析】由對話中女子表示I need any office supplies（我需要辦公用品），可知女子所需要的是日常辦公所需的文具用品，故答案選(A)。女子在對話中詢問其中一名男子：「需要辦公用品要找誰」，是要找人，並非主動要求「申請表格」，故選項(B)並非適當的答案。

57 What is Murphy responsible for?
(A) Recruitment.
(B) Product inventory.
(C) Equipment maintenance.
(D) Office supplies.

Murphy負責什麼事務？
(A) 人才招募。
(B) 產品庫存。
(C) 設備維護。
(D) 辦公用品。

【類型】提問細節題型

【詞彙】
recruitment 人才招募／
inventory 存貨／
equipment 設備

【正解】(D)

【解析】對話中女子詢問Mike「需要辦公用品要找誰」，Mike對此回覆Murphy，並接著表示He's in charge of consumable office supplies.（他負責消耗性辦公用品），可知Murphy負責管理消耗性的辦公用品，答案選(D)。

58 Look at the form. Which item won't the woman get right away?
(A) Filing box.
(B) Staples.
(C) Staplers.
(D) Thumbtacks.

請看表格。哪一個品項女子無法立刻拿到？
(A) 檔案盒。
(B) 釘書針。
(C) 檔案夾。
(D) 大頭釘。

【類型】圖表對照題型

【詞彙】
stapler 釘書機

【正解】(A)

【解析】Murphy在對話中表示只要有庫存的文具物品，一經申請馬上就能拿到。而由本題所附表格內容看來，女子申請了四項文具用品，在庫存狀況欄位中，file box是呈現「無庫存狀態」，可知女子無法立刻拿到「檔案盒」，故答案為(A)。

男 妳在填寫的表格是什麼？

女 這個？這是補休申請表。我要用休假代替加班費。

男 為什麼？妳上個月幾乎天天工作超過十個小時。如果妳申請加班費可以賺好多錢哩！

女 我知道啊，但我此刻只想離開工作休息一下。我可不想過勞死。

男 妳說得對。儘管休假去吧。妳休假時我可以幫妳代理職務。

女 真的嗎？太謝謝你了！

★

補休單			
姓名	日期	時間	總時數
Diana Jones	2017/11/30	13:00-18:00	5
代理人簽名			*Tim Leonard*

【詞彙】
comp leave (compensatory leave) 補休／in lieu of 代替／die from overwork 過勞死

Questions 59-61 refer to the following conversation.

M What's that form you're filling out?

W This? It's the comp leave request form. I'm going to take time off in lieu of overtime pay.

M Why? You worked over 10 hours almost every day last month. You will be getting a lot of money if you declare overtime pay.

W I know, but all I want at the moment is to get away from work and relax. I don't want to die from overwork.

M You're right. Go ahead and take some time off. I can cover for you at work during your leave.

W Really!? Thanks a lot!

★

Compensatory Leave Form			
Name:	Date:	Time:	Total hours
Diana Jones	2017/11/30	13:00-18:00	5
Substitute's signature			*Tim Leonard*

女子正在申請什麼？
(A) 產假。
(B) 補休假。
(C) 年假。
(D) 婚假。

【類型】詢問主題題型

【詞彙】
maternity leave 產假／marriage leave 婚假

【正解】(B)

---

59 What is the woman applying for?
(A) Maternity leave.
(B) Compensatory leave.
(C) Annual leave.
(D) Marriage leave.

【解析】由對話中女子表示她正在填comp leave request form（補休申請單），可知她想要申請補休假，故答案為(B)。

60 What's the relationship between the speakers?
(A) Coworkers.
(B) Teacher and student.
(C) Classmates.
(D) Doctor and patient.

【解析】由對話中兩人交談時所出現的comp leave request（補休申請）、cover for you（幫你代理職務）等關鍵字詞，可推測兩人應為同事關係，因為只有同事才能幫忙代理工作，其他關係如(B)的「師生」、(C)的「同班同學」或(D)的「醫生病人」都無法代理彼此的工作，故選(A)。

兩位說話者是什麼關係？
(A) 同事
(B) 師生
(C) 同班同學
(D) 醫生與病患

【類型】說話者關係題型

【正解】(A)

---

61 Look at the form. How long will the woman be absent from work?
(A) Five hours.
(B) Two days.
(C) One week.
(D) A whole morning.

【解析】由表格內容顯示女子在補休申請單上所填寫的總補休時數為「5」，可知女子將請「五小時」的補休假，故答案為(A)。

請看表格。女子將缺勤多久時間？
(A) 五個小時。
(B) 兩天。
(C) 一週。
(D) 一整個上午。

【類型】圖表對照題型

【詞彙】
absent from work 缺勤

【正解】(A)

女 Smith先生，Williams先生剛打電話來說他必須取消明天的會面。

男 不過他這週應該要跟我們簽約的。他有說為何要取消會面嗎？

女 沒有，不過他問我們是否可以把時間重新安排在下星期某個時間。Williams先生說他會配合你有空的時間。問題是，你下星期的行程已經滿了。

男 不過，我們得儘快簽到這份合約。想辦法從我的行程中擠一點時間來吧。

女 那我就安排一個工作午餐會吧。我立刻打電話到他辦公室確認日期和時間。

【詞彙】
accommodate 給……方便／
availability 可利用性／
squeeze 擠／luncheon 午餐會

Questions 62-64 refer to the following conversation.

W Mr. Smith, Mr. Williams just called and said he had to cancel his appointment tomorrow.

M But he's supposed to sign the contract with us this week. Did he say why he would cancel the appointment?

W No, but he asked whether we could reschedule it sometime next week. Mr. Williams said he would accommodate your availability. The problem is, your schedule next week is full.

M Well, we need to get this contract signed as soon as possible. Try to squeeze some time out of my schedule.

W Then I'll schedule a business luncheon. I'll call his office to confirm the date and time right away.

Williams先生是誰？
(A) 一位客戶。
(B) 一位作家。
(C) 一位公車司機。
(D) 一個親戚。

【類型】詢問對方身份題型

【詞彙】
relative 親戚

【正解】(A)

---

62 Who is Mr. Williams?
(A) A client.
(B) A writer.
(C) A bus driver.
(D) A relative.

【解析】由對話中男子表示需要跟Williams先生簽定合約，可推測Williams先生應該與他們有工作業務上的往來，選項中以(A)為最有可能的答案，故選(A)。

63 Why is the man eager to meet with Mr. Williams?
(A) To ask for a raise.
(B) To get the contract signed.
(C) To cancel his order.
(D) To postpone an appointment.

【解析】由對話中男子表示：we need to get this contract signed as soon as possible（我們必須儘快簽到這份合約），並要求女子想辦法從滿檔的行程中硬擠時間出來，可知男子希望能進快讓Williams先生完成簽約的動作，故正解為(B)。

男子為何急著與Williams先生碰面？
(A) 要求加薪。
(B) 請他簽約。
(C) 取消訂單。
(D) 延遲會面時間。

【類型】詢問原因題型

【詞彙】
raise 加薪

【正解】(B)

64 When will the man meet Mr. Williams next week?
(A) During lunchtime.
(B) After work.
(C) Before work.
(D) During the weekend.

【解析】對話最後女子表示I'll schedule a business luncheon（我來安排一個工作午餐會），luncheon是指正式的午餐，而business luncheon即指一邊工作一邊吃午餐的工作午餐會。由此可知男子下週與Williams先生會在午餐時間碰面，故選(A)。

男子將於下週何時跟Williams先生碰面？
(A) 午餐時間。
(B) 下班後。
(C) 上班前。
(D) 週末期間。

【類型】詢問細節題型

【正解】(A)

女 週會是在十點開始，不是嗎？

男 它已經被移到下午了。妳沒收到會議更改通知信嗎？

女 我不記得收過有關會議的任何信件。你可以轉寄給我嗎？

男 當然可以。會議議程沒有變，不過時間和地點都改了。好了，我剛剛已經寄給你了。

女 收到了。謝謝。

★

	原定	更新
會議時間	二月 12 10 a.m - 12 p.m.	二月 12 2 p.m.- 4 p.m.
會議地點	會議室	3113室

【詞彙】
forward 轉寄

Questions 65-67 refer to the following conversation.

W The weekly meeting started at 10, didn't it?

M It's been moved to this afternoon. Didn't you get the notice letter for change of meeting?

W I don't remember receiving any email regarding the meeting. Could you forward the mail to me?

M Sure thing. The meeting agenda remains unchanged, but the time and location have both been changed. OK. I sent it to you.

W Got it. Thanks.

	original	rearranged
Meeting time	Feb 12 10 a.m -12 p.m.	Feb 12 2 p.m.- 4 p.m.
Meeting location	Meeting Room	Room 3113

我們對會議有何認知？
(A) 它被延後了。
(B) 它被取消了。
(C) 它被提前了。
(D) 它被中斷了。

【類型】段落主題題型

【詞彙】
postpone 延後／
advance 提前／interrupt 打斷

【正解】(A)

---

65 What do we know about the meeting?
   (A) It's been postponed.
   (B) It's been cancelled.
   (C) It's been advanced.
   (D) It's been interrupted.

【解析】女子在對話一開始向男子確認「週會是在十點開始，不是嗎？」男子對此表示It's been moved to this afternoon.（已經被移到下午），可知週會時間由早上十點移到下午，因此是被延後了，故答案為(A)。

66 What did the woman ask the man to do?
(A) Forward her the notice letter.
(B) Tell her when the meeting is held.
(C) Help her find the meeting room.
(D) Modify the meeting agenda.

【解析】男子在對話中以女子表示否定疑問句詢問女子「難道沒收到會議更改通知信嗎？」於是女子向男子提出Could you forward the mail to me?（可以轉寄那封信給我嗎？）的請求，故答案為(A)。

女子要求男子做什麼？
(A) 轉寄通知信給她。
(B) 告訴她會議時間。
(C) 幫她找會議室。
(D) 修改會議議程。

【類型】提問細節題型

【正解】(A)

---

67 Look at the form. When will the meeting start?
(A) At 10 a.m.
(B) At 12 p.m.
(C) At 2 p.m.
(D) At 4 p.m.

【解析】由本題所附圖表內容，可看出會議原定時間為上午十點至中午十二點，重新安排後的時間為下午兩點至下午四點，可知會議將在下午兩點開始，故答案為(C)。

請看表格。會議將於何時開始？
(A) 上午十點。
(B) 中午十二點。
(C) 下午兩點。
(D) 下午四點。

【類型】圖表對照題型

【正解】(C)

女	現在來討論下一個議程一定價。Billy，你有什麼看法？
男 A	我擔心因為我們的價格太高會流失顧客。
女	你對這有何看法呢，Darren？
男 B	是這樣的，我有幾個新客戶在手上，而且才跟其中一個成交了一份訂單。所以我不認為有這個問題。
男 A	但是對手售價比我們低是不爭的事實。
男 B	不過我們有很棒的產品線，而且我們提供高標準的品質。事實上我比較關心顧客滿意度的問題。我的客戶們都很重視售後服務。
女	對的，Darren，那才是重點。

Questions 68-70 refer to the following conversation.

Woman　Now, the next item on the agenda... the pricing. Billy, what's on your mind?

Man A　I'm worried that we'll lose customers because our prices are too high.

Woman　What's your take on this, Darren?

Man B　Well, I'm getting several new clients and I just closed a deal with one of them. So I don't think there's a problem.

Man A　But it's true that we're being undersold by our competitors.

Man B　We have a great product line and we offer a high standard of quality. I'm actually more concerned about customer satisfaction. My clients all care about after-sales service.

Woman　Yes. Darren. That's the point.

女子在會議中扮演的角色為何？
(A) 主席
(B) 記錄者
(C) 計時者
(D) 召集人

【類型】說話者身份題型

【詞彙】
moderator 會議主席／
note-taker 做記錄者／
timekeeper 計時員／
convener 召集人

【正解】(A)

68 What role is the woman playing in the meeting?
(A) The moderator.
(B) The note-taker.
(C) The timekeeper.
(D) The convener.

【解析】由對話中女子負責控制會議流程以及指示與會者發言的動作看來，其在會議中的角色應為類似「主席」的身份，因此(A)為最適當的答案。由對話內容並無法判斷女子是否為會議的「召集人」，也看不出女子有負責做「記錄」或「計時」，因此選項(B)(C)(D)皆可直接刪除不考慮。

69 What did the two men disagree on?
(A) The marketing strategy.
(B) The prices of the products.
(C) The promotion campaign.
(D) The sales target.

兩位男子對何者意見分歧？
(A) 行銷策略
(B) 產品價格
(C) 促銷活動
(D) 業績目標

【類型】詢問細節題型

【解析】對話一開始女子便表示進入pricing（定價）這個議題。兩名男子在對話中分別對產品的定價發表了不同的意見及看法，因此可知兩名男子對「產品價格」意見分歧，故選(B)。

【詞彙】
disagree 不同意／
marketing strategy 行銷策略／
campaign 活動／target 目標

【正解】(B)

70 What does the woman think matters most?
(A) After-sales service.
(B) Sales pitch.
(C) Sales performance.
(D) Work attitude.

女子認為何者最重要？
(A) 售後服務。
(B) 推銷辭令。
(C) 業績表現。
(D) 工作態度。

【類型】提問細節題型

【解析】對話中的一名男子在肯定公司產品線及產品品質後，表示「關心顧客滿意度」而且「客戶都很重視售後服務」。女子隨即以That's the point. 表示對方「說到了重點」，透露了女子對此説法的認同，因此可知女子認為售後服務很重要，故選(A)。其他選項都未在對話中被提及，因此可以不用考慮。

【詞彙】
sales pitch 推銷辭令

【正解】(A)

Directions: You will hear some talks given by a single speaker. You will be asked to answer three questions about what the speaker says in each talk. Select the best response to each question and mark the letter (A), (B), (C) or (D) on your answer sheet. The talks will not be printed in your test book and will be spoken only one time.

男 今天,我既開心又難過。我開心是因為Schmidt先生被拔擢為紐約分公司的經理。他過去十年來在工作上的奉獻是大家有目共睹的,他的優異表現絕對值得這個肯定。他出色的領導能力也證明了自己是這個職位的最佳人選。然而,我很難過我們必須跟Schmidt先生道別。他離開我們辦公室對我們來說是一大損失。我們將會非常想念這個超級能幹的財務金融專家。現在就讓我們敬Larry Schmidt一杯酒。恭喜你啦,Schmidt先生!

【詞彙】
recognition 肯定／
dedication 奉獻／
adequate 稱職的／
farewell 道別／
capable 能幹的

Questions 71-73 refer to the following talk.

Man Today, I'm both happy and sad. I'm happy because Mr. Schmidt has been promoted to the manager of the New York branch. He deserves this recognition as his outstanding performance and his dedication at work for the past ten years is obvious to us all. His brilliant leadership also proves himself the most adequate person for this position. However, I am sad that we have to say farewell to Mr. Schmidt. His absence from our office is a big loss for us. We are going to miss this exceptionally capable financial professional so much. Let's now drink a toast to Larry Schmidt. Congratulations, Mr. Schmidt!

71 What most likely is this occasion?
(A) A welcoming party.
(B) A farewell party.
(C) A funeral ceremony.
(D) A ground-breaking ceremony.

【解析】由談話中男子先提及Schmidt先生被晉升為紐約分公司經理，接著表示we have to say farewell to Mr. Schmidt（我們必須跟Schmidt先生道別），可推測這應該是一個餞別餐會，故選(B)。

這最有可能是什麼場合？
(A) 迎新派對
(B) 歡送會
(C) 葬禮
(D) 破土典禮

【類型】談話背景題型

【詞彙】
funeral 葬禮／
ground-breaking 破土

【正解】(B)

---

72 Why is Mr. Schmidt leaving?
(A) He was promoted.
(B) He was fired.
(C) He resigned.
(D) He's been headhunted.

【解析】由Mr. Schmidt has been promoted to the manager of the New York branch（Schmidt先生已經被晉升為紐約分公司經理）這句話可知Schmidt先生獲得職務晉升，即將前往紐約分公司任職，因此選項中以(A)為最適當的答案。

Schmidt先生為何要離開？
(A) 他被晉升了。
(B) 他被開除了。
(C) 他離職了。
(D) 他被挖角了。

【類型】詢問原因題型

【詞彙】
resign 辭職／
headhunt 挖角；獵人頭

【正解】(A)

---

73 How long has Mr. Schmidt been working for this company?
(A) Five years.
(B) Ten years.
(C) Fifteen years.
(D) Twenty years.

【解析】由男子在這段談話中提到his dedication at work for the past ten years is obvious to us all（他在過去十年對工作的奉獻是我們有目共睹的），如果能抓到這句話的關鍵字ten years，便能很快選出這題的正確答案(B)。

Schmidt先生在這家公司工作多久了？
(A) 五年
(B) 十年
(C) 十五年
(D) 二十年

【類型】詢問細節題型

【正解】(B)

女子 嗨，各位。我很高興能在各位第一天上班就認識各位。我希望你們對於到愛德森電器來上班都感到很興奮。在你們的手冊上你們可以看到我們三天訓練活動的時間表。如你所見，在今天的上半天，我們的人事部的同仁會為向你們介紹我們的聘雇相關事宜。我相信這三天的活動能幫助各位順利融入我們的公司。現在我就把時間交給Sally。

★新進員工訓練活動

	星期三	星期四	星期五
9:00–12:00	人事部聘雇相關事宜説明	人事部休假政策説明	人事部員工考覈説明
12:00–1:30	午餐時間		
1:30–5:00	各部門整體工作內容介紹	各部門部門政策／程序及工作期許	新進員工歡迎會

Questions 74-76 refer to the following talk and program.

Woman Hi, everyone. It's a great pleasure for me to meet you all on your first day at work. I hope you are all very excited about your new employment with Edson Electric. In your manual you'll find the schedule of our three-day orientation program. As you can see, in the first half of the day, our Human Resources staff will make an introduction of our employment related issues. I believe the three-day program can help you successfully integrate into our organization. Now I'd like to hand over to Sally.

★New Employee Orientation Program

	Wednesday	Thursday	Friday
9:00–12:00	HR-Employment Issues Introduction	HR- Leave policy	HR- Employee performance evaluation
12:00–1:30	Lunch Time		
1:30–5:00	Your Department – Overall work of the department	Your Department – Department policies, procedures and job expectations	New Employee Welcoming Party

聽話者最有可能是誰？
(A) 新進員工
(B) 工作面試官
(C) 工作應徵者
(D) 大學新生

【類型】聽話者身份題型

【詞彙】
interviewer 面試官／
applicant 應徵者

【正解】(A)

74 Who most likely are the listeners?
(A) New employees.
(B) Job interviewers.
(C) Job applicants.
(D) New college students.

【解析】由女子在談話一開始便表示It's a great pleasure for me to meet you all on your first day at work（很高興你們第一天上班認識你們）可知她説話的對象是「第一天來上班的人」，即「新進員工」，故答案為(A)。

75 How long is the new-hire orientation?
(A) One day.
(B) Two days.
(C) Three days.
(D) Five days.

【解析】由女子在談話中提到…… the schedule of our three-day orientation program （我們為期三天的訓練活動的時間表），可知這次的新進員工訓練活動時間為三天，故選(C)。

新進員工訓練時間多長？
(A) 一天
(B) 兩天
(C) 三天
(D) 五天

【類型】詢問細節題型

【正解】(C)

---

76 Look at the program. When will the welcoming party take place?
(A) Tuesday
(B) Wednesday
(C) Thursday
(D) Friday

【解析】由本題所附時間表上所示內容，可看出新進員工歡迎會將會在星期五下午舉行，故正確答案為(D)。

請看計畫表。歡迎會將在何時舉行？
(A) 星期二
(B) 星期三
(C) 星期四
(D) 星期五

【類型】圖表對照題型

【正解】(D)

女 我要問各位一個問題：你們
有多少人覺得自己剛進公司
的時候，是在受到完整的訓
練和指導，在完全準備好的
情況下開始上班？如果你覺
得你是，請舉手。好的。看
來我們之中並沒有很多人認
為自己得到應該有的訓練。
這表示，我們的新進員工訓
練活動無法在第一天上班時
提供新進員工足夠的工作資
訊。因此，我們下一個小時
將會討論如何讓我們的新進
員工能更有自信且更自在地
開始他們的新工作。

【詞彙】
sufficient 充足的

聽話者如何回答說話者的問題？
(A) 用手語。
(B) 用簡訊。
(C) 用電子郵件。
(D) 以舉手方式。

【類型】提問細節題型

【詞彙】
sign language 手語／
text message 文字簡訊／
show of hands 舉手

【正解】(D)

Questions 77-79 refer to the following talk.

W Let me ask you a question: How many of you feel that you were well trained and guided, and that you were fully prepared for the work you were hired to do when you enter the company? Put up your hands if you think you do. OK. Looks like not many of us believe they received as much training as they should have. Which means, our new-hire training program does not provide our new employees with sufficient career resources in the very first day of work. So, we'll spend the next hour discussing how to make our new employees more confident and comfortable with their new jobs.

---

77 How did the listeners answer the speaker's question?
(A) By sign language.
(B) By text messages.
(C) By e-mails.
(D) By show of hands.

【解析】說話者在提出問題之後，要聽話者Put up your hands if you think you do.（覺得是的請舉手），put up one's hand即「舉起手」之意，因此可知聽話者是以「舉手」的方式回答問題，故選(D)。

78 What was the woman's point?
- (A) The new-hire training was insufficient.
- (B) The company is understaffed.
- (C) The comment was unconstructive.
- (D) The punishment was unfair.

【解析】女子所發表的這段篇談話,整體脈絡是以「員工職前訓練不足」為中心,從一開始的提問、舉手回答的結果以及女子做出的結論,都表示該公司所提供給新進員工的訓練不充分,因此答案選(A)。

女子發言的重點是什麼?
(A) 新人訓練不充足。
(B) 公司人力不足。
(C) 批評沒有建設性。
(D) 懲處不公平。

【類型】詢問重點題型

【詞彙】
insufficient 不充足的／
understaffed 人力不足的／
comment 批評／
unconstructive 沒有建設性的／
punishment 處罰

【正解】(A)

---

79 What's the purpose of the meeting?
- (A) Improve new employee training.
- (B) Assign meeting roles.
- (C) Select a party organizer.
- (D) Design a questionnaire.

【解析】由女子在談話最後表示 spend the next hour discussing how to make our new employees more confident and comfortable with their new jobs(如何使我們的新員工對新工作感到更自信與自在),可知會議目的是要討論出一個使新人訓練活動更好的做法,故選(A)。

此會議的目的為何?
(A) 加強新人訓練。
(B) 分配會議職務。
(C) 選出派對負責人。
(D) 設計一份問卷。

【類型】詢問目的題型

【詞彙】
organizer 負責人／
questionnaire 問卷

【正解】(A)

女 嗨，我的名字是Michelle Chang，是潔比化妝公司的業務代表。我們是上海專業化妝品製造龍頭之一，我們的產品包括各種化妝產品，如唇膏、唇線筆、唇蜜、眼影、眼線筆、睫毛膏、遮瑕膏、粉底以及化妝工具及護膚系列產品。我們已經跟歐洲與亞洲一些知名國際品牌合作好幾十年了，因此我們有自信能滿足您的需要及要求。這是我的名片，如果您有任何問題，請在任何時間打電話與我聯絡。

★

✒ 潔比化妝品公司. ✑

業務代表
Michelle Chang
公司電話/02-9876-5432
　　　　(9 a.m. – 6 p.m.)
行動電話/0912345678
電子郵件/Michelle.
　　　　Miller@jpcosmetics.com

【詞彙】

representative 代表／

cosmetics 化妝品／

manufacturer 製造商／

makeup 化妝／lipstick 唇膏／

lip liner 唇線筆／

lip gloss 唇蜜／

eye shadow 眼影／

eyeliner 眼線筆／

mascara 睫毛膏／

concealer 遮瑕膏／

foundation 粉底／

business card 名片／

inquiry 問題

Questions 80-82 refer to the following talk and card.

W Hi, my name is Michelle Chang, the sales representative from J&P's Cosmetics Inc. We are one of the leading professional cosmetics manufacturers in Shanghai. Our products include all kinds of makeup products, such as lipstick, lip liner, lip gloss, eye shadow, eyeliner, mascara, concealer, foundation as well as makeup kit and skin care series. We have been collaborating with some famous international brands in Europe and Asia for decades; therefore we are confident that we can satisfy your needs and requirements. This is my business card. If you have any inquiries, please contact me by the number anytime.

★

✒ J&P's Cosmetics Inc. ✑

Sales Representative
Michelle Chang
　Office/02-9876-5432 (9 a.m. – 6 p.m.)
　Mobile/0912345678
　Email/Michelle.Miller@jpcosmetics.com

---

80 Who most likely is the woman talking to?
(A) Her neighbor.
(B) A potential customer.
(C) Her boss.
(D) A police officer.

女子最有可能在跟誰說話？
(A) 她的鄰居。
(B) 一名潛在顧客。
(C) 她的老闆。
(D) 一名警員。

【解析】由女子在談話中極力向對方推薦公司及公司產品，並在最後遞上名片，請對方隨時與他聯繫，可知女子認為對方應該是可能會對公司產品有興趣的人，因此選項中以(B)的「潛在顧客」最有可能，故選(B)。

【類型】詢問聽話者身份題型

【詞彙】
potential 潛在的

【正解】(A)

---

81 What's the purpose of the woman's talk?
(A) Make a new friend.
(B) Find a new client.
(C) Explore investment opportunities.
(D) Job-hop to another company.

女子說話的目的為何？
(A) 交個新朋友。
(B) 找到新客戶。
(C) 探測投資機會。
(D) 跳槽到另一間公司。

【解析】由女子在談話最後遞給對方自己的名片，並歡迎對方任何時候與他聯繫，可知女子希望能與對方有業務上的合作關係，選項中以(B)的「找到新客戶」為最有可能的答案，故選(B)。

【類型】詢問目的題型

【詞彙】
explore 探索／job-hop 跳槽

【正解】(B)

---

82 Look at the business card. When does the woman's working day start?
(A) 6:00 a.m.
(B) 8:00 a.m.
(C) 9:00 a.m.
(D) 10:00 a.m.

請看名片。女子上班日幾點開始？
(A) 上午六點。
(B) 上午八點。
(C) 上午九點。
(D) 上午十點。

【解析】女子所附上的名片上顯示兩個聯絡電話，公司電話後面有註明時間為上午九點至下午六點，可知此應為女子會在公司的時間，推測女子上班的時間應該是上午九點，故選(C)。

【類型】圖表對照題型

【正解】(C)

男 好的，我相信你們大家一定都對這趟旅行感到很興奮吧！在你們開始打包行李之前，請檢查你的護照，確認護照有至少六個月的效期，否則你們將無法獲准進入這個國家。這很重要，所以我要再提醒你們一次。現在請打開你們的行前手冊到第八頁。這是一張你們在出發前至少一星期前需要做的事項核對清單。我們現在一起花幾分鐘瀏覽這份清單。

★

核對清單	
1. 護照效期	☐
2. 提高信用卡消費額度	☐
3. 台幣兌換美金	☐
4. 取得國際電信服務	☐
5. 取得插座變流器	☐

【詞彙】
validity 效期／permit 允許／
pre-departure manual 行前手冊／
checklist 核對清單／
spending limit 消費額度／
outlet 電源插座／
converter 變流器

Questions 83-85 refer to the following talk and checklist.

M OK. I'm sure all of you are very excited about your trip! Before you start packing, check your passport and make sure it has at least six months of validity, otherwise you will not be permitted to enter the country. This is very important, so I'd like to remind you once again. Now please open your pre-departure manual to page 8. This is a checklist of what you need to do at least one week before you leave for the trip. Let's take a few minutes to look through the checklist together...

★

Checklist	
1. passport validity	☐
2. increase credit card spending limit	☐
3. exchange NT dollars for US dollars	☐
4. get international phone service	☐
5. get an outlet converter	☐

這最有可能是何種場合？
(A) 行前說明會
(B) 新進員工說明會
(C) 新生說明會
(D) 家長座談會
【類型】談話場合題型

【詞彙】
pre-departure orientation
行前說明會／
parent-teacher conference
家長座談會

【正解】(A)

---

83 What most likely is this occasion?
    (A) A pre-departure orientation.
    (B) A new staff orientation.
    (C) A new student orientation.
    (D) A parent-teacher conference.

【解析】由談話中幾個關鍵字詞如trip（旅行）、passport（護照），並且男子要求聽話者打開pre-departure manual（行前手冊），可推測這應該是一個旅行前的「行前說明會」，故答案為(A)。

226

84 What industry does the speaker work in?
(A) Logistics
(B) Semiconductor
(C) Financial
(D) Tourism

【解析】由整篇談話內容幾乎都是與旅行有關，可推測說話的男子應該是從事與旅遊相關的行業，故答案為(D)。

說話者最有可能從事哪一種行業？
(A) 物流業
(B) 半導體業
(C) 金融業
(D) 旅遊業

【類型】說話者身份題型

【詞彙】
industry 行業／
logistics 物流業／
semiconductor 半導體業／
tourism 旅遊業

【正解】(D)

---

85 Look at the checklist. Which country are the listeners most likely to visit?
(A) Thailand.
(B) Japan.
(C) South Korea.
(D) Guam.

【解析】由本題所附核對清單上的內容中，可看到一條「將台幣兌換為美金」的項目，可知聽話者將會需要使用美金。選項中的四個國家中，只有(D)的「關島」以美金為通用貨幣，故最有可能的答案為(D)。泰國的通用貨幣為Baht（泰銖）；日本的通用貨幣為Yen（日圓）；南韓的通用貨幣為Won（韓元）。

請看核對清單。聽話者最有可能要去哪裡？
(A) 泰國
(B) 日本
(C) 南韓
(D) 關島

【類型】圖表對照題型

【詞彙】
Thailand 泰國／Guam 關島

【正解】(D)

W 我是萊徹斯特時尚的Anita。Pica女士，非常謝謝你早先時候的來信詢問我們是否能幫您的新品牌設計商標。我們很高興地告訴您，我們可以的，因為我們在過去八年期間幫全國超過五十個名牌服飾設計過商標，而且從未讓我們的顧客失望過。如果您想看一些設計，好做進一步的考慮，請您打1234-5678這個電話給我，並告訴我何時方便我們去拜訪您。再次感謝您，並希望能很快有您的消息。

【詞彙】
logo 商標／
designer clothing 名牌服飾／
fail 使失望／consideration 考慮

Questions 86-88 refer to the following voice message.

W This is Anita Wang at Leicester Fads. Thank you, Mrs. Pica, for your email earlier asking if we could design a logo for your new brand. We are happy to tell you that we can do this as we have designed logos for more than fifty designer clothing brands in the country over the past eight years and we never failed our customers. If you would like to see some designs for your further consideration, please phone me at 1234-5678 and tell me what is the most convenient time for us to visit you. Thank you again and we look forward to hearing from you soon.

這通語音留言的目的為何？
(A) 提供工作機會
(B) 回覆詢問
(C) 訂定會議時間
(D) 發出邀請

【類型】詢問目的題型

【詞彙】
voice message 語音留言／
reply 回覆

【正解】(B)

86 What's the purpose of this voice message?
　　(A) To offer a job.
　　(B) To reply to an inquiry.
　　(C) To schedule a meeting.
　　(D) To give an invitation.

【解析】由女子在這段訊息中表示Thank you... for your email earlier asking if we could...（謝謝您早些時候的來信詢問我們是否能……）可知對方先前有以電子郵件聯絡她，女子接著表示We are happy to tell you that we can do this...（我們很高興告訴您我們可以……）以此回覆對方電子郵件的詢問，因此這通語音留言的目的，很清楚地是一通回覆對方詢問的訊息，故選(B)。

87 What type of business is Leicester Fads?
(A) Travel agency
(B) Interior design
(C) Logo design
(D) Book publisher

【解析】由女子在訊息中提到 we have designed logos... over the past eight years（我們在過去八年……設計商標……）的關鍵字 design logos（設計商標），可知這家公司應該是做「商標設計」的行業，故答案為(A)。

Leicester Fads為何種工作行業？
(A) 商標設計
(B) 室內設計
(C) 旅行社
(D) 圖書出版

【類型】提問細節題型

【詞彙】
interior design 室內設計

【正解】(C)

---

88 How does the speaker wish the listener to contact her?
(A) By e-mail.
(B) By telephone.
(C) By text.
(D) By voice message.

【解析】由女子在訊息最後表示 please phone me at...（請撥打……給我），可知女子希望對方能直接打電話聯絡他，故答案為(B)。

說話者希望聽話者以何種方式聯絡她？
(A) 寫電子郵件
(B) 打電話
(C) 傳簡訊
(D) 留語音留言

【類型】提問細節題型

【正解】(B)

男 首先，我想謝謝你們所有人撥出時間來參加尾牙派對。今晚我們非常高興萊德公司的朋友能來與我們一起慶祝這個盛會。這是個讓我們忘掉煩憂，盡情玩樂的時刻。為了讓今晚更加愉快，我們邀請了幾位流行歌手及樂團一起來。你們可以在你們的座位上看到今晚的節目單。別忘了將你們的抽獎券投入抽獎箱，因為我們為大家準備了很棒的獎品喔！現在讓我們歡迎五月天！

節目單	
19:00 – 19:10	開場
19:10 – 19:40	五月天
19:40 – 19:50	第一次抽獎
19:50 – 20:10	蔡依林
20:10 – 20:30	林俊傑
20:30 – 20:40	第二次抽獎
20:40 – 20:50	晚會結束

【詞彙】
festivities 盛會／
enjoyable 愉快的／
raffle ticket 抽獎券／
drawing box 抽獎箱

Questions 89-91 refer to the following talk and program.

M First of all, I'd like to thank all of you for taking the time to come to our year-end party. Tonight we are very delighted to have our friends from Ryder Company to celebrate the festivities with us. It is time we forget our worries and have fun. To make this evening the most enjoyable, we have invited several popular singers and bands over. You can find the program for tonight on your table. Don't forget to put your raffle ticket into the drawing box because we've got some very amazing prizes for you! Now let's welcome Mayday!

Program		
19:00 – 19:10	Opening
19:10 – 19:40	Mayday
19:40 – 19:50	First Lucky Draw
19:50 – 20:10	Jolin
20:10 – 20:30	JJ
20:30 – 20:40	Second Lucky Draw
20:40 – 20:50	Closing

聽話者被鼓勵做什麼？
(A) 明年工作更努力。
(B) 向老闆舉杯敬酒。
(C) 上台表演。
(D) 參加抽獎活動。

【類型】提問細節題型

【正解】(D)

89 What are the listeners encouraged to do?
    (A) To work harder in the next year.
    (B) To drink a toast to the boss.
    (C) To perform on the stage.
    (D) To participate in the lucky draw.

【解析】由男子在談話最後提醒聽話者Don't forget to put your raffle ticket into the drawing box（別忘了將抽獎券放入抽獎箱），可知男子鼓勵聽話者積極參加抽獎活動，故選(D)。

90 Who is going to perform at the festivities?
(A) Some employees.
(B) A magician.
(C) Popular singers.
(D) A circus.

【解析】男子在談話中提到「有邀請流行歌手及樂團過來」，而且每桌還有節目表演單，可知這些受邀的流行歌手及樂團將會在此尾牙活動中表演，故選(C)。

誰將在盛會上表演？
(A) 一些員工
(B) 一位魔術師
(C) 流行歌手
(D) 一個馬戲團

【類型】提問細節題型

【詞彙】
magician 魔術師／
circus 馬戲團

【正解】(C)

91 Look at the program. How many times will the lucky draw take place?
(A) Only once
(B) Twice
(C) Three times
(D) Four times

【解析】由本題附上的節目單內容，看到19:40及20:30分別會有一次抽獎活動，因此可知抽獎活動將會舉行兩次，故選(B)。

請看節目表。抽獎活動將舉行幾次？
(A) 只有一次
(B) 兩次
(C) 三次
(D) 四次

【類型】圖表對照題型

【正解】(B)

男 那麼，現在終於到了你們發表口頭報告的時候。我希望你們都做好準備，因為你們的口頭報告佔這門科目總成績的百分之廿五。你們每個人都只有十分鐘的時間可以報告你們研究和分析的結果。請嚴格將報告時間控制在十分鐘之內。當時間到時，即使你報告還沒結束，也不能夠再繼續，當然，這將會影響你的成績。你們將會以學號的先後順序來做報告。現在就讓我們開始吧！

★

報告順序	
A001	Jenny Liu
A002	Sophia Tsai
A003	Doris Yang
A004	James Wang
A005	Peter Song

【詞彙】
oral presentation 口頭報告／
account for 說明／
allocate 分配／confine 限制／
student number 學號

這段話發生在何處？
(A) 加油站
(B) 餐廳
(C) 教室
(D) 麵包店

【類型】詢問地點題型
【詞彙】
bakery 烘焙坊

【正解】(C)

232

Questions 92-94 refer to the following talk and list.

M Well, it's finally time for you to give your oral presentation. I hope you are all well prepared as your oral presentation accounts for 25% of your overall grade of this course. Each one of you is only allocated 10 minutes to present the result of your research and analysis. Please strictly confine your presentation to 10 minutes. When the time is up, you will not be able to continue even if you haven't finished your presentation, and, of course, it will affect your grade. You will be presenting in the order of your student number. Now let's begin.

★

Presentation order	
A001	Jenny Liu
A002	Sophia Tsai
A003	Doris Yang
A004	James Wang
A005	Peter Song

92 Where is this talk taking place?
(A) In a gas station.
(B) In a restaurant.
(C) In a classroom.
(D) In a bakery.

【解析】由男子在談話中提到grade（分數）、course課程及student number（學號）等關鍵字，可知這個談話的背景環境應該發生在與學校或教育課程相關的地方，選項中以(C)為最有可能發生此談話的地點，故選(C)。

93 What is the length of each presentation?
    (A) An hour.
    (B) Half an hour.
    (B) A quarter.
    (D) Ten minutes.

【解析】由男子在談話中表示Please strictly confine your presentation to 10 minutes.（請將報告嚴格控制在十分鐘內），可知每一段報告時間只有十分鐘，故正解為(D)。

每一段報告時間多長？
(A) 一小時
(B) 半小時
(C) 一刻鐘
(D) 十分鐘

【類型】詢問細節題型

【詞彙】
 quarter （一）刻

【正解】(D)

---

94 Look at the list. Who will be the last one to present?
    (A) Jenny
    (B) Peter
    (C) Sophia
    (D) Doris

【解析】由本題所附表格上所示內容，可知順序排在最後一個的學生為Peter，故答案為(B)。

請看名單。誰將是最後一個做報告的人？
(A) Jenny
(B) Peter
(C) Sophia
(D) Doris

【類型】圖表對照題型

【正解】(B)

女　歡迎來到崔斯頓貿易公司。我是Lillian，很高興你們大老遠從東京過來參訪本公司。我們會盡最大努力讓您兩天的參訪行程有意義及值得。今天我將會帶你們參觀我們新蓋好的總部大樓。現在我發給你們的是本大樓的樓層總覽表。如果您看這張表，會看到資訊處理中心位在一樓。這正是我們現在所在的地方，而且我們將會從這裡展開我們的參觀行程。

樓層總覽
3F　主管辦公室
2F　員工辦公室
1F　資訊處理中心
GF　入口/接待處
B1　員工餐廳
B2　停車場

【詞彙】
corporation 公司／
worthwhile 值得的／
headquarters building 總部大樓／
hand out 發出／
floor guide 樓層總覽／
information-processing center
資訊處理中心

Questions 95-97 refer to the following talk and floor guide.

W Welcome to Tristan Trading Corporation. I am Lillian, and I am so glad that you have come all the way from Tokyo to visit our company. We will try our best to make your two-day visit meaningful and worthwhile. Today I will show you around our newly built headquarters building. What I am handing out to you right now is the floor-guide of this building. If you look at the guide, you will find the information-processing center on the first floor. This is where we are, and where we will be starting our tour.

Floor Guide
3F　Executive office
2F　Staff office
1F　Information-processing center
GF　Entrance/Reception
B1　Staff Cafeteria
B2　Parking lot

95 Who are the listeners?
(A) Visitors from Tokyo.
(B) New employees.
(C) New interns.
(D) Family members of the staff.

【解析】女子在談話中的這句I am so glad that you have come all the way from Tokyo to visit our company（很高興各位大老遠從東京來參觀本公司），就已經點出了聽話者的身份為「東京來的參觀者」，故答案為(A)。

聽話者是誰？
(A) 來自東京的訪客。
(B) 新員工。
(C) 新實習生。
(D) 員工家屬。

【類型】詢問聽話者身份題型

【正解】(A)

---

96 Which section will the speaker introduce first?
(A) Research and development center.
(B) Information-processing center.
(C) Main conference hall.
(D) Staff lounge.

【解析】談話最後女子向聽者介紹目前所在之處為information-processing center（資訊處理中心），且表示「我們將從這裡開始參觀」，可知選項(B)為正確答案。

說話者會首先介紹哪個部分？
(A) 研究發展中心
(B) 資訊處理中心
(C) 主會議廳
(D) 員工休息室

【類型】提問細節題型

【詞彙】
research and development center 研究發展中心／
conference hall 會議廳／
staff lounge 員工休息室

【正解】(B)

---

97 Look at the floor guide. What is on the first basement floor?
(A) The executive office.
(B) The staff office.
(C) The parking lot.
(D) The staff cafeteria.

【解析】由本題所附總覽表所示內容來看，選項(A)的「主管辦公室」位於三樓；選項(B)的「員工辦公室」位於二樓；選項(C)的「停車場」位於地下二樓；選項(D)的「員工餐廳」位於地下一樓。因此可知正確答案為(D)。

請看樓層總覽表。何者位在地下一樓？
(A) 主管辦公室
(B) 員工辦公室
(C) 停車場
(D) 員工餐廳

【類型】圖表對照題型

【詞彙】
basement floor 地下樓層

【正解】(C)

男 各位早安。在我們會議開始
之前，我希望各位見見我
們部門的新實習生，Brian
Sunders先生。Sunders先
生目前是在東亞大學主修電
腦工程的大四學生。雖然
Sunders先生還是一位學生，
卻已經拿到電腦軟體設計丙
級技術士的執照。他將會在
這一年與我們一起工作。希
望你們在這場會議之後都能
花一點時間跟他打招呼。

【詞彙】
intern 實習生／
senior student 大四學生／
Level C Technician for
computer software design
電腦軟體設計丙級技術士

Questions 98-100 refer to the following talk.

M Good morning, everyone. Before we start out meeting, I would like you to meet the new intern of our department, Mr. Brian Sunders. Mr. Sunders is currently a senior student majoring in computer engineering in East Asia University. While Mr. Sunders is still a student, he already got the Level C Technician for computer software design license. He will be working with us this year. I hope you can all take some time to say hello to him after this meeting.

本篇談話的目的為何？
(A) 推出一個新產品。
(B) 介紹一位實習工程師。
(C) 歡迎一位新經理。
(D) 表揚一位員工。

【類型】詢問目的題型

【詞彙】
commend 表揚

【正解】(B)

98 What's the purpose of the talk?
　(A) To launch a new product.
　(B) To introduce an intern engineer.
　(C) To welcome a new manager.
　(D) To commend an employee.

【解析】I'd like you to meet sb. 是用來向人「介紹某人」的常用句型，男子在談話一開始即表示I would like you to meet the new intern of our department（我想讓你們認識我們部門的新實習生），可知這篇談話的目的是在「介紹實習生」，故答案為(B)。

99 What's the intern's professional specialty?
(A) Computer software design.
(B) Machinery maintenance.
(C) Marketing and advertising.
(D) Graphic design.

【解析】男子在談話中提到新來的實習生在大學主修電腦工程，且已取得「電腦軟體設計丙級技術士」的執照，因此選項中最有可能是該實習生專長的應為「電腦軟體設計」，故(A)為正解。

實習生的專長是什麼？
(A) 電腦軟體設計。
(B) 機器維修。
(C) 行銷與廣告。
(D) 平面設計。

【類型】提問細節題型

【詞彙】
machinery maintenance
機器維修／advertising 廣告／
graphic design 平面設計

【正解】(A)

---

100 What are the listeners encouraged to do after the meeting?
(A) Teach the intern a lesson.
(B) Take the intern to lunch.
(C) Make the intern feel welcome.
(D) Show the intern around.

【解析】由男子在介紹完新實習生之後，表示希望聽話者能夠take some time to say hello to him（花點時間跟他打招呼），可知他是在鼓勵聽話者能主動與實習生交談，選項中以(C)所表示的「讓實習生感到受歡迎」是最適當的答案，故選(C)。

聽話者被鼓勵在會議後做什麼？
(A) 給實習生一個教訓。
(B) 帶實習生去午餐。
(C) 讓實習生感到受歡迎。
(D) 帶實習生到處參觀。

【類型】提問細節題型

【詞彙】
teach sb. a lesson
給某人一個教訓／
show sb. around
帶某人到處參觀

【正解】(C)

New TOEIC Listening 　Analysis 3
新多益聽力全真模擬試題解析第3回

(A) 孩子們在到處玩。
(B) 一隻野狗走過去。
(C) 沒人跟男子說話。
(D) 有些人正在看男子作畫。

【類型】單人照片題型

【詞彙】
street dog 野狗

【正解】(C)

01 (A) Kids are playing around.
　　(B) A street dog is walking by.
　　(C) No one is talking to the man.
　　(D) Some people are watching the man painting.

【解析】新制多益聽力測驗的照片題，除了會測驗應試者對照片內容的描述能力外，也會測驗應試者「看到了什麼」。即使是單人照片，重點也不一定總是放在唯一的主角上，反而會放在背景環境，因此在選擇答案時，不要只盯著照片中的人物看，而錯過正確的描述選項。照片中，我們可以看到一名男子坐在地上作畫，並未(C)與人交談；四周並無(A)孩童奔跑，亦無(B)野狗行經；從照片中也看不出(D)有人正在看男子作畫，故選項中以(C)的描述最為適當。

(A) 馬兒在工作。
(B) 馬兒在打盹兒。
(C) 馬兒在吃東西。
(D) 馬兒在奔跑。

【類型】兩人以上照片題

【詞彙】
take a nap 打盹兒

【正解】(A)

02 (A) The horse is working.
　　(B) The horse is taking a nap.
　　(C) The horse is eating.
　　(D) The horse is running.

【解析】本題雖然有多人出現在照片中，但重點放在拉觀光馬車的「馬兒」上。選項(A) 描述照片中的馬兒「正在工作」，是正確答案。其他選項的描述皆不符照片內容。

(A) 女子看起來很悲傷。
(B) 女子穿著一件裙子。
(C) 女子留著短髮。
(D) 女子正在微笑。

【類型】單人照片題

【正解】(C)

03 (A) The woman looks sad.
　　(B) The woman is wearing a skirt.
　　(C) The woman has short hair.
　　(D) The woman is smiling.

【解析】對照片中女子的客觀描述中，只有(C)「女子蓄短髮」是正確的，故為正解。由於女子背對著鏡頭，無法確認其臉部表情，因此(A)與(D)皆非適當描述；照片中只能看到女子上半身，無法得知該女子是否著裙子，因此(B)亦非適當答案。

(A) 幼苗正被栽種。
(B) 幼苗正被澆水。
(C) 幼苗正被踐踏。
(D) 幼苗正被碾碎。

【類型】人物／景物照片題

【詞彙】
seedling 幼苗／plant 栽種／
water 給水／trample 踐踏／
crush 碾碎；壓壞

【正解】(A)

04 (A) The seedling is being planted.
　　(B) The seedling is being watered.
　　(C) The seedling is being trampled.
　　(D) The seedling is being crushed.

【解析】圖為兩人照片，觀察照片中人物對圖片中植物幼苗所做的事，便能判斷(A)是正確描述。照片中的女孩們並沒有對幼苗做出(B)「澆水」、(C)「踐踏」以及(D)「碾壓」等動作，因此(B)(C)(D)所述皆不符照片內容。

(A) 女子是一名理髮師。
(B) 女子是一名芭蕾女伶。
(C) 女子是一名歌手。
(D) 女子是一名售貨員。

【類型】兩人以上照片題型

【詞彙】
barber 理髮師／
ballerina 芭蕾女伶／
salesclerk 售貨員

【正解】(A)

05 (A) The woman is a barber.
   (B) The woman is a ballerina.
   (C) The woman is a singer.
   (D) The woman is a salesclerk.

【解析】照片為兩人照片，由女子正在幫男子理髮，以此判斷女子的職業的話，選項(A)「理髮師」是最有可能的答案，故正解為(A)。

(A) 他們在表演魔術。
(B) 他們在演奏樂器。
(C) 他們在問彼此問題。
(D) 他們在海灘上玩。

【類型】多人照片題型

【詞彙】
perform 表演／
magic trick 魔術／
musical instrument 樂器

【正解】(B)

06 (A) They are performing magic tricks.
   (B) They are playing musical instruments.
   (C) They are asking each other questions.
   (D) They are playing on the beach.

【解析】圖為多人照片，由照片中的人物皆手持樂器做出演奏的動作，可判斷(B)「他們正在演奏樂器」為正確答案。選項(A)的「表演魔術」及選項(D)的「在海灘上玩」皆與照片不符；照片中的人物彼此也未有交談的動作，因此(C)的描述亦不正確。

▶ PART 2

Directions: You will hear a question or statement and three responses spoken in English. They will not be printed in your test book and will be spoken only one time. Select the best response to the question or statement and mark the letter (A), (B) or (C) on your answer sheet.

Example

You will hear:

Did you have dinner at the restaurant yesterday?

You will also hear:

(A) Yes, it lasted all day.

(B) No, I went to a movie with my girlfriend.

(C) Yes, the client was nice.

The best response to the question "Did you have dinner at the restaurant yesterday?" is choice (B), "No, I went to a movie with my girlfriend," so (B) is the best answer. You should mark answer (B) on your answer sheet.

---

07 Can you spell your last name, please?
  (A) You're right. It's Woodfield.
  (B) Sure. C-O-O-P-E-R, Cooper.
  (C) I don't have a nickname.

【解析】題目提出spell your last name（拼出你的姓）的要求，只有選項(B)確實將Cooper這個姓逐字拼出來，是為正解。選項(A)為詢問「是否姓Woodfield」的肯定回覆，而(C)為詢問「暱稱為何」的回覆，故皆非適當答案。

可以請你拼你的姓嗎？
(A) 你說得對。是Woodfield。
(B) 當然。C-O-O-P-E-R，Cooper。
(C) 我沒有小名。

【類型】yes/no疑問句題型

【詞彙】
last name 姓／
nickname 小名；暱稱

【正解】(B)

你不能在這棟大樓裡吸菸。
(A) 好。這是我的身分證件。
(B) 抱歉，我不知道。
(C) 我沒有點那道菜。

【類型】陳述句題型

【正解】(B)

08 You're not allowed to smoke in this building.
　(A) OK. Here is my ID.
　(B) Sorry, I didn't know that.
　(C) I didn't order that.

【解析】題目為對「不能在大樓內吸菸」這項規定的陳述，選項(B)對違反此規定「道歉」，並表示自己對此規定「並不知情」，是最適當的回應，故為正確答案。選項(A)是用來回應「出示身分證件之要求」，而(C)則是在「服務生送錯餐點」的情況下所使用的回應，皆與本題陳述句無關。

你今天幫花園澆水了嗎？
(A) 不，我不渴。
(B) 對，這是個花園派對。
(C) 對，我剛澆了。

【類型】現在完成式疑問句題型

【詞彙】
thirsty 口渴／
garden party 花園派對

【正解】(C)

09 Have you watered the garden today?
　(A) No, I'm not thirsty.
　(B) Yes, it's a garden party.
　(C) Yes, I just did.

【解析】本題疑問句以現在完成式的時態，詢問是否「已經完成幫花園澆水」這個動作。選項(C)以過去簡單式回答「剛剛澆過」，表示「已經做過這個動作」，故為正確答案。water這個字在本問句中作動詞解，為「給……澆水」之意，而不是做名詞「水」解，所以不要一聽到water 就忙著回答跟「喝水」有關的選項(A)。garden指的是「花園」，但是問句是以garden統稱花園裡面的所有花草植栽，因此不要聽到garden就直接選跟garden有關的選項(B)。

我覺得這牛奶聞起來怪怪的。
(A) 噢，它兩天前就過期了。
(B) 那個真的是太貴了。
(C) 對，我們牛奶快喝完了。

【類型】陳述句題型

【詞彙】
expire 到期／run out of 用完

【正解】(A)

10 The milk doesn't smell right to me.
　(A) Oh, it expired two days ago.
　(B) That's really too expensive.
　(C) Yes, we're running out of milk.

【解析】本題陳述句表示「牛奶聞起來不太對」，選項(A)表示牛奶「兩天前就過期」，呼應「牛奶味道怪異」的陳述，是最適當的答案。陳述句中並未提及「價格」，因此選項(B)可以刪除不考慮。選項(C)表示「牛奶快喝完」，亦跟題目陳述內容無關。

11 How would you like your hair cut today?
(A) No, I don't have scissors.
(B) Just trim off the split ends, please.
(C) I don't know any of your hair stylists.

【解析】本題為以how為句首，詢問對方對「頭髮怎麼剪」有何想法的疑問句。選項(A)回答「沒有剪刀」與選項(C)回答「不認識任何髮型設計師」，均為答非所問的回應。選項(B)表示「只要修剪髮尾即可」，是最適當的回覆，故為正解。

您今天頭髮想要怎麼剪？
(A) 不，我沒有剪刀。
(B) 請幫我剪掉髮尾分岔就好。
(C) 我不認識你們任何一個髮型師。

【類型】how 疑問句題型

【詞彙】
trim off 修剪／
split end 分岔髮尾／
hair stylist 髮型設計師

【正解】(B)

---

12 How long do you stay open today?
(A) We will stay for a week.
(B) Sorry, I can't open it.
(C) We close at 10 p.m.

【解析】 以how long為句首的疑問句，主要是要問「多久時間」。本題疑問句有小小陷阱，應試者必須正確理解疑問句的意思，才能夠選出正確答案。疑問句中的動詞stay在此不做「停留」解，而是「保持」的意思；open為形容詞，意指「開門營業的」，stay open即「保持營業狀態」之意。選項(A)中的stay表「停留」，選項(B)中的open為動詞，表「打開」，兩個選項內容皆與問句不符。選項(C)的close指「打烊」，此選項表示「我們晚上十點打烊」，適當回覆「營業時間多長」，故為正解。

你們今天會開到什麼時候？
(A) 我們會停留一個星期。
(B) 抱歉，我打不開。
(C) 我們晚上十點關門。

【類型】how long疑問句題型

【詞彙】
open 營業／close 打烊

【正解】(C)

---

13 Is there a dress code?
(A) Oh, it's a costume party.
(B) No, it's pretty hot today.
(C) It's in your wardrobe.

【解析】題目問dress code（服裝密碼），意思是想知道某個場合是否有「服裝規定」。選項(A)回答「這是個變裝派對」，也就是必須「變裝」參加的意思，是最適當的答案。如果應試者不慎將題目中的code聽成cold（冷的），可能就會被誤導，選到(B)這個錯誤的答案。題目並不是要問某物的所在地，因此選項(C)表示「在衣櫃裡」亦不是所需要的答案。

有服裝規定嗎？
(A) 噢，這是個變裝派對。
(B) 不，今天蠻熱的。
(C) 它在你的衣櫃裡。

【類型】be 動詞疑問句題型

【詞彙】
dress code 服裝規定／
costume party 變裝派對／
wardrobe 衣櫥、衣櫃

【正解】(A)

加★部分為多益新題型以及相關小提醒，考生要特別注意喔！ 243

你什麼時候要交這篇報告？
(A) 截止期限是九月八日。
(B) 在走廊盡頭。
(C) 我會在六點左右到達。

【類型】when 疑問句題型

【詞彙】
submit 提交／
deadline 截止期限／
hallway 走道

【正解】(A)

14 When should you submit the paper?
(A) The deadline is September 8th.
(B) At the end of the hallway.
(C) I will arrive around six.

【解析】聽到以when為句首的疑問句，便可知本題要問的是「何時」應該提交報告。選項(B)的回答與「地點」有關；選項(C)的回答應用在回覆「何時抵達」，均與問句內容無關。選項(A)表示「截止期限為九月八日」，可知報告應該在九月八日前提交，故為正解。

請在離開辦公室前關掉電燈。
(A) 好。
(B) 不，謝了。
(C) 一點也不。

【類型】祈使句題型

【詞彙】
switch off 關掉

【正解】(A)

15 Please switch off the light before leaving the office.
(A) Will do.
(B) No, thanks.
(C) Not at all.

【解析】本題為前面加了please使語氣委婉的祈使句題型，希望對方能在離開辦公室前關掉電燈。選項(A)以省略主詞 I 的口語方式回答「我會做這件事」，是正確答案。選項(B)與選項(C)皆不是祈使句的適當回覆方式，故不選。

誰正在用會議室？
(A) 它在三樓。
(B) 它是空的。
(C) 很好，謝謝。

【類型】who 疑問句題型

【詞彙】
conference room 會議室／
vacant 空的

【正解】(B)

16 Who is using the conference room?
(A) It's on the third floor.
(B) It's vacant.
(C) Pretty well. Thanks.

【解析】題目以who為句首，詢問「誰」在使用會議室。選項(A)的回答與「地點」有關，可直接刪除不考慮。選項(B)以 It's vacant.（它是空的）表示會議室「沒有人在用」，是最適當的回答，故為正解。選項(C)是用在回覆「問候」時的回答，與疑問句想要問的「是誰」完全無關。

17 We're gonna have the party in the yard.
　(A) No, but thanks for asking.
　(B) I need a few more minutes.
　(C) What if it rains?

【解析】題目為表示「我們將在院子裡開派對」的陳述。be gonna 即be going to之口語說法。由於派對將在「院子裡」舉行，因此可知此派對是個戶外派對。選項(C)的what if...為表示「萬一⋯⋯；要是⋯⋯怎麼辦」的句型用法，此處未雨綢繆的詢問「萬一下雨怎麼辦？」為最適合本陳述句的反應，故為正確答案。

我們將在院子舉行派對。
(A) 不，但是謝謝你的關心。
(B) 我還需要幾分鐘。
(C) 萬一下雨怎麼辦？

【類型】陳述句題型

【詞彙】
yard 院子

【正解】(C)

---

18 What is the fastest way to get to the airport?
　(A) Definitely by subway.
　(B) Two hours in advance.
　(C) It's just a block away.

【解析】本題以what疑問詞為句首，詢問到機場最快的方式「為何」。選項(A)表示「當然是地鐵」，適當回應了此問句，故為正解。選項(B)的回答與「時間」有關，選項(C)的回答與「距離」有關，皆非適合本問句的答案。

到機場最快的方式是什麼？
(A) 絕對是搭地鐵。
(B) 提前兩小時。
(C) 它只有一個路口遠。

【類型】what 疑問句題型

【正解】(A)

---

19 I'd like a smoked salmon sandwich.
　(A) It's Sunday.
　(B) Make it two.
　(C) Not really.

【解析】本題陳述句通常用在「點餐」，表示「我要點○○。」選項(A)回答「星期天」與選項(C)回答「並不是」，與本題陳述句均無直接關係，故不考慮。選項(B)表示Make it two.（製作兩份），通常是另一個一同前往用餐的人用來表示「我也要點一樣的」的表達方法，故為正解。

我要一份燻鮭魚三明治。
(A) 是星期天。
(B) 來兩份。
(C) 並不是。

【類型】陳述句題型

【詞彙】
smoked salmon sandwich
煙燻鮭魚三明治

【正解】(B)

噢，老天啊！你全身濕透了！
(A) 對，今天會下雨。
(B) 對啊。我應該要帶把傘的。
(C) 不，它們不是我的襪子。

【類型】陳述句題型

【詞彙】
soaked 濕透的

【正解】(B)

20 Oh, my. You're soaked through!
(A) Yes, it will rain today.
(B) Yeah. I should have brought an umbrella.
(C) No, they're not my socks.

【解析】本題陳述句中的soaked為soak（浸泡；使濕透）的過去分詞，亦即「濕透了的」之意。be soaked through就是be completely wet的口語用法，意指「全身濕透」。由陳述句所述內容可知，「對方全身濕透」是已經發生的事，選項(A)的回答，時態是未來式，因此不需考慮。選項(C)回答「不是我的襪子」，更是答非所問。選項(B)以「should＋現在完成式」表示「應做而未做之事」，指自己「應該要帶把雨傘才對」，是最適當的回答，故為正解。

你會去部門聚餐嗎？
(A) 在瑪麗的熟食咖啡店。
(B) 這個星期五晚上。
(C) 除非我完成專案報告。

【類型】will疑問句題型

【詞彙】
department dinner 部門聚餐／
project report 專案報告

【正解】(C)

21 Will you go to the department dinner?
(A) It's held at Marie's Deli Cafe.
(B) This Friday night.
(C) Only if I finish the project report.

【解析】本題是以will為句首的yes/no疑問句，詢問「是否將會參加部門聚餐」。選項(A)的回答與「地點」有關，選項(B)的回答與「時間」有關，均未正面回答本題疑問句。選項(C)的only if通常用在「條件句」的句型中，意指「唯有在某種情況下，才有可能發生某事」；這裡表示「除非我完成專案報告」才會去，是最適當的回應，故為正解。

我們何時會僱用新辦公室秘書？
(A) 很久以前。
(B) 這個月底前。
(C) 好，馬上來。

【類型】when 疑問句題型

【詞彙】
office secretary 辦公室秘書

【正解】(B)

22 When will we hire a new office secretary?
(A) A long time ago.
(B) By the end of this month.
(C) Yes, in a minute.

【解析】本題為以when為句首的疑問句，詢問「何時會聘用新辦公室秘書」，句中的助動詞will說明這是個會發生在未來時間的事。選項(B)回答「在這個月底之前」，是最適當的回答，故為正解。選項(A)回答「很久以前」，時間與問句不符；選項(C)回答「是，馬上」則是答非所問。

23 How does Mr. Taylor want us to ship his order?
    (A) The sooner the better.
    (B) Three tons of rubber raw material.
    (C) By DHL express.

【解析】本題為以how為句首的疑問詞，主要問詢問「以什麼方式」。選項(C)回答「以DHL快遞方式」寄送，是最適當的回答，故為正解。選項(A)會用來回答以when為句首的疑問句，而選項(B)的回答則是用在回覆以what為句首的疑問句，故皆不需考慮。

Taylor先生希望我們用什麼方式寄出他的貨品？
(A) 越快越好。
(B) 三噸的橡膠原料。
(C) 用DHL快遞。

【類型】how 疑問句題型

【詞彙】
rubber raw material 橡膠原料

【正解】(C)

---

24 Why didn't you attend the weekly meeting this morning?
    (A) At 10 a.m.
    (B) In Room 201.
    (C) My car broke down.

【解析】本題為以why為句首的疑問句，要問的是沒有參加週會的「原因」。選項(A)的回答與when（時間）有關；選項(B)的回答與where（地點）有關，因此皆不需考慮。選項(C)表示「車子拋錨」，適當提供本題疑問句一個合理的原因，是為正解。

你今天早上為何沒參加週會？
(A) 上午十點。
(B) 在201室。
(C) 我的車拋錨了。

【類型】why 疑問句題型

【詞彙】
break down 拋錨、故障

【正解】(C)

---

25 Congratulations on your promotion!
    (A) I didn't mean to.
    (B) Thanks. I won't fail you.
    (C) That's not true.

【解析】「congratulations on 某事」為向某人表達恭賀之意的句型用法。本題旨在向對方「祝賀職務晉升」，選項(B)以Thank you.表達對此祝賀的感謝，是為最適當的回應，故為正解。後面加上I won't fail you.（我不會讓您失望的），顯示向他祝賀的人可能是「讓他升職的人」，合情合理。選項(A)是用在「推卸責任」時的反應，而選項(C)則是用在「否認某件事」，都不是適合本題的答案。

恭喜你升職啦！
(A) 我不是故意的。
(B) 謝謝。我不會讓你失望的。
(C) 那不是真的。

【類型】表達祝賀題型

【詞彙】
promotion 晉升

【正解】(B)

我們有多少時間可以吃午餐？
(A) 在得來速。
(B) 在員工餐廳。
(C) 不到半小時。

【類型】詢問時間長短題型

【詞彙】
drive-thru 得來速／
staff cafeteria 員工餐廳

【正解】(C)

26 How much time do we have for lunch?
(A) At the drive-thru.
(B) At staff cafeteria.
(C) Less than half an hour.

【解析】聽到how much time ...便可知本題是要問「有多少時間」可以吃午餐。選項(A)與(B)的回答都與where「地點」有關，故不需考慮。選項(C)回答「少於半小時」，可判斷是最適當的答案，故為正解。

你跟Kingston先生的會面是約幾點？
(A) 明天下午三點。
(B) 我不想去。
(C) 時間越來越晚了。

【類型】時間疑問題型

【正解】(A)

27 What time is your appointment with Mr. Kingston?
(A) Three p.m. tomorrow.
(B) I don't wanna go.
(C) It's getting late.

【解析】疑問詞what後面接的名詞，就是此類疑問句想要問的重點，what time即「什麼時間」、「在何時」。選項(A)明確回答「明天下午三點」是為正解。選項(B)答非所問，而選項(C)則是用來表示「時間不早了」的常用句，均非本題適當的回應。

你的專案進行得怎麼樣了？
(A) 對，我很確定。
(B) 蠻順利的。
(C) 你有所不知。

【類型】how 疑問句題型

【詞彙】
go on 進展

【正解】(B)

28 How is your project going on?
(A) Yes, I'm pretty sure.
(B) Pretty well.
(C) You have no idea.

【解析】go on在本疑問句中為表示「取得進展」之意，通常以現在進行式的方式使用在how疑問句中，以關心「某人或事的發展狀況如何」，本題疑問句即在詢問「你的專案怎麼樣了？」選項(B)回答Pretty well.（蠻順利的）是選項中最適當的回答，是為正解。選項(A)是用來回答yes/no 疑問句；選項(C)的You have no idea.（你有所不知）通常是用來作為「即將開始抱怨某事」的開頭語，故以上兩個選項皆非適當答案。

29 Is the conference room ready for the meeting?
  (A) Yes, I will be on time.
  (B) No, it's a bit delayed.
  (C) Yes, it's all set.

會議室已經準備好可以開會了嗎？
(A) 好，我會準時。
(B) 不，它有點延遲了。
(C) 是，都準備好了。

【類型】yes/no 疑問句題型

【正解】(C)

【解析】本題以be動詞為句首的疑問句問的是「會議室是否已經準備好可以開會了」。選項(A)回答「我會準時」，主詞與疑問句不同，不需考慮；選項(B)是用來回覆「是否會準時」的回應，故亦非適當回答。選項(C)的set在此做形容詞用，表「準備好的」，因此all set即表示「全都準備好了」，是正確答案。

---

30 I'm getting married next month!
  (A) Are you serious?
  (B) I didn't do it.
  (C) Sounds interesting.

我下個月要結婚了！
(A) 你是認真的嗎？
(B) 不是我做的。
(C) 聽起來很有意思。

【類型】陳述句題型

【正解】(A)

【解析】本題為陳述「我要結婚了」這個事實的表述句。選項(B)的回答通常用在「推卸責任」的情況下，而選項(C)的回答則是用在對「某介紹或說明」表示「很有意思」，均不適合用來回應本題陳述句。選項(A)以Are you serious?（你是說真的嗎？）表達對此通知「感到意外」，並希望透過反問的方式向對方確定事情真偽，是合情合理的回應，故為正解。

---

31 I can't believe we got the contract.
  (A) Switch your phone off, please.
  (B) We should go celebrate.
  (C) You're gonna pay for that.

我不敢相信我們拿到合約了。
(A) 請將你的手機關機。
(B) 我們應該去慶祝。
(C) 你會付出代價的。

【類型】陳述句題型

【詞彙】
contract 合約／celebrate 慶祝／
pay for 為……付出代價

【正解】(B)

【解析】本題陳述「我們已經拿到合約」這個事實，並在前面加上I can't believe表達對此事實的發生感到驚訝。選項(A)表示「請將手機關機」，文不對題；選項(C)表示「你將付出代價」亦非在常理下適合用來回覆本句的反應，故皆可刪除不考慮。選項(B)對此陳述，提出「我們應該去慶祝一下」的建議，符合情理，故為正解。

男A 所以,你們可以具體地跟我說明你們的行銷策略嗎?

女 嗯,是這樣的,我們將會在新品上市六星期之前,開始在報章雜誌以及主要網站上打廣告。

男B 同時,我們將開始在各大捷運車站及百貨公司開始發送免費樣品。

男A 你們計劃何時開始宣傳活動?

女 六月初。我們將會僱用兼職業務員來幫忙。

男B 上市那天會有一個上市記者會,而且我們目前打算要邀請一位彩妝師來為一位模特兒上妝,不過這還在討論中。

男A 很好。感謝你們對這件事的努力。我們兩星期後再開會。

【詞彙】
launch press conference
上市記者會／
makeup artist 彩妝師／
under discussion 在討論中／
reconvene 再集會

▶ PART 3

Directions: You will hear some conversations between two people. You will be asked to answer three questions about what the speakers say in each conversation. Select the best response to each question and mark the letter (A), (B), (C) or (D) on your answer sheet. The conversations will not be printed in your test book and will be spoken only one time.

Questions 32-34 refer to the following conversation.

Man A So, can you tell me specifically about your marketing strategy?

Woman Well, we'll start advertising in the newspapers, magazines and on major sites six weeks prior to the launch.

Man B At the same time, we'll begin handing out our free samples at major MRT stations and department stores.

Man A When do you plan to begin promotions?

Woman At the beginning of June. We'll hire some part-time sales personnel to help.

Man B There'll be a launch press conference on launch day, and we're thinking of inviting a makeup artist to apply makeup on a model, but it's still under discussion.

Man A Good. I appreciate the effort you've put into this. We'll reconvene in two weeks.

32 What are the speakers talking about?
    (A) An investment project.
    (B) Marketing strategy.
    (C) Product quality.
    (D) Cost reduction.

【解析】由對話中第一位男子表示希望知道your marketing strategy（你們的行銷策略），接著其他兩位對話者便在對話中針對marketing strategy作說明，可知這段對話是以「報告行銷策略」為主軸發展的，因此正解為(B)。

說話者在談論什麼？
(A) 一樁投資案。
(B) 行銷策略。
(C) 產品品質。
(D) 降低成本。

【類型】主題提問題型

【詞彙】
reduction 降低

【正解】(B)

---

33 Who's going to help with the promotions?
    (A) Part-time sales personnel.
    (B) Colleagues from other departments.
    (C) College students.
    (D) The makeup artist.

【解析】由對話中女子表示We'll hire some part-time sales personnel to help. 可知他們將會僱用「兼職銷售員」來協助促銷活動，故正解為(A)。

誰將協助促銷？
(A) 兼職銷售員
(B) 其他部門的同仁
(C) 大學生
(D) 彩妝師

【類型】提問細節題型

【正解】(A)

---

34 When will the speakers have a meeting again?
    (A) The day after tomorrow.
    (B) Next Monday.
    (C) Tuesday morning.
    (D) Two weeks later.

【解析】由對話最後男子表示We'll reconvene in two weeks.（我們兩週後再開一次會），可知下次開會時間是兩星期後，故正解為(D)。

說話者何時會再次開會？
(A) 後天
(B) 下週一
(C) 週二上午
(D) 兩週後

【類型】提問細節題型

【正解】(D)

女 你確定這家二手書店就是 Jerry推薦的嗎？

男 對啊。他說那家書店在花店和超商中間啊。

女 好吧，看來它今天沒開。真可惜。

男 等一下！門上有個標牌。我們來看看上面寫什麼。

女 嗯……它說這家店每個營業日中午午休會關閉。我們可以在馬路對面的咖啡店等，晚點再過來。

男 好主意。

★

茉莉二手書店

星期一～星期六營業

上午10點 – 下午7點

午休 下午12:30 – 下午3:30

Questions 35-37 refer to the following conversation and sign.

W Are you sure this is the second-hand bookstore that Jerry recommended?

M Yes. He said the bookstore is between a flower store and a convenience store.

W Well, looks like it is closed today. Too bad.

M Wait! There's a sign on the door. Let's see what it says.

W Hmm... it says the store is closed for a lunch break every business day. We can wait at the cafe on the opposite side of the street and come back later.

M Good thinking.

★

Jasmine Second-hand Bookstore

Open Monday-Saturday

10 a.m. – 7:00 p.m.

Lunch break 12:30 p.m. – 3:30 p.m.

說話者在哪裡？
(A) 在花店。
(B) 在公車上。
(C) 在書店門口。
(D) 在超商裡。

【類型】提問細節題型

【正解】(C)

35 Where are the speakers?
　　(A) At the flower store.
　　(B) On the bus.
　　(C) In front of the bookstore.
　　(D) In a convenience store.

【解析】由對話中兩人看著貼在店門上的標牌，可知兩人應該是正在書店的門口，故正解為(C)。

36 According to the conversation, why is the bookstore closed?
(A) It's time for the lunch break.
(B) The staff is on annual leave.
(C) It's currently undergoing renovation.
(D) It has been relocated.

【解析】由女子看了門口上的標示，表示the store is closed for a lunch break（店家因午休而閉店），可知店家沒開門的原因是因為「現在是午休時間」，故正解為(A)。

根據對話內容，這家書店為何關著？
(A) 現在是午休時間。
(B) 員工正在放年假。
(C) 它正在進行翻修。
(D) 它已經搬遷了。

【類型】提問細節題型

【詞彙】
renovation 翻修／relocate 搬遷

【正解】(A)

---

37 Look at the sign. What time is this conversation most likely to take place?
(A) 11:30 a.m.
(B) 12:45 p.m.
(C) 4:00 p.m.
(D) 6:15 p.m.

【解析】由標牌上表示午休時間為12:30~3:30，可知對話中的兩人應該是在這段時間內來到店門口，並發生這段對話。選項中只有(B)符合這段時間，故正解為(B)。

請看標牌。這段對話最有可能發生在幾點？
(A) 上午十一點三十分。
(B) 下午十二點四十五分。
(C) 下午四點。
(D) 下午六點十五分。

【類型】圖表對照題型

【正解】(B)

Questions 38-40 refer to the following conversation.

Man A   OK. Let's get started. Teresa, you can start your presentation.

Woman   Good. Regarding the outlet mall investment project, ...

Man A   Hold on a sec, Teresa. There's a lot of static.

Man B   I can hardly hear what is being said. The reception is bad here.

Woman   How's it now? Can you hear me better?

男 A   好。我們就開始吧。Teresa，妳可以開始妳的簡報了。

女   好。關於這個暢貨中心投資案……

男 A   Teresa，等等。有很多靜電干擾。

男 B   我沒辦法聽到妳說什麼。這裡收訊很差。

女   現在呢？可以聽得比較清楚了嗎？

男 B	不。我還是沒辦法聽得很清楚，而且圖表因為扭曲的砌塊看起來很不清楚。	Man B	No. We still can't hear you perfectly, and the chart looks fuzzy with the distorted building blocks.
女	你可以找資管部的人來修理一下嗎？	Woman	Could you get someone from MIS to fix it?
男 A	嗯，給我們一些時間把問題處理好。三十分鐘後再重新開會吧。	Man A	Well, give us some time to get the problem fixed. Let's reconvene in thirty minutes.

【詞彙】
static 靜電干擾／
reception 收訊／
fuzzy 模糊不清的／
distorted 扭曲的／
reconvene 再開會

現在最可能正在進行什麼事？
(A) 視訊會議
(B) 表演試鏡
(C) 慈善義賣
(D) 精品拍賣

【類型】對話主題題型

【詞彙】
video conference 視訊會議／
audition 試鏡／charity 慈善／
boutique 精品／auction 拍賣

【正解】(A)

38 What most likely is taking place?
　　(A) A video conference.
　　(B) An acting audition.
　　(C) A charity sale.
　　(D) A boutique auction.

【解析】由對話中其中一名男子要求女子開始做簡報，隨即打斷她表示有static（干擾）而聽不清楚；此外，女子簡報用的圖表也因為出現扭曲砌塊而fuzzy（不清楚），可知這場簡報應該不是面對面的簡報，而是透過視訊進行，選項中以(A)所表示的「視訊會議」最有可能，故為正解。

女子正試著做什麼事？
(A) 籌劃一場展覽。
(B) 做一篇簡報。
(C) 安排一次會面。
(D) 訂一張飛機票。

【類型】提問細節題型

【詞彙】
exhibition 展覽

【正解】(B)

39 What is the woman trying to do?
　　(A) Organize an exhibition.
　　(B) Give a presentation.
　　(C) Schedule an appointment.
　　(D) Book a flight ticket.

【解析】由對話中男子對女子表示「可以開始簡報」，可知女子正要向兩位男士做簡報，故選項(B)為正解。

40 What did the speakers decide to do?
(A) Cancel the appointment.
(B) Proceed with the meeting later.
(C) Discuss in private.
(D) Give up trying.

【解析】由對話最後其中一名男子表示Let's reconvene in thirty minutes.（三十分鐘後再開會），可知他們決定暫停會議，先處理訊號問題，三十分鐘後再繼續開會，故正確答案為(B)。

說話者決定怎麼做？
(A) 取消約會。
(B) 稍晚再繼續開會。
(C) 私下討論。
(D) 放棄嘗試。

【類型】提問細節題型

【詞彙】
proceed with 繼續進行／
in private 私下

【正解】(B)

Questions 41-43 refer to the following conversation.

M Good morning, Daphne, this is Vincent.

W Oh hey, Vincent, what's up?

M I'm not feeling well today. I have a bad cough and I think I have a fever.

W Oh, I'm so sorry to hear that. Would you like a day off?

M Yeah, I think I need it. I'm wondering if you could cover for me today.

W I can do that. Anything you need me to take care of?

M Yes. Mr. Barrymore from the printing house will come around 10. Please hand him the paper bag on my desk. Thanks for your help.

W Sure thing. Get well soon.

男　早安，Daphne，我是Vincent。

女　噢，嘿，Vincent，有什麼事嗎？

男　我今天不太舒服。我咳得很嚴重，而且我覺得我發燒了。

女　噢，很難過聽到這樣的事。你想要休息一天嗎？

男　對，我覺得我需要。不知道妳今天能不能代理我的工作？

女　我可以啊。有什麼你要我處理的事嗎？

男　有。印刷廠的Barrymore先生十點左右會來。請妳把我桌上的紙袋拿給他。謝謝妳幫忙。

女　當然好。早日康復噢。

【詞彙】
cover for sb. 幫某人代理工作

男子為何打電話？
(A) 請病假。
(B) 取消約會。
(C) 邀請朋友。
(D) 訂餐廳座位。

【類型】對話主題題型

【詞彙】
call in sick 打電話請病假

【正解】(A)

41 Why is the man calling?
(A) To call in sick.
(B) To cancel an appointment.
(C) To invite a friend.
(D) To reserve a table.

【解析】由男子在對話中表示自己覺得不舒服，並且需要a day off（休一天假），可知男子是打電話來請病假的。call in sick即「打電話請病假」的片語用法，正解為(A)。

女子將做什麼？
(A) 去拜訪男子。
(B) 頂替男子的工作。
(C) 去看醫生。
(D) 照顧男子。

【類型】提問細節題型

【詞彙】
pay a visit to sb. 拜訪某人

【正解】(B)

42 What will the woman do?
(A) Pay a visit to the man.
(B) Cover the man's work.
(C) Go to the doctor.
(D) Take care of the man.

【解析】由對話中男子詢問女子可否幫他代理工作，女子表示同意，可知女子將要頂替男子的工作，正確描述為(B)。

男子的訪客何時會來？
(A) 九點
(B) 十點
(C) 中午左右
(D) 五點以前

【類型】提問細節題型

【正解】(B)

43 When will the man's visitor come?
(A) At 9.
(B) At 10.
(C) Around noon.
(D) By five.

【解析】由對話中男子表示印刷公司的Mr. Barrymore會在十點左右來，可知正確答案為(B)。

Questions 44-46 refer to the following conversation and coupon.

W I don't feel like cooking tonight. Let's eat out.

M OK. What would you like to eat?

W Anything but fast food. I'm so tired of it.

M Wanna try the new Thai restaurant next to the glasses store?

W Why not? But it seems expensive.

M Don't worry. Look what I've got. A colleague of mine gave me a coupon for that restaurant. It's gonna save us a bundle.

W Great! Give me five minutes to get changed.

M Take your time!

★

erer **Thai Thai** *erer*

Buy 1 Entree
Get 1 Entree **Free**

Valid until Jan 31, 2018

女 我今晚不想做飯。我們出去吃吧。

男 好啊。你想吃什麼？

女 只要不是速食什麼都可以。我對它超膩了。

男 要不試試眼鏡行隔壁那家新泰式餐廳？

女 好啊。不過看起來好像很貴。

男 別擔心。你看我有什麼。我一個同事給我一張那家餐廳的優惠券。可以幫我們省一筆錢。

女 太棒了！給我五分鐘換衣服。

男 慢慢來吧！

★

erer 泰泰 *erer*

主菜**買一送一**

有效至2018年一月31

---

44 What does the man suggest for dinner?
(A) Fast food.
(B) His signature dish.
(C) Thai cuisine.
(D) Street food.

【解析】對話中男子詢問Wanna try the new Thai restaurant...?（要不要試試……新泰國餐廳），可知他建議吃泰國菜，選項(C)的cuisine 指「菜餚」，Thai cuisine即「泰國料理」，因此選項(C)為正解。

男子建議晚餐吃什麼？
(A) 速食
(B) 他的拿手菜。
(C) 泰式料理
(D) 路邊攤食物

【類型】提問細節題型

【詞彙】
signature dish 拿手菜／
cuisine 菜餚

【正解】(C)

男子從何處得到優惠券？
(A) 餐廳
(B) 雜誌
(C) 網站
(D) 同事

【類型】提問細節題型

【正解】(D)

45 Where did the man get the coupon?
(A) From the restaurant.
(B) From a magazine.
(C) From the website.
(D) From his colleague.

【解析】由男子表示A colleague of mine gave me a coupon for that restaurant.可知男子的優惠券是同事給的，答案為(D)。

請看優惠券。優惠券何時到期？
(A) 一月一日。
(B) 兩週後。
(C) 一月底。
(D) 一月最後一個星期天。

【類型】圖表對照題型

【詞彙】
expire 到期

【正解】(C)

46 Look at the coupon. When will the coupon expire?
(A) January the first.
(B) In two weeks.
(C) The end of January.
(D) The last Sunday of January.

【解析】由優惠券下方表示Valid until Jan 31, 2018，可知這張優惠券到2018年一月31 前有效，也就是一月底到期，故正解為(C)。

男　剛是誰在跟妳通電話？

女　那是Selfridge先生。他希望我們立刻進行合約事宜。

男　我相信他一定這麼希望。好，這是一份大合約，所以我們最好開始擬定條款內容，並確定涵蓋所有基本要素。時間範圍是什麼？

女　Selfridge先生希望我們最晚這星期五之前就可以把合約寄給他。

Questions 47-49 refer to the following conversation.

M　Who was that on the phone?

W　It was Mr. Selfridge. He wants us on the contract immediately.

M　I'm sure he does. Well, this is a big contract, so we'd better start working on the terms and conditions and make sure all bases are covered. What's the timeline?

W　Mr. Selfridge hopes that we mail him the contract by this Friday at the latest.

M Wow! We don't have much time left, then. I guess we both have to work overtime this week.

W It seems so.

男　哇！那我們沒剩多少時間了。我想我們兩個這星期都得加班了。

女　看來是這樣。

【詞彙】
timeline 時間表

---

47 Who most likely is Mr. Selfridge?
(A) The boss of the speakers.
(B) A supplier that the speakers work with.
(C) The father of the woman.
(D) The guard of the office building.

【解析】由對話中女子表示Mr. Selfridge希望能趕快把合約簽好，可推測Mr. Selfridge應該是跟他們有業務往來的人，選項中以(B)為最有可能的答案，故(B)為正解。

Selfridge先生最有可能是誰？
(A) 說話者的老闆。
(B) 跟說話者合作的供貨商。
(C) 女子的父親。
(D) 辦公大樓的警衛。

【類型】提問細節題型

【正解】(B)

---

48 What can we know about the contract?
(A) It's urgent.
(B) It needs modification.
(C) It's been signed.
(D) It's already been sent to Mr. Selfridge.

【解析】由對話中男子表示要趕快擬定條款內容，而且女子提到Mr. Selfridge希望星期五之前就把合約給他，可知這份合約應該很趕，選項中以(A)所述最符合對話內容，故為正解。

我們對這份合約知道什麼？
(A) 它很緊急。
(B) 它需要修改。
(C) 它已經被簽好了。
(D) 它已經被送去給Selfridge先生了。

【類型】提問細節題型

【詞彙】
modification 修改

【正解】(A)

女子在對話最後表示什麼？
(A) 他們將必須工作很晚。
(B) 他們可以慢慢來。
(C) 她可以自己處理這件事。
(D) Selfridge先生太苛求了。

【類型】提問細節題型

【詞彙】
demanding 要求高的

【正解】(A)

49 What does the woman imply at the end of the conversation?
(A) They will have to work late.
(B) They can take their time.
(C) She can take care of this by herself.
(D) Mr. Selfridge is too demanding.

【解析】男子在對話中表示他們這星期可能都要work overtime（加班工作），女子以It seems so.表示「看來是如此」，可知他們將工作得很晚，選項(A)為正解。

男　嗨，我上星期跟你們買了這條長褲，但我想退貨。

女　可以請問是什麼問題嗎？

男　呃，我穿起來不是很合身。它對我來說太緊了。

女　你想要換一條尺寸大一點的嗎？

男　不。我想要全額退貨。

女　噢，好吧。你有帶收據嗎？

男　當然。在這裏。

女　喔，抱歉，先生。我們只接受購買七天之內的退貨。所以我恐怕沒辦法接受這件商品的退貨。

★

靚裝
男子服飾有限公司

收銀員：喬安　2017年五月26日3:55:43P

1 黑色西裝褲　　　　$2,599

總金額　　　　　　$ 2,599
現金交易　　　　　$ 2,599

感謝您的惠顧！

Questions 50-52 refer to the following conversation and the receipt.

M　Hi, I bought the trousers from you last week, but I'd like to return it.

W　May I know what the problem is?

M　Uh, they don't fit me perfectly. They are a bit too tight for me.

W　Would you like to exchange them for a larger size?

M　No. I want to return it for a full refund.

W　Well, OK. Do you have your receipt with you?

M　Sure. Here it is.

W　Oh, sorry, sir. We only accept returns within 7 days of purchase. So I'm afraid we cannot accept this return.

★

Looking Sharp
Men's Clothing, Co. Ltd.

Cashier: Joanne　　26-May-2017 3:55:43P

1 Black Suit Trousers　　　　$2,599

Total　　　　　　　$ 2,599
Cash Sale　　　　　$ 2,599

Thank you!

50 Where most likely does the woman work?
(A) At the post office.
(B) On the flight.
(C) In a local school.
(D) In a clothing store.

【解析】由女子正在處理男子所購買的長褲退貨事宜，可知女子最有可能在服飾店工作，故正解為(D)。

女子最有可能在哪裡工作？
(A) 在郵局
(B) 在飛機上
(C) 在一間當地學校
(D) 在一間服飾店。

【類型】提問細節題型

【正解】(D)

---

51 What can we know about the man?
(A) He works with the woman.
(B) He bought a watch at the store.
(C) He wants to return an item he bought.
(D) He is looking for a shirt to go with his trousers.

【解析】由男子在對話中表示自己買了一件長褲，但是I'd like to return it.（我想退貨），可知(C)為正解。

我們對男子有何所知？
(A) 他跟女子一起工作。
(B) 他在這家店買了一隻手錶。
(C) 他想要退他買的一件商品。
(D) 他正在找一件搭配褲子的襯衫。

【類型】提問細節題型

【正解】(C)

---

52 Look at the receipt. What most likely is the date when this conversation takes place?
(A) 28-May-2017.
(B) 30-May-2017.
(C) 1-June-2017.
(D) 3-June-2017.

【解析】由收據上顯示交易時間為五月26日，以此往後推算七天，可知到六月一日前都是可以退貨的時間。但是對話中女子卻表示已經超過七天可退貨時間了，可知這段對話應該是發生在六月一日以後，選項(D)為最有可能的答案，故為正解。

請看收據。這段對話發生的日期最有可能是幾號？
(A) 五月二十八日。
(B) 五月三十日。
(C) 六月一日。
(D) 六月三日。

【類型】圖表對照題型

【正解】(D)

男　我們跟Larry和他太太是約幾
　　點？

女　十二點。我們早了一小時
　　多。這表示我們還有時間可
　　以去搭個短程的渡輪。

男　好主意。我一直都想搭船遊
　　曼哈頓一圈。

女　我們在渡輪總站附近找個停
　　車位，然後再去買船票。

男　妳在說什麼呀？渡輪是免費
　　的！

女　噢，真的嗎？我不知道耶。
　　免費搭渡輪聽起來更棒了！
　　我等不及了。

男　我讓你在這下車吧。我停車
　　的時候妳可以查一下渡輪時
　　刻表。

★

Monday through Friday	
Leave	Back
8:00	9:05
9:30	10:35
10:45	11:50
11:15	12:20

【詞彙】
ferry 渡輪／terminal 總站

Questions 53-55 refer to the following conversation and timetable.

M　When is our appointment with Larry and his wife?

W　Twelve. We're more than an hour early. That means we still have time to go for a short ferry ride.

M　Great idea. I've always wanted to take a boat ride around Manhattan.

W　Let's find a parking space near the ferry terminal before we buy ferry tickets.

M　What are you talking about? The ferry is free!

W　Oh, is it? I didn't know that! A free ferry ride sounds even better! I can't wait.

M　I'll drop you off here. You can check out the ferry timetable while I'm parking the car.

Monday through Friday	
Leave	Back
8:00	9:05
9:30	10:35
10:45	11:50
11:15	12:20

這段對話發生在何處？
(A) 在他們的車上。
(B) 在火車站裡。
(C) 在飛機上。
(D) 在渡輪上。

【類型】提問細節題型

【正解】(A)

53 Where did the conversation take place?
　　(A) In their car.
　　(B) At the train station.
　　(C) On the flight.
　　(D) On a ferry.

【解析】由對話中說話者表示要找parking space（停車位），可推測他們應該正在車子裡，故正解為(A)。

54 What will the woman do next?
(A) Buy the ferry tickets.
(B) Give Larry a call.
(C) Check out the ferry schedule.
(D) Park the car.

【解析】由對話中男子表示要女子下車先去查看ferry timetable（渡輪時間表），可知女子接下來應該是會去做這件事，故正解為(C)。

女子接下來要做什麼？
(A) 買船票。
(B) 打電話給Larry。
(C) 查看渡輪時刻表。
(D) 停車。

【類型】提問細節題型

【正解】(C)

55 Look at the schedule. Which ferry should the speakers take?
(A) The one that leaves at 8:00.
(B) The one that leaves at 9:30.
(C) The one that leaves at 10:45
(D) The one that leaves at 11:15.

【解析】由對話內容可知說話者跟朋友十二點有約，而他們早了一小時多到。再對照渡輪時刻表，他們必須在十二點之前回來，因此只有十點四十五分出發的那班渡輪符合他們的需求，故正解為(C)。

請看時刻表。說話者應該要搭哪一班遊輪？
(A) 八點開船的那一班。
(B) 九點半開船的那一班。
(C) 十點四十五分開船的那一班。
(D) 十一點十五分開船的那一班。

【類型】提問細節題型

【正解】(C)

男 A　台北國際書展又要開始了。

男 B　今年的書展時間出來了嗎？

女　　出來了，它時間排在十一月一日到十一月十四日。

男 A　今年我們必須要儘快拿到一個攤位，因為它們很快就會被搶光。

男 B　對。而且我們需要一個大一點的攤位，因為我們需要大一點的展示區。

男 A　我們不是真的需要一個大一點的攤位。我覺得我們去年的攤位蠻令人滿意的呀。

女　　你知道，大一點的攤位表示較高的價錢。我們真的得把有限的預算納入考慮。

【詞彙】
display area 展示區／
take... into consideration
將……納入考慮

Questions 56-58 refer to the following conversation.

Man A　The Taipei International Book Fair is coming soon.

Man B　Has this year's book fair been scheduled?

Woman　Yes. it's scheduled from November 1 to November 14.

Man A　This year we need to get a booth as soon as possible because they go very fast.

Man B　Yeah. And we need a bigger booth this year because we will need a larger display area.

Man A　We don't really need a bigger booth. I think the space we had last year was pretty satisfactory.

Woman　Well, a bigger booth means a higher price. We really need to take our limited budget into consideration.

這段對話主要在討論什麼？
(A) 要看哪一部電影
(B) 在書展中取得一個攤位。
(C) 書展將在何處舉辦。
(D) 如何到達展覽館。

【類型】對話主題題型

【詞彙】
exhibition hall 展覽館

【正解】(B)

56 What is mainly discussed in this conversation?
　(A) Which movie to watch.
　(B) Getting a booth at the fair.
　(C) Where the book fair will be held.
　(D) How to get to the exhibition hall.

【解析】由對話內容可知台北國際書展即將展開，且對話主軸繞著書展「攤位」發展，可知這段對話重點是在討論「要在書展拿到攤位」，故正解為(B)。

57 Which information is NOT provided in the conversation?
(A) The name of the fair.
(B) The duration of the fair.
(C) The price of the booth.
(D) The location of the fair.

【解析】對話中提到的Taipei International Book Fair已經清楚表示這個「書展名稱」，且可知此展覽為在「台北」舉辦。對話中女子表示書展期間為11月1日至11月14日，因此我們也得到展覽期間的資訊。唯一不知道的就是選項(C)所指的「攤位價格」，故正解為(C)。

對話中並未提供哪一項資訊？
(A) 展覽名稱。
(B) 展覽期間。
(C) 攤位價格。
(D) 展覽地點。

【類型】提問細節題型

【詞彙】
duration 期間

【正解】(C)

---

58 What did the woman imply at the end of the conversation?
(A) They need the set up the exhibition within the budget.
(B) They can have a booth as big as they wish.
(C) There's no need to worry about the budget.
(D) She can negotiate with the sponsor for a better price.

【解析】由女子表示We really need to take our limited budget into consideration.這句話的關鍵字為limited budget（有限的預算）；女子這句話意在表示「選擇攤位時要把有限的預算考慮進去」，因此選項中以(A)所述與女子這句話的意思最相近，故(A)為最適當的答案。

女子在對話最後是什麼意思？
(A) 他們需要在預算內完成佈展。
(B) 他們想要多大的攤位都可以。
(C) 沒有必要擔心預算的事。
(D) 她可以跟主辦單位協調一個更優惠的價格。

【類型】提問細節題型

【詞彙】
sponsor 主辦人

【正解】(A)

男 嗨，我想訂一張到溫哥華的機票。

女 你想要什麼時候出發跟回來呢？

男 我想在下週六七月二十二日出發，八月三日回來。

女 你有比較喜歡的航空公司嗎？還有你想要搭什麼艙等？

男 福爾摩沙航空，豪華經濟艙。

女 我立刻為您查詢可搭的航班。好的，先生，您的機票已經訂好了。詳細的航班資訊會在幾分鐘內會以電子郵件寄給您。

男 謝謝。

★

日期	航班	出發/抵達	起飛時間
七月 22	FA1330	TPE/YVR	9:35
八月 3	FA1331	YVR/TPE	13:40

Questions 59-61 refer to the following conversation and table.

M Hi, I'd like to book a flight to Vancouver.

W When would you like to leave and return?

M I'd like to leave next Saturday, the twenty-second of July, and return on the third of August.

W Do you have a preferred airline? And what class?

M Formosa Airline and luxury economy class, please.

W I'll check the flight availability for you immediately. OK, sir, your flight is booked. The detailed information of your flight will be emailed to you within a few minutes.

M Thanks.

★

Date	Flight	From/To	Departure Time
July 22	FA1330	TPE/YVR	9:35
August 3	FA1331	YVR/TPE	13:40

男子將會使用什麼交通工具去溫哥華？
(A) 火車
(B) 遊覽車
(C) 飛機
(D) 地下鐵

【類型】提問細節題型

【詞彙】
transportation 交通工具

【正解】(C)

59 What type of transportation will the man use to get to Vancouver?
(A) Train
(B) Coach
(C) Plane
(D) Subway

【解析】由男子表示他要book a flight（訂機票），可知他的交通工具為飛機，故(C)為正解。

60 What job does the woman probably do?
(A) Travel agent
(B) Aircraft mechanic.
(C) Mail carrier
(D) Flight attendant

女子可能從事什麼工作？
(A) 旅行代辦人
(B) 飛機維修師
(C) 郵差
(D) 空服員

【解析】由對話內容可知女子幫男子完成訂機票的動作，因此可推測女子最有可能的身份是travel agent（旅行社代辦人員），故正解為(A)。

【類型】說話者身份題型

【正解】(A)

---

61 Look at the table. What time will the man's flight leave the airport on July 22?
(A) At 7:35.
(B) At 9:35.
(C) At 11:40.
(D) At 13:40.

請看圖表。男子的飛機七月廿二日這天幾點會離開機場？
(A) 七點三十五分
(B) 九點三十五分
(C) 十一點四十分
(D) 下午一點四十分。

【解析】由航班資料表所示，男子七月廿二日的班機出發時間為9:35，因此答案為(B)。

【類型】圖表對照題型

【詞彙】
departure 離境

【正解】(B)

女　早安。我需要三張票給兩位
　　大人跟一個小孩。

男　小孩幾歲？

女　他十四歲。

男　十六歲以下的孩童可以免費
　　參觀博物館。

女　太好了！那就兩張成人票。

男　三十二鎊。

女　沒問題。給你。這張票可以
　　看所有展覽嗎？

男　這票只能看固定展覽。臨時
　　展覽的門票另外收費。這是
　　你的門票和地圖。

女　謝謝。地圖是免費的嗎？

男　對，那是送的。

【詞彙】

regular 固定的／
temporary 臨時的／
separately 個別的／
complimentary 贈送的

Questions 62-64 refer to the following conversation.

W Good morning. I need three tickets for two adults and one child, please.

M How old is the child?

W He's fourteen.

M Children under 16 years old can visit the museum for free.

W Great! Two adult tickets, then.

M That would be 32 pounds.

W Sure. Here you are. Does the ticket include all exhibitions?

M The ticket is only for regular exhibitions. Admission for temporary exhibitions will be charged separately. Your tickets and the map.

W Thanks. Is the map free?

M Yes, it's complimentary.

這段對話發生在何處？
(A) 售票亭
(B) 電影院
(C) 圖書館裡
(D) 月台上

【類型】對話地點題型

【正解】(A)

62 Where did this conversation take place?
(A) At the ticket booth.
(B) In the cinema.
(C) In a library.
(D) On the platform.

【解析】由對話內容可知女子正在買票，故這段對話發生的地點應為ticket booth（售票亭），正解為(A)。

63 What can we learn from this conversation?
(A) Admission is free for children under 16.
(B) All children should be accompanied by an adult.
(C) Admission is free to all visitors on Fridays.
(D) The museum does not open on the weekends.

【解析】由對話中男子表示Children under 16 years old can visit the museum for free.可知十六歲以下孩童可免費參觀博物館，故正解為(A)。其他選項所述皆未在對話中提及，故不考慮。

我們可以從這段對話知道什麼？
(A) 十六歲以下的孩童免入場費。
(B) 所有孩童都應該由一位大人陪同。
(C) 每週五所有人都可免費入場參觀。
(D) 這間博物館週末沒有開放。

【類型】提問細節題型

【詞彙】
admission 入場門票／
accompany 陪同

【正解】(A)

64 What did the woman get for free?
(A) An adult ticket.
(B) A family ticket.
(C) A map of the museum.
(D) A ticket for the temporary exhibition.

【解析】由對話內容可知男子將一份地圖連同門票一起給女子，女子詢問地圖是不是免費的，男子回答it's complimentary（贈送的），可知女子免費得到一份地圖，正解為(C)。

女子免費得到什麼？
(A) 一張成人票。
(B) 一張家庭票。
(C) 一張博物館地圖。
(D) 一張臨時展覽的票。

【類型】提問細節題型

【正解】(C)

男　嗨，Miranda。謝謝你大老遠從台中過來。請坐。

女　謝謝。很高興再次見到你。我想你一定已經聽說我們上次跟你訂購的平板電腦賣得很好吧。

男　對啊。它們如我預料地一樣非常暢銷。

女　沒錯，這就是為什麼我們想要再跟你們訂一批貨。這次我們打算下一筆兩萬台的訂單。

男　那可真是一筆大訂單啊，我得說。妳希望這筆訂單何時交貨呢？

女　希望可以在年底前交貨，而且我們希望可以比上次的訂單價格低個百分之五。

【詞彙】
batch 批／
go like hot cakes 非常暢銷

Questions 65-67 refer to the following conversation.

M　Hi, Miranda. Thanks for coming all the way from Taichung. Please have a seat.

W　Thanks. It's nice to see you again. I bet you have already heard that the last batch of notepads we ordered from you is selling well.

M　Yes, I have. They are going like hot cakes just like I predicted.

W　Exactly, and that's why we'd like to order another batch from you. This time we're thinking to place an order of twenty thousand units.

M　That's a very huge order, I must say. When do you want this order to be delivered?

W　Hopefully by the end of the year, and we are expecting five percent less than our previous order.

女子來訪的目的為何？
(A) 推銷一個新產品。
(B) 做新產品簡報。
(C) 來下訂單。
(D) 來應徵一份工作。

【類型】對話主題題型

【正解】(C)

65 What is the purpose of the woman's visit?
　(A) To sell a new product.
　(B) To give a new product presentation.
　(C) To place an order.
　(D) To interview for a job.

【解析】由女子在對話中並未與男子多做寒暄，而是直接將話題帶到「上次跟你訂購的平板」，並接著表示we'd like to order another batch from you （我們想跟你訂另一批貨），可知女子來訪的目的是為了下訂單，故正解為(C)。

66 Why does the woman want to order the same products again?

(A) The previous ones are broken.

(B) She wants to buy them as gifts.

(C) They're flying off the shelves.

(D) They're on sale now.

【解析】由兩個對話者在對話中提到上次訂購selling well（賣得很好）以及這些商品go like hot cakes（非常暢銷），可知女子會想再追加訂單，是因為這些商品賣得很好，故正解為(C)。

女子為何想要再次訂購同樣的產品？

(A) 之前的產品已經壞了。

(B) 她想買來當禮物送人。

(C) 它們賣得很好。

(D) 它們現在正在特價。

【類型】提問細節題型

【詞彙】

fly off the shelves

暢銷；銷售一空

【正解】(C)

---

67 What request did the woman make?

(A) Bring down the price.

(B) Offer her the position.

(C) Compensate for her loss.

(D) Grant her leave for two days.

【解析】女子說明希望交貨日期之後，接著表示we are expecting five percent less than our previous order（希望價格能是上一批訂單的九五折），也就是希望對方能再降價，故正解為(A)。

女子提出什麼請求？

(A) 降價。

(B) 提供她這個職務。

(C) 賠償她的損失。

(D) 准她休兩天假。

【類型】提問細節題型

【詞彙】

bring down 降低／

compensate 賠償

【正解】(A)

女　不好意思。我覺得我的雞排沒有煮熟。你看！它還是粉紅色的。我真不敢相信我等了快一個小時，居然等到這樣的東西。

男A　噢，我很抱歉。我會把它拿回廚房，再幫您重做一份。

女　不用麻煩了。我沒辦法再等一小時。

男B　女士，很抱歉這道菜讓您不滿意。我是這間餐廳的主廚。請給我們一個機會彌補錯誤。如果你可以給我十分鐘，我保証會為您端上您吃過最好吃的雞排，而且，您今天晚上吃的所有東西都由餐廳請客。

女　這樣啊，好吧。

【詞彙】
chicken fillet 雞排／
unsatisfactory 令人不滿的／
on the house 店家請客

Questions 68-70 refer to the following conversation.

Woman Excuse me. I think my chicken fillet is undercooked. Look! It's still pink. I can't believe this is what I get after waiting for nearly an hour.

Man A Oh, I'm sorry. I'll send it back to the kitchen and make you another one.

Woman Don't bother. I can't for wait for another hour.

Man B I'm sorry, ma'am, that this dish is unsatisfactory. I am the chef of this restaurant. Please kindly give me a chance to fix our mistake. If you could give us ten minutes, I promise you'll be served with the best chicken fillet you've ever had, and everything you have tonight will be on the house.

Woman Well, alright.

女子對她的食物感覺如何？
(A) 滿意的
(B) 感謝的
(C) 不滿的
(D) 懷疑的

【類型】提問細節題型

【詞彙】
grateful 感謝的／
dissatisfied 不滿的／
doubtful 懷疑的

【正解】(C)

68 How did the woman feel about her food?
　(A) Satisfied.
　(B) Grateful.
　(C) Dissatisfied.
　(D) Doubtful.

【解析】由女子表示自己的雞排undercooked（沒煮熟），不相信自己居然等了快一小時還等到沒熟的雞排，可知女子的感覺是很不滿的，答案為(C)。

69 What did the restaurant chef offer the woman?
(A) A free dinner.
(B) Some coupons.
(C) A part-time job.
(D) A 10 percent discount.

【解析】由餐廳主廚在對話中表示everything you have tonight will be on the house，這句話最後的on the house即表示「由店家請客」的片語用法，因此可知餐廳主廚提供女子免費晚餐，答案為(A)。

餐廳主廚提供女子什麼？
(A) 一頓免費晚餐。
(B) 一些優惠券。
(C) 一個兼職工作。
(D) 九折優惠。

【類型】提問細節題型

【正解】(A)

---

70 What is the woman going to do next?
(A) Leave the restaurant.
(B) Wait for ten more minutes.
(C) Go to the restroom.
(D) Pack the leftovers.

【解析】餐廳廚師提出希望女子給他十分鐘親自做雞排，而女子表示alright（好吧），可知女子將會再等十分鐘，答案為(B)。

女子接下來將要做什麼？
(A) 離開餐廳。
(B) 再多等十分鐘。
(C) 去洗手間。
(D) 打包剩菜。

【類型】提問細節題型

【詞彙】
leftovers 剩菜

【正解】(B)

Directions: You will hear some talks given by a single speaker. You will be asked to answer three questions about what the speaker says in each talk. Select the best response to each question and mark the letter (A), (B), (C) or (D) on your answer sheet. The talks will not be printed in your test book and will be spoken only one time.

Questions 71-73 refer to the following talk and chart.

M Our plans enable our users to do all the things, include data, minutes and texts in Taiwan without any extra cost. What's more, our plans are flexible so that you can change your plan each month or even cancel anytime you wish. We'll recommend the right plan for you according to your telecommunication usage. As we don't do contracts, all you need to do is to get a SIM card, and activate it whenever you need it. Here's the table of our most popular plans.

★

Price per month	Data	Minutes	Texts
NT$299	100 MB	150	300
NT$499	1 GB	250	500
NT$899	3 GB	500	Unlimited
NT$1,299	Unlimited	Unlimited	Unlimited

男 我們的方案可以讓我們的使用者在台灣境內不花任何額外費用就做所有事情,包括使用數據、行動通話、簡訊傳輸等。而且,我們的方案很有彈性,所以你可以每個月改變方案,甚至任何時候只要你想要,都可以取消。我們會根據你的電信用量推薦適合你的方案。因為我們不簽合約,你所需要做的事情就是取得一張用戶辨識卡,並在任何你需要的時候啟用它就可以了。這張表就是我們最受歡迎的方案。

★

每月價格	數據量	行動通話 (分鐘)	簡訊 (則)
NT$299	100 MB	150	300
NT$499	1 GB	250	500
NT$899	3 GB	500	不限
NT$1,299	不限	不限	不限

【詞彙】
flexible 彈性的／
telecommunication usage
電信用量／do contract 簽合約／
SIM (Subscriber identity
module) 用戶辨識卡／
activate 啟用

71 What industry is the speaker most likely to work in?
(A) Telecom industry.
(B) Clothing industry.
(C) Food processing industry.
(D) Renovation industry

【解析】由說話者提到data（行動數據）、minutes（行動通話時間）以及texts（簡訊傳輸）等關鍵字來做公司的電信方案說明，可知說話者應該是在電信業服務，故正解為(A)。

說話者最可能從事哪一種行業？
(A) 電信業
(B) 服飾業
(C) 食物加工業
(D) 裝修行業

【類型】說話者身份題型

【詞彙】
telecom 電信／
food processing 食物加工／
renovation 裝修

【正解】(A)

72 According to the speaker, what is true about their plans?
(A) They are 2-year contracted plans.
(B) They don't include data.
(C) They can be cancelled anytime.
(D) They are unchangeable.

【解析】由男子表示他們的方案包含data（行動數據）、minutes（通話分鐘）以及texts（簡訊傳輸），而且他們don't do contracts（不用簽合約），can be canceled anytime（可隨時取消）而且每個月都可以更改方案，可知選項中只有(C)符合男子所述，正解為(C)。

根據說話者所說，有關他們的方案何者正確？
(A) 它們是要簽兩年合約的方案。
(B) 它們不包含數據用量。
(C) 它們可以隨時取消。
(D) 它們是不能變更的。

【類型】提問細節題型

【詞彙】
contracted 簽約的／
unchangeable 不可改變的

【正解】(C)

73 Look at the table. Which plan includes unlimited data, minutes and texts?
(A) The $299 plan
(B) The $499 plan
(C) The $899 plan
(D) The $1299 plan

【解析】由表格內容所示，數據用量、通話分鐘及簡訊傳輸都是unlimited（不限）的方案為每個月電信費用$1299的方案，故正解為(D)。

請看表格。哪一個方案的數據、通話分鐘、簡訊傳輸都不限用量？
(A) 299方案
(B) 499方案
(C) 899方案
(D) 1299方案

【類型】圖表對照題型

【正解】(D)

女　這是福爾摩沙航空EJ3031
　　飛往沖繩班機的最後一
　　次登機廣播。預定搭乘
　　EJ3031班機前往沖繩的乘
　　客Christopher Kristpan以
　　及Nicholas Hoffman請現在
　　立刻就前往廿五號登機門。
　　最後的檢查已經完成，機長
　　將會在五分鐘左右下令關閉
　　艙門。我再重複一次，乘客
　　Christopher Kristpan以及
　　Nicholas Hoffman請前往廿
　　五號登機門。登機門即將關
　　閉。謝謝您。

【詞彙】
boarding call 登機廣播／
proceed to 前往

Questions 74-76 refer to the following announcement.

W　This is the final boarding call for Formosa Airlines flight EJ3031 to Okinawa. Passengers Christopher Kristpan and Nicholas Hoffman booked on flight EJ3031 to Okinawa please now proceed to Gate 25 immediately. The final checks are being completed and the captain will order for the doors of the aircraft to close in approximately five minutes time. I repeat. Passengers Christopher Kristpan and Nicholas Hoffman please proceed to Gate 25 for boarding. The gate is about to close. Thank you.

說話者為何要發佈這則廣播？
(A) 年終特賣即將開始。
(B) 有兩位乘客登機遲到。
(C) 商店馬上就要打烊了。
(D) 生日派對馬上就要開始了。

【類型】廣播主題題型

【正解】(B)

74 Why is the speaker making this announcement?
(A) The year-end sale is about to start.
(B) Two passengers are late for boarding.
(C) The store is about to close soon.
(D) The birthday party will begin soon.

【解析】由女子催促兩位乘客立刻前往登機，可推測有兩位乘客沒有在預定時間內前往登機，故(B)為正解。

75 According to the announcement, what's going to happen in five minutes?
(A) The airplane will start to land.
(B) The airplane will take off.
(C) The door of the airplane will be closed.
(D) The inflight entertainment will be available.

【解析】由女子在廣播中表示the captain will order for the doors of the aircraft to close in approximately five minutes time（機長將在五分鐘左右下令關閉艙門），可知五分鐘後機艙門即將關閉，故正解為(C)。

根據廣播內容，五分鐘後會發生什麼事？
(A) 飛機將要開始降落。
(B) 飛機將要起飛。
(C) 機艙門將會關閉。
(D) 機上娛樂將開始提供。

【類型】提問細節題型

【詞彙】
land 落地／take off 起飛／
inflight entertainment 機上娛樂

【正解】(C)

---

76 Where are we most likely to hear this announcement?
(A) On the airplane.
(B) On the train station.
(C) In the department store.
(D) At the airport lounge.

【解析】由廣播一開始即說明這是一則登機廣播，可知這是要通知候機室等候搭機的乘客可以登機的廣播，因此最有可能在airport lounge（機場候機室）聽到這則廣播，答案為(D)。

我們最有可能在何處聽到這則廣播？
(A) 飛機上
(B) 火車站
(C) 百貨公司
(D) 機場候機室

【類型】詢問地點題型

【詞彙】
airport lounge 機場候機室

【正解】(D)

女 哈囉，大家好。首先我要
歡迎你們，並感謝各位今
天的出席。很遺憾Robbie
今天因為感冒在家休息，
不能加入我們，所以
Jennifer將會代替他做會議
記錄。我現在發下去的是
今天的議程，你們可以在
上面可以看到我們今天要
討論的主題。如你所見，
我們在這兩小時會議中要
做的事情很多，所以我們
現在應該要開始了。

★

	議程
9:00-9:20	上次會議記錄檢討
9:20-9:40	露比的專案簡報
9:40-10:00	表決提案預算
.	
.	
.	
12:00	休會

【詞彙】
stand in 代替／
minutes 會議記錄／
agenda 議程／
adjournment 休會

Questions 77-79 refer to the following talk and agenda.

W Hello, everyone. First I'd like to welcome you all and thank everyone for attending today. Unfortunately, Robbie cannot join us today because he is home with the flu, so Jennifer will be standing in to take the minutes. What I am passing around right now are the copies of the agenda, on which you can see the main topics that we will discuss today. As you can see, we have a lot to cover in this two-hour meeting, so we should get started now.

★

Meeting Agenda	
9:00-9:20	Review last meeting's minutes
9:20-9:40	Ruby's project presentation
9:40-10:00	Vote on proposed budget
.	
.	
.	
12:00	Adjournment

這是個什麼樣的集會？
(A) 大學同學會
(B) 記者會
(C) 部門會議
(D) 晚餐聚會

【類型】談話主題題型

【正解】(C)

77 What type of assembly is this?
(A) A college reunion.
(B) A press conference.
(C) A department meeting.
(D) A dinner gathering.

【解析】由談話內容提到需要take the minutes（做會議記錄），而選項中的四個聚會，只有department meeting（部門會議）是最有可能需要做會議記錄的集會，故選項(C)是最有可能的答案。

78 What would Robbie be in charge of if he were able to attend the meeting?
(A) Taking the minutes.
(B) Hosting the meeting.
(C) Reserving the meeting room.
(D) Making copies of the agenda.

如果羅比能夠來參加會議的話，他將會負責什麼？
(A) 會議記錄
(B) 主持會議
(C) 訂會議室
(D) 影印議程表

【解析】說話者提到Robbie時，表示他今天因為感冒不能與會，所以由Jennifer代替他做會議記錄，由這句話可知「做會議記錄」原本是Robbie該做的工作，故可知如果Robbie有來開會，就會負責做會議記錄，答案為(A)。

【類型】提問細節題型

【詞彙】
host 主持

【正解】(A)

---

79 Look at the agenda. What will be decided in the meeting?
(A) Where to hold the department dinner.
(B) The proposed budget.
(C) The chairman of the next meeting.
(D) The date of new product launch.

請看議程。何者將會在會議中決定？
(A) 舉辦部門聚餐的地點
(B) 提案預算
(C) 下次會議主席
(D) 新品上市日期

【解析】由本題所附的會議議程內容，可知其中一項議程為vote for the proposed budget（表決提案預算），vote for即表示「投票表決」的片語，可知在此次會議中將會以投票表決的方式決定提案預算，故答案為(B)。

【類型】圖表對照題型

【詞彙】
chairman 主席

【正解】(B)

男　各位女士先生，歡迎來到
　　永鮮超市。如果您或您家
　　人喜歡海鮮，您今天就走
　　運了！海鮮商品包括各式
　　魚類、蝦子、蛤蜊、淡
　　菜、牡蠣還有最重要的毛
　　蟹都將舉辦限時特賣！我
　　們海鮮區的所有商品都是
　　五折！對，你沒聽錯！海
　　鮮區所有商品都只要半
　　價！今天的限時特賣時間
　　只有一小時，從上午十點
　　到十一點。五分鐘後就要
　　開始了！請別錯過囉！

【詞彙】
be in luck 走運／
flash sale 限時特賣

Questions 80-82 refer to the following talk.

M　Ladies and gentlemen, welcome to Always Fresh Supermarket. If you or your family loves seafood, you're in luck today! There will be a flash sale on all our seafood, including a variety of fish, shrimp, clams, mussels, oysters and most important of all, hairy crab! Everything in our seafood section is fifty percent off! Yes, you heard me! Everything at seafood section is half off! This flash sale is only happening for one hour today, from 10 a.m to 11 a.m. It will start in five minutes! Don't miss it!

說話者最有可能在何處工作？
(A) 一間海鮮餐廳
(B) 一間海鮮加工廠
(C) 一間當地超市
(D) 一個觀光夜市

【類型】說話者身份題型

【詞彙】
processing plant 加工廠

【正解】(C)

80 Where most likely is the speaker working?
　　(A) In a seafood restaurant.
　　(B) In a seafood processing plant.
　　(C) In a local supermarket.
　　(D) In a tourist night market.

【解析】由說話者一開始就表示welcome to Always Fresh Supermarket，可知他最有可能在超市工作，選項中最有可能的地點就是(C)的「當地超市」。

81 What's the purpose of this talk?
(A) To announce an employee's retirement.
(B) To convene an impromptu meeting.
(C) To announce a flash sale.
(D) To cancel an appointment.

【解析】由男子表示There will be a flash sale（將會有一場限時特賣），並開始針對特賣內容及特賣時間作說明，可知這篇談話主要是要宣布這場限時特賣的活動，故正解為(C)。

這篇談話的目的為何？
(A) 宣布一名員工退休的消息。
(B) 召集一個臨時會議。
(C) 宣布限時特賣的活動。
(D) 取消一個約會。

【類型】詢問主題題型

【詞彙】
retirement 退休／
impromptu 臨時的

【正解】(C)

---

82 Which of the following can be bought at half price during the sale?
(A) Salmons and squids
(B) Beef and pork
(C) Cheese and milk
(D) Tissue and toothpaste

【解析】由公告內容可知這是一場所有海鮮商品五折的seafood flash sale（海鮮限時特賣），選項中只有(A)的鮭魚及軟絲是屬於海鮮，故正解為(A)。

下列何者在特賣中可以以半價買到？
(A) 鮭魚和軟絲
(B) 牛肉和豬肉
(C) 乳酪和牛奶
(D) 衛生紙和牙膏

【類型】提問細節題型

【詞彙】
salmon 鮭魚／squid 軟絲

【正解】(A)

女　嗨，大家好！您現在所收看的是家庭廚師Susanna！我是您的家庭廚師，Susanna。誰不愛吃美麗又美味的炒蛋呢？今天我們就要來用英式方法做炒蛋！現在我來將鍋子中火加熱。很快地把這些蛋打散。加一小團優質奶油。現在把蛋汁……直接下鍋，只要加一點鹽就好。我現在要用像這樣的一支小鏟，來撥動蛋汁，靜置五秒鐘，然後再撥一次。現在你可以看到蛋汁已經開始凝固，有些人喜歡加進牛奶或鮮奶油。但如果你做法正確，你根本不需要加任何東西。

【詞彙】
scrambled egg 炒蛋／
a la 以……方式，whisk 攪打／
glob 一點／spatula 鏟；刮刀／
set 凝固

Questions 83-85 refer to the following talk.

W Hi, everyone! You're now watching *Home chef, Susanna*, and I'm your home chef, Susanna. Who doesn't love beautiful and delicious scrambled eggs? Today, we're gonna cook scrambled eggs a la the English way. We're gonna go on to medium heat. Just whisk these eggs up. I'm gonna go in with a nice glob of butter. Now egg mixture... straight in, just with a little salt. I'm gonna move it around with a spatula like this, leave it for five seconds, and move it again. Now you can see the egg beginning to set. Some people like to put milk or cream in, but if you cook it right, you don't need any of that.

女子最有可能正在做什麼？
(A) 賣小鏟子
(B) 推銷一種新奶油
(C) 拍攝一支烹飪影片
(D) 在廚房幫她媽媽

【類型】提問主題題型

【詞彙】
film 拍攝

【正解】(C)

83 What most likely is the woman doing?
(A) Selling spatulas.
(B) Promoting a new butter.
(C) Filming for a cooking video.
(D) Helping her mom in the kitchen.

【解析】由女子表示「我們今天要來做炒蛋」，可知女子應該正在烹飪。如果是在廚房幫媽媽做菜，應該不會對步驟逐一解釋。因此最有可能的選項應該是(C)。

84 What is the woman demonstrating?
(A) How to cook English scrambled eggs.
(B) How to cook scrambled eggs in different ways.
(C) How to choose perfect eggs for scrambled eggs.
(D) How to fried eggs without oil or butter.

【解析】由女子表示we're gonna cook scrambled eggs a la the English way.（我們將用英式方式做炒蛋），可知女子正在示範如何做英式炒蛋，故正解為(A)。

女子正在做什麼示範？
(A) 如何做英式炒蛋
(B) 如何用不同方式做炒蛋。
(C) 如何為炒蛋選擇完美的蛋。
(D) 如何不用油或奶油煎蛋。

【類型】提問細節題型

【正解】(A)

85 What did the woman imply at the end?
(A) Cream is the key to scrambled eggs.
(B) Cream and milk are not really necessary.
(C) Most people like creamy scrambled eggs.
(D) Her scrambled eggs recipe is the best.

【解析】女子在最後提到有人喜歡加入牛奶和鮮奶油，但表示 if you cook it right, you don't need any of that（如果你做法正確，就不需要那些東西），可知女子認為牛奶和鮮奶油都不是必須的。故正解為(B)。

女子在最後做何暗示？
(A) 鮮奶油是炒蛋的關鍵。
(B) 鮮奶油和鮮奶並非真的需要。
(C) 大部份人都喜歡奶油炒蛋。
(D) 她的炒蛋食譜是最棒的。

【類型】提問細節題型

【正解】(B)

男　好，我們提供很多在世界各個最具異國風情的地點的蜜月套裝行程。這個列表上所有套裝行程的價格都包含整趟旅程的交通、住宿、門票及餐點費用。除此之外，我們還可以依據你個人的偏好和興趣，為你量身定做旅行計劃。例如，你可以決定你旅行的天數，還有你想要參觀的特定旅遊景點或你想做的特定活動。請看看我們的套裝行程，有任何問題儘管問我。

★

	天數	行程價格	
印度	5 天	NT$ 56,000	
泰國	4 天	原本 NT$ 25,000	現在 NT$ 18,000
馬爾地夫	12 天	NT$ 120,000	
義大利及希臘	14 天	NT$ 180,000	

【詞彙】
exotic 異國的／
transportation 交通／
accommodation 住宿／
admission 門票／
customize 訂做；客製／
preference 偏好／
tourist attraction 觀光景點

Questions 86-88 refer to the following talk and table.

M　Well, we offer a wide range of honeymoon packages to the most exotic locations around the world. The package prices of all the packages on this list include transportation, accommodations, admissions and meals during your trip. Besides, we can also customize these plans according to your preferences and interests. For example, you can decide on the length of your trip, and the specific tourist attractions you want to visit or specific activities you want to do. Please take a look at our packages and feel free to ask me any questions.

★

	Days	Package price	
India	5 days	NT$ 56,000	
Thailand	4 days	was NT$ 25,000	now NT$ 18,000
Maldives	12 days	NT$ 120,000	
Italy & Greece	14 days	NT$ 180,000	

86 Who most likely is the man speaking to?
(A) A newlywed couple.
(B) A group of elementary school students.
(C) His wife.
(D) His dentist.

【解析】由男子在談話中主要在介紹honeymoon package（蜜月套裝行程），根據常理，蜜月旅行行程的目標顧客應該是新婚夫妻，因此推測男子說話的對象最有可能是剛新婚的夫婦，故(A)為正解。

男子最有可能在跟誰說話？
(A) 一對新婚夫妻。
(B) 一群小學生。
(C) 他的妻子。
(D) 他的牙醫。

【類型】提問細節題型

【詞彙】
newlywed 新婚的

【正解】(A)

87 According to the man, what's the distinguishing feature of their packages?
(A) They are private tour packages.
(B) They can be cancelled anytime.
(C) The prices include tips for local guides.
(D) They can be customized.

【解析】由男子的說話內容提到we can also customize these plans according to your preferences and interests（我們還能根據你的偏好和興趣來為您客製旅行計劃），可知選項(D)所述正確，是為正解。其他選項內容皆與男子所言不符。

根據男子所言，他們的套裝行程有何特色？
(A) 它們是私人旅遊套裝行程。
(B) 它們可以隨時取消。
(C) 費用包含當地旅遊導遊小費。
(D) 它們可以客製化。

【類型】提問細節題型

【詞彙】
feature 特色

【正解】(D)

88 Look at the table. Which package is this travel agency promoting?
(A) The package to Thailand.
(B) The package to Italy and Greece.
(C) The package to India.
(D) The package to the Maldives.

【解析】由圖表所示四個行程的價格中，泰國的行程原價25000元，現在是18000元，可知目前泰國的行程正在促銷中，故正解為(A)。

請看表格。這家旅行社正在促銷哪個行程？
(A) 泰國行程
(B) 義大利及希臘行程
(C) 印度行程
(D) 馬爾地夫行程

【類型】圖表對照題型

【正解】(A)

男 如果您需要一個可以尾牙聚餐的好地點，就是水晶中國餐廳，別再找了。位在台北市金融區中心，我們寬敞的用餐區可以容納三十至兩百五十人。水晶中國餐廳不僅提供有現代化視聽系統及舞台的絕佳用餐包廂，而且還有口味多變化的菜單能滿足每個人的胃口。想知道關於我們團體活動更多的費用訊息，請上www.crystalchinese.com 網站查詢。

★

	容納人數	費用 （含餐點/飲料/設備）
祥龍廳	30 人	NT$ 30,000/4 小時
鳳凰廳	50 人	NT$ 55,000/4 小時
麒麟廳	100人	NT$ 120,000/4 小時
水晶廳	250人	NT$ 280,000/4 小時

【詞彙】
year-end banquet 尾牙餐會／
look no further than...
別再找了，就是……／
financial district 金融區／
accommodate 可容納……／
audiovisual system 試聽系統／
appetite 胃口

這篇談話的目的為何？
(A) 幫一家餐廳打廣告。
(B) 推銷一個新產品。
(C) 恭喜一對夫婦結婚。
(D) 表達感激之情。

【類型】提問主題題型

【詞彙】
advertise 打廣告／
gratitude 感激之情

【正解】(A)

Questions 89-91 refer to the following talk and table.

M If you need a great place for the year-end banquet, look no further than Crystal Chinese Restaurant. Situated in the heart of the financial district in Taipei City, we have spacious dinning areas that can accommodate from 30 to 250 people. Not only does Crystal Chinese Restaurant provide great dinning rooms equipped with modern audiovisual systems and stages, but also a diverse menu that can please everyone's appetite. Please check it out for more information about our rates for group events on www. crystalchinese.com.

★

	accommodates	rates (meal/drinks/equipment)
Dragon Hall	30 people	NT$ 30,000/4 hours
Phoenix Hall	50 people	NT$ 55,000/4 hours
Kylin Hall	100 people	NT$ 120,000/4 hours
Crystal Hall	250 people	NT$ 280,000/4 hours

89 What is the purpose of this talk?
(A) To advertise a restaurant.
(B) To promote a new product.
(C) To congratulate a couple on their wedding.
(D) To express gratitude.

【解析】由這篇談話主要在介紹一家中國餐廳，最後還提供網站資訊，讓聽話者可以做進一步查詢，可知說話者應該是在幫這家中國餐廳做廣告宣傳，正解為(A)。

90 What do we know about the restaurant according to the talk?
(A) It provides authentic Italian food.
(B) It provides modern audiovisual equipment.
(C) It is a great place to enjoy a quiet breakfast.
(D) It is a one-star Michelin restaurant.

【解析】由這是一則有關一家中國餐廳的廣告，故不可能賣道地的義大利菜；而且廣告一開始就說這是個適合舉辦year-end banquet（尾牙餐會）的地方，因此並非一個可以享受安靜早餐的餐廳；廣告中僅提到餐廳有「現代化視聽設備」以及「口味多樣化的菜單」，並未提及這是一間Michelin（米其林）餐廳，因此除了選項(B)之外，其他選項所述皆與內容不符。正解為(B)。

根據本段談話，我們對此餐廳有何認識？
(A) 它提供道地的義大利菜。
(B) 它提供現代的視聽設備。
(C) 它是適合享受一頓安靜早餐的好地方。
(D) 它是一家米其林一星餐廳。

【類型】提問細節題型

【詞彙】
authentic 道地的／
Michelin 米其林

【正解】(B)

91 Look at the table. Which of the following has the greatest capacity?
(A) Dragon Hall
(B) Phoenix Hall
(C) Kylin Hall
(D) Crystal Hall

【解析】由圖表內容可知，Crystal Hall能容納250人用餐，是所有包廂中可容納人數最多的，故(D)為正解。

請看表格。下列何者能容納最多人？
(A) 祥龍廳
(B) 鳳凰廳
(C) 麒麟廳
(D) 水晶廳

【類型】圖表對照題型

【詞彙】
capacity 容量

【正解】(D)

女 嗨，Steven。我是Lauren，打來回你電話。你早上打來時我正在開會，剛剛才聽到你的留言。很開心而且很榮幸受邀參加你的喬遷派對，我很高興地告訴你我要接受你的邀請。我等不及要看看你的新公寓了。我會帶一瓶酒和一些點心過去。不過我有個問題。開普敦街到底在哪裡？聽到留言打個電話給我吧。拜拜。

【詞彙】
housewarming party 喬遷派對／
invitation 邀請／
give sb. a ring 打個電話給某人

Questions 92-94 refer to the following message.

W Hi, Steven. This is Lauren returning your call. I was in the middle of a meeting when you called this morning and just heard your message. Well, I'm very glad and honored to be invited to your housewarming party, and I'm pleased to tell you that I will accept your invitation. I can't wait to see your new apartment. I'll bring a bottle of wine and some snacks over. But I have a question. Where exactly is Cape Town Street? Give me a ring when you hear my message. Bye.

女子正在做什麼？
(A) 她正在訂位。
(B) 她正在記留言。
(C) 她正在留語音留言。
(D) 她正在取消一個約會。

【類型】提問主題題型

【詞彙】
voice message 語音留言

【正解】(C)

92 What is the woman doing?
(A) She is making a reservation.
(B) She is taking a message.
(C) She is leaving a voice message.
(D) She is cancelling an appointment.

【解析】由最後女子表示Give me a ring when you hear my message（聽到留言打個電話給我）可推測女子現在應該是正在錄語音留言，故選項(C)所述正確，是為正解。

93 What can we learn from the message?

(A) The woman is having a party.

(B) The woman is going on a vacation.

(C) The woman is looking for a job.

(D) The woman will attend a party.

【解析】女子在留言中提到很高興受邀參加對方的喬遷派對，可知她並不是要辦派對的人，選項(A)可先刪除；女子接著表示I will accept your invitation（我接受你的邀請），可知女子將會出席這場派對，選項(D)所述正確，故為正解。選項(B)(C)皆與留言內容不符。

我們可以從這則留言得知什麼？

(A) 女子要辦派對。

(B) 女子要去度假。

(C) 女子正在找工作。

(D) 女子將出席一場派對。

【類型】提問細節題型

【正解】(D)

---

94 Which of the following information is provided in the message?

(A) The purpose of the party.

(B) The time of the party.

(C) The location of the party.

(D) The dress code of the party.

【解析】由留言內容，僅能知道Steven邀請Lauren參加他的喬遷派對，關於派對時間、地點及服裝規定等均未提及，因此這則留言僅提供有關「舉辦派對之目的」的訊息，故正解為(A)。雖然留言最後有提到Cape Town Street（開普敦街），但並無法表示這個地方就是舉辦派對的地方。

這則留言提供了下列哪一項訊息？

(A) 派對目的

(B) 派對時間

(C) 派對地點

(D) 派對服裝規定

【類型】提問細節題型

【正解】(A)

男 好的，雖然我們沒有明文的服裝規定，我認為有必要特別提出來，因為我們的工作需要大量與客戶面對面，因此我們在工作場合的服裝應該要能表現出專業形象。我們的外在形象必須讓我們的客戶及顧客，覺得他們可以信任我們的判斷和建議。不需要穿整套西裝，但是一定要穿正裝長褲，以及有扭扣的襯衫。領帶可以選擇性搭配。白板上列出的項目可能會讓你看起來比較不專業。不要穿它們來上班。

★

不要穿這些來上班—
1. 短褲
2. 背心上衣
3. 涼鞋
4. 運動鞋

【詞彙】
dress code 服裝規定／
attire 服裝／reflect 反映；表現出／
stick with 堅持／
dress pants 正裝長褲／
button-down shirt 有扭扣的襯衫／
optional 隨意的

這篇談話主要是關於什麼？
(A) 公司的服裝政策。
(B) 服飾店的退貨政策。
(C) 網站的隱私政策。
(D) 公司的休假政策。

【類型】提問主題題型

【詞彙】
privacy policy 隱私政策

【正解】(A)

Questions 95-97 refer to the following talk.

M Well, even though we don't have a written dress code, I believe it is necessary to point out that our workplace attire should reflect professional appearance, as our job involves lots of face time with clients. Our appearance needs to make our clients and customers feel that they can trust our judgment and recommendations. A full suit is unnecessary, but always stick with dress pants and button-down shirts. Ties are optional. Items listed on the board may make you look less professional. Don't wear them to work.

★

Don't wear these to work—
1. shorts
2. tank tops
3. sandals
4. sports shoes

95 What is this talk mainly about?
(A) The company's dress code policy.
(B) The clothing store's return policy.
(C) The website's privacy policy.
(D) The company's leave policy.

【解析】由談話一開始出現的關鍵字dress code（服裝規定），可知這篇談話是與公司服裝規定有關，故(A)為最有可能的答案。其他選項所述皆未在談話中出現，故不用考慮。

96 How does the speaker expect the listeners to look at workplace?
(A) Neat
(B) Casual
(C) Friendly
(D) Professional

說話者希望聽話者在工作場合看起來如何？
(A) 整潔
(B) 隨性
(C) 友善
(D) 專業

【解析】由說話者表示工作場合所穿的服裝應該要能reflect professional appearance（表現專業外觀），也就是希望聽話者在工作場合能看起來professional（專業），故正解為(D)。

【類型】提問細節題型

【正解】(D)

---

97 Look at the list. Which of the following is unacceptable in this company?
(A) Trousers
(B) Ties
(C) Sleeveless shirts
(D) Necklaces

請看列表。在這家公司不能穿戴以下何者上班？
(A) 長褲
(B) 領帶
(C) 無袖襯衫
(D) 項鍊

【解析】談話中說話者表示一定要穿dress pants（正裝長褲），因此選項(A)符合要求，可先刪除；ties（領帶）是optional（非必要的），可知要佩戴領帶是可以的，故選項(B)亦可刪除；列表中所列出的項目中出現了tank top，可知「背心式的上衣」是不被接受的，因此(C)的「無袖襯衫」不能穿來上班，故為正解。選項(D)的necklace（項鍊）屬於配飾，談話及列表中均未提及，故不需考慮。

【類型】圖表對照題型

【詞彙】
trousers 長褲／
sleeveless 無袖的

【正解】(C)

女　所有員工注意。由於本辦公大樓發生無預警的停電，所有機器都已經停止運作。電路工程師說要到明天才能恢復供電。因為我們大部份的人的工作都無法沒有網路和電腦，因此我們不得不宣布停班一天。公司會在三十分鐘內關閉，所以我們所有人都必須在十點之前離開。別忘了電梯現在不能用，所以我們全都得走樓梯。

【詞彙】
power failure 停電／
electrical technician
電力工程技術員

Questions 98-100 refer to the following announcement.

W　Attention all staff. Due to an unexpected power failure in this office building, all machines are shut down. According to the electrical technician, we won't be getting the power back until tomorrow. Since most of us cannot work without the Internet and computers, we have no choice but to announce a day off. The office will be closed in thirty minutes so all of us need to leave by 10. Well, don't forget that the elevators are not available right now so we all need to take the stairs.

為什麼辦公室要關閉？
(A) 停電了
(B) 有個颱風要來了
(C) 淹水了
(D) 剛發生一場地震

【類型】提問細節題型

【詞彙】
blackout 停電

【正解】(A)

98 Why will the office be closed?
　　(A) There's a blackout.
　　(B) A typhoon is coming.
　　(C) It's flooded.
　　(D) An earthquake just occurred.

【解析】由談話一開始便出現的關鍵詞彙power failure（停電），可知辦公大樓停電，blackout亦為「停電」之意，故正確答案為(A)。

99 What are the listeners asked to do?
(A) Assemble in the meeting room.
(B) Hand in their reports immediately.
(C) Leave the office in thirty minutes.
(D) Work overtime tonight.

【解析】說話者表示「辦公室會在三十分鐘內關閉」，因此所有人必須在十點前離開，因此可知所有人都必須在辦公室關閉之前離開，故選項(C)所述為正解。

聽話者被要求做什麼？
(A) 在會議室集合
(B) 立刻交報告
(C) 在三十分鐘內離開辦公室
(D) 今天晚上加班

【類型】提問細節題型

【詞彙】
assemble 集合／
work overtime 加班

【正解】(C)

---

100 How will the listeners reach the ground floor?
(A) Take the elevators
(B) Take the escalators
(C) Use the emergency ladder
(D) Take the stairs

【解析】由最後一句the elevators are not available right now（電梯現在不能用）so we all need to take the stairs（所以我們都得走樓梯）可知得走樓梯下樓。故(D)為正解。

聽話者將如何到達地面樓層？
(A) 搭電梯
(B) 搭手扶梯
(C) 使用逃生梯
(D) 走樓梯

【類型】提問細節題型

【詞彙】
elevator 電梯／
escalator 電扶梯／
emergency ladder 逃生梯

【正解】(D)

New TOEIC Listening Analysis 4
新多益聽力全真模擬試題解析第4回

(A) 這是一個超市。
(B) 這是一個美食攤位。
(C) 這是一個烘焙坊。
(D) 這是一輛餐車。

【類型】多人照片題型

【詞彙】
food booth 美食攤位／
bakery 烘焙坊／food truck 餐車

【正解】(B)

01 (A) It's a supermarket.
　　(B) It's a food booth.
　　(C) It's a bakery.
　　(D) It's a food truck.

【解析】在本題照片中可以看到一個臨時搭建的棚子，並且由攤位上寫著Burger（漢堡），以及照片左邊有寫著Menu的牌子，可判斷此為一個熟食攤位，故正確答案為(B)。

(A) 電車目前暫停服務。
(B) 電車是空的。
(C) 人們正在上電車。
(D) 電車的車門是關的。

【類型】人物與景物題型

【詞彙】
tram 有軌電車

【正解】(D)

02 (A) The tram is not in service.
　　(B) The tram is empty.
　　(C) People are boarding the tram.
　　(D) The tram's doors are closed.

【解析】本題照片很清楚地為一輛輕軌電車。透過電車的玻璃窗可以看見電車內有不少乘客，可知選項(A)與(B)所述並不符合照片內容；此外電車的門並沒有打開，沒有看到乘客上下車，故可知選項(C)非正確描述，而選項(D)的描述因符合照片內容，故為正解。

(A) 女侍正在接受點菜。
(B) 女侍正在清理桌面。
(C) 女侍正在掃地。
(D) 女侍正在抹桌子。

【類型】人物照片題型

【詞彙】
sweep 掃／wipe 抹

【正解】(B)

03 (A) The waitress is taking orders.
    (B) The waitress is cleaning the table.
    (C) The waitress is sweeping the floor.
    (D) The waitress is wiping the table.

【解析】出現人物照片題型，且人物為重點時，要特別留意人物的動作。本題照片中的女服務生站在一張空桌子旁邊，因為沒有客人，因此不可能正在幫客人點菜；觀察女服務生的動作，可知她並不是在掃地，也不是在擦桌子，而是在清理桌面上的餐盤，因此選項中以(B)之描述最符合照片內容，故選(B)。

(A) 男子將要求婚。
(B) 一場婚禮正在進行。
(C) 人們正在吃大餐。
(D) 婚禮在教堂舉行。

【類型】多人照片題型

【詞彙】
propose 求婚／
wedding ceremony 婚禮／
feast 筵席

【正解】(B)

04 (A) The man is going to propose.
    (B) A wedding ceremony is going on.
    (C) People are having a feast.
    (D) The wedding is held in a church.

【解析】在照片題中，除了觀察照片中人物的動作、景物的陳設以及人與四周環境的互動情況等之外，有時候也會測試應試者對照片背景情境的理解能力。在本題的照片中，可以看到一名穿著新娘禮服的女子，因此判斷這是一個與「婚禮」有關的照片。照片中的男子並沒有出現選項(A)所提到的「求婚」的動作，也沒有看到選項(C)所描述的「人們吃大餐」，故此二選項都可直接刪除不考慮。由照片背景來看，並沒有明顯的「教堂」象徵，因此選項(D)的描述亦不適合。此照片只能看到一對新人正在向一名年長的婦人行跪拜禮，可推測這應該是婚禮儀式之一，故以選項(B)所描述的「婚禮正在進行中」最為恰當，故(B)為正解。

(A) 男孩正在玩牌。
(B) 男孩正在爬樹。
(C) 男孩正盯著螢幕。
(D) 男孩正在講電話。

【類型】單人照片題型

【詞彙】
stare at 盯著……看

【正解】(C)

05 (A) The boy is playing cards.
(B) The boy is climbing a tree.
(C) The boy is staring at the screen.
(D) The boy is talking on the phone.

【解析】出現單人照片題型時，要特別注意照片中人物的動作。此題照片中的男孩正在用滑鼠玩著電腦上的遊戲，眼睛盯著電腦螢幕不放，因此選項中以(C)之描述最符合照片內容，故選(C)。

(A) 有一個黑板。
(B) 有一個白板。
(C) 有一顆足球。
(D) 有一間樹屋。

【類型】多人照片題型

【詞彙】
blackboard 黑板／
whiteboard 白板／
tree house 樹屋

【正解】(B)

06 (A) There is a blackboard.
(B) There is a whiteboard.
(C) There is a football.
(D) There is a tree house.

【解析】在新制多益聽力測驗中，也常測驗應試者「看到了什麼」，因此在多人照片題型中，除了要注意人物的動作之外，也要留心照片中出現的事物。如本題的多人照片中，並沒有出現選項(A)提及之「黑板」、選項(C)提及之「足球」或選項(D)提及之「樹屋」，而是出現選項(B)提及之「白板」，故(B)為正解。

> **PART 2**

Directions: You will hear a question or statement and three responses spoken in English. They will not be printed in your test book and will be spoken only one time. Select the best response to the question or statement and mark the letter (A), (B) or (C) on your answer sheet.

Example

You will hear:

Did you have dinner at the restaurant yesterday?

You will also hear:

(A) Yes, it lasted all day.

(B) No, I went to a movie with my girlfriend.

(C) Yes, the client was nice.

The best response to the question "Did you have dinner at the restaurant yesterday?" is choice (B), "No, I went to a movie with my girlfriend," so (B) is the best answer. You should mark answer (B) on your answer sheet.

---

07 Why are you in such a hurry?

    (A) I don't wanna miss my bus.

    (B) It's not worth the wait.

    (C) Yes, I have a reservation.

【解析】以疑問詞why為句首的疑問句，要問的是「原因」。本題詢問對方「如此匆忙的原因」，只有選項(A)表示的「我不想錯過公車」，是最可能的原因，故為正解。選項(B)與(C)的回答均答非所問，故不選。

你為何這麼匆忙？

(A) 我不想錯過公車。

(B) 這不值得等待。

(C) 是的，我有訂位。

【類型】why 疑問句題型

【詞彙】

  in a hurry 匆忙的；趕忙的

【正解】(A)

你決定要僱用那個人了沒？
(A) 不，我還沒有下決定。
(B) 不，他有點不舒服。
(C) 不，他的分數比我高。

【類型】現在完成式疑問句題型

【詞彙】
under the weather 不舒服

【正解】(A)

08 Have you decided whether or not to hire that guy?
    (A) No, I haven't made a decision yet.
    (B) No, he's a little bit under the weather.
    (C) No, his score is higher than mine.

【解析】以現在完成式為時態做疑問句時，主要是為問對方「完成某事了沒」。本題疑問句以動詞decide問「僱用那個人的決定做好了沒？」選項(A)以名詞decision回答「還沒有決定」，為最適當的回應，故為正解。選項(B)的weather乍聽之下與題目中的whether有點像，小心不要被誤導；選項(C)也是刻意以發音與題目中的hire相似的higher來混淆應試者，要小心不要上當。

你多久出差一次？
(A) 自從上個月。
(B) 每兩個月。
(C) 不是太久之前。

【類型】how often 疑問句題型

【詞彙】
travel for business 出差

【正解】(B)

09 How often do you travel for business?
    (A) Since last month.
    (B) Every other month.
    (C) Not too long ago.

【解析】以How often為句首的疑問句主要是要詢問事件發生的「頻率」。本題問的是「多久出差一次」，也就是「出差的頻率」。選項(A)與(C)都是用來回答「過去發生的事」，故可直接刪除不考慮。選項(B)的「every+一段時間」為表示「每隔多長一段時間即發生一次」的頻率副詞片語用法，every other+時間名詞，則為「每隔一（時間）」之意，故every other month即「每隔一個月」，也就是「兩個月一次」，故為正解。

你晚上打算做什麼？
(A) 謝謝你的關心。
(B) 我的車拋錨了。
(C) 我會去健身房。

【類型】what疑問句題型

【詞彙】
up to sth. 忙於某事

【正解】(C)

10 What are you up to tonight?
    (A) Thanks for asking.
    (B) My car broke down.
    (C) I'll hit the gym.

【解析】以what為句首的疑問句要問的是「什麼」。本題疑問句中的be up to sth. 為表示「忙於某事」的片語用法，如果後面接未來時間副詞，則有詢問對方將來某個時間「將要做某事」之意，因此這題要問的是「你晚上要做什麼」。選項(A)是用在回應「關心式的詢問」如How is your mom?（你母親好嗎？）或是用在「拒絕邀請後」，感謝對方提出邀請時。選項(B)回答「車子拋錨」，完全答非所問。選項(C)的hit the gym並不是指「打健身房」，而是表示「去健身房」的口語說法，故(C)是最適當的答案。

11 Victor is going downtown to meet his client this afternoon.
(A) When is he coming back?
(B) I haven't seen her today.
(C) I'll just have a cup of tea.

Victor今天下午要去市區見客戶。
(A) 他什麼時候回來？
(B) 我今天還沒見到她。
(C) 我只要喝一杯茶。

【類型】陳述句題型

【正解】(A)

【解析】不同於有特定疑問詞如when/where/how/who等疑問句，陳述句的回應比較沒有必須回答「時間」、「地點」、「方式」、「對象」等限制，因此遇到陳述句題型時，必須選出一個能呼應陳述句所述內容，且合情合理的回答。本題陳述句表示「Victor今天要去見客戶」，選項(A)反問「他何時回來」，意在詢問「Victor何時從市區見完客戶回來」，是最適當的回應，故為正解。選項(B)與(C)之回應均與陳述句內容無關，故不選。

12 How do you like the candidate we interviewed this morning?
(A) A candlelit dinner sounds great.
(B) He was the strongest of all.
(C) It will arrive on schedule.

你覺得我們今天早上面試的那個應徵者怎麼樣？
(A) 一頓燭光晚餐聽起來很棒。
(B) 他是所有人中條件最好的。
(C) 它會按照預定時間抵達。

【類型】詢問意見題型

【詞彙】
candidate 應徵者、候選人／
candlelit 燭光的／
on schedule 按照預定時間的

【正解】(B)

【解析】以疑問詞how為句首的疑問句主要是在問「如何」、「怎麼樣」，本題疑問句要問的是「你覺得今天早上面試的應徵者如何」，也就是在問對方對此人的「意見、看法」。選項(B)回應「他是所有人中最強的」，意在表示「此人是所有應徵者中條件最好的」，是最適合的答案。選項(A)與(C)均答非所問，其中選項(A)中的candlelit（燭光的）乍聽之下會跟題目中的candidate混淆，要小心不要被誤導。

13 Why don't we meet up tomorrow to discuss the project?
(A) It took me three weeks to finish it.
(B) How about 10 a.m. at my office?
(C) No, I never go to sleep before 10 p.m.

我們何不明天碰個面討論一下這個案子？
(A) 我花了三個星期才完成。
(B) 早上十點在我辦公室如何？
(C) 不，我從來沒在晚上十點前就寢。

【類型】why否定疑問句題型

【詞彙】
meet up 碰面

【正解】(B)

【解析】以why為句首的疑問句要問的是「原因」，但是以why not為句首的疑問句，表示「為何不做……？」則是在向對方「提出建議」，並邀請對方對此建議發表看法。因此本題疑問句主要是在建議「明天碰面討論案子」，選項(B)以另一個以how about為句首的疑問句提出建議「早上十點在我辦公室如何」，在此疑問句中不僅透露了贊成「明天碰面」這個建議，並且進一步建議了「碰面的時間與地點」，是最適合的答案，故為正解。

你知道Kingston女士的分機號碼是幾號嗎？
(A) 不知道。
(B) 她的秘書。
(C) 你答對了。

【類型】間接疑問句題型

【詞彙】
extension number 分機號碼

【正解】(A)

14 Do you know what Ms. Kingston's extension number is?
(A) No idea.
(B) Her secretary.
(C) You are correct.

【解析】本題是一個間接疑問句，以do you know（你知不知道）接以what為疑問詞所引導的疑問句，想問對方「知不知道……分機號碼」。選項(B)與(C)既未回答「知不知道」也未提到問句中想問的「分機號碼」，可知答非所問。選項(A)的回答「No idea」，是省略了主詞及動詞I have，用來表示「我不知道」的口語用法，雖為非正式用語，卻是最適當的回應，故為正解。

郵局今天幾點開？
(A) 八點吧，我猜。
(B) 那是昨天的事。
(C) 偶爾。

【類型】詢問時間題型

【詞彙】
open for business 開門營業／
once in a while 偶爾

【正解】(A)

15 What time is the post office open for business today?
(A) Eight, I guess.
(B) That was yesterday.
(C) Once in a while.

【解析】以what time為句首的疑問句，主要是要問「時間」。本題疑問句問的是郵局今天開門營業的「時間」，問句中已清楚提到today，因此選項(B)回答yesterday可以直接刪除不考慮。疑問句要問的並非「某件事發生的頻率」，因此選項(C)的頻率副詞once in a while（偶爾）亦不適合。選項(A)以Eight回覆「八點」，並加上表示「不十分確定」的I guess（我猜），是最適當的回答，故為正解。

我很欣賞我們新助理的工作效率。
(A) 我也是這麼想。
(B) 不，他還在等。
(C) 喔，我可能會遲到。

【類型】陳述句題型

【詞彙】
be impressed with 對……有深刻印象；受……感動／
work efficiency 工作效率

【正解】(A)

16 I'm very impressed with our new assistant's work efficiency.
(A) My thoughts exactly.
(B) No, he's still waiting.
(C) Well, I might be late.

【解析】本題以陳述句「我很欣賞新助理的工作效率」表達對新助理工作效率的肯定。選項(A)的My thoughts exactly.（我也是這麼想的）是一個簡化過的口語表達法，完整的句子應為My thoughts are exactly the same as yours.（我的想法跟你的一模一樣），是最適合本陳述句的回應，故為正解。

17 I have no idea where we are right now.
   (A) We're lost, aren't we?
   (B) That's a great idea.
   (C) I put it on your desk.

【解析】I have no idea意指「我不知道」。本題題目為表示「我不知道我們現在在哪裡」的陳述句。選項(B)的idea指「主意、點子」，與題目中的idea指「理解、明白」並不相同，乃答非所問。選項(C)的回答更是與本題陳述句毫不相關。選項(A)的附加疑問句呼應了題目所表示的「不知身在何處」，以反問「我們迷路了，對吧」的方式想要確定迷路的事實，故為正解。

我不知道我們現在在哪裡。
(A) 我們迷路了，對吧？
(B) 那真是一個好主意。
(C) 我把它放在你桌上。

【類型】陳述句題型

【正解】(A)

---

18 You should find yourself a new apartment.
   (A) On the third floor.
   (B) I'm thinking about it.
   (C) I can't remember.

【解析】本題為利用助動詞should（應該）向對方提出「應該做某事」的建議。選項(A)是用來回答「地點」，而選項(C)則答非所問。選項(B)表示「正在考慮」對方的建議，是最適當的回答，故為正解。

你應該幫自己找間新公寓。
(A) 在三樓。
(B) 我有在考慮。
(C) 我記不得了。

【類型】提出建議題型

【正解】(B)

---

19 Can I have our bill, please?
   (A) Yes, in a minute.
   (B) No beers tonight.
   (C) I'll call him later.

【解析】本題疑問句向對方提出「請給我我們的帳單」之請求。選項(A)回答「好」，並以in a minute（馬上、立刻）表示「會立刻送上帳單」，是最適當的回答，故為正解。選項(B)的beer（啤酒）聽起來跟題目中的bill很容易混淆，要注意尾音的差別。

麻煩給我我們的帳單，好嗎？
(A) 好，馬上。
(B) 今晚沒啤酒喝。
(C) 我晚點會打給他。

【類型】yes/no 疑問句題型

【詞彙】
 bill 帳單／beer 啤酒

【正解】(A)

我今天覺得不太舒服。
(A) 我需要再五分鐘。
(B) 很高興你喜歡。
(C) 你何不休息一天？

【類型】陳述句題型

【正解】(C)

---

20 I'm not feeling very well today.
    (A) I need five more minutes.
    (B) I'm glad you like it.
    (C) Why don't you take a day off?

【解析】本題為表示「我覺得不舒服」的陳述句，選項(C)的 take 一段時間off為表示「休息（一段時間）」的片語用法，這裡針對「身體不舒服」這一點，向對方提出「何不休息一天」的建議，是最適當的回應，故為正解。

主管會議會在哪裡舉行？
(A) 三星期後。
(B) 有關人事改組。
(C) 在總公司。

【類型】where 疑問句題型

【詞彙】
executive meeting 主管會議／
take place 發生／personnel
reorganization 人事改組／
headquarters 總公司；總部

【正解】(C)

---

21 Where will the executive meeting take place?
    (A) In three weeks.
    (B) About personnel reorganization.
    (C) At the headquarters.

【解析】本題以疑問詞where為句首，要問主管會議舉行的「地點」。選項(A)可用來回答主管會議舉行的「時間」，而選項(B)可用來回答主管會議的「討論內容」，但皆不適合用來回應本題疑問句。選項中只有(C)為與地點有關之回答，是為正解。

誰負責專案評估？
(A) 我們的評估小組。
(B) 一切都進行順利。
(C) 讓我查查行程表。

【類型】who疑問句題型

【詞彙】
in charge of 負責／
evaluation 評估／
assessment 評估

【正解】(A)

---

22 Who is in charge of project evaluation?
    (A) Our assessment team.
    (B) Everything goes well.
    (C) Let me check my schedule.

【解析】本題以疑問詞who為句首，要問負責專案評估的人是「誰」。選項(A)雖未指出人名，卻以「人」所組成的「團隊、小組」，表示專案評估工作由「評估小組」負責，是為正解。選項(C)要查的是schedule（時程表），而非與負責專案評估有關的人員配置表，故非適當的答案。

23 Would you like to leave a message?
(A) Yes, you can use it now.
(B) Just tell him his wife called.
(C) The escalator is out of order.

你想要留言嗎？
(A) 對，你現在可以用了。
(B) 跟他說他太太有打來就行了。
(C) 手扶梯故障了。

【解析】take a message指「記下留言」，而leave a message則為「留下留言」。本題以Would you like to... 詢問對方「是否想要留言」。選項(A)與(C)的回答均與「是否要留言」無關，而選項(B)表示「跟他說他太太打來」，簡單交待了留言內容，是為正解。

【類型】詢問意願題型

【詞彙】
message 訊息／
escalator 電扶梯

【正解】(B)

---

24 I'm wondering if you could cover my shift for the next three days.
(A) No, I haven't heard of it before.
(B) Sure. Are you going on a vacation?
(C) Actually, I have a date today.

我想知道接下來三天你能不能幫我代班。
(A) 不，我以前沒聽過。
(B) 當然。你要去度假嗎？
(C) 其實我今天有約會。

【解析】本題雖無疑問詞，卻為一個間接疑問句。I'm wondering if... 為表示「不知道……」的句型用法，if在這裡不做表條件的「如果」，而是做與whether同義的「是否」解。這題想問的是：我想知道「未來三天你是否能幫我代班」，時間清楚表明是在「未來三天」，因此選項(B)回答「今天有約會」，在時間上就已經與問句不符，不需考慮。選項(A)回答內容與問句無關，亦可直接刪除。選項(B)明確回答Sure。後面的問句是在問對方三天不來上班是不是要去度假，符合情理，故為正解。

【類型】間接問句題型

【詞彙】
cover one's shift 幫某人代班／
go on a vacation 去度假

【正解】(B)

---

25 When will the new office assistant start working?
(A) The first day of next month.
(B) That sounds exciting.
(C) I don't think they know each other.

新的辦公室助理什麼時候要開始上班？
(A) 下個月第一天。
(B) 那聽起來很令人興奮。
(C) 我不認為他們認識對方。

【解析】本題疑問句以when為句首，要問的是新辦公室助理「何時」開始上班。選項(A)表示「下個月第一天」，為正確答案。其他兩個回應皆與本題疑問句無關，故不考慮。

【類型】when疑問句題型

【詞彙】
office assistant 辦公室助理

【正解】(A)

加★部分為多益新題型以及相關小提醒，考生要特別注意喔！ 303

我可以私下跟你談談嗎？
(A) 是，我尊重那一點。
(B) 噢，你不需要這麼做的。
(C) 當然。是有關什麼事？

【類型】提出請求題型

【詞彙】
have a word with sb.
與某人談話／in private 私下／
respect 尊重

【正解】(C)

26 Could I have a word with you in private?
　　(A) Yes, I respect that.
　　(B) Oh, you shouldn't have.
　　(C) Sure. What's it about?

【解析】本題以助動詞could為句首，客氣委婉地提出想跟對方私下談話的請求，選項(C)以sure 表示答應請求，並進一步詢問對方要談的事「與什麼有關」，是最適當的回應，故為正解。

你知道他們明年要結束東京分公司嗎？
(A) 是，我經常去那兒。
(B) 不，我還不認識他。
(C) 不。我第一次聽說。

【類型】間接疑問句題型

【正解】(C)

27 Did you know that they're closing the Tokyo Branch next year?
　　(A) Yes, I visit there very often.
　　(B) No, I haven't met him yet.
　　(C) No. This is news to me.

【解析】題目中的動詞close在此作「（永久性地）關閉（某個組織）」解，本題以間接疑問句的方式詢問對方「是否知道公司要結束東京分公司這件事」。選項(A)與(B)的回應皆答非所問，選項(C)以This is news to me.（這對我來説是個新聞）表示自己「對此並不知情」，故為正解。

你需要多久時間修改企劃案？
(A) 是，問題已經解決了。
(B) 大概兩小時。
(C) 儘管休息一下吧。

【類型】how much 疑問句題型

【詞彙】
revise 修改／proposal 企劃案

【正解】(B)

28 How much time do you need to revise the proposal?
　　(A) Yes, the problem has been fixed.
　　(B) About two hours.
　　(C) Just take a break.

【解析】遇到how為句首的疑問句時，要注意how後面接了什麼，如how many問的是「數量」、how often問的是「頻率」、how long問的是「多久」，而本題的how much time則是在問對方修改企劃案需要「多少時間」。選項(B)以About two hours. 回答「大概（需要）兩小時」，是最適當的回應，故為正解。

29 Have you got any plans for the weekend?
(A) Yes, that's all.
(B) Here is my ticket.
(C) Nope. Any suggestions?

你週末有任何計劃嗎？
(A) 是，就這些了。
(B) 這是我的票。
(C) 沒。有什麼建議嗎？

【解析】題目中的have you got... 為do you have... 的另一種表達方式，本題疑問句即是在問對方「週末有沒有任何計劃」。選項(A)通常是用來回答購物或點餐時店員詢問「就這些嗎？」時，而(B)則是用在有人提出出示票券請求時，可知以上兩個選項均與本題疑問句無關。選項(C)的nope為表示否定的口語用法，並接著詢問對方「有沒有任何建議」，符合常理，顧為正解。

【類型】yes/no 現在完成式疑問句題型

【正解】(C)

30 Where would you like me to put these files?
(A) By the courier.
(B) By the window.
(C) By five o'clock.

你希望我把這些檔案放在哪裡？
(A) 用快遞。
(B) 窗戶邊。
(C) 五點前。

【解析】本題疑問句以where為句首，要問的是希望將檔案放在「何處」。三個選項雖然都是用by這個介系詞，但是意義大不相同。選項(A)的courier為「快遞員」，by courier意指「交由快遞員寄送」，是用來回答物品運送的「方式」；選項(B)的by為地方介系詞，表示「在……旁邊」，by the window 即「在窗戶邊」，是用來表示物品所在「位置」；選項(C)的by為時間介系詞，表示「在……之前」，by five o'clock即「五點之前」，是用來表示動作應完成的「時間」。由上可知只有選項(B)回答了本題疑問句所想知道的「何處」，故為正解。

【類型】where 疑問句題型

【詞彙】
courier 快遞員

【正解】(B)

31 Didn't you use to work in our Los Angeles Branch?
(A) Yes, for two years.
(B) Yes, I will be there.
(C) It didn't work out.

你不是曾經在洛杉磯分部工作過嗎？
(A) 對，兩年的時間。
(B) 對，我會去那裡。
(C) 它沒有成功。

【解析】以否定助動詞為句首的疑問句，通常是要向對方「確認某已知之事」。本題以否定助動詞didn't為句首，詢問對方「不是曾經在LA分公司工作嗎」。選項(A)肯定回答，並進一步表示在該處工作「長達兩年時間」，是最適當的回答。選項(B)是用來回答「是否會去某地」，而選項(C)則是單純陳述某事「沒有結果」，兩者皆與題目所問無關。故(A)為正解。

【類型】否定疑問句題型

【詞彙】
used to 過去曾經／
work out 成功；有結果

【正解】(A)

PART 3

Directions: You will hear some conversations between two people. You will be asked to answer three questions about what the speakers say in each conversation. Select the best response to each question and mark the letter (A), (B), (C) or (D) on your answer sheet. The conversations will not be printed in your test book and will be spoken only one time.

Questions 32-34 refer to the following conversation.

M Good morning. I have an appointment with Mr. Chen at 10 o'clock.

W May I have your name, please?

M My name is Gordon Hsieh. I'm here for the interview.

W Yes. Could you follow me to the reception room? We have some forms for you to fill in first.

M Sure. I was told that there's also a written test.

W Right. You will take the written test after you finish the paperwork.

M Got it. Thanks.

男　早。我跟陳先生約十點。

女　請問你的大名是？

男　我的名字是Gordon謝。我是來面試的。

女　是。你可以跟我來會客室嗎？我們有些表格要先讓你填寫。

男　好。我被告知還要做筆試。

女　對。你在完成這些書面作業之後就會開始做筆試了。

男　明白了。謝謝。

【詞彙】
reception room 接待室／
written test 筆試／
paperwork 書面作業

32 Who most likely is the woman?
(A) A flight attendant.
(B) A taxi driver.
(C) A stay-at-home mother.
(D) A receptionist.

【解析】由對話內容可知男子是前來面試的應徵者，而女子則負責招呼接待這位面試者。關於女子的身份，選項中最有可能的就是公司的櫃檯接待人員，選項(A)(B)(C)皆不可能在公司機關單位做招呼面試者這件事，故正解為(D)。

女子最有可能是誰？
(A) 一名空服員
(B) 一名計程車司機
(C) 一名全職母親
(D) 一名櫃檯接待人員

【類型】說話者身份題型

【詞彙】
stay-at-home mother 全職母親／
receptionist 接待人員

【正解】(D)

---

33 What is the man's purpose of his visit?
(A) To interview for a job.
(B) To attend a conference.
(C) To meet his client.
(D) To collect his parcel.

【解析】由男子在對話中表示I'm here for the interview.（我是來這兒面試的），可知男子來訪的目的是為了要面試工作，故正解為(A)。

男子來訪的目的為何？
(A) 來面試一份工作
(B) 來出席一場會議
(C) 來見他的客戶
(D) 來領他的包裹

【類型】內容主題題型

【正解】(A)

---

34 What is the man going to do next?
(A) Fill in some forms.
(B) Take the written test.
(C) Talk to Mr. Chen.
(D) Interview some applicants.

【解析】雖然對話中有提到written test（筆試），但是女子在對話中表示We have some forms for you to fill in first.（有些表格要先讓你填），並表示書面作業完成後才進行筆試，可知男子接下來要做的事情應該是先填表格，故正解為(A)。

男子接下來將要做什麼？
(A) 填寫一些表格。
(B) 做筆試。
(C) 跟陳先生談話。
(D) 面試一些應徵者。

【類型】提問細節題型

【正解】(A)

女　好的，Zawaski先生。你的履歷上寫著你承辦酒席的經驗很豐富，對嗎？

男A　是的。我在一家本地的餐廳工作了五年。我一開始是學徒，在兩年後就被指定為二廚了。

男B　如你所知，我們正在找一個有定點酒席經驗的人。我們的主廚必須能夠堅持嚴格預算，為大量賓客烹飪及提供飲食服務。

女　你覺得這是你想要的挑戰嗎？

男A　當然。我很樂意接受。

男B　很好。你什麼時候可以開始上班？

【詞彙】
extensive 大量的／
catering 承辦酒席／
apprentice 學徒／
senior cook 二廚／
location catering 外燴／
adhere to 堅持

Questions 35-37 refer to the following conversation.

Woman　OK, Mr. Zawaski. Your resume says that you have extensive experience in catering, right?

Man A　Yes. I had worked in a local restaurant for five years. I began as an apprentice, and was designated as the senior cook after two years.

Man B　As you know, we're looking for someone with experience of location catering. Our chef must be capable of cooking and catering for large numbers of guests adhering to strict budgets.

Woman　Do you think this is the challenge you're looking for?

Man A　Absolutely. I'm willing to take it.

Man B　Good. When can you start?

這是什麼樣的場合？
(A) 協商會議
(B) 工作面試
(C) 專案簡報
(D) 學術研討會

【類型】對話情境題型

【詞彙】
negotiation conference
協商會議／
academic seminar 學術研討會

【正解】(B)

35 What kind of occasion is this?
(A) A negotiation conference
(B) A job interview
(C) A project presentation
(D) An academic seminar.

【解析】由對話中的關鍵字resume（履歷）以及對話最後一句When can you start?（你什麼時候可以開始上班？），可推測這則對話應該是在進行一場工作面試。正解為(B)。

36 Which of the following position is the man applying for?
(A) The headwaiter
(B) The manager
(C) The chef
(D) The accountant

【解析】由對話中女子在解釋職務要求時，提到Our chef must...（我們的主廚必須要……），可知男子應徵的職務應該是chef（主廚），正解為(C)。

男子正在應徵下列哪一個職務？
(A) 領班
(B) 經理
(C) 主廚
(D) 會計

【類型】提問細節題型

【詞彙】
headwaiter 服務生領班

【正解】(C)

37 What does the man mean at the end of the conversation?
(A) The applicant has been offered the job.
(B) The applicant should wait a week for the result.
(C) They are interviewing more applicants later.
(D) The applicant doesn't meet their requirements.

【解析】面試官之一的男子在對話最後表示「很好。你何時可以開始上班？」，按常理可推測男子有意給予男子工作機會，因此詢問他何時可以到職，選項中以(A)所述為最有可能的答案，故選(A)。

在對話最後，男子說的話是什麼意思？
(A) 應徵者得到工作機會了。
(B) 應徵者要等一星期才能得知結果。
(C) 他們稍晚會面試更多應徵者。
(D) 應徵者不符合他們的要求條件。

【類型】對話結果題型

【詞彙】requirement 要求條件

【正解】(A)

男　嘿，Jenny，幹嘛一張臭臉？

女　我真不敢相信我的休假申請又被拒絕了。我好期待要跟家人一起休假的。

男　如果我沒記錯的話，這已經是第二次他們拒絕讓妳休假了。

女　沒錯！上次Wellington女士因為工作量太大，沒准我假。

男　那她這次的理由是什麼？

女　她說研發部沒有人可以替補我的工作。

男　那不公平。休年假是妳的權利，我覺得妳應該跟Wellington女士談談，解決這個問題。

【詞彙】
reject 拒絕／disapprove 不准／
workload 工作量／
R&D (=research and
development) 研發

Questions 38-40 refer to the following conversation.

M Hey, Jenny, why the long face?

W I can't believe my leave request has been denied. I was so looking forward to a vacation with my family.

M If I remember it right, this is the second time they rejected your leave request.

W Exactly! Last time Ms. Wellington disapproved my holiday request because of heavy workload.

M And what's her reason this time?

W She said no one in the R&D department could cover my work.

M That's unfair. It's your right to take annual leave. You should talk with Ms. Wellington to work this out.

女子覺得如何？
(A) 不高興
(B) 困惑
(C) 感恩
(D) 不情願

【類型】提問細節題型

【詞彙】
appreciated 感謝的／
reluctant 不甘不願的；勉強的

【正解】(A)

38 How does the woman feel?
　　(A) Upset
　　(B) Confused
　　(C) Appreciated
　　(D) Reluctant

【解析】由對話一開始男子問女子Why the long face?（為何拉長一張臉），而這通常是當一個人感覺不高興或生氣時會有的表情，因此可知女子心情應該是不高興的，答案為(A)。

39 Which most likely is the woman's job?
(A) An insurance sales agent
(B) An R&D engineer
(C) A librarian
(D) An interior designer

女子的工作最有可能是什麼？
(A) 保險業務人員
(B) 研發工程師
(C) 圖書館員
(D) 室內設計師

【解析】由對話中女子提到上次提出休假申請被拒絕的理由是no one in the R&D department could cover my work（研發部門沒有人能替代我的工作），可知女子應該是在R&D部門工作，選項中最有可能的答案就是R&D工程師，故正解為(B)。

【類型】提問細節題型

【詞彙】
insurance sales agent 保險業務人員／librarian 圖書館員／interior designer 室內設計師

【正解】(B)

---

40 What does the man suggest the woman do?
(A) Resign her position.
(B) Find a decent job.
(C) Speak with her boss.
(D) Revise the contract.

男子建議女子做什麼？
(A) 辭去她的職務。
(B) 找個像樣的工作。
(C) 跟她的主管談談。
(D) 修改合約內容。

【解析】由對話中男子建議女子應該talk with Ms. Wellington to work this out，work sth. out為表示「解決某個問題；找出解決某事的方法」，talk with sb.即「與某人討論」，與選項(C)的speak with同義。由對話內容可知Wellington女士能夠決定要不要批准女子的休假申請，可推測此號人物應該是女子的主管。最適當的答案為(C)。

【類型】提問細節題型

【詞彙】
resign 辭去／decent 像樣的／revise 修改

【正解】(C)

女　Carl，我想召開一個會議討論辦公室翻修計劃。你今天下午可以訂一間會議室嗎？

男　當然。妳希望我預約幾點的會議室呢？

女　一點到三點之間的時間吧。會議大約會開一個小時。

男　妳有特別喜歡哪個會議室嗎？

女　只要能容納十五個人，哪個會議室對我來說都沒差。

男　我知道了。我會跟Joanne查一下哪間會議室可以用，再向妳回報。

★會議室預約表

二月八日	G011室 (6人)	1011室 (10人)	2011室 (18人)	3011室 (25人)
12:00-14:00		行銷部	研發部	人資部
14:00- 16:00	企劃部			財務部

【詞彙】
renovation 翻修／
accommodate 容納／
availability 可用性／
reservation 預約

Questions 41-43 refer to the following conversation and table.

W　Carl, I want to call a meeting to discuss the office renovation plan. Can you book a meeting room this afternoon?

M　Sure. What time do you want me to reserve the meeting room for?

W　Sometime between one and three o'clock. The meeting will take about one hour.

M　Do you have a preferred meeting room?

W　It makes no difference to me, as long as the room can accommodate as many as fifteen people.

M　Got it. I'll check the availability of the meeting rooms with Joanne and get back to you soon.

★Meeting Rooms Reservation Table

08-Feb	Room G011 (6 people)	Room 1011 (10 people)	Room 2011 (18 people)	Room 3011 (25 people)
12:00-14:00		Marketing Dep.	R&D Dep.	HR Dep.
14:00- 16:00	Planning Dep.			Finance Dep.

女子正計劃做什麼？
(A) 召集一場會議。
(B) 將會議延期。
(C) 將會議提前。
(D) 取消一場會議。

【類型】提問細節題型

【詞彙】
convene 召開／
postpone 延後／advance 提前

【正解】(A)

41 What is the woman planning to do?
(A) To convene a meeting.
(B) To postpone a meeting.
(C) To advance a meeting.
(D) To cancel a meeting.

【解析】call a meeting為表示「召開會議」的片語用法。女子在對話一開始便表示I want to call a meeting（我想召開一場會議），選項(A)的動詞convene即「召集」會議之意，符合女子的意圖，正解為(A)。

42 How long will the meeting last?
(A) Approximately one hour.
(B) At least two hours.
(C) Only ten minutes.
(D) No more than three hours.

【解析】由女子在對話中表示The meeting will take about one hour.（會議會開大約一小時），可知會議將持續大約一小時的時間，故正解為(A)。

這場會議將持續多久？
(A) 大約一小時。
(B) 至少兩小時。
(C) 只要十分鐘。
(D) 不會超過三小時。

【類型】提問細節題型

【正解】(A)

43 Look at the table. Which room will the man probably book for the meeting?
(A) Room G011
(B) Room 1011
(C) Room 2011
(D) Room 3011

【解析】女子在對話中提到會議室的唯一條件為 as long as the room can accommodate as many as fifteen people（只要能容納十五個人），可知這間會議室的容納人數不能小於15人，表格中只有可容納18人的2011室在一點至三點這個時段是沒有人訂的，故正解為(C)。

請看表格。男子可能訂哪個會議室開會？
(A) G011室
(B) 1011室
(C) 2011室
(D) 3011室

【類型】圖表對照題型

【正解】(C)

男	婚禮企劃公司的Nikki Sunders 打來說我們得在這星期五之前決定婚宴地點。
女	噢，我可以晚點在想那件事嗎？我正試著列出那天我們要邀請的賓客名單呢。
男	妳估計會有多少賓客出席呢？
女	可能有六十到七十個吧。所以我們需要一個至少能容納七十個賓客的場地。
男	Nikki剛傳給我這個。妳稍早提過妳一直都夢想一個戶外花園婚禮。所以我們應該選哪一個已經很明顯了。

★

玫瑰峰莊園	30 位賓客	室內/戶外泳池
加州飯店	10-50 位賓客	室內/戶外海灘
西林恩農莊	80 位賓客	戶外花園
白廊莊園	60-200 位賓客	室內

【詞彙】
venue 場地／estimate 估計

Questions 44-46 refer to the following conversation and table.

M Nikki Sunders from the wedding planning company called and said that we need to decide on the wedding venue no later than this Friday.

W Oh, can I think about that later? I'm trying to list out all the guests we're gonna invite for the day.

M How many guests do you estimate will attend?

W Probably 60 to 70. So we need a place that accommodates at least 70 guests.

M Well, Nikki just sent me this. You mentioned earlier that you've always dreamed of an outdoor garden wedding. So it's obvious which one we should go for.

★

Rosemont Manor	30 guests	Indoor/ Outdoor Pool
California Hotel	10-50 guests	Indoor/ Outdoor Beach
West Lynn Farm	80 guests	Outdoor Garden
Whitehall Estate	60- 200 guests	Indoor

根據對話內容，說話者正在為什麼做計劃？
(A) 他們的蜜月旅行
(B) 一年一度的家人團聚
(C) 一次部門聚餐
(D) 他們的結婚喜宴

【類型】背景情境題型

【詞彙】
reunion 再團聚／
reception 宴會

【正解】(D)

44 According to the conversation, what are the speakers planning for?
(A) Their honeymoon trip.
(B) An annual family reunion.
(C) A department dinner.
(D) Their wedding reception.

【解析】由對話內容可知女子正在列賓客邀請名單，而且還必須決定wedding venue（婚禮場地），可知說話者應該是正在為了他們的結婚喜宴做準備，故正解為(D)。

45 What does the man urge the woman to do?
(A) Decide on the venue.
(B) Send the invitations.
(C) Return Nikki's call.
(D) Pick a wedding dress.

【解析】由男子在對話中轉告女子we need to decide on the wedding venue no later than this Friday（我們必須在星期五之前決定婚禮場地），並且引導對話，讓女子縮小場地的選擇範圍，可知男子正在催女子決定場地地點，答案為(A)。

男子催促女子做什麼？
(A) 決定地點
(B) 發出邀請
(C) 回Nikki電話
(D) 挑一件結婚禮服

【類型】提問細節題型

【正解】(A)

46 Look at the table. Which location will the couple most likely choose?
(A) Rosemont Manor
(B) West Lynn Farm
(C) California Hotel
(D) Whitehall Estate

【解析】女子表示婚禮場地必須能容納至少70位賓客；加上男子表示女子先前提過夢想辦一場花園婚禮，而表格上的四個地點，只有West Lynn Farm符合以上兩個條件，因此最有可能獲選為婚宴地點，故正解為(B)。

請看表格。這對夫婦最有可能選擇哪個地點？
(A) 玫瑰峰莊園
(B) 西林恩農莊
(C) 加州飯店
(D) 白廊莊園

【類型】圖表對照題型

【正解】(B)

男A	Tracy，妳的寶寶預產期是什麼時候？	**Questions 47-49 refer to the following conversation.**

男A	Tracy，妳的寶寶預產期是什麼時候？
女	三月十二日。
男B	只剩六週了。妳打算什麼時候請產假？
女	這個嘛，我今年可以放七天年假，所以我想要在休產假前先休年假。我打算二月十日就開始放假，不過Freeman先生還沒有批准我的休假申請。
男A	別擔心。我相信他會的。
男B	妳休假時誰要代理妳的工作？
女	Jessica。

Questions 47-49 refer to the following conversation.

ManA	Tracy, when is your baby due?
Woman	March 12.
Man B	Only six more weeks to go! When are you planning to take maternity leave?
Woman	Well, I'm entitled to seven days of yearly leave this year, so I'd like to take my annual leave before maternity leave. I'm thinking to start my leave from February 10, but Mr. Freeman hasn't approved my leave application yet.
Man A	Don't worry. I'm sure he will.
Man B	Who's gonna cover your position while you're on leave?
Woman	Jessica.

【詞彙】
due 到期的／
maternity leave 產假／
be entitled to 享有／
leave application 休假申請

Tracy為何正在計劃休長假？
(A) 她將出國進修。
(B) 她將要生寶寶。
(C) 她將出國度假。
(D) 她將要動手術。

【類型】提問細節題型

【正解】(B)

47 Why is Tracy planning to take a long leave from work?
(A) She's going abroad for further study.
(B) She's going to have a baby.
(C) She's going on a vacation abroad.
(D) She's going to have a surgery.

【解析】由對話以Tracy何時休maternity leave（產假）為主軸，因此可知Tracy休假的原因是因為她的孩子即將出生，故正解為(B)。

48 According to the conversation, which statement is true?

(A) Tracy is going to have her first baby.
(B) Tracy is on her annual leave at the moment.
(C) Tracy hasn't applied for her leave yet.
(D) Tracy will give birth to her baby in about six weeks.

【解析】由Tracy在對話中說出自己的預產期之後,男同事表示Only six weeks to go(只剩六星期了),可知Tracy將在大約六週後生下寶寶,正解為(D)。其他選項所述皆與對話內容不符。

根據對話內容,哪項敘述正確?
(A) Tracy將要迎接她的第一個寶寶。
(B) Tracy此刻正在休年假。
(C) Tracy還沒有提出休假申請。
(D) Tracy將在大約六週後生下寶寶。

【類型】提問細節題型

【詞彙】
give birth to sb. 生下某人

【正解】(D)

---

49 What does the man mean?

(A) Tracy's leave application will be approved.
(B) Tracy shouldn't take her annual leave now.
(C) He didn't receive Tracy's leave application.
(D) Tracy's boss won't grant her leave.

【解析】本題是要根據男子所說的Don't worry. I'm sure he will.(別擔心,我相信他會的)這句話來推測男子所要表示的意思。由前文Tracy表示Freeman先生還沒批准她的休假申請,男子表示「他會的」,意即「Freeman先生將會准妳的假」,故正解為(A)。

男子所言是什麼意思?
(A) Tracy的休假申請將會被核准。
(B) Tracy不應該現在就休年假。
(C) 他沒有收到Tracy的休假申請。
(D) Tracy的主管不會准她假。

【類型】提問細節題型

【詞彙】
grant sb.'s leave 准某人休假

【正解】(A)

女　哈囉，Norwaski先生。我是杰狄運動用品專賣店的Cathy。我是打電話來告訴你我們已經收到您的訂單了。

男　噢，嗨，Cathy。好。我幾分鐘前剛完成付款。

女　對，您的付款已經成功。我想跟你說你的訂單已經受理而且已經在今天寄出了。

男　太好了。所以我明天就會收到我的有氧健身車了，對不對？

女　對，如果你明天下午五點前沒收到，請立刻通知我們。

男　好。謝謝。我等不及了。

Questions 50-52 refer to the following conversation.

W Hello, Mr. Norwaski. This is Cathy from J&D Sports Equipment Shop. I'm calling to inform you that we have received your order.

M Oh, hi, Cathy. Good. I just completed my payment a few minutes ago.

W Yes, your payment was successful. I'd like to tell you that your order was processed and shipped today.

M Great. So I will receive my aero bike tomorrow, right?

W Yes. Please let us know immediately if you don't receive it by 5 p.m. tomorrow.

M OK. Thanks. I can't wait.

女子為何要打這通電話？
(A) 催促男子繳付帳款。
(B) 請求男子提前出貨。
(C) 取消一筆她稍早下的訂單。
(D) 告訴男子他們已經寄出他訂的東西。

【類型】提問細節題型

【正解】(D)

---

50 Why is the woman calling?
　　(A) To urge the man to make the payment.
　　(B) To request the man to advance the delivery.
　　(C) To cancel an order she made earlier.
　　(D) To tell the man they have shipped his order.

【解析】女子在對話中向男子表示他的訂單已經processed and shipped（受理且寄出），因此可知選項(D)所述符合對話內容，故(D)為正解。

51 According to the conversation, which statement is true?

    (A) The man has received his purchase.

    (B) The woman hasn't received the payment.

    (C) The delivery will be delayed for 24 hours.

    (D) The man's order has been delivered.

【解析】由女子表示Your payment was successful（付款成功），可知女子應該已經收到貨款，故選項(B)可先刪除。女子在對話中表示訂單已經受理，商品也已經寄出，會在明天下午五點前送達，因此選項(A)(C)皆不符對話內容，只有選項(D)所述正確，故(D)為正解。

根據對話內容，哪項敘述正確？

(A) 男子已經收到訂購的東西。

(B) 女子尚未收到貨款。

(C) 出貨將會延遲24小時。

(D) 男子的訂單已經出貨了。

【類型】提問細節題型

【正解】(D)

---

52 When can the man expect to get his aero bike?

    (A) No later than 5 o'clock tomorrow.

    (B) By 5 p.m. today.

    (C) In two weeks.

    (D) Within 7 days.

【解析】由女子在對話最後表示Please let us know immediately if you don't receive it by 5 p.m. tomorrow.（如果明天下午五點前沒收到，請通知我們），可知男子訂購的東西應該會在明天下午五點之前送到，正解為(A)。

男子何時預計可以拿到他的有氧健身車？

(A) 明天下午五點之前。

(B) 今天五點以前。

(C) 兩星期之後。

(D) 七天之內。

【類型】提問細節題型

【正解】(A)

女 嗨，我想寄這個包裹。

男 包裹裡是什麼？

女 只有一些書和衣服。

男 我要秤一下你的包裹。可以請你把它放在秤台上嗎？

女 沒問題。這包裹的運費多少錢？

男 是這樣的，運費是根據重量來收費。這包裹的費用是110元。

女 好的。這裡是110元。謝謝。

★ 一般郵資/普通包裹

重量	費用
5公斤以下	70
10公斤以下	90
15公斤以下	110
20公斤以下	135

【詞彙】
platform scale 檯秤

Questions 53-55 refer to the following conversation and table.

W Hi, I'd like to send this parcel.

M What's inside the parcel?

W There are only some books and clothes.

M I need to weigh your parcel. Could you put it on the platform scale, please?

W Sure. How much is the shipping cost of this parcel?

M Well, the shipping cost is charged by weight. The price of this parcel will be $110.

W OK. Here's $110. Thanks.

★ Ordinary Postage Rates/ Surface Parcel

Weight	Rate
Up to 5 kg	70
Up to 10 kg	90
Up to 15 kg	110
Up to 20 kg	135

這段對話最可能發生在何處？
(A) 郵局
(B) 體育館
(C) 銀行
(D) 電視台

【類型】對話背景題型

【詞彙】
stadium 體育館

【正解】(A)

53 Where most likely is this conversation taking place?
(A) In a post office.
(B) At the stadium.
(C) In a bank.
(D) At a TV station.

【解析】由對話內容可知這裡是可以寄運包裹的地方，除了民間宅配機構之外，最有可能提供郵務服務的就是郵局，故正解為(A)。

54 How did the man decide the postage rate of the parcel?
(A) According to its superficial measurements.
(B) According to its weight.
(C) According to the items inside.
(D) According to the distance to the delivery destination.

男子如何決定包裹寄運價格？
(A) 根據面積
(B) 根據重量
(C) 根據內容物
(D) 根據運送距離

【類型】提問細節題型

【詞彙】
postage rate 郵資費用／
superficial measurement 面積

【正解】(B)

【解析】由對話中男子表示the shipping cost is charged by weight（運費根據重量收費），可知包裹的重量將決定運費多寡，正解為(B)。

---

55 Look at the table. How much does the parcel probably weigh?
(A) 3.8 kg
(B) 8.5 kg
(C) 13.6 kg
(D) 18.7 kg

請看表格。這個包裹可能有多重？
(A) 3.8公斤
(B) 8.5公斤
(C) 13.6公斤
(D) 18.7公斤

【類型】圖表對照題型

【正解】(C)

【解析】男子表示女子的包裹運費為110元，而由本題所附的包裹重量價格對照表可知10-15公斤之內的包裹收費皆為110元，超過15公斤就要收135元，因此選項中以(C)的13.6公斤符合110元的重量標準，故正解為(C)。

女　哈囉，先生。可以請您將托
　　盤餐桌放下來嗎？

男　噢，當然。抱歉。

女　沒關係。您想要雞肉還是豬
　　肉呢？

孩　我的兒童餐呢？

男　安靜，Simon。它待會就來
　　了。我要豬肉，麻煩你。

孩　我現在好餓噢。我沒辦法等
　　了。

女　兒童餐已經要送來了。只是
　　你需要多一點點耐心，因為
　　它會帶著一個驚喜來噢！

孩　一個驚喜？耶！

女　你的日式豬排飯，先生。請
　　享用。

【詞彙】
tray table 托盤餐桌／
kid's meal 兒童餐

Questions 56-58 refer to the following conversation.

Woman Hello, sir. Would you please put down your tray table?

Man Oh, sure. Sorry.

Woman No problem. Would you like chicken or pork?

Boy What about my kid's meal?

Man Quiet, Simon. It will come later. I'll have pork please.

Boy I'm hungry now! I can't wait!

Woman The kid's meal is on the way. You just need to have a bit more patience, because it's gonna come with a surprise.

Boy A surprise? Yay!

Woman Your Japanese pork chop with rice, sir. Please enjoy.

這段對話最有可能發生在何處？
(A) 自助餐廳
(B) 飛機上
(C) 美食廣場
(D) 速食餐廳

【類型】對話背景題型

【詞彙】
buffet restaurant 自助餐廳／
food court 美食廣場

【正解】(B)

---

56 Where most likely is the conversation taking place?
(A) In a buffet restaurant.
(B) On an airplane.
(C) At the food court.
(D) In a fast food restaurant.

【解析】由女子在對話中第一句提到的關鍵字tray table（托盤餐桌），即可知說話者正在飛機上，因為一般只有飛機上的餐桌是可折起貼在前方座位後面的托盤餐桌，故正解為(B)。

57 According to the conversation, what is true about the man?
(A) He is the captain of the flight.
(B) He is a flight attendant.
(C) He is the boy's father.
(D) He likes pork better than chicken.

根據對話內容，關於男子，何者正確？
(A) 他是這班飛機的機長。
(B) 他是一名空服員。
(C) 他是男孩的父親。
(D) 他喜歡豬肉勝過雞肉。

【解析】雖然由男子知道男孩的名字，並且請他安靜，可推測兩人應該是彼此認識，但卻沒有更多資訊可以確定兩人之間的關係，因此選項(C)並不是最適當的描述。男子在雞肉與豬肉兩種餐點中，選擇了豬肉，可知比起雞肉，男子更喜歡豬肉，因此選項(D)為正解。由對話內容可推測男子應該是乘客，並非機長，而且也不是空服員，因此選項(A)(B)皆不需考慮。

【類型】提問細節題型

【詞彙】
captain 機長

【正解】(D)

58 What do we know about the boy's meal?
(A) It's meat-free.
(B) It comes with a gift.
(C) It's complimentary.
(D) It's undercooked.

關於男孩的餐點，我們知道什麼？
(A) 它是沒有肉的。
(B) 它會附上一份禮物。
(C) 它是免費贈送的。
(D) 它沒有煮熟。

【解析】由女子在對話中對kid's meal的描述中只提到it's gonna come with a surprise（它將附有一個驚喜），並未提到餐點內容，因此選項(A)(D)皆可先刪除不考慮；依常理，飛機上的餐點費用都是包含在機票費用內的，因此並非免費贈送，故(C)亦不正確。有些飛機上的兒童餐，除了餐點之外，還會附上一個小玩具，這對孩子來說是一個額外的驚喜，因此選項(B)為最有可能的答案，正解為(B)。

【類型】提問細節題型

【詞彙】
complimentary 贈送的

【正解】(B)

女　我已經飽到喉嚨了。

男A　我這個也吃不完。我們把剩菜打包當明天中餐吧。

女　不好意思。可以給我們兩個外帶餐盒打包剩菜嗎？

男B　當然可以。但為了怕你們不知道所以跟您說一下，我們已經不再提供免費外帶餐盒了。

男A　什麼意思？

男B　餐廳規定每個外帶餐盒要收費五元。

女　這我覺得不合理，不過好吧，我就買兩個外帶餐盒，因為我不想浪費食物。

【詞彙】

up to one's throat 飽到喉嚨了／
takeout box 外帶餐盒

Questions 59-61 refer to the following conversation.

Woman　I'm stuffed.

Man A　I can't finish this either. Let's pack the leftovers for tomorrow's lunch.

Woman　Excuse me. Can you please give us two takeout boxes for the leftovers?

Man B　Sure. But in case you don't know, we don't provide free takeout boxes anymore.

Man A　What do you mean?

Man B　It's this restaurant's policy to charge NT$5 for each takeout box.

Woman　It seems unreasonable for me, but alright, I'll buy two takeout boxes because I don't want to waste the food.

這段對話正在進行什麼事？
(A) 說話者正在決定要點什麼。
(B) 說話者正在討論要去哪裡吃。
(C) 說話者正在抱怨食物。
(D) 其中兩位說話者想要打包食物。

【類型】內容主題題型

【正解】(D)

59 What is taking place in this conversation?
　(A) The speakers are deciding what to order.
　(B) The speakers are discussing where to eat.
　(C) The speakers are complaining about the food.
　(D) Two of the speakers want to pack their food.

【解析】由對話內容可推知有兩位用餐者因為吃不下，正向服務生要外帶餐盒要打包剩菜，因此正確描述為(D)，故(D)為正解。

60 Which statement about the restaurant is true?
(A) It doesn't provide takeout service.
(B) It provides home delivery service.
(C) It doesn't provide free takeout boxes.
(D) It encourages customers to bring leftovers home.

【解析】由對話中服務生表示we don't provide free takeout boxes anymore（我們不再提供免費外帶餐盒），可知正確答案為(C)。

關於這家餐廳哪項敘述正確？
(A) 它不提供外帶服務。
(B) 它提供宅配到府服務。
(C) 它不提供免費外帶餐盒。
(D) 它鼓勵顧客帶剩菜回家。

【類型】提問細節題型

【詞彙】
home delivery 宅配

【正解】(C)

61 How does the woman see the restaurant's takeout policy?
(A) Advantageous
(B) Irrational
(C) Embarrassing
(D) Appropriate

【解析】針對餐廳對外帶餐盒收費這個規定，女子表示It seems unreasonable for me，可知女子認為這個規定並不合理，unreasonable與irrational這兩個形容詞都可以用來表示「荒謬的；不合理的」，故(B)為正解。

女子怎麼看餐廳的外帶規定？
(A) 有利的
(B) 不合理的
(C) 令人尷尬的
(D) 恰當的

【類型】提問細節題型

【詞彙】
advantageous 有利的／
irrational 荒謬的

【正解】(B)

女　嗨，Eddie，我是布萊頓化妝品公司的Amanda。

男　哈囉 Amanda。我正好要打給妳呢。謝謝妳寄給我妳們最新的型錄。它剛寄到。

女　不客氣。欸，其實我是打電話來跟你說我們剛剛在型錄裡發現一些錯誤。

男　是喔？

女　對啊。抱歉。我現在正傳真有錯的項目還有更正單給你。

男　好。正在收了。

★

頁數	商品編號	產品名稱	錯誤	更正
4	EM10023	眼線筆	$1,299	$1,099
8	FD20139	粉底液	5色	3色
15	CC50288	氣墊粉餅	防曬係數15	防曬係數50

【詞彙】
catalogue 型錄／error 錯誤／
description 敘述／
correction 訂正／
eyeliner marker 眼線筆／
foundation 粉底液／
cushion compact 氣墊粉餅

Questions 62-64 refer to the following conversation and the list.

W　Hi, Eddie, this is Amanda from Brighten Cosmetics.

M　Hello, Amanda. I was just about to call you. Thanks for sending me your latest catalogue. It just arrived.

W　You're welcome. Well, actually, I am calling to tell you that we just found a few errors in it.

M　You did?

W　Yeah. Sorry about that. I'm faxing the list of items with incorrect descriptions as well as the corrections to you right now.

M　OK. Receiving.

★

Page	Item No.	Product Name	error	correction
4	EM10023	Eyeliner Marker	$1,299	$1,099
8	FD20139	Foundation	5 shades	3 shades
15	CC50288	Cushion Compact	SPF 15	SPF 50

女子來電目的為何？
(A) 宣布新產品上市。
(B) 為目錄裡的錯誤致歉。
(C) 再次確認她的飯店訂房。
(D) 提醒男子未付帳款。

【類型】提問細節題型

【詞彙】
unsettled 未付清的

【正解】(B)

62 Why is the woman calling?
(A) To announce a new product launch.
(B) To apologize for the errors in the catalogue.
(C) To reconfirm her hotel reservation.
(D) To remind the man of his unsettled payment.

【解析】對話中女子表示I am calling to tell you that we just found a few errors in it.（我是打來告訴你我們發現裡面幾個錯誤），並且在後面對話中表示Sorry about that（抱歉），可知這通電話的目的是為了型錄中出錯致歉，故正解為(B)。

63 By what means did the woman send the corrections to the man?
(A) By a courier
(B) By freight
(C) By fax
(D) By email

女子用什麼方式將修改單傳給男子？
(A) 快遞
(B) 貨運
(C) 傳真
(D) 電子郵件

【解析】由I'm faxing the... corrections to you right now.（我現在正把……訂正傳真過去給你）這句話，可知女子是用「傳真」的方式將型錄訂正傳給男子，正解為(C)。

【類型】提問細節題型

【詞彙】
courier 快遞／freight 貨運

【正解】(C)

---

64 Look at the list. Which item has been mispriced?
(A) Eyeliner marker
(B) Foundation
(C) Cushion compact
(D) None of the above.

請看清單。哪一個商品標價錯誤？
(A) 眼線筆
(B) 粉底液
(C) 氣墊粉餅
(D) 以上皆非

【解析】題目中的misprice意指「給錯標價」。清單上的三個錯誤中，只有eyeliner marker的錯誤是標價上出錯，由原本的$1299改為$1099，其他兩個錯誤都是產品敘述上出錯，故正解為(A)。

【類型】圖表對照題型

【詞彙】
misprice 標錯價格

【正解】(A)

女 哈囉。我想租個一家四口用的帳篷，從一月三日起租三個晚上。

男 沒問題。妳要找的是哪一種形式的帳篷，圓頂帳、快速帳、充氣帳、隧道帳、錐形帳還是拖車帳？

女 呃，……基本款的圓頂帳就可以了。

男 當然。妳的預算是多少？

女 喔，我真的希望不要是租金會超過每晚700元的。

男 我們來看一下這張表格，找出適合妳的帳篷。

★圓頂帳租金表

品牌	價格/每晚
The North Face	800
Marmot	1200
MSR	900
Big Agnes	650

Questions 65-67 refer to the following conversation.

W Hello. I'd like to rent a tent for a family of four for three nights from January 3.

M Certainly. What type of tent are you looking for, a dome tent, an instant tent, an inflatable tent, a tunnel tent, a teepee or a trailer tent?

W Uh, ...I'll just go for a basic dome tent.

M Sure. Your budget?

W Well, I surely hope the rent is not anything more than $700 per night.

M Let's check the table for a right tent for you.

★Rates for Dome Tents

Brands	Rates/per night
The North Face	800
Marmot	1200
MSR	900
Big Agnes	650

說話者位在何處？
(A) 帳篷租借行
(B) 飯店大廳
(C) 營地
(D) 度假勝地

【類型】對話者身份題型

【正解】(A)

65 Where are the speakers?
　(A) At a tent rental shop
　(B) At the hotel lobby
　(C) At the campsite
　(D) At a holiday resort

【解析】由本段對話以rent a tent（租借帳篷）為發展主軸，可知說話者應該是在一個有提供帳篷租借的地方，選項中最有可能的地點即帳篷租借行，故正解為(A)。

66 According to the conversation, which statement is true?
(A) The woman can't afford a teepee.
(B) The woman's budget for the tent rent is limited.
(C) The woman prefers a tunnel tent.
(D) The woman will buy a family tent.

根據對話內容,哪項敘述正確?
(A) 女子買不起圓錐形帳篷。
(B) 女子租帳篷的預算有限。
(C) 女子比較喜歡隧道帳。
(D) 女子將會買一個家庭帳。

【類型】提問細節題型

【正解】(B)

【解析】由對話內容可知女子的目的是要「租帳篷」而不是「買帳篷」,因此選項(A)(D)都可先刪去不選。女子在回應男子想要租什麼帳篷的問題時,回答要go for a dome tent(選擇圓頂帳),片語go for在這裡為「選擇,寧要」之意,可知選項(C)所述亦不正確。女子在回應男子有關預算問題時,表示hope the rent is not anything more than $700 per night(希望租金不要超過一晚七百),可推知女子是有租借帳篷的預算的,故正解為(B)。

---

67 Look at the table. Which tent will the woman probably rent?
(A) The North Face one
(B) The Marmot one
(C) The MSR one
(D) The Big Agnes one

請看表格。女子可能會租哪一個帳篷?
(A) North Face牌的帳篷
(B) Marmot 牌的帳篷
(C) MSR 牌的帳篷
(D) Big Agnes 牌的帳篷

【類型】圖表對照題型

【正解】(D)

【解析】由表格上的帳篷租金價格看來,只有Big Agnes品牌的帳篷每晚租金$650,符合女子的預算,因此女子最有可能會租這個牌子的帳篷,正解為(D)。

男 嗨，Emily。妳要到這裡了嗎？

女 喔，Jerry，我很抱歉。我應該要早點打給你的。我們的午餐會我去不成了。

男 發生什麼事了？

女 我老闆剛剛召開了一個緊急會議。我沒辦法缺席。

男 噢，那我們的會怎麼辦？妳知道採購電子零件的合約這個星期就要簽好呀。

女 我知道。我們把它延到明天可以嗎？明天同一時間。

男 好吧。到時候見。

Questions 68-70 refer to the following conversation.

M Hi, Emily. Are you on your way here yet?

W Oh, Jerry, I'm sorry. I should have called you earlier. I won't be able to make it to our luncheon.

M What happened?

W My boss just called an emergency meeting. I can't be absent.

M Well, what about our meeting? You know the contract for the purchase of electronic instruments needs to be signed by this week.

W I know. Is it okay if we put it off until tomorrow? The same time tomorrow.

M Alright. See you then.

說話者正在做什麼？
(A) 問路
(B) 重新安排會面
(C) 跟彼此爭執
(D) 抱怨他們的工作

【類型】內容主題題型

【正解】(B)

68 What are the speakers doing?
　(A) Asking directions.
　(B) Rescheduling their meeting.
　(C) Arguing with each other.
　(D) Complaining about their work.

【解析】由對話內容可知女子因為臨時要開會，無法前往赴約，因此跟男子協調，將會面時間延至明天，故正解為(B)。

69 Why can't the woman make it to the appointment with the man?
(A) She has to attend a more important meeting.
(B) She is not feeling very well today.
(C) She got trapped in the traffic jam.
(D) She hasn't had the contract ready.

【解析】女子在對話中表示她的老闆just called an emergency meeting（剛召開緊急會議）而她不能缺席，可知這個緊急會議比她與男子的午餐會更重要，故正解為(A)。其他選項所述與對話內容不符，故不需考慮。

女子為何要延後與男子的約會？
(A) 她必須出席一場更重要的會議。
(B) 她今天覺得不太舒服。
(C) 她被困在交通堵塞裡了。
(D) 她還沒有將合約準備好。

【類型】提問細節題型

【詞彙】
trap 堵塞

【正解】(A)

---

70 When will the speakers meet up?
(A) Sometime next week.
(B) At lunchtime tomorrow.
(C) At two o'clock this afternoon.
(D) This Friday evening.

【解析】女子在對話一開始表示I won't be able to make it to our luncheon.（我無法去成我們的午餐會了），luncheon指的是「與午餐同時進行的會議」。由兩人對話最後將會面時間改到 the same time tomorrow（明天同一時間），可知明天也將是午餐時間會面，故正解 (B)。

說話者將會在何時碰面？
(A) 下星期某個時間
(B) 明天午餐時間
(C) 今天下午兩點
(D) 這個星期五晚上

【類型】提問細節題型

【正解】(B)

Directions: You will hear some talks given by a single speaker. You will be asked to answer three questions about what the speaker says in each talk. Select the best response to each question and mark the letter (A), (B), (C) or (D) on your answer sheet. The talks will not be printed in your test book and will be spoken only one time.

Questions 71-73 refer to the following message.

W Good morning, Mrs. Tung. This is Vicky calling from Hans Appliance Shop. We received your letter complaining about the defective electric rice cooker. We are sorry for delivering an imperfect product and will send you a replacement today. The shipment will arrive at the same delivery address around three this afternoon. Our courier will retrieve the defective item at the same time. If three o'clock is not a convenient time for you, please return my call as soon as possible. Thank you very much.

女 早安，童太太。我是漢斯家電行的Vicky。我們收到您關於瑕疵電鍋的抱怨信函了。我們很抱歉寄了一個有瑕疵的商品，而且今天就會寄一個替換品過去給您。貨會在今天下午三點左右送達同一個寄件地址。我們的快遞也會同時將瑕疵商品取回。如果三點這個時間對您來說不方便，請您立刻回電給我。非常感謝您。

【詞彙】
defective 有瑕疵的／
electric rice cooker 煮飯電鍋／
imperfect 有瑕疵的、不完美的／
replacement 替換品／
shipment 運輸的貨物／
retrieve 取回、收回

71 Why is the woman leaving this message?
(A) To complain about the defective product.
(B) To explain for the late delivery.
(C) To apologize for the unsatisfactory product.
(D) To request for a replacement.

【解析】女子在留言中表示We are sorry for delivering an imperfect product...（我們對於寄給您有瑕疵的商品感到抱歉……）可知女子留言的目的是要向對方致歉，正解為(C)。

女子為何要留這通留言？
(A) 為了抱怨瑕疵品。
(B) 為了解釋延遲交貨的原因。
(C) 為了不符要求的產品致歉。
(D) 為了要求更換品。

【類型】訊息重點題型

【正解】(C)

---

72 How does the woman deal with the complaint about faulty products?
(A) Send a replacement immediately.
(B) Accept returns unconditionally.
(C) Refund the money to customers.
(D) Compensate customers for their loss.

【解析】由這段訊息中，女子在為寄出瑕疵品道歉之後，表示... will send you a replacement today（今天將會送替換品給您），可知她處理投訴瑕疵產品的方式為立刻寄替換品給顧客，幫顧客換貨。正解為(A)。

女子如何處理有關瑕疵產品的投訴？
(A) 立刻寄上替換品。
(B) 無條件接受退貨。
(C) 退錢給顧客。
(D) 賠償顧客損失。

【類型】提問細節題型

【詞彙】
unconditionally 無條件地／
refund 退款／compensate 賠償

【正解】(A)

---

73 According to this message, which statement is incorrect?
(A) The replacement will arrive today.
(B) The courier will withdraw the faulty item.
(C) The shop is responsible for their products.
(D) Mrs. Tung was pleased with the rice cooker.

【解析】訊息留言一開始即表示We received your letter complaining...（我們收到您來信抱怨……），可知童太太對收到的產品並不滿意，選項(D)所述並不正確，故為正解。

根據這段留言，哪項敘述不正確？
(A) 更換品將會在今天送達。
(B) 快遞會回收瑕疵品。
(C) 店家對他們的產品負責。
(D) 童太太對電鍋很滿意。

【類型】提問細節題型

【詞彙】
withdraw 取回

【正解】(D)

加★部分為多益新題型以及相關小提醒，考生要特別注意喔！

男 女士們，早安！謝謝你們的等待！終於到了我們一年一度的清倉特賣了！這是一年之中最適合買任何東西的時刻。所有你在店內看到的商品今天全部都打三折！對，只有今天！請容我提醒各位，在您購買所有商品之前，一定要先試穿試戴，因為我們不接受任何出清商品的退貨。我們有足夠的試衣間，就在結帳櫃檯旁邊。感謝您的耐心。現在請將你們的購物推車準備好吧！

【詞彙】
fitting room 試衣間／
checkout counter 結帳櫃檯／
shopping trolley 購物推車

這間店最可能是賣什麼的？
(A) 家用電器
(B) 女性服飾
(C) 男性運動服裝
(D) 童書及玩具

【類型】廣播背景題型

【詞彙】
accessory 飾品／
sportswear 運動服裝

【正解】(B)

Questions 74-76 refer to the following announcement.

M Good morning, ladies! Thanks for waiting! It's finally time for our yearly clearance sale! It is the best time to buy anything during the year. All items you see in the store are 70% off today! Yes, for today only! Please allow me to remind you that you must try on everything before you buy it, as we do not accept returns on any clearance items. We have plenty of fitting rooms right next to the checkout counter. Thanks for your patience. Now please get your shopping trolleys ready!

74 What most likely is this store selling?
    (A) Household appliances
    (B) Women's clothes and accessories
    (C) Men's sportswear
    (D) Children's books and toys

【解析】一開始說話者打招呼的對象就是ladies（女士們），因此推測這家店的主要目標顧客為女性；此外，說話者提醒聽話者要在購買商品前先try on everything（試穿或試戴每件商品），可推斷這應該是一間女性的服飾店，最有可能的答案為(B)。

75 According to this talk, what is going to take place?
(A) A beauty contest
(B) A job fair
(C) An annual clearance sale
(D) An opening ceremony

【解析】由男子在廣播中表示It's finally time for our yearly clearance sale!（終於到了我們一年一度清倉特賣的時候），因此正解為(C)。

根據這段談話，什麼事件即將開始進行？
(A) 選美比賽
(B) 職業博覽會
(C) 年度出清特賣
(D) 開幕典禮

【類型】內容主題題型

【詞彙】
beauty contest 選美比賽

【正解】(C)

76 Why should the listeners try on everything before they buy it?
(A) No returns on clearance items
(B) There are plenty of fitting rooms.
(C) In case they don't know their sizes.
(D) Not all items are in stock.

【解析】說話者在廣播中提醒所有人在購物之前要先試穿試戴，原因是we do not accept returns on any clearance items（不接受出清商品退貨），故此題正解為(A)。

為什麼聽話者應該要在買每樣東西前先試穿？
(A) 出清商品不能退貨
(B) 有足夠的試衣間
(C) 以免他們不知道自己的尺寸
(D) 並非所有商品都有存貨

【類型】提問細節題型

【詞彙】
in case 以免／
in stock 有存貨的

【正解】(A)

男 女士先生們，歡迎光臨歡樂地遊樂園。我知道你們全都很期待能在歡樂地玩得很開心。在你們衝向你們最喜歡的遊樂設施之前，容我提醒各位，牛仔饒舌歌手從十點到四點，每兩小時就會在新公園廣場為您演出。同時，別忘了園內有很多值得一看的活動和節目表演。你們可以在園區地圖找到每日的活動時刻表。現在樂園開門了！各位請開心地玩吧！

★固定節目

胡迪的奇幻旅行	上午10:00 /下午13:00
歡笑製造公司	上午11:00 /下午15:00
動物們的華麗遊行	下午3:00
煙火秀	下午8:30

Questions 77-79 refer to the following greetings and schedule

M Welcome, ladies and gentlemen, to Joy Land Amusement Park. I know all of you are looking forward to having fun at Joy Land. Before you rush to your favorite park attractions, allow me to remind you the Cowboy Rappers will perform for you on New Park Square every two hours from 10 to 4. Also, don't forget that there are many events and shows worth seeing in this park. You can find our daily events schedule on the park map. Now the park is open! Have fun everyone!

★**Regular Entertainments**

Magical Trip with Hoody	10:00 a.m./13:00 p.m.
Laughter Maker Company	11:00 a.m./15:00 p.m.
Animals' Fantasy Parade	3:00 p.m.
Fireworks Show	8:30 p.m.

根據談話，何者每隔一小時會進行一次？
(A) 胡迪的奇幻旅行
(B) 動物們的華麗遊行
(C) 牛仔饒舌歌手的表演
(D) 歡笑製造公司

【類型】提問細節題型

【正解】(C)

77 According to the talk, what takes place every other hour?
(A) Magical Trip with Hoody
(B) Animals' Fantasy Parade
(C) Cowboy Rappers' show
(D) Laughter Maker Company

【解析】「every other＋時間單位」為「每隔二（時間單位）」的表示法。由the Cowboy Rappers will perform... every two hours（牛仔饒舌歌手每兩個小時就會表演）這句話，可知每隔兩小時就會表演一次的是Cowboy Rappers，故正解為(C)。

78 Where can the event schedule be found?
(A) At the entrance of the park
(B) On the map of the park
(C) Behind the ticket
(D) On the cover of the manual

【解析】由You can find our daily events schedule on the park map.（你可以在園區地圖上找到每日活動時刻表），可知答案為(B)。

哪裡可以找到活動時刻表？
(A) 樂園入口
(B) 園區地圖
(C) 門票後面
(D) 手冊封面

【類型】提問細節題型

【詞彙】
entrance 入口／manual 小冊子

【正解】(B)

79 Look at the schedule. When does the park give a fireworks display?
(A) 10:00 a.m.
(B) 11:00 a.m.
(C) 3:00 p.m.
(D) 8:30 p.m.

【解析】由時刻表上的各項活動時間看來，可知煙火秀的表演時間是在晚上八點半，故正解為(D)。

請看時刻表。樂園何時會放煙火秀？
(A) 上午10:00
(B) 上午11:00
(C) 下午3:00
(D) 下午8:30

【類型】圖表對照題型

【詞彙】
display 表演

【正解】(D)

女 嗯，我必須說我真的非常為你們所作的報告感到驕傲。謝謝你們所有人對這次報告所付出的努力。報告內容非常的具教育性，我相信在場的每個人一定跟我一樣印象深刻。現在，在我們結束今天的座談會之前，我們要宣布海報競賽的獲勝者。我希望每個人都投票了。那麼在這裡我要歡迎美中生態研究中心的副院長Jason Molly來做這項宣布。

【詞彙】
wrap up 完成、結束／
symposium 座談會／
deputy director 副院長

Questions 80-82 refer to the following talk.

W Well, I must say that I am very proud of the presentation that you made. Thank you all for the effort you've put into the presentation. It was very informative and I'm sure everyone here is as impressed as I am. Now before we wrap up our symposium, we're gonna announce the winner of our poster competition. I hope everybody voted. So here I'd like to welcome Jason Molly, the deputy director of the US-China Ecology Research Center, to make this announcement.

這是個什麼樣的場合？
(A) 就職典禮
(B) 科學座談會
(C) 頒獎典禮
(D) 大學畢業典禮

【類型】談話背景題型

【詞彙】
induction 就職／
commencement 畢業典禮

【正解】(B)

---

80 What kind of occasion is this?
   (A) An induction ceremony
   (B) A scientific symposium
   (C) An award ceremony
   (D) A university commencement

【解析】由女子在致辭時提到before we wrap up our symposium（在我們結束座談會之前），可知這是一場symposium（座談會），因此選項中最可能的答案就是選項(B)的科學座談會，故正解為(B)。

81 Who most likely is the speaker?
(A) The host of the symposium
(B) The supervisor of the presentation
(C) The winner of the poster competition
(D) The director of the Ecology Research Center

說話者最有可能是什麼身份？
(A) 座談會的主持人
(B) 簡報的指導者
(C) 海報比賽的獲勝者
(D) 生態研究中心的負責人

【解析】由說話者的致辭內容除了為活動做總結，並且介紹頒獎人上台，可推斷其應為這場活動的主持人，故正解為(A)。說話者在致辭中，表達對做簡報者的讚許，但並沒有更多資訊顯示她是簡報的指導者，故(B)不是最適當的答案。

【類型】說話者身份題型

【詞彙】
supervisor 指導者

【正解】(A)

82 What is Jason Molly going to do?
(A) To announce the winner of the poster competition.
(B) To give a presentation about his ecology research.
(C) To give his comments on the presentation.
(D) To answer the questions from the audience.

Jason Molly將要做什麼？
(A) 宣布海報競賽的優勝者
(B) 做有關他生態研究的簡報
(C) 對簡報發表他的評論
(D) 回答現場觀眾的問題

【解析】說話者在這段致辭中表示要宣布海報競賽的優勝者，接著歡迎Jason Molly來做這項宣布，可知Jason Molly將要宣布海報競賽的優勝者，正解為(A)。

【類型】提問細節題型

【詞彙】
comment 評語／audience 觀眾

【正解】(A)

女 這款抗皺眼霜是我們今年最暢銷的產品。它是用海藻、小黃瓜、蘆薈的萃取物、荷荷巴油以及乳木果油製成的。這高效配方能立即緊實、明亮、滑順並滋潤脆弱的眼睛周圍皮膚；而且，它還有助於消除黑眼圈和眼睛下方的眼袋。我自己本身也有使用這款眼霜，我可以跟你說它真的有效。事實上，我們大部份的客人幾乎都能立刻就發現改變。今天是你的幸運日，因為如果你今天買兩瓶，我們就會免費送你一瓶！

【詞彙】

anti-wrinkle 抗皺／
seaweed 海藻／
cucumber 小黃瓜／aloe 蘆薈／
extract 萃取物／
jojoba oil 荷荷巴油／
Shea butter 乳木果油／
potent 高效的

Questions 83-85 refer to the following talk.

W This anti-wrinkle eye cream is our best-selling product of the year. It is made of seaweed, cucumber, aloe extracts, jojoba oil and Shea butter. The potent formula is instantly firming, brightening and tightening, smoothing and moisturizing the delicate eye area; what's more, it helps diminish dark circles and under-eye bags. I'm using this eye cream myself, and I can tell that it really works. In fact, most of our customers notice changes almost immediately. This is your lucky day, because if you buy two today, we are giving you another one for free!

說話者正在做什麼？
(A) 推銷一款眼霜
(B) 幫她的書做廣告
(C) 示範使用一台麵包機
(D) 介紹一個新朋友

【類型】內容主題題型

【正解】(A)

83 What is the speaker doing?
(A) Promoting an eye cream
(B) Advertising for her book
(C) Demonstrating a bread machine
(D) Introducing a new friend

【解析】由說話者說話內容以介紹anti-wrinkle eye cream（抗皺眼霜）為主軸，並在最後說明促銷方案為買二送一，可知說話者正在推銷眼霜，答案為(A)。

84 Where most likely is the speaker giving a talk like this?
  (A) In a tourist information center
  (B) At the airport check-in counter
  (C) At the ticket booth of a museum
  (D) At a department store skin care product counter

【解析】由說話者介紹眼霜給客人，可推測說話者應該是在展售眼霜的地點做這樣的介紹，選項中最有可能展售眼霜的地點就是百貨公司保養品櫃檯，因此(D)為最適當的答案。

說話者最有可能在何處發表像這樣的談話？
(A) 遊客資訊中心
(B) 機場報到櫃檯
(C) 博物館售票亭
(D) 百貨公司保養品專櫃

【類型】說話背景題型

【詞彙】
tourist information center
遊客資訊中心／counter 專櫃

【正解】(D)

85 What special offer can the listeners get?
  (A) 20 percent off
  (B) Free delivery service
  (C) Buy two, get one free
  (D) Buy one, get one half price

【解析】由說話者在最後表示buy two today, ...another one for free（今天買二，送一），因此正解為(C)。

聽話者可以得到什麼特別優惠？
(A) 八折
(B) 免運服務
(C) 買二送一
(D) 買一件，第二件半價

【類型】提問細節題型

【正解】(C)

男　很高興向各位宣布，從下週一起兩週，校內將會舉辦一連串的職業博覽會。這對各位來說是個可以跟一些全國頂尖企業的老闆在一個非正式場合裡碰面，並知道你可能會有興趣在大學最後一年之後任職的公司，有提供哪些工作及實習職位的好機會。想知道更多詳細訊息，請看佈告欄上的貼文。這種機會並不是天天都有的，所以不要錯過了！

★2018春季學期

三月5-7日 上午11點-下午4點	工程／科技業
三月8-9日 上午11點-下午4點	投資銀行
三月12-13日 上午11點-下午4點	法律及會計
三月14-16日 上午11點-下午4點	媒體業／新聞工作

【詞彙】
internship 實習職位

Questions 86-88 refer to the following announcement and post.

M　I'm very pleased to announce that there will be a series of job fairs on campus for two weeks, starting next Monday. It will be a good opportunity for you all to meet with employers from some top companies nationwide in an informal setting and learn about job and internship opportunities offered by the companies where you might be interested to work following your final year in college. Please see the post on the bulletin board for more detailed information. This kind of opportunity doesn't occur every day so don't miss it!

★Spring Semester 2018

Mar 5-7 11am-4pM	Engineering/Technology
Mar 8-9 11am-4pM	Investment Banking
Mar 12-13 11am-4pM	Law & Accounting
Mar 14-16 11am-4pM	Media/journalism

說話者最有可能正在跟誰說話？
(A) 大一新生
(B) 大二生
(C) 大三生
(D) 大四生

【類型】說話對象題型

【詞彙】
fresher(=freshman) 新生、新鮮人／sophomore 二年級生／junior 三年級生／senior 四年級生

【正解】(D)

86 Who most likely is the speaker talking to?
(A) College freshers
(B) College sophomores
(C) College juniors
(D) College seniors

【解析】由說話者提到It will be a good opportunity for you... following this final year in college. 這句的關鍵詞：this final year in college（在大學的這最後一年），可知說話者的說話對象是針對大學最後一年的學生，也就是大四學生，故正解為(D)。

87 What will take place in school from next Monday?
(A) A series of job fairs
(B) An educational exhibition
(C) An International travel fair
(D) An auto show

下週一起校園將舉行什麼活動？
(A) 一系列就業博覽會
(B) 一場教育展覽會
(C) 一場國際旅遊展
(D) 一場車展

【解析】由説話者一開始就表示there will be a series of job fairs on campus（校內將會有一連串的工作博覽會），campus指「校園」，on campus即「校內」，故可知正解為(A)。

【類型】內容主題題型

【詞彙】
educational exhibition 教育展覽會／travel fair 旅遊展／auto show 車展

【正解】(A)

---

88 Look at the post. When should those who are interested in working in journalism attend the fair?
(A) March 6
(B) March 10
(C) March 12
(D) March 15

請看貼文。有興趣在新聞界工作的人應該在哪一天參加博覽會？
(A) 三月六日
(B) 三月十日
(C) 三月十二日
(D) 三月十五日

【解析】由貼文內容看來，可知與媒體及新聞工作相關的工作博覽會時間是在三月14-16日，選項(D)的三月15日符合這個時間，故為正解。

【類型】圖表對照題型

【正解】(D)

女 嘿，Linda，我是Nancy。我需要妳幫公司午餐會跟老張餐廳訂外帶。妳剛不在座位上，所以我就留了張紙條在妳桌上。請照著清單點餐。老張餐廳不提供外送服務，所以妳必須自己去拿午餐。別忘了要收據，才能報公帳。餐點必須在十二點之前為午餐會準備好。謝謝妳的幫忙。

★

老張餐廳 電話: 20233035	
	數量
豬肉飯	3
炸雞腿飯	5
豬排飯	8
素食便當	6

【詞彙】
takeout 外帶／
reimbursement 報銷費用

Questions 89-91 refer to the following message and the note.

W Hey, Linda, this is Nancy. I need you to order takeout from Old John's Restaurant for the office luncheon. You weren't at your desk so I left a note on your desk. Please order according to the list. The Old John's doesn't provide delivery service, so you have to pick up the lunch by yourself. Don't forget to ask for a receipt in order to claim for reimbursement. Meals must be ready for the luncheon by 12 o'clock. Thanks for your help.

★

The Old John's Restaurant Tel: 20233035	
	Quantity
Rice with stewed pork	3
Rice with fried chicken leg	5
Rice with pork chop	8
Vegetarian lunch box	6

這通語音留言的目的為何？
(A) 要求聽話者幫忙跑腿。
(B) 訂購午餐外送。
(C) 傳達感激之意。
(D) 通知聽話者開會。

【類型】內容主題題型

【詞彙】
run errands 跑腿辦事

【正解】(A)

89 What is the purpose of this voice message?
(A) To ask the listener to run an errand.
(B) To order lunch delivery.
(C) To convey gratitude.
(D) To notify the listener of the meeting.

【解析】由留言內容，説話者指示「訂午餐外帶」，且要自己去拿，可知這通留言的目的是要指示聽話者幫忙跑腿辦事，正解為(A)。

90 Why does the listener need to ask for a receipt?
(A) To return the purchase later.
(B) To apply for reimbursement.
(C) To file a tax return.
(D) To keep track of her business expenses.

聽話者為何要索取收據？
(A) 為了退回購買的東西。
(B) 為了申請銷帳。
(C) 為了報稅。
(D) 為了了解工作開銷。

【類型】提問細節題型

【解析】由說話者在留言中表示ask for a receipt in order to claim for reimbursement（要收據已做申請公帳之用），可知索取收據的目的是為了要報公帳，故正解為(B)。

【詞彙】
file 申請／tax return 退稅／
keep track of 了解……動態

【正解】(B)

---

91 Look at the note. How many people will attend the luncheon?
(A) 8 people
(B) 14 people
(C) 22 people
(D) 30 people

請看紙條。將會有多少人參加午餐會？
(A) 八人
(B) 十四人
(C) 二十二人
(D) 三十人

【類型】圖表對照題型

【解析】由午餐訂購數量加起來一共有22個餐盒，可推知參加午餐會的人數會有二十二人。正解為(C)。

【正解】(C)

女　好。現在讓我們進入下一個議程：尾牙派對籌備。再一次地，企劃部將會負責這次盛會的統籌。今年，派對將會獎勵傑出員工的頒獎典禮後，於社區禮堂舉行。所以我們將會分成兩組，分別準備這兩場活動。你們可以在白板上的表格看到自己是屬於哪一組。目前為止有任何問題嗎？

★

典禮組		派對組	
組長	Jason	組長	Kyle
組員	Heidi	組員	Larson
	Steven		Wendy
	Billy		Amelia
	Daniel		Max
	Rosie		Sam

【詞彙】
awarding ceremony 頒獎典禮／
respectively 分別地

Questions 92-94 refer to the following talk and table.

W　OK. Let's move on to the next agenda item: Year-end party preparation. Again, the Planning Department will be in charge of overall arrangements for this occasion. This year, the party will be held in the Community Hall, following the awarding ceremony in which some outstanding staff will be rewarded. So we will be divided into two teams and prepare for the two events respectively. You can see which team you belong to from the table on the board. Any questions so far?

★

Ceremony Team		Party Team	
Leader:	Jason	Leader:	Kyle
Members:	Heidi	Members:	Larson
	Steven		Wendy
	Billy		Amelia
	Daniel		Max
	Rosie		Sam

這個會議的參與者是誰？
(A) 研發部員工
(B) 企劃部員工
(C) 行銷部員工
(D) 人資部員工

【類型】談話背景題型

【正解】(B)

92 Who are the participants of this meeting?
(A) The R&D Department staff
(B) The Planning Department staff
(C) The Marketing staff
(D) The HR Department staff

【解析】說話者在發言中提到今年的派對統籌仍是由 Planning Department（企劃部）負責，接著以第一人稱表示 We will be divided into two teams（我們將分成兩組），來籌備活動，故可知參與這個會議的人是企劃部的員工，正解為 (B)。

93 Who will be commended in the awarding ceremony?
(A) Outstanding staff
(B) Senior staff
(C) The winner of the competition
(D) Employees with perfect attendance

【解析】由the awarding ceremony in which some outstanding staff will be rewarded（傑出員工會在頒獎典禮中獲得頒獎）這一句可知這個頒獎典禮是要獎勵傑出員工的，故正解為(A)。

誰將會在頒獎典禮中受到表揚？
(A) 傑出員工
(B) 資深員工
(C) 比賽優勝者
(D) 全勤員工

【類型】提問細節題型

【詞彙】
perfect attendance 全勤

【正解】(A)

---

94 Look at the table. Who will be in charge of the year-end party?
(A) Mike
(B) Jason
(C) Max
(D) Kyle

【解析】由人員分組表所示，派對組的組長為Kyle，因此可知Kyle為尾牙派對的負責人，正解為(D)。

請看表格。誰將負責尾牙派對？
(A) Mike
(B) Jason
(C) Max
(D) Kyle

【類型】圖表對照題型

【正解】(D)

男 呃，嗨，我是Oliver Benson。
我昨天在你們的網站上訂購
了一台咖啡機，訂單編號
AF019240259。我希望現在
變更交貨內容還不算太遲，因
為我想請你們將我訂購的東西
直接送到我的公司，而不是訂
單上所寫的地址。我的公司是
在Brax路上的Maxwell 大廈三
樓。如果因為做變更而有額外
收費的話，請直接從我帳上扣
款，謝謝。

Questions 95-97 refer to the following message.

M Uh, hi, this is Oliver Benson. I ordered a coffee maker on your website yesterday, and the order number is AF019240259. I hope it's not too late to make a delivery change because I would like you to deliver my order directly to my office instead of the address stated on the order form. My office is on the third floor of Maxwell Mansion on Brax Street. If there's an additional fee for the change please directly charge it to my account. Thanks.

這通留言的目的為何？
(A) 更改送貨地址
(B) 更改交貨日期
(C) 確認訂單內容
(D) 請求開立收據

【類型】內容主題題型

【正解】(A)

95 What is the purpose of this message?
(A) To change the delivery address
(B) To change the delivery date
(C) To confirm the order
(D) To request an invoice

【解析】由說話者表示希望對方deliver my order directly to my office instead of the address stated on the order form（直接將訂購的東西送到公司，而非訂單上所寫的地址），可知這通留言的目的是要變更送貨地點，故正解 (A)。

96 Where does the speaker want his order to be delivered?
(A) His office
(B) The hotel he is staying in
(C) His parents' place
(D) Directly to the airport

【解析】由留言表示I would like to ask you to deliver my order directly to my office（希望請你們將我訂的東西直接送到公司），可知他希望東西可以送到公司來，正解為(A)。

說話者希望他訂購的商品可以被送到哪裡？
(A) 他的公司
(B) 他住的飯店
(C) 他爸媽的住處
(D) 直接送到機場

【類型】提問細節題型

【正解】(A)

---

97 By what means will the speaker pay for the additional fee?
(A) By cash
(B) By credit card
(C) Through direct debit
(D) By his stored value card

【解析】說話者在留言最後表示如果有additional fee（額外收費），就directly charge it to my account（直接從帳戶扣款），charge money to sb.'s account 即表示「從某人帳戶直接扣款」之意。direct debit指「用現金帳戶直接付款」，因此正解為(C)。

說話者將會用什麼方法支付額外費用？
(A) 現金
(B) 信用卡
(C) 直接扣款
(D) 儲值卡

【類型】提問細節題型

【正解】(C)

男 謝謝你們給我這個機會向各位介紹我們公司。我們是一家專門從事廚房電器用品的設計與製造的製造商。我們的產品在過去十年主要是外銷至歐美。兩年前我們開始將事業擴展到亞洲，現在在上海、北京、曼谷、臺北以及大阪都有分店。目前我們正在尋找可信賴的代理商，將我們的產品行銷至印度，我們想知道您是否對跟我們合作有興趣。

Questions 98-100 refer to the following talk.

M Thanks for giving me this opportunity to introduce our company. We are a manufacturer specialized in designing and manufacturing kitchen appliances. Our products were mainly exported to Europe and the United States in the past ten years. We started expanding our business to Asia two years ago, and now we have agents in Shanghai, Beijing, Bangkok, Taipei and Osaka. We are currently looking for a reliable agent to market our products in India, so we're wondering if you are interested in working with us.

說話者最有可能在跟誰說話？
(A) 工作應徵者
(B) 潛在事業夥伴
(C) 旅行社代辦人員
(D) 目標顧客

【類型】目標對象題型

【正解】(B)

98 Who most likely is the speaker talking to?
(A) Job applicants
(B) Potential business partners
(C) Travel agents
(D) Target customers

【解析】說話者在最後表示we're wondering if you are interested in working with us（我們想知道您是否有興趣與我們合作），可知他的說話對象是可能與他們公司有合作關係的人，因此選項(B)的「潛在事業夥伴」，是最有可能的答案，故為正解。

99 What is the speaker doing?
(A) Promoting a new product
(B) Introducing a new friend
(C) Recommending a restaurant
(D) Seeking a sales agent

【解析】說話者在介紹完公司之後，直接表示We are currently looking for a reliable agent to market our products...（我們正在找一個可以幫我們行銷產品的可靠代理商），故可知正解為(D)。

說話者正在做什麼？
(A) 推銷新產品
(B) 介紹一位新朋友
(C) 推薦一家餐廳
(D) 尋求一個業務代理商

【類型】內容主題題型

【正解】(D)

100 According to the talk, where does the company plan to market their products?
(A) South Korea
(B) India
(C) Singapore
(D) The Philippines

【解析】由說話者表示We are currently looking for a reliable agent ... in India （我們正在找……印度境內的……可靠代理商），可推測這間公司計劃將他們的產品行銷至India（印度），故正解為(B)。

根據這段談話，這家公司計劃在哪裡銷售他們的產品？
(A) 南韓
(B) 印度
(C) 新加坡
(D) 菲律賓

【類型】提問細節題型

【正解】(B)

New TOEIC Listening Analysis 5
新多益聽力全真模擬試題解析第5回

(A) 他們牽著手走路。
(B) 他們在尋找對方。
(C) 他們在野餐。
(D) 他們正在遛狗。

【類型】兩人照片題型

【詞彙】
hand in hand 牽手／
walk the dog 遛狗

【正解】(A)

01 (A) They are walking hand in hand.
   (B) They are looking for each other.
   (C) They are having a picnic.
   (D) They are walking their dog.

【解析】照片主題明顯為人物時，要特別注意人物的動作。本題照片中的兩人牽著彼此的手走著，並沒有其他特別的動作，而且四周也沒有其他人或動物。因此選項(A)的描述最符合照片內容，故選(A)。

(A) 現在正在舉行賽馬。
(B) 警察們正在巡邏。
(C) 孩子們在四周玩耍。
(D) 他們其中一人落馬了。

【類型】人物景物題型

【詞彙】
horse race 賽馬／
on patrol 巡邏

【正解】(B)

02 (A) A horse race is taking place.
   (B) The policemen are on patrol.
   (C) Kids are playing around.
   (D) One of them fell off a horse.

【解析】本題照片內容算是相當清楚明確，可以看到身著制服的警察騎著馬。由於照片中並未出現選項(A)所述之「賽馬」情事，也沒有看到選項(C)提到的「孩子」，更沒有選項(D)提及之「落馬」畫面，因此選項(B)的「警員巡邏」是最符合照片內容的描述，故為正解。

(A) 人們在等著入座。
(B) 一名服務生正在伺候進餐。
(C) 一對夫妻正在等桌子。
(D) 還有一張桌子空著。

【類型】多人照片題型

【詞彙】
wait on table 伺候進餐

【正解】(D)

03 (A) People are waiting to be seated.
(B) A waiter is waiting on table.
(C) A couple is waiting for their table.
(D) There is still a table available.

【解析】遇到多人照片題時，重點除了照片中人物的動作以及人物與四周環境的互動關係之外，有時候也會測驗應試者觀察與人物無關之背景環境的能力。本題照片中的所有人都在餐廳內完成入座的動作，沒有出現還在等著入座或等桌子的客人，因此選項(A)與(C)可以先刪除不考慮。此外照片中並未看到服務生隨侍在桌邊，因此選項(B)亦不是正確描述。照片右方可以看到有一張空桌，符合選項(D)之描述，故(D)為正解。

(A) 船員們正試著揚起帆。
(B) 車子在公路上拋錨。
(C) 渡輪搭載著一群人。
(D) 人們正等著上船。

【類型】人物景物題型

【詞彙】
hoist 升起／ferry 渡輪／
board 上（船、車、飛機等）

【正解】(C)

04 (A) The sailors are trying to hoist the sails.
(B) The car broke down on the highway.
(C) The ferry carried a bunch of people.
(D) People are waiting to board the ship

【解析】本題照片為一艘載滿乘客的渡輪在河面上航行，因此選項(B)可以優先刪除。觀察照片中的這艘渡輪，並未出現選項(A)所提及之「船員」，也沒有「揚帆」的動作，因此(A)亦不正確；照片中的船已經離岸，沒有人還在等著上船，故(D)所述亦不符合照片內容。只有選項(C)表示的「渡輪載著一群人」是最符合照片內容的描述，故為正解。

加★部分為多益新題型以及相關小提醒，考生要特別注意喔！　353

(A) 有隻狗正在找食物吃。

(B) 這個人獨自在那裡。

(C) 男子正試著找停車位。

(D) 現在正下著傾盆大雨。

【類型】單人照片題型

【詞彙】

rain cats and dogs 下傾盆大雨

【正解】(B)

05 (A) There's a dog looking for food.

(B) The person is there alone.

(C) The man is trying to find a parking space.

(D) It's raining cats and dogs.

【解析】本題照片為一個人躺在戶外長椅上，圖中並未看到動物，圖中人物也並非開著車，因此選項(A)(C)均不正確；照片中雖看不出晴空萬里，但是並未有「傾盆大雨」的情形，因此選項(D)亦為錯誤描述。選項(B)描述照片中的人只有自己一人，最符合照片內容，故為正解。

(A) 他們正在過馬路。

(B) 他們正坐在長凳上。

(C) 他們正斜靠在牆上。

(D) 他們正站在陽傘下。

【類型】多人照片題型

【詞彙】

bench 長椅／

lean against 斜倚著／

parasol 陽傘

【正解】(D)

06 (A) They are crossing the street.

(B) They are sitting on a bench.

(C) They are leaning against the wall.

(D) They are standing under a parasol.

【解析】照片主角超過一人時，要注意觀察照片人物的互動、動作及所在背景環境。本題照片中的三個人正在一個大陽傘下談話，並非選項(A)之「正在過馬路」；照片中的人是「站著」，而且並沒有站在牆邊，因此選項(B)及(C)所述皆不正確。只有選項(D)所述符合照片內容，是為正解。

▶ **PART 2**

Directions: You will hear a question or statement and three responses spoken in English. They will not be printed in your test book and will be spoken only one time. Select the best response to the question or statement and mark the letter (A), (B) or (C) on your answer sheet.

Example

You will hear:

Did you have dinner at the restaurant yesterday?

You will also hear:

(A) Yes, it lasted all day.

(B) No, I went to a movie with my girlfriend.

(C) Yes, the client was nice.

The best response to the question "Did you have dinner at the restaurant yesterday?" is choice (B), "No, I went to a movie with my girlfriend," so (B) is the best answer. You should mark answer (B) on your answer sheet.

---

07 When should we submit the assignment?
  (A) September 8th is the deadline.
  (B) As long as you can afford it.
  (C) Mr. Taylor will do it.

【解析】本題要問應該繳交指定作業的「時間」，選項(A)明確告知繳交作業的deadline（最後期限），是為正解。選項(B)與(C)答非所問，不需花時間考慮。

我們什麼時候要繳交指定作業？
(A) 九月八日是截止日期。
(B) 只要你負擔得起。
(C) 泰勒先生會去做。

【類型】when疑問句題型

【詞彙】
submit 繳交／
assignment 指定作業

【正解】(A)

你可以把電視音量調低一點嗎？
(A) 我很抱歉拒絕你。
(B) 噢，當然。抱歉那麼大聲。
(C) 好，我可以跟你一起看。

【類型】yes/no 疑問句題型

【詞彙】
turn down 關小、調低；拒絕

【正解】(B)

08 Could you turn down the TV a little bit?
    (A) I'm sorry to turn you down.
    (B) Sure. Sorry for being loud.
    (C) Yes, I can watch it with you.

【解析】片語動詞turn down有很多用法，通常看後面的受詞是什麼，就能知道是哪一個用法。問句中的turn down為「將（音量或強度）關小、調低」之意，本題以過去式助動詞could禮貌地詢問對方是否能將音量調低，選項(B)肯定回答，並對聲音那麼大表示歉意，是最適當的回應，故為正解。選項(A)雖使用同一個片語動詞turn down，卻是「拒絕（他人）」的意思，因此並非適當回應。選項(C)答非所問，故不考慮。

我有一點小東西要給你。
(A) 好，但只能一點點。
(B) 他們看起來不像。
(C) 噢，你不該這麼做的。

【類型】陳述句題型

【詞彙】
alike 相像的

【正解】(C)

09 I've got a little something for you.
    (A) OK, but only a little.
    (B) They don't look alike.
    (C) Aww, you shouldn't have.

【解析】本題以現在完成式為時態，表示為對方準備了禮物。選項(C)以should not＋現在完成式為時態，意指「應該不要做，卻已經做了」來表示「對方實在不需要這麼做」。這句話通常用在收到別人的禮物或餽贈時，客氣地表示「不好意思讓對方破費或特別準備禮物」的說法，故(C)為最適當的答案。

請把你的電話轉到靜音模式。
(A) 我已經這麼做了。
(B) 你聽到我說的了。
(C) 我不是故意的。

【類型】祈使句題型

【詞彙】
silent mode 靜音模式

【正解】(A)

10 Please switch your phone to silent mode.
    (A) I already did.
    (B) You heard me.
    (C) I didn't mean it.

【解析】本題為句首加了please的祈使句，表達希望對方「將手機轉靜音」的要求。選項(A)以過去簡單式表示「已經這麼做了」，是最適當的回應，故為正解。選項(B)意指「你已經聽到我說的話了」，表示「不想再次重複已經說過的話」，與選項(C)一樣答非所問

11 This job involves heavy business travel.
(A) I can live with that.
(B) I travel once a month.
(C) I'm between jobs.

【解析】本題為描述工作內容「需要大量出差」之陳述。選項(B)回答「旅行頻率」；選項(C)的between jobs（待業中）為表示「身處失業狀態」的委婉表示法，亦與題目陳述無關。選項(A)表示I can live with that. 是用來表示「我可以接受」的口語用法，因此是最適當的回應。

這份工作需要經常出差。
(A) 我可以接受。
(B) 我一個月旅行一次。
(C) 我目前待業中。

【類型】陳述句題型

【詞彙】
involve 需要；包含／
heavy 大量的／business travel
出差（因公旅行）／
between jobs 待業中

【正解】(A)

---

12 I think we should buy a car.
(A) The taxi will be here in five minutes.
(B) I don't think we can afford it.
(C) I can't remember where we parked it.

【解析】I think＋名詞子句，為表達個人意見或看法時所使用的句型。本題陳述句表示「我認為我們應該買輛車」。由於「車子」乃高單價物品，因此選項(B)亦以I don't think＋名詞子句，表達個人意見，表示「我不認為我們買得起」，是最合情合理的回應。afford指「買得起；負擔得起」。

我認為我們應該買輛車。
(A) 計程車五分鐘會到。
(B) 我不認為我們買得起。
(C) 我不記得把車停哪兒了。

【類型】陳述句題型

【正解】(B)

---

13 What's wrong with the chicken?
(A) It's apparently undercooked.
(B) You deserve a promotion.
(C) Just keep it tidy and neat.

【解析】What's wrong with sb./sth.? 是用來詢問「某人或某事有什麼不對勁？」的問句句型。本題問的是「雞肉有什麼問題」，選項(B)(C)的回答與「雞肉」無關，不需考慮。選項(A)以apparently undercooked（明顯沒煮熟）回答，是最適當的回應，故為正解。

雞肉有什麼問題嗎？
(A) 它很明顯沒煮熟。
(B) 你值得獲得晉升。
(C) 保持乾淨整齊就對了。

【類型】What疑問句題型

【詞彙】
undercooked 沒煮透的／
deserve 值得／promotion 晉升

【正解】(A)

可以再跟我說一次你的名字嗎？
(A) 是3130-1234。
(B) 在第一街上。
(C) 是Zack。

【類型】yes/no 疑問句題型

【正解】(C)

晚餐算我的。
(A) 不，我們各付各的。
(B) 不，它不在那裡。
(C) 大概七點左右。

【類型】陳述句題型

【詞彙】
go Dutch 各付各的

【正解】(A)

我們去那間泰國餐廳吃晚餐，好嗎？
(A) 好，我會原諒你。
(B) 好。我會訂位。
(C) 好。我會準時到。

【類型】附加疑問句題型

【詞彙】
forgive 原諒／
reservation 訂位／on time準時

【正解】(B)

---

14 Can I have your name again?
(A) It's 3130-1234.
(B) It's on the First Street.
(C) It's Zack.

【解析】Can I have your name?（我可以知道你的名字嗎？）是比What's your name?（你叫什麼名字？）更有禮貌地詢問對方名字的方式。問句最後加上副詞again，可知說話者希望對方再告訴他一次，因此選項(C)回答It's Zack.（我的名字是Zack）是最適當的回答。選項(A)回答「電話號碼」，選項(B)回答「所在位置」，皆答非所問。

15 The dinner is on me.
(A) No, let's go Dutch.
(B) No, it's not there.
(C) Around seven o'clock.

【解析】on這個介系詞在此作「由……支付」解，這題陳述句是在表示「這頓晚餐的費用由我付」，選項(A)否定這個提議，表示Let's go Dutch.（我們各付各的）是選項中最適當的回答，故為正解。

16 Let's have dinner at that Thai restaurant, shall we?
(A) OK. I'll forgive you.
(B) OK. I'll make a reservation.
(C) OK. I'll be there on time.

【解析】Let's do sth. ... 為用來表示提議的句型，在提議之後加上附加問句shall we? 則是詢問對方對此提議的看法。選項(B)回答OK，並接著表示「我來訂位」，是最適當的回應，故為正解。

17 Who fixed the printer?
　　(A) James did.
　　(B) Tomorrow morning.
　　(C) Why not?

【解析】本題問的是修好印表機的「人」，選項(A)表示James做了修印表機這件事，是最適當的回應，故為正解。

誰把印表機修好了？
(A) 是James。
(B) 明天早上。
(C) 好啊。

【類型】who 疑問句題型

【正解】(A)

---

18 Can we take a 10-minute break?
　　(A) I don't see why not.
　　(B) Yes, it's been delayed.
　　(C) I didn't mean to break it.

【解析】本題以助動詞can為疑問句句首，意在請求對方同意。問句中的break做名詞解，表「休息」，take a break為「休息一下」的片語用法，take a ten-minute break即「休息十分鐘」之意。選項(C)的break作動詞解，表「打破」，與問句無關；選項(B)回答「時間延誤了」，亦答非所問。選項(A)的see表「理解」，I don't see why not. 意指「我不知道為什麼不行」，也就是「當然可以」的意思，是最適當的回答。

我們可以休息十分鐘嗎？
(A) 當然可以。
(B) 對，它被延誤了。
(C) 我不是故意打破的。

【類型】yes/no 疑問句題型

【詞彙】
break （名詞）休息；（動詞）打破

【正解】(A)

---

19 How early should we arrive at the airport?
　　(A) We depart from Terminal 2.
　　(B) You should have arrived earlier.
　　(C) Two hours before departure.

【解析】本題疑問詞雖不是when，但是疑問詞how接時間副詞early，便是要問「要多早」，是另一種詢問時間的方式。選項(A)是用來回答「從哪一個航廈起飛」，選項(B)以should＋完成式的時態，表示對方「應該早到卻沒有早到」的事實，亦沒有回答問題。選項(C)回答「起飛之前兩小時」就應該要到機場，是最適當的回應，故為正解。

我們應該多早抵達機場？
(A) 我們從第二航廈起飛。
(B) 你應該要早點到的。
(C) 起飛前兩小時。

【類型】how 疑問句題型

【詞彙】
terminal 航廈／departure 離境

【正解】(C)

你多久洗一次衣服？
(A) 一星期一次。
(B) 那是不能吃的。
(C) 兩星期之前。

【類型】how often 疑問句題型

【詞彙】
laundry 待洗的衣服／
edible 可以吃的

【正解】(A)

20 How often do you do your laundry?
　　(A) Once a week.
　　(B) It's not edible.
　　(C) Two weeks ago.

【解析】how often疑問句要問的是事情發生的「頻率」，選項(B)答非所問，不需考慮；選項(C)是用來回答「某事在過去哪個時間點發生」。只有選項(A)的「一星期一次」，有確實告知「多久洗一次衣服」，是為正解。

你什麼時候會發出婚禮邀請？
(A) 是在大皇宮酒店。
(B) 下個月某個時間。
(C) 你一定是在開我玩笑吧。

【類型】when疑問句題型

【詞彙】
give out 分發／sometime
（過去或將來）某一時候

【正解】(B)

21 When will you give out your wedding invitations?
　　(A) It's at Grand Palace Hotel.
　　(B) Sometime next month.
　　(C) You must be kidding me.

【解析】本題要問的是發出婚禮邀請的「時間」，選項中只有(C)的回答與時間有關，sometime指過去或未來的「某個時候」，表示尚未決定確定的時間，但會是在next month（下個月），故為正解。

你認為Barrymore先生會准我的休假申請嗎？
(A) 我也認不出他來。
(B) 他回來之前我不會離開。
(C) 如果你沒有好理由就不會。

【類型】間接疑問句題型

【詞彙】
grant 准予／
leave request 休假申請／
recognize 認出

【正解】(C)

22 Do you think Mr. Barrymore would grant my leave request?
　　(A) I can't recognize him either.
　　(B) I won't leave until he comes back.
　　(C) Not if you don't have a good reason.

【解析】本題為以do you think 後接直接問句Would Mr. Barrymore grant my leave request的間接問句題型，目的是為詢問對方看法。選項(C)以if條件句回應：「如果你沒有好理由，就不會准」，表達了自己的看法，是最適當的回應，故為正解。

23 When will our office assistant return to work?
  (A) From the post office.
  (B) You must have the receipt.
  (C) Probably next week.

【解析】when 疑問句題型要問的是「時間」，選項中只有 (C)的回答與時間有關，表示「可能下星期」，故為正解。

我們的辦公室助理何時會回來上班？
(A) 從郵局。
(B) 你必須要有收據。
(C) 可能是下星期。

【類型】when 疑問句題型

【詞彙】
office assistant 辦公室助理／
return 返回／receipt 收據

【正解】(C)

---

24 The food here is not as good as I expected.
  (A) You should bring an umbrella.
  (B) It's acceptable to me.
  (C) Get well soon.

【解析】本題雖未直接抱怨餐點難吃，但是以 not as goo as I expected（不如我所期待的好）來表示「餐點不如預期」。選項(A)與(C)之回答均不適合用來回應這個句子；選項(B)並未對此予以附和，而是提出相反看法：「對我來說是可以接受的」，表示餐點並不糟糕，是最適當的回應，故為正解。

這兒的餐點沒有我期待的好吃。
(A) 你應該帶把雨傘。
(B) 我覺得還可以接受。
(C) 祝你早日康復。

【類型】敘述句題型

【詞彙】
acceptable 可接受的／
as good as 如……一樣好

【正解】(A)

---

25 I didn't know that the meeting time had changed.
  (A) I wasn't informed, either.
  (B) It's been moved to another room.
  (C) It only takes a few minutes.

【解析】本題直述句表示對於「會議時間已經更改」一事「並不知情」。選項(A)以被動語態表示「我也沒有收到通知」，意即「自己也對此事不知情」，是最適當的回應，故 (A)為正解。

我不知道會議時間已經改了。
(A) 我也沒收到通知。
(B) 它已經被移到另一間了。
(C) 它只要花幾分鐘時間。

【類型】敘述句題型

【詞彙】
inform 通知

【正解】(A)

我不認為我負擔得起這房租。

(A) 你可以找個室友啊。

(B) 這絕對值得努力。

(C) 我把它們放在架子上了。

【類型】敘述句題型

【詞彙】
rent 房租／roommate 室友／
effort 努力／shelf 架子

【正解】(A)

26 I don't think I can afford the rent.

(A) You can find a roommate.

(B) It definitely worth the effort.

(C) I put them on the shelf.

【解析】題目為間接否定句，表示「我負擔不起這房租」。選項(A)提議find a roommate（找個室友），暗示對方可以找個人一起合租，分擔房租，是最適當的回答，故為正解。

你在哪兒找到我的手錶的？

(A) 它要1500元。

(B) 現在三點半了。

(C) 你把它放在我桌上。

【類型】where 疑問句題型

【正解】(C)

27 Where did you find my watch?

(A) It's $1500.

(B) It's half past three.

(C) You put it on my desk.

【解析】where疑問句要問的是「地點」。本題問句問「手錶是在哪裡找到的」，選項(A)回答「價錢」，選項(B)回答「時間」，皆答非所問。選項(C)表示「你把它放在我桌上」，表示手錶是在「我的桌上」發現的，是最適當的答案。

現在六點了沒？

(A) 我不知道時間。

(B) 我沒時間做那件事。

(C) 不，那不是個時鐘。

【類型】be動詞疑問句題型

【正解】(A)

28 Is it six o'clock yet?

(A) I don't have the time.

(B) I don't have time for that.

(C) No, it's not a clock.

【解析】疑問句後面加上表示「已經」的副詞yet，是用來詢問「……了沒有？」本題疑問句問的是「六點了沒？」選項(B)的回答雖與「時間」有關，但卻是答非所問；因為題目有提到o'clock，應試者如果沒有稍加留意可能就會被選項(C)回答中的clock（時鐘）誤導。選項(A)表示I don't have the time.這句話是在表示「我沒有可以表達時間的東西」，也就是「我不知道幾點」的意思，對本題問句來說是最適當的回答，故為正解。

29 The bus runs every ten minutes, doesn't it?
    (A) No, it's not that far.
    (B) Only during the rush hour.
    (C) Yes, this is our stop.

【解析】附加疑問句的功能是用來確認前面敘述句內容是否正確。本題問句想確認「公車是不是十分鐘來一班」，選項(A)的回應與「距離」有關，而選項(C)的回應答非所問。選項(B)表示「只有尖峰時間」是十分鐘一班車，是最適當的回應，故為正解。

這班公車每十分鐘一班，不是嗎？
(A) 不，沒有那麼遠。
(B) 只有尖峰時間如此。
(C) 對，這是我們的站。

【類型】附加疑問句題型

【詞彙】
rush hour 尖峰時間

【正解】(B)

---

30 Where are you going for your honeymoon trip?
    (A) For eight days.
    (B) In January.
    (C) Australia.

【解析】以where為句首的疑問句主要是要問「地點」或「位置」。題目問「蜜月旅行的地點」，選項(C)回答「澳洲」，是最適當的答案，故為正解。選項(A)是用來回應「有幾天」的答案；而選項(B)是用來回應「何時去」的答案。

你們要去哪裡蜜月旅行？
(A) 八天。
(B) 一月。
(C) 澳洲。

【類型】where疑問句題型

【詞彙】
honeymoon 蜜月

【正解】(C)

---

31 How's the weather in Singapore?
    (A) You'll need a map.
    (B) It's out of battery.
    (C) Extremely hot.

【解析】題目要問的是weather（天氣），選項中只有(C)的回答與天氣有關，故答案為C。

新加坡天氣怎麼樣？
(A) 你將會需要一份地圖。
(B) 這已經沒電了。
(C) 非常的熱。

【類型】how 疑問句題型

【詞彙】
out of battery 電池沒電

【正解】(C)

Directions: You will hear some conversations between two people. You will be asked to answer three questions about what the speakers say in each conversation. Select the best response to each question and mark the letter (A), (B), (C) or (D) on your answer sheet. The conversations will not be printed in your test book and will be spoken only one time.

女　這是報價單。

男　謝了。看起來很不錯。我相信Willies先生會對你們提供的折扣很滿意的。

女　那麼我想我可以期待很快就能收到你們的訂單，對嗎？

男　那是當然的，如果沒有意外的話。

女　太好了。我一收到你們的訂單就會立刻跟你確認藍牙耳機的交貨細節了。

★報價單

數量	貨號／明細	單位標價 （新台幣）	折扣	單位淨價 （新台幣）
5,000	CT-S20BH8 運動藍牙耳機	2,500.00	40%	1,500
總價				7,500,000

【詞彙】
quotation 報價單／
bluetooth headphone 藍牙耳機／
Qty（=quantity）數量／
unit list price 單位報價／
unit net price 單位淨價

Questions 32-34 refer to the following conversation and quotation.

W Here's the quotation.

M Thanks. This looks good. I'm sure Mr. Willies will be happy with the discount you offer.

W So I guess I can expect to receive your purchase order pretty soon, right?

M That's for sure, if nothing goes wrong.

W Good. I will confirm the details regarding the delivery on your bluetooth headphones as soon as we receive your order.

★Quotation

Qty	Item/Description	Unit List Price (NT$)	Discount	Unit Net Price (NT$)
5,000	CT-S20BH8 sports bluetooth headphones	2,500.00	40%	1,500
Total				7,500,000

32 What did the woman give the man?
(A) The quotation
(B) The signed contract
(C) The purchase order
(D) The invoice

女子給男子什麼東西？
(A) 報價單
(B) 簽好的合約
(C) 訂單
(D) 發票

【解析】對話一開始，女子便對男子表示Here's the quotation.（報價單在這裏）可知女子拿給男子「報價單」，正解為(A)。

【類型】主題內容題型

【詞彙】
invoice 發票

【正解】(A)

---

33 What are the speakers doing?
(A) Negotiating the order
(B) Wrapping up a deal
(C) Confirming the delivery date
(D) Inquiring about prices

說話者正在做什麼？
(A) 商議訂單內容
(B) 完成交易
(C) 確認交貨日期
(D) 詢問價格

【解析】由女子提供報價單，並詢問是否可以很快拿到訂單，男子表示肯定，可推測兩位對話者已經經過了詢價及協商階段，故(A)(D)可以先刪除不考慮。由女子在對話最後表示「收到訂單後馬上確認交貨細節」，因此還沒到進行選項(C)的「確認交貨日期」階段，故(C)也可以刪除。由於這項交易只剩下「下訂單」這個步驟，可知兩人已經來到了完成生意交易的階段，因此選項中以(B)為最適當的答案。

【類型】內容主題題型

【正解】(B)

---

34 Look at the quotation. How much discount has the man got?
(A) 20%
(B) 30%
(C) 40%
(D) 50%

請看報價單。男子得到多少折扣？
(A) 八折
(B) 七折
(C) 六折
(D) 五折

【解析】由報價單上Discount（折扣）那一欄顯示40%，可知賣方提供了六折的折扣，故正解為(C)。

【類型】圖表對照題型

【正解】(C)

男 妳今天又要加班了嗎？

女 不。我要跟朋友一起吃晚餐，所以我大約六點左右就會下班了。你呢？

男 我沒辦法準時下班。我還有一些工作要趕。

女 不能留到明天再做嗎？

男 最好不要。完成期限快到了，而我已經進度落後了。

女 不要工作過度了。稍作休息其實可以讓你工作成效更好。

男 我知道。好啦，我最好現在就回去工作。祝妳夜晚愉快囉！

【詞彙】
knock off 下班／put off 拖延／overwork oneself 過度工作

Questions 35-37 refer to the following conversation.

M Are you going to work overtime again today?

W No. I'm going to have dinner with my friends, so I'll knock off around six. What about you?

M I can't leave work on time. I've still got some work to catch up on.

W Can't you put it off until tomorrow?

M I'd better not. The deadline is approaching and I'm already behind schedule.

W Don't overwork yourself. Taking a little break can actually help you work more productively.

M I know. Well, I'd better get back to work now. Have a nice evening!

說話者的關係是什麼？
(A) 高中同班同學
(B) 工作上的同事
(C) 生意上的夥伴
(D) 住在隔壁的鄰居

【類型】對話者關係題型

【正解】(B)

35 What's the relationship between the speakers?
   (A) High school classmates
   (B) Colleagues at work
   (C) Business partners
   (D) Next-door neighbors

【解析】由說話者一個表示「不加班」，一個表示「工作進度落後，必須加班」，且自己必須回去工作，按常理，可推測說話者的關係最有可能是公司同事，其他選項的關係都不太可能有類似對話內容的討論，故正解為(B)。

36 Why can't the man get off work on time?
(A) He wants to get his job done on schedule.
(B) He has to run errands for his boss.
(C) He is covering for the woman.
(D) He has an appointment with a client.

【解析】男子在對話中表示I've still got some work to catch up on（有一些工作要趕），而且自己有一點behind schedule（進度落後），可知男子必須留下來加班的原因是希望自己工作能趕上應有的進度，正解為(A)。

男子為何不能準時下班？
(A) 他想如期將工作完成。
(B) 他要幫老闆跑腿辦事。
(C) 他要幫女子代班。
(D) 他跟一位客戶有約。

【類型】提問細節題型

【詞彙】
on schedule 按時

【正解】(A)

37 What will the man do next?
(A) Talk to his boss.
(B) Leave work early.
(C) Proceed with his work.
(D) Have dinner with the woman.

【解析】由男子在對話最後表示I'd better get back to work（我最好回去工作），可知男子要回去繼續進行暫時中斷的工作，正解為(C)。 proceed with sth. 是用來表示「繼續進行突然中斷的活動」的片語用法。

男子接下來將要做什麼？
(A) 跟老闆談談。
(B) 提早下班。
(C) 繼續工作。
(D) 跟女子一起晚餐。

【類型】提問細節題型

【詞彙】
proceed with 繼續

【正解】(C)

Questions 38-40 refer to the following conversation.

Man A	Good news! We have achieved the sales targets this month.
Man B	Really? It's only the middle of the month!
Woman	Thanks to the big order from that French automobile company.
Man A	You can say that again. It never occurred to me that they would purchase 10,000 radiator at one go.

男 A　好消息！我們已經達成這個月的業績目標了。

男 B　真的？現在才月中而已呢！

女　　真是多謝那筆法國汽車公司的大訂單了。

男 A　你說的沒錯。我從沒想過他們會一口氣訂購一萬個散熱器。

| 男B | 如果我們繼續努力，我們非常有可能會贏得這個月最佳團體業績獎。 | Man B | If we keep up the good work, it's very likely that we'll win the best group performance this month. |
| 女 | 哇！我已經可以聞到業績獎金的味道了！ | Woman | Wow! I can smell the sales bonus already! |

【詞彙】
radiator （汽車的）散熱器／
at one go 一次、一口氣／
sales bonus 業績獎金

說話者可能為下列哪間公司工作？
(A) 廚房家電製造廠
(B) 化妝品公司
(C) 汽車零件製造廠
(D) 圖書出版社

【類型】提問細節題型

【詞彙】
hardware 硬體／
manufacturer 製造廠／
auto parts 汽車零件

【正解】(C)

38 Which of the following do the speakers probably work for?
(A) A kitchen appliance manufacturer
(B) A cosmetics company
(C) An auto parts manufacturer
(D) A book publisher

【解析】由對話中提到一筆一萬個radiator（散熱器）的大訂單的買主是一家法國汽車公司，可知這家公司應該是經營與汽車零件生產或販售有關的事業，因此最有可能的答案為(C)。其他選項的營業內容均不太像是會跟汽車公司有生意往來的公司，故不需考慮。

說話者如何如此快速地達到月業績目標？
(A) 他們都是專業的業務員。
(B) 他們採用新的銷售策略。
(C) 他們設定實際的銷售目標。
(D) 他們得到一筆大訂單。

【類型】提問細節題型

【詞彙】
realistic 實際的

【正解】(D)

39 How did the speakers achieve the monthly sales targets so fast?
(A) They were all professional salespeople.
(B) They adopted a new sales strategy.
(C) They set realistic sales goals.
(D) They received a huge order.

【解析】對於這個月才到一半就已經達到本月業績目標，女子表示Thanks to the big order from...（謝謝……的大訂單），可推斷業績目標如此快速達成，跟他們接到一筆大訂單有關，正解為(D)。

40 What is the woman expecting?
(A) The sales incentive
(B) A long-planned vacation
(C) A raise in her salary
(D) A promotion at work

女子正在期待什麼？
(A) 業績鼓勵
(B) 一次計劃已久的休假
(C) 加薪
(D) 工作晉升

【解析】女子在對話最後表示I can smell the sales bonus already（我已經可以聞到業績獎金的味道），暗示獎金似乎已經近在眼前，可知女子很期待能拿到業績獎金，incentive 指「鼓勵、刺激」，而獎金亦為鼓勵方式之一，故正解為 (A)。

【類型】提問細節題型

【詞彙】
incentive 獎勵

【正解】(A)

Questions 41-43 refer to the following conversation.

Woman	How much annual bonus are we gonna get this year?
Man A	Last year the company only gave a 0.5-month year-end bonus.
Man B	The company's profits rose by 35% this year. So there's a good chance that we can expect a large annual bonus this year.
Woman	If we can get a year-end bonus of three months this year, I will definitely budget a portion of it for a trip to Hawaii.
Man A	When will they make the announcement?
Man B	Not sure yet. Let's just wait and see.

女	我們今年會拿到多少年終獎金啊？
男A	去年公司只給了半個月的年終獎金。
男B	公司今年的營收上升了百分之卅五。所以我們今年很有可能可以拿到一大筆年終獎金喔。
女	如果我們可以拿到一筆三個月的年終獎金，我絕對會拿一部份去夏威夷旅遊。
男A	他們什麼時候會宣布啊？
男B	還不確定呢。我們等著瞧吧。

【詞彙】
annual bonus 年終獎金

說話者在討論什麼？
(A) 年終獎金
(B) 員工旅遊
(C) 尾牙餐會
(D) 部門會議

【類型】內容主題題型

【正解】(A)

41 What are the speakers talking about?
    (A) The annual bonus
    (B) The staff trip
    (C) The year-end banquet
    (D) The department meeting

【解析】由本篇對話從頭到尾以annual bonus（年終獎金）為主軸，可知說話者在討論「年終獎金」，正解為(A)。

根據對話內容，哪項敘述正確？
(A) 公司從不發年終獎金
(B) 公司今年的獲利下降
(C) 公司今年的生意成長
(D) 公司不發現金紅利

【類型】提問細節題型

【詞彙】
cash bonus 現金紅利

【正解】(C)

42 According to the conversation, which statement is true?
    (A) The company never gives away annual bonuses.
    (B) The company's profit fell this year.
    (C) The company's business grew this year.
    (D) The company doesn't give cash bonuses.

【解析】由對話中其中一名男子表示The company's profits rose by 35% this year.（公司今年獲利上升35%），可知公司今年的營收成長，選項(C)所述正確，故為正解。

年終獎金什麼時候會宣布？
(A) 還不確定
(B) 不會晚於十二月廿三日
(C) 最快下週一
(D) 最慢這星期五

【類型】提問細節題型

【詞彙】
uncertain 不確定的

【正解】(A)

43 When will the annual bonus be announced?
    (A) It remains uncertain
    (B) No later than December 23
    (C) Next Monday at the earliest
    (D) This Friday at the latest

【解析】對話中對於何時宣布年終獎金一問，其中一名男子表示Not sure yet（還不清楚），可知還不知道什麼時候會宣布，故正解為(A)。

Questions 44-46 refer to the following conversation and graph.

M The Sporting Goods Show is finally over.

W I think we did a good job at this year's trade show.

M Exactly. I didn't expect to receive so many orders during the show.

W Well, I must say the location of our booth has greatly contributed to our sales volumes.

M True. But it's undeniable that our excellent after-sales service was an important selling point. None of our competitors can offer a three-year warranty.

W Can't agree more. I'm sure Mr. Cardings will be very pleased when he sees our sales performance.

★

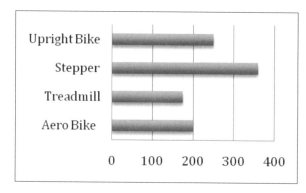

男　運動用品展終於結束了。

女　我覺得我們今年的商展表現很不錯。

男　的確是。我沒想到展示期間會拿到那麼多訂單。

女　這個嘛，我必須說我們攤位的地點對我們的銷售量有很大的貢獻。

男　千真萬確。不過不能否認我們優秀的售後服務是個很重要的賣點。我們沒有一個競爭對手可以提供三年的保固。

女　不能同意更多了。我相信Cardings先生看到我們的銷售表現時會很開心的。

★

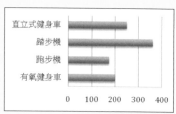

【詞彙】
sales volume 銷售量／
warranty 保固／
upright bike 直立式健身車／
stepper 踏步機／
treadmill 跑步機／
aero bike 有氧健身車

有關說話者，我們知道什麼？
(A) 他們正在準備一場商展。
(B) 他們計畫一起去看表演。
(C) 他們是銷售健身器材的。
(D) 他們對他們的攤位不滿意。

【類型】提問細節題型

【正解】(C)

44 What do we know about the speakers?
(A) They are preparing for a trade show.
(B) They plan to go to a show together.
(C) They sell gym equipment.
(D) They are not happy with their booth.

【解析】選項(A)(B)所述與對話內容不符，可先刪除不考慮。由兩人在對話中表示the location of our booth（我們攤位的地點）對銷售量有很大貢獻，可知他們對攤位地點很滿意，故選項(D)所述亦不正確。對話一開始的The Sports Goods Show is finally over（運動用品展終於結束了）這句話，可推測對話者很可能是參與運動用品展的廠商，很有可能是賣健身用品的，故正解為(C)。

他們產品的賣點是什麼？
(A) 較好的品質
(B) 較低的價格
(C) 多功能
(D) 較長的保固期

【類型】提問細節題型

【詞彙】
multiple 多重的

【正解】(D)

45 What is the selling point of their products?
(A) Better quality
(B) Lower price
(C) Multiple functions
(D) Longer warranty

【解析】對話中男子提到他們產品重要的賣點是excellent after-sales service（良好的售後服務），並接著說明：None of our competitors can offer a three-year warranty.（我們的競爭對手沒有一個能提供三年保固），可知他們的保固期是優於競爭產品的賣點，正解為(D)。

請看圖表。哪一個是商展賣得最好的產品？
(A) 立式健身車
(B) 踏步機
(C) 跑步機
(D) 有氧健身車

【類型】圖表對照題型

【正解】(B)

46 Look at the graph. Which is the best-selling product at the show?
(A) Upright bike
(B) Stepper
(C) Treadmill
(D) Aero bike

【解析】由直條圖所顯示的數據，代表踏步機銷售量的直條圖是最長的，可知踏步機是這次商展中銷售量最多的產品，故正解為(B)。

Questions 47-49 refer to the following conversation.

M So, what brings you here?

W My lower teeth on the left side have been sensitive lately.

M When was the last time you had a teeth cleaning?

W I can't remember. Probably two years ago.

M Well, the first thing I'm gonna do... is to give your teeth a thorough cleaning so as to remove the plaque from your teeth.

W Plaque... does that mean I have gum disease?

M Not really, but if you don't take good care of your teeth, you will, sooner or later.

男　那麼，你為什麼來這兒呀？

女　我下排牙齒右邊最近有點敏感。

男　你上次洗牙是什麼時候的事？

女　我不記得了。可能是兩年前吧。

男　喔，首先我要做的事情……就是幫你的牙齒好好的洗一下，好幫你去除牙齒上的牙菌斑。

女　牙菌斑……這意思是我有牙周病嗎？

男　並不是，不過如果你不照顧好自己的牙齒，你遲早會有的。

【詞彙】
sensitive 敏感的／
teeth cleaning 洗牙／
plaque 牙菌斑；牙垢／
gum disease 牙周病

---

47 Where is this conversation taking place?
　(A) At a dental clinic
　(B) At the Health Insurance Bureau
　(C) In a pharmacy
　(D) In the Counselors' Office

【解析】由男子在對話中提到要幫女子做teeth cleaning（洗牙），可知這個地方應該是個牙科診所，正解為(A)。

這段對話發生在何處？
(A) 牙科診所
(B) 建保局
(C) 藥房
(D) 輔導室

【類型】對話背景題型

【詞彙】
dental clinic 牙科診所／
Health Insurance Bureau
建保局／pharmacy 藥房

【正解】(A)

男子最有可能是什麼身份？

(A) 外科醫師

(B) 內科醫師

(C) 護理師

(D) 牙醫師

【類型】說話者身份題型

【正解】(D)

48 Who most likely is the man?

 (A) A surgeon

 (B) A physician

 (C) A nurse

 (D) A dentist

【解析】teeth cleaning「洗牙」是只有「牙醫師」方能從事的醫療行為，故男子最有可能是一名「牙醫師」，正解為(D)。

女子接下來要接受什麼？

(A) 心臟手術

(B) 整形手術

(C) 洗牙

(D) 拔牙

【類型】提問細節題型

【詞彙】

plastic surgery 整形手術／
tooth extraction 拔牙

【正解】(C)

49 What will the woman undergo next?

 (A) A heart surgery

 (B) A plastic surgery

 (C) A teeth cleaning

 (D) A tooth extraction

【解析】由對話中男子表示他要做的第一件事情，就是幫女子的牙齒做一次thorough cleaning（徹底的清洗），可知女子接下來將要接受teeth cleaning（洗牙），正解為(C)。

男 嗨，我想租一輛車。

女 沒問題。你想要租哪一種車？

男 一輛可載八個人的中型運動休旅車。

女 當然。要租多久？

男 三天。我這個星期六下午五點前會還。

女 非常好。這張表列出我們所有運動休旅車的租金。稅和保險都已經有含在租金裡了。

男 我可以在不同地點還車嗎？像是機場？

Questions 50-52 refer to the following conversation.

M Hi, I'd like to rent a car.

W No problem. What kind of car would you like to rent?

M A mid-size SUV with a capacity of eight.

W Sure. For how long?

M Three days. I'll return it by five this Saturday.

W Lovely. This table displays the rents of all our SUVs. Tax and insurance are both included.

M Can I drop it off at a different location, like the airport?

W Sorry, the car has to be returned to the same location.

女　抱歉，車子必須要在同個地點還車喔。

★

	Max Capacity	Daily Rates (NT$)
GMC Acadia	7	2,500
Honda Pilot	8	3,000
Mazda CX9	7	2,750
Volkswagen Atlas	7	2,800

★

	最大載客量	每日租金（新台幣）
GMC Acadia	7	2,500
Honda Pilot	8	3,000
Mazda CX9	7	2,750
Volkswagen Atlas	7	2,800

【詞彙】
SUV（= sport utility vehicle）運動型休旅車／
max capacity 最大載客量

50 What does the man need?
(A) An SUV for eight people
(B) A sports car
(C) A convertible car
(D) A camper

【解析】男子在對話中表示自己想要租A mid size SUV with a capacity of eight（可載八人的中型運動休旅車），故正解為(A)。

男子需要什麼？
(A) 一輛八人座運動型休旅車
(B) 一輛跑車
(C) 一輛敞篷車
(D) 一輛露營車

【類型】提問細節題型

【詞彙】
sports car 跑車／
convertible car 敞篷車／
camper 露營車

【正解】(A)

51 According to the conversation, which statement is true?
(A) The man wants a full-sized car.
(B) The cars are insured.
(C) The man reserved a car three days ago.
(D) All mid size cars are reserved.

【解析】由女子給男子看中型運動休旅車租金表時，表示Tax and insurance are both included.（稅和保險費都含在裡面），可知車子是已經有保險的，正解為(B)。

根據對話內容，哪項敘述正確？
(A) 男子想要一輛大型車。
(B) 車子有保車險。
(C) 男子三天前訂了一輛車。
(D) 所有中型車都被預訂了。

【類型】提問細節題型

【詞彙】
full size 大型的

【正解】(B)

請看表格。哪一輛車符合男子的需求？
(A) GMC Acadia
(B) Honda Pilot
(C) Mazda CX9
(D) Volkswagen Atlas

【類型】圖表對照題型

【正解】(B)

52 Look at the table. Which one meets the man's requirements?
(A) GMC Acadia
(B) Honda Pilot
(C) Mazda CX9
(D) Volkswagen Atlas

【解析】由男子在對話中表示自己需要可載八個人的中型運動休旅車，對照表格中每款車的最大載客量，可知只有Honda Pilot這款車符合他的需求，故正解為(B)。

女　你要確定帶足夠的保暖內衣喔。

男　好。我還需要什麼東西？

女　別忘了在你的打包清單上加上厚羽絨外套、暖和的手套和圍巾。

男　這只是個五天的旅行而已。我還以為我可以輕裝出遊。

女　如果你是在一月中去倫敦，就不行。

男　你覺得我會需要雨衣和雨鞋嗎？

女　你會的。如果你不希望大部分時間都在室內度過，就為幾場雨做好準備吧。

【詞彙】
thermal 保暖的／
down jacket 羽絨外套

Questions 53-55 refer to the following conversation.

W　Make sure you bring enough thermal underwear.

M　OK. What else do I need?

W　Don't forget to add a heavy down jacket, warm gloves and a scarf onto your packing list.

M　It's just a five-day trip. I thought I could pack light.

W　Not if you're visiting London in Mid-January.

M　Do you think I will need a raincoat and waterproof boots?

W　You will. If you don't want to spend most of your time indoors, be prepared for a few showers.

53 What is the man going to do?
(A) Pack for a trip
(B) Go shopping with the woman
(C) Buy some warm clothes
(D) Book a flight

【解析】男子在對話中詢問女子自己應該要帶什麼東西，女子在回答時提到關鍵字packing list（打包清單），而且從男子提到這只是個五天的trip（旅行），可知男子應該是將為了旅行而作打包行李的動作，正解為(A)。

男子將要做什麼？
(A) 為旅行打包行李
(B) 跟女子去逛街
(C) 買些暖和的衣服
(D) 訂機票

【類型】內容主題題型

【正解】(A)

54 According to the conversation, which statement is true?
(A) The man is going on a business trip.
(B) The woman is helping the man pack.
(C) The man is visiting London in the winter.
(D) The man will spend a long time in London.

【解析】由對話內容聽來，女子只是建議男子該打包什麼衣物，並未幫男子打包；男子並未提到自己旅行的目的；而由It's just a five-day trip.（這只是個五天的旅行）這句話知道男子只會在倫敦旅行五天，因此選項(A)(B)(D)皆非適當的敘述。由女子表示 ...you're visiting London in Mid January（你將在一月中拜訪倫敦），可知男子是在一月，也就是冬季時節去倫敦，正確敘述為(C)。

根據對話內容，哪項敘述正確？
(A) 男子將要去出差。
(B) 女子正在幫男子打包。
(C) 男子會在冬天拜訪倫敦。
(D) 男子將在倫敦待很久。

【類型】提問細節題型

【正解】(C)

55 What does the woman mean?
(A) The man should take a shower.
(B) There's a good chance it will rain in London.
(C) It's a bad idea to visit London in the winter.
(D) She prefers outdoor activities.

【解析】shower意指「陣雨」，女子在對話最後建議男子應be prepared for a few showers 即表示「應為幾場陣雨做好準備」，暗示倫敦很有可能會下雨，正解為(B)。

女子所言是什麼意思？
(A) 男子應該要沖個澡。
(B) 倫敦很有可能會下雨。
(C) 冬天去倫敦不是個好主意。
(D) 她比較喜歡戶外活動。

【類型】提問細節題型

【詞彙】
take a shower 沖澡

【正解】(B)

男A　嗨，我們需要一張兩人的座位。

男B　你們有訂位嗎？

女　你們不接受訂位，不是嗎？

男B　我們現在接受了。是這樣的，我們現在客滿。你們介意候位嗎？

男A　要等多久呢？

男B　我們有九十分鐘的用餐時間限制，所以三十分鐘後就會有幾張桌子空出來了。

女　好。我們等。

【詞彙】

table time limit 用餐時間限制

Questions 56-58 refer to the following conversation.

Man A　Hi, we need a table for two.

Man B　Do you have a reservation?

Woman　You don't take reservations, do you?

Man B　We do now. Well, we're full right now. Do you mind waiting?

Man A　How long is the wait?

Man B　We have a table time limit of 90 minutes, so there should be a few tables available in thirty minutes.

Woman　OK. We'll wait.

這段對話正在進行什麼事？

(A) 兩個人正在等用餐座位。

(B) 一名女子正在打電話訂位。

(C) 一名男子正邀請他的朋友晚餐。

(D) 一名男子正在機場為朋友送行。

【類型】內容主題題型

【詞彙】

see sb. off 為某人送行

【正解】(A)

56 What is taking place in this conversation?

(A) Two people are waiting for a table.

(B) A woman is calling to get a reservation.

(C) A man is inviting his friends for dinner.

(D) A man is seeing his friends off at the airport.

【解析】由對話內容聽到對話中中的一男一女正在一間目前客滿的餐廳，與安排座位的服務生對話，並決定等候空桌，因此可知選項(A)敘述符合對話內容，是正確答案。

57 According to the conversation, what do we know about the restaurant?
(A) It doesn't take reservations.
(B) It has a table time limit.
(C) It's not open for business yet.
(D) It doesn't serve alcohol.

【解析】由對話內容可知這家餐廳目前客滿，而且可能是帶位服務生的男子表示餐廳現在是接受訂位的，可知選項(A)(C)所述都是錯誤的，可先刪除不考慮。對話中並未提到是否提供酒精飲料，因此不能確定(D)所述是否正確。由其中一名男子表示We have a table time limit of 90 minutes（我們有九十分鐘的用餐時間限制），可知這家餐廳是有用餐時間限制的，正解為(B)。

根據對話內容，我們對這家餐廳有何認識？
(A) 它不接受訂位。
(B) 它有用餐時間限制。
(C) 它尚未開放營業。
(D) 它不提供酒精飲料。

【類型】提問細節題型

【正解】(B)

58 How long do the speakers have to wait for a free table?
(A) At least an hour.
(B) Probably 90 minutes.
(C) About half an hour.
(D) It depends.

【解析】雖然店家的用餐時間限制為九十分鐘，但男子表示there should be a few tables available in thirty minutes（三十分鐘後應該就會有幾張桌子空出來），可知有一批客人可能在三十分鐘後就會達到限制用餐時間，因此說話者可能等約半小時就可以有座位，正解為(C)。

說話者需要等多久才能等到一張空桌？
(A) 至少一小時
(B) 可能要九十分鐘
(C) 大約半小時
(D) 要看情況

【類型】提問細節題型

【正解】(C)

女　你可以跟我介紹一下你們的會員方案嗎？

男　當然可以啊。我們有很多彈性會員方案。你可以選擇不簽約的每月制會員方案、一日暢用方案或是定期會員方案。

女　你們也有學生會員方案，對不對？

男　對，我們有。妳目前是在大學就讀的學生嗎？

女　對，我是。

男　很好。妳很幸運，因為我們這個月正推出學生專用優惠方案。有了會員資格妳就可以使用我們在美國各地的健身房內所有健康及健身設備。

★

學生會員	折扣
12個月制	20%
6個月制	15%
3個月制	10%
每月滾動制	5%

【詞彙】
membership 會員／
package 方案／
fixed-term 定期的／
access 使用

Questions 59-61 refer to the following conversation and table.

W Could you introduce me your membership packages?

M Sure. We have a wide range of flexible membership options. You can choose a monthly membership without a contract, a day pass or a fixed-term membership.

W You also have student membership, don't you?

M Yes, we do. Are you currently a student in the university?

W Yes, I am.

M Good. You're in luck, as we're offering exclusive deals for students this month. With the membership you'll get full access to all the health and fitness facilities in any of our gyms around the U.S.

★

Student Membership	Discount
12-month	20%
6-month	15%
3-month	10%
Monthly rolling	5%

59 What does the woman want to join?
(A) A gym
(B) A drama club
(C) A band
(D) The army

女子想要加入什麼？
(A) 健身房
(B) 話劇社
(C) 樂團
(D) 軍隊

【解析】女子請男子向她介紹會員方案，對話最後男子表示有了這個會員資格，女子就能get full access to all the health and fitness facilities in any of our gyms（得到使用我們任何一間健身房的健康及健身設備），由關鍵字gyms（健身房）可知女子想參加的是健身房會員，答案為(A)。

【類型】內容主題題型

【正解】(A)

60 Which membership package is the woman interested in?
(A) A no contract monthly membership
(B) A day pass
(C) A fixed-term membership
(D) A student membership

女子對哪項會員方案有興趣？
(A) 無合約月制會員
(B) 一日暢用制會員
(C) 定期合約制會員
(D) 學生會員

【解析】男子一開始先向女子介紹三種會員方案，包括無合約的每月會員、一日制會員以及定期會員，但女子卻對這三種方案沒有興趣，直接問男子有關student membership（學生會員）的方案，可知女子應該是對「學生會員方案」有興趣。

【類型】提問細節題型

【正解】(D)

61 Look at the table. Which package offers the biggest discount?
(A) The monthly rolling membership
(B) The three-month membership
(C) The six-month membership
(D) The 12-moth membership

請看表格。哪個方案提供最大優惠？
(A) 逐月滾動會員
(B) 三個月會員
(C) 半年制會員
(D) 全年制會員

【解析】由本題所附顯示四種會期的學生會員所提供的會費折扣，以12個月會期提供20%的折扣最高，可知全年制會員的優惠最多，正解為(D)。

【類型】圖表對照題型

【正解】(D)

女　不好意思。我的行李沒有出現在我抵達的行李轉檯上。

男　請讓我看一下妳的行李票，好嗎？

女　當然。在這兒。

男　女士，我剛剛查詢了您的行李狀態。您的行李有在您的班機上，但因為某些原因沒有到達正確的行李轉檯。

女　那我現在該怎麼做？

男　請稍等幾分鐘，讓作業人員追蹤它的下落。抱歉造成您的不便。

女　只要不是不見了就沒關係。

【詞彙】
carousel 行李轉檯／
luggage ticket 行李票／
track down 追蹤

Questions 62-64 refer to the following conversation.

W Excuse me. My luggage didn't show up on the carousel on my arrival.

M Can I have a look at your luggage ticket, please?

W Sure. Here it is.

M Ma'am, I just checked your luggage status. Your luggage was on your flight but for some reason didn't make it to the right carousel.

W So what do I do now?

M Please wait a few minutes for the staff to track them down. Sorry for the inconvenience.

W It's okay as long as it's not missing.

說話者在哪裡？
(A) 外幣兌換櫃檯
(B) 機場報到櫃檯
(C) 行李提領處
(D) 免稅商店

【類型】對話地點題型

【詞彙】
luggage claim area 行李提領處

【正解】(C)

62 Where are the speakers?
(A) At the currency exchange counter
(B) At the airport check-in counter
(C) At the luggage claim area
(D) In the duty free shop

【解析】由關鍵字carousel（行李轉檯），以及luggage ticket（行李票），可推測女子應該是下了飛機要提領行李，因此最有可能發生這段對話的地點應為「機場的行李提領處」，正解為(C)。

63 What do we know about the woman?
(A) She missed her connecting flight.
(B) She couldn't find her luggage.
(C) She was forced to give up her seat.
(D) She was charged for her overweight luggage.

【解析】女子在對話一開始便表示她的行李沒有出現在行李轉檯上，可知她無法找到自己的行李，答案為(B)。

關於女子我們知道什麼？
(A) 她錯過了轉接的班機。
(B) 她找不到她的行李。
(C) 她被迫放棄座位。
(D) 她因行李超重被收費。

【類型】提問細節題型

【詞彙】
connecting flight 轉接班機／
overweight 超重的

【正解】(B)

---

64 What happened to the woman's luggage?
(A) It was put on a wrong flight.
(B) It didn't make the flight.
(C) It wasn't put on the right carousel.
(D) Someone else took it by mistake.

【解析】男子查詢了女子的行李狀態後，表示行李的確有被放上女子搭的飛機，因此選項(A)(B)皆可以先刪除不選。對話中並沒說行李是被人誤拿了，所以選項(D)亦非適當答案。女子表示行李didn't make it to the right carousel（沒有到正確的行李轉檯），可推測行李可能是被誤放到其他班機的行李轉檯上了，故正解為(C)。

女子的行李發生什麼事？
(A) 它被放上錯誤的班機。
(B) 它沒搭上飛機。
(C) 它沒被放在正確的輸送帶上。
(D) 其他人拿錯了。

【類型】提問細節題型

【詞彙】
by mistake 錯誤地

【正解】(C)

男A	先生，不好意思。我們正試著買一瓶汽水，但這自動販賣機吃了我們的錢。

男B	這台機器最近機能有點失常。我還以為它已經修好了。

女	我們剛投入了一個五十元硬幣，但是這機器沒有給我們我們要的東西。

男A	我們可以退錢嗎？

男B	你得到服務台去填退款申請單。作業人員會處理你們的申請。

女	如果這機器不能運作，你們真應該張貼一張標示，以免大家去使用它呀。

【詞彙】
vending machine 自動販賣機／
malfunction 發生故障；
機能失常／refund 退錢

Questions 65-67 refer to the following conversation.

Man A	Excuse me, sir. We were trying to buy a soda, but the vending machine ate our money.
Man B	This machine has been malfunctioning recently. I thought it was fixed.
Woman	We just inserted a 50-dollar note, but the machine didn't give us what we asked for.
Man A	Can we get a refund?
Man B	You need to fill out a refund request form at the service counter. The staff will process your request.
Woman	If it's not working, you should really put up a sign to keep people from using it.

這對情侶想在哪裡買飲料？
(A) 便利商店
(B) 自動販賣機
(C) 街上攤販
(D) 超級市場

【類型】對話背景題型

【正解】(B)

65 Where did the couple try to buy a drink?
　　(A) In a convenience store
　　(B) From a vending machine
　　(C) From a street vendor
　　(D) In a supermarket

【解析】由對話內容可知這對情侶是想在vending machine（自動販賣機）買汽水，故正解為(B)。

66 What's wrong with the machine?
(A) It gives the wrong change.
(B) It won't take debit cards.
(C) It won't take cash.
(D) It is out of order.

【解析】對話中並未提到這台販賣機會找錯零錢，也未提到這台販賣機是用什麼方式收費，故選項(A)(B)(C)皆不是適當答案。男子表示自動販賣機ate our money（吃了我們的錢），另一名男子也表示the machine has been malfunctioning（這機器機能失常），因此可判斷這台販賣機應該是out of order（故障了），正解為(D)。

這機器出了什麼問題？
(A) 它給錯誤的找零。
(B) 它不收現金卡。
(C) 它不收現金。
(D) 它故障了。

【類型】提問細節題型

【正解】(D)

67 What does the woman mean?
(A) The machine needs an out-of-order sign.
(B) The machine needs to be discarded.
(C) She can fix the machine by herself.
(D) She will compensate the man for his loss.

【解析】女子在對話最後表示如果機器不能運作，就應該要貼張告示，提醒人們這台機器「out of order（故障）」，而不要去使用它。因此選項(A)所述是最適當的答案。

女子所言是什麼意思？
(A) 這台機器需要一張故障標牌。
(B) 這台機器需要被丟掉。
(C) 她可以自己把機器修好。
(D) 她會賠償男子他的損失。

【類型】提問細節題型

【詞彙】
discard 丟棄／
compensate 賠償

【正解】(A)

男A 我剛突然想到下週五就是
Clinton先生最後一天上班
了。

女 他一直都是個很好共事的
好同事。我們應該幫他辦
一場歡送會。

男B 我們來辦個驚喜派對，共
度愉快時光吧。

男A 我贊成。歡送會不一定要
搞得離情依依。

女 我來訂個會議室辦派對。
Jeremy，你可以為Clinton
先生致個歡送詞嗎？

男B 致詞真不是我擅長的事。
不過我可以為這個場合訂
蛋糕、準備禮物和鮮花。

【詞彙】
going away party 歡送會／
sentimental 感傷的／
farewell speech 歡送詞

Questions 68-70 refer to the following conversation.

Man A It just occurred to me that next Friday is Mr. Clinton's last day at work.

Woman He's been a great colleague to work with. We should throw him a going away party.

Man B Let's make it a surprise party and have fun.

Man A I agree. A going away party doesn't have to be sentimental.

Woman I'll reserve a meeting room for the party. Can you give a farewell speech for Mr. Clinton, Jeremy?

Man B Giving a speech is really not my thing. But I can order the cake, gifts and flowers for the occasion.

說話者在計劃什麼？
(A) 一場學術演講
(B) 一場慶生派對
(C) 一場葬禮儀式
(D) 一場歡送會

【類型】內容主題題型

【詞彙】
scholarly 學術的／
farewell party 歡送會

【正解】(D)

68 What are the speakers planning?
(A) A scholarly presentation
(B) A birthday celebration
(C) A funeral ceremony
(D) A farewell party

【解析】女子在對話中表示我們應該幫他辦一場going away party（歡送派對），也就是選項(D)的farewell party（歡送派對），其他兩位男士也針對舉辦歡送會提供想法和意見，可知他們正在為這場歡送會作計劃，答案為(D)。

69 How will the going away party be?
(A) Sad
(B) Joyful
(C) Awkward
(D) Emotional

【解析】由其中一名男子在對話中提到要把派對弄成一個驚喜派對，並且have fun（玩得愉快），可知這場歡送會應該會充滿笑聲，故正解為(B)。

這將會是怎樣的一場歡送會？
(A) 悲傷的
(B) 歡樂的
(C) 尷尬的
(D) 情緒激動的

【類型】提問細節題型

【正解】(B)

70 What will the woman do in preparation for the party?
(A) Send the invitation
(B) Bake a cake
(C) Reserve a venue
(D) Buy a gift

【解析】由女子在對話中表示I'll reserve a meeting room for the party.（我來訂個會議室開派對），可知女子將會負責訂派對場地，答案為(C)。

女子將會做什麼來為派對做準備？
(A) 寄送邀請函
(B) 烤蛋糕
(C) 訂場地
(D) 買禮物

【類型】提問細節題型

【詞彙】
in preparation for sth.
作為……的準備／venue 場地

【正解】(C)

Directions: You will hear some talks given by a single speaker. You will be asked to answer three questions about what the speaker says in each talk. Select the best response to each question and mark the letter (A), (B), (C) or (D) on your answer sheet. The talks will not be printed in your test book and will be spoken only one time.

男 各位午安！很高興在此宣布我們今年的年度員工旅遊將會在十月底舉行。確實的時間會晚一點決定。我們目前正在決定旅遊地點，員旅籌備小組需要各位的協助參與。這裡是旅遊地點的選項，以及每人大約旅遊費用。請在明天下午三點前投票給你最想去的地點。投票結果將會在這星期四的會議中宣布。

★ 投票結果

地點	票數
墾丁	22
宜蘭	34
阿里山	18
台南	12

Questions 71-73 refer to the following talk and table.

M Good afternoon, everyone! I'm pleased to announce that our annual company trip this year will take place at the end of October. The exact dates will be decided later. The Staff Travel Preparation Group is currently in the process of deciding the destination for the trip, and we're seeking your input. We have four trip destination options. Please vote for your most preferred destinations by 3 p.m. tomorrow. The result will be announced in Thursday's meeting.

★ Result of the vote

Place	Votes
Kenting	22
Yilan	34
Alishan	18
Tainan	12

71 Which event will take place at the end of October?
(A) Re-election of directors
(B) Opening anniversary celebration
(C) Annual company trip
(D) Company sports fest

【解析】由our annual company trip this year will take place at the end of October（我們今年的年度公司旅遊將十月底舉行）這句話，可知正確答案為(C)。

十月底將會舉行什麼活動？
(A) 董事改選
(B) 開幕週年慶
(C) 年度公司旅遊
(D) 公司運動會

【類型】提問細節題型

【詞彙】
re-election 改選／
director 董事／
sports fest 運動會

【正解】(C)

---

72 What will the speakers vote for?
(A) The destination of the trip
(B) The dates of the trip
(C) The leader of the preparatory group
(D) The location of the staff dinner

【解析】由本段談話提到Please vote for your most preferred destinations（請投票選出你最想去的地點），可知聽話者被要求投票選出旅遊地點，正解為(A)。

聽話者將要投票選什麼？
(A) 旅遊地點
(B) 旅遊日期
(C) 籌備小組的組長
(D) 員工聚餐地點

【類型】提問細節題型

【正解】(A)

---

73 Look at the table. Which place is selected as the trip destination?
(A) Kenting
(B) Yilan
(C) Alishan
(D) Tainan

【解析】由表格所顯示的投票票數，宜蘭得到的票數34票，領先其他地點票數，可知宜蘭被選為旅遊地點，正解為(B)。

請看表格。哪個地方被選為旅遊地點？
(A) 墾丁
(B) 宜蘭
(C) 阿里山
(D) 台南

【類型】圖表對照題型

【正解】(B)

女　各位，請注意我這裡一下好嗎？為了加強我們的顧客服務技巧，我們將會在下週三上午舉辦一場客服研討會。這場兩小時的研討會將會涵蓋包括電話技巧、抱怨解決以及建立顧客忠誠度這些議題。這不是強制參加的，但我們真的很希望每個人都能參加這場研討會，因為它能幫助各位改進客服方面的技巧及策略。對參加這場研討會有興趣的人，請在這星期之前到接待櫃檯登記。

【詞彙】
workshop 研討會／
customer loyalty 顧客忠誠度／
compulsory 強制性的

Questions 74-76 refer to the following announcement.

W Guys, may I have your attention please? In order to strengthen our customer service skills, we're having a customer service workshop next Wednesday morning. The two-hour workshop will cover issues including telephone skills, complaint resolution and building customer loyalty. It's not compulsory, but we do hope that everyone can join us at the workshop, because it can help you improve your skills and strategies in terms of customer service. Those who are interested in attending this workshop please sign up at the reception desk by the end of this week.

這場專題研討會主要是關於什麼？
(A) 如何加強顧客服務技巧
(B) 如何激勵員工更努力工作
(C) 如何提升工作效率
(D) 如何改善時間管理技巧

【類型】內容主題題型

【詞彙】
motivate 激勵／
work efficiency 工作效率／
time management 時間管理

【正解】(A)

74 What is the workshop mainly about?
(A) How to strengthen customer service skills
(B) How to motivate employees to work harder
(C) How to enhance work efficiency
(D) How to improve time management skills

【解析】由談話中表示we're having a customer service workshop（我們將舉辦一場顧客服務研討會），可知這場研討會是與顧客服務有關，選項中只有(A)與顧客服務有關，故(A)為最有可能的答案。

75 Which of the following will not be included in the workshop?
(A) Telephone skills
(B) Complaint resolution
(C) Building customer loyalty
(D) Interpersonal skills

【解析】這段話提到這場兩小時的研討會包含telephone skills, complaint resolution and building customer loyalty這三個議題，並不包括選項(D)的「人際技巧」，故可知正解為(D)。

研討會不包含下列哪一項內容？
(A) 電話技巧
(B) 處理投訴
(C) 建立顧客忠誠度
(D) 人際技巧

【類型】提問細節題型

【詞彙】
interpersonal 人際的

【正解】(D)

76 Which statement about the workshop is NOT true?
(A) It's a two-hour training program.
(B) It's optional.
(C) It will take place next Wednesday morning.
(D) The registration ends today.

【解析】由這段談話最後表示please sign up at the reception desk by the end of this week（請在這週結束前到櫃檯登記），可知登記參加這場研討會的時間是到這週結束前截止，選項(D)所述與談話內容不符，故為正解。

有關研討會敘述，哪一項不正確？
(A) 它是個兩小時的訓練課程。
(B) 它是選擇性參加的。
(C) 它將在下週三上午舉行。
(D) 登記報名將在今天結束。

【類型】提問細節題型

【詞彙】
optional 可選擇的

【正解】(D)

嗨，Daniel，我是Lily。我是打來提醒你明天的會議的。我希望你已經預訂一間會議室了。是這樣的，我已經把明天我們會議會需要的文件以電子郵件寄給你了。請你影印足夠的份數發給每個人了。別忘了你要在會議開始之前把視聽設備準備好。還有，你必須做座位安排，讓與會者可以按照會議桌上的名牌入座。目前應該就是這些事了。拜。

★

附件 (4)
1.　上回會議記錄
2.　會議議程
3.　團隊業績月報
4.　預算提案

Questions 77-79 refer to the following message and picture.

W Hi, Daniel. This is Lily. I'm calling to remind you of tomorrow's meeting. I hope you have reserved a meeting room. Well, I've emailed you the documents that we'll need in the meeting. Please make enough copies for everyone. Don't forget that you need to have the video equipment ready by the time the meeting starts. Also, you need to make seating arrangement and make the participants sit according to their nametags on the meeting table. I think that's all for now. Bye.

★

Attachments (4)
1.　Last meeting's minutes
2.　Meeting agenda
3.　Team monthly sales report
4.　budget proposal

說話者正在做什麼？
(A) 記留言
(B) 留留言
(C) 訂會議室
(D) 邀請男子參加會議

【類型】主題提問題型

【正解】(B)

77 What is the speaker doing?
(A) Taking a message
(B) Leaving a message
(C) Reserving a meeting room
(D) Inviting the man for the meeting

【解析】由內容判斷說話者並非在記留言，選項(A)可先刪除不考慮。選項(C)(D)亦不符談話內容。由這段談話內容推測應該是在交代待辦事項，因此說話者應該是在留語音留言，正解為(B)。

78 According to the message, which is Daniel not responsible for?
(A) Reserving a meeting room
(B) Making seat arrangements
(C) Getting the video equipment ready
(D) Sending invitation notices

【解析】由留言內容沒有交代Daniel發會議通知，可知這應該不是Daniel所負責的工作，故選(D)。

根據留言內容，哪一項不是Daniel負責的？
(A) 訂會議室
(B) 安排座位
(C) 準備視聽設備
(D) 發出會議通知

【類型】提問細節題型

【詞彙】
be responsible for 負責……

【正解】(D)

79 Look at the picture. Which is not included in the attachments?
(A) The last meeting's minutes
(B) Meeting agenda
(C) Presentation outline
(D) Budget proposal

【解析】由圖片中顯示的四項附件標題，並不包含presentation outline（簡報大綱），可知正解應為(C)。

請看圖片。哪一項不包含在附件裡？
(A) 上回會議記錄
(B) 會議議程
(C) 簡報大綱
(D) 預算提案

【類型】圖表對照題型

【詞彙】
outline 大綱

【正解】(C)

男　好。現在讓我重複一次您的訂位資料。您是以Whitefield先生的名義預訂今天晚上七點鐘四位大人兩位小孩的座位。您的聯絡電話號碼為0912345678。我們將會為您保留座位十五分鐘。怕您不知道，在此告訴您我們最近有調整過自助晚餐的價格。細節都公佈在我們的網站上了。非常期待今晚能為您及您的貴賓提供服務。

	時間	價格
平日	17:30-21:00	$580（每位大人）$290（每位小孩）
週末及假日	17:00-22:00	$650（每位大人）$320（每位小孩）

Questions 80-82 refer to the following talk and table.

M OK. Let me repeat your table reservation details. You reserved a table for four adults and two children this evening at 7 p.m. in the name of Mr. Whitefield. Your contact phone number is 0912345678. We will hold your table for only 15 minutes past your booking time. In case you don't know, we have recently adjusted the prices for our dinner buffet. More details can be found on our website. Thank you very much for making the reservation. We look forward to being of service to you and your guests this evening.

★

	Time	Prices
Weekdays	17:30-21:00	$580 (per adult) $290 (per child)
Weekend & Holiday	17:00-22:00	$650 (per adult) $320 (per child)

說話者正在做什麼？
(A) 預訂一張桌子
(B) 進行預訂
(C) 取消預訂
(D) 接受預訂

【類型】主題提問題型

【正解】(D)

80 What is the speaker doing?
　　(A) Booking a table
　　(B) Making a reservation
　　(C) Canceling a reservation
　　(D) Taking a reservation

【解析】由說話者重複訂位資訊，並提醒聽話者訂位只保留十五分鐘，因此可推測說話者應該是正在接受預訂，正解為(D)。

81 What type of restaurant is this?
(A) A fast food restaurant
(B) A barbecue restaurant
(C) A buffet restaurant
(D) A bistro

這是間什麼形式的餐廳？
(A) 速食餐廳
(B) 烤肉餐廳
(C) 自助餐廳
(D) 小酒館

【解析】由説話者提到we have recently adjusted the prices for our dinner buffet（我們最近調整了自助晚餐的價格），其中關鍵字dinner buffet（自助晚餐）透露這家餐廳應該是一家自助餐廳，故正解為(C)。

【類型】提問細節題型

【詞彙】
bistro 小酒館

【正解】(C)

82 Look at the table. What's the price for dinner buffet per adult during the weekdays?
(A) $580
(B) $290
(C) $650
(D) $320

請看表格。平日每位成人的自助晚餐價格是多少？
(A) $580
(B) $290
(C) $650
(D) $320

【解析】由表格上所顯示的平日價格，每位大人是$580，因此正解為(A)。

【類型】圖表對照題型

【正解】(A)

女　嘿，媽，我有個消息，而且我希望妳是第一個知道的。聽之前先深呼吸一我跟Gary訂婚了！我知道妳現在一定在尖叫，但冷靜下來，好嗎？我跟Gary不會辦訂婚派對，因為我們打算在八月辦婚禮。我下個星期會回家。我等不及要給妳一個大擁抱，並且讓你看看我的戒指。噢，當然妳未來的女婿也會跟我一起回去。愛妳喲！

【詞彙】
engagement party 訂婚派對／
plan on 打算

Questions 83-85 refer to the following message.

W Hey, Mom, I've got some news and I want you to be the first one to know. Take a deep breath before you hear this – Gary and I are engaged! I know you must be screaming right now, but calm down, OK? Gary and I are not gonna have an engagement party because we're planning on having our wedding in the coming August! I will come home next week. I can't wait to give you a big hug and show you the ring. Well, of course your future son-in-law will be coming with me. Love you.

關於說話者，我們知道什麼？
(A) 她懷孕了。
(B) 她得到第一個工作機會。
(C) 她工作面試很成功。
(D) 她被求婚了。

【類型】提問細節題型

【詞彙】
pregnant 懷孕的／
propose 求婚

【正解】(D)

83 What do we know about the speaker?
(A) She got pregnant.
(B) She got her first job offer.
(C) She nailed the job interview.
(D) She has been proposed.

【解析】由說話者表示自己有個消息，即Gary and I are engaged!（我跟Gary訂婚了），可推測Gary可能向她求婚，而她答應了，因此訂下婚約，選項(D)為最有可能的答案，故為正解。選項(C)的nail sth.表示「幹得好」。

84 What is the purpose of this message?
(A) To share happy news
(B) To announce pregnancy
(C) To express gratitude
(D) To give a warning

這通留言的目的是什麼？
(A) 分享喜訊
(B) 宣布懷孕
(C) 表達感謝
(D) 提出警告

【解析】由説話者表示我有個消息，而且希望你第一個知道，可知他是要分享一個消息；接著説話者表示自己已經訂婚了，可知這通留言的目的是要分享一個喜訊，故正解為(A)。其他選項所述皆與留言內容不符。

【類型】內容主題題型

【詞彙】
pregnancy 懷孕

【正解】(A)

85 According to the message, what will take place in the coming August?
(A) An engagement party
(B) A wedding banquet
(C) A graduation ceremony
(D) An opening tea party

根據留言內容，即將到來的八月會發生什麼事？
(A) 訂婚派對
(B) 結婚喜宴
(C) 畢業典禮
(D) 開幕茶會

【解析】由留言內容提到we're planning on having our wedding in the coming August（我們打算在八月舉行婚禮），可知八月將會有一個結婚喜宴，故正解為(B)。

【類型】提問細節題型

【正解】(B)

男　嗨，Paula，進來吧。請坐。我已經看過妳昨天交的執行企劃書了。寫得很好，很簡單明瞭，而且非常有力地證明妳的論點。整體來說我認為這是一份很合宜的一份提案，不過如果妳可以將妳的想法結合相關市場部分，並且定義產品將能如何鎖定我們的市場，這份提案就會更具可行性。妳可以根據我的反饋意見做修改，並且在這星期之前給我修訂的版本嗎？

【詞彙】
implementation proposal
執行企劃書／make one's point
證明主張、論點／
segment 部分／
feedback 回饋意見

Questions 86-88 refer to the following talk.

M Hi, Paula, come on in. Please take a seat. I've reviewed the Implementation Proposal that you turned in yesterday. It was well written, comprehensible, and made your points about the plan very effectively. Overall, I think this is a very reasonable proposal, but if you can organize your ideas into related market segments and define how the product will target our markets, this proposal will be even more workable. Could you revise it according to my feedback and give me the modified version by this week?

男子正在做什麼？
(A) 要求他的秘書幫他跑腿辦事
(B) 提供一名員工意見回饋
(C) 面試一位工作應徵者
(D) 向他的老闆提出可行的計劃

【類型】內容主題題型

【正解】(B)

86 What is the man doing?
(A) Asking his secretary to run his errands
(B) Providing feedback to an employee
(C) Interviewing a job candidate
(D) Showing his boss a workable plan

【解析】由説話者表示I've reviewed your Implementation Proposal（我已經看過你的執行企劃書），並針對企劃書內容提供正面的肯定以及可以使它更具可行性的提議，可知説話者正在針對企劃書內容提出意見回饋，故選(B)。

87 What does the speaker ask the listener to do?
(A) Estimate the cost of developing the product
(B) Work on the launch plan
(C) Rewrite her proposal
(D) Integrate her ideas into the market

【解析】由說話者表示if you can organize your ideas into related market segments...（如果你能將想法與相關市場部分做結合），就會使這份提案更具可行性，因此可知說話者是在建議對方將她的想法與市場做結合，選項(D)符合所述，故為正解。

說話者要求聽話者做什麼？
(A) 估算開發產品的成本
(B) 規劃上市計劃
(C) 重寫提案
(D) 將想法與市場結合

【類型】提問細節題型

【詞彙】
estimate 估算／
integrate sth. into... 使合併

【正解】(D)

88 When is the listener expected to turn in a revision?
(A) In two weeks
(B) By the end of this week
(C) By next meeting
(D) By the end of this month

【解析】由本段談話最後提出give me the modified version by this week（這星期以前將修改過的版本給我）的要求，可知聽話者應該在這星期之內提交提案修正版，故正解為(B)。

聽話者何時應提交修正版？
(A) 兩週後
(B) 這週結束前
(C) 下次會議前
(D) 這個月底前

【類型】提問細節題型

【詞彙】revision 修正版

【正解】(B)

女 我是Brenda Brown。我是
打來表達我強烈的憤怒。我
就直接說重點了。我最近發
現我的照片在未經我同意的
情況下被使用在你們的廣告
中。這已經造成我極大的不
便和困擾，因為我從未答應
當你們的品牌代言人。無論
理由是什麼，你們已經侵犯
我的肖像權，而我正認真考
慮要對你們公司採取法律行
動。我要在廿四小時之內聽
到你們的回應，否則我絕對
會訴諸法律，而你們必須得
負擔後果。

【詞彙】
resentment 憤怒／
cut to the chase 直接說重點／
permission 同意／
consent 同意／
brand ambassador 品牌代言人／
portraiture right 肖像權

Questions 89-91 refer to the following message.

W This is Brenda Brown. I'm calling to express my strong resentment. I'll just cut to the chase. I recently found that my photo was being used in your advertisement without my permission. This has caused me a lot of inconvenience and troubles, as I never consented to be your brand ambassador. Whatever your reason is, you have violated my portraiture right, and I am seriously considering taking legal actions against your company. I expect a response within 24 hours, otherwise I will take an action at law for sure and you will have to bear the consequence.

說話者聽起來如何？
(A) 很興奮
(B) 很憤怒
(C) 很懊悔
(D) 很困窘

【類型】提問細節題型

【詞彙】
furious 盛怒的／
regretful 後悔的

【正解】(B)

89 How does the speaker sound?
(A) Excited
(B) Furious
(C) Regretful
(D) Embarrassed

【解析】說話者一開始就表明I'm calling to express my strong resentment（我是打來表達我強烈的憤怒），名詞resentment意指「憤怒」，而選項(B)的furious亦是用來表達「感到憤怒」的形容詞，故(B)為正解。

90 What is the purpose of this call?
(A) To announce a promotion
(B) To offer an apology
(C) To make a complaint
(D) To claim a insurance

【解析】由說話者表示自己是打來「表達憤怒」，隨後陳述造成不滿的原因，可知這通電話的目的是在「抱怨」，故正解為(C)。

這通電話的目的為何？
(A) 宣布升遷消息
(B) 表達歉意
(C) 提出抱怨
(D) 保險索償

【類型】內容主題題型

【詞彙】
insurance 保險

【正解】(C)

---

91 When is the listener supposed to make a response?
(A) Within 12 hours
(B) Within 24 hours
(C) Within 48 hours
(D) Within 72 hours

【解析】由說話者表示I expect a response within 24 hours（我要在廿四小時內得到回應），可知聽話者應該在廿四小時內作出回應，正解為(B)。

聽話者何時應該做出回應？
(A) 十二小時之內
(B) 廿四小時之內
(C) 四十八小時之內
(D) 七十二小時之內

【類型】提問細節題型

【正解】(B)

男　好，現在大家聽我說。音樂會在二十分鐘後就會開始了。帶位員會在表演開始時將所有的門都關起來，所以強烈建議各位現在去上個洗手間，否則就得等到中場休息。這是音樂會的節目單，裡面提供音樂會上會表演的曲目細節。如果你需要一份的話，現在還有足夠的時間可以去入口買。只是要確定你在表演開始前五分鐘回來。

★

春季音樂會

D小調第三號小提琴奏鳴曲，作品108

布拉姆斯 (1833-1897)

=== 中場休息 (20分鐘) ===

A大調小提琴奏鳴曲，作品FWV 8

法朗克 (1822-1890)

【詞彙】
usher 帶位員／
intermission 中場休息／
piece 曲目

Questions 92-94 refer to the following talk and program.

M OK, now everyone please listen to me. The concert will begin in twenty minutes. The ushers will close all the doors at the beginning of the performance, so it is highly recommended that you go to the restroom right now otherwise you will have to wait until intermission. This is the concert program, which gives detailed information about the pieces to be performed at the concert. If you need one, there's still plenty of time for you to get it at the entrance. Just make sure you come back five minutes before the scheduled start time.

★

Spring Concert

Sonata No. 3 in D minor, Op. 108

Johannes Brahms (1833-1897)

=== Intermission (20 minutes) ===

Sonata in A Major, FWV 8

Cêser Franck (1822-1890)

二十分鐘後將會開始什麼活動？
(A) 音樂會
(B) 足球賽
(C) 嘉年華遊行
(D) 廟會

【類型】主題內容題型

【詞彙】
carnival 嘉年華／
religious 宗教的

【正解】(A)

92 What will start in twenty minutes?
　　(A) A music concert
　　(B) A football match
　　(C) A carnival parade
　　(D) A religious festival

【解析】由說話者一開始便表示The concert will begin in twenty minutes.（音樂會二十分鐘後就會開始），可知答案為(A)。

93 What are the listeners advised to do?
(A) Silence their phones
(B) Get a concert program
(C) Go to the restroom
(D) Buy souvenirs at the gift shop

聽話者被勸告做什麼事？
(A) 將手機靜音
(B) 買一份音樂節目單
(C) 去上洗手間
(D) 到禮品店買紀念品

【解析】說話者表示it is highly recommended that you go to the restroom（強烈建議你們去上個洗手間）；it is highly recommended that ...為表示「強力建議某事」的句型用法。因此可知說話者建議聽話者「去上廁所」，正解為(C)。

【類型】提問細節題型

【詞彙】
silence 使安靜／
souvenir 紀念品

【正解】(C)

94 Look at the program. How long is the intermission?
(A) Five minutes
(B) Ten minutes
(C) Fifteen minutes
(D) Twenty minutes

請看節目單。中場休息時間多長？
(A) 五分鐘
(B) 十分鐘
(C) 十五分鐘
(D) 二十分鐘

【解析】由節目單上顯示intermission（中場休息）的時間為 20 minutes（二十分鐘），可知答案為(D)。

【類型】圖表對照題型

【正解】(D)

女 在我們會議結束之前，我有件事情要宣布。如你們大部份人可能已經知道的，我即將在下個月轉調到南京總公司去了。Jennifer將會接替我擔任人事部主任一職。我希望你們能給予她相同的支持與協助。我從大學畢業起就在這間分公司工作了，因此對我來說要說再見真的不容易。跟各位共事的感覺非常美好。希望我們能保持聯絡。

【詞彙】
headquarters 總部／
succeed 接替；繼承

Questions 95-97 refer to the following announcement.

W Before we wrap up the meeting, I have an announcement to make. As most of you may have known, I am transferring to the Nanjing headquarters next month. Jennifer will succeed me as the Director of HR Department. I hope you can give her the same support and assistance. I have been working in this branch since I graduated from university, so it's really not easy for me to say goodbye. It's been a great experience working with you all. I hope we can stay in touch.

這則宣布主要是關於什麼？
(A) 喬遷通知
(B) 營業時間異動
(C) 暫停營業通知
(D) 人事異動

【類型】內容主題題型

【詞彙】
temporary closure 暫時歇業

【正解】(D)

95 What is this announcement mainly about?
(A) A notice of relocation
(B) A change of business hours
(C) A notice of temporary closure
(D) A change of personnel

【解析】由說話者表示自己即將調職，並介紹接任人選，可知這是一則有關人事異動的宣布，故正解為(D)。

96 What information is not given in this announcement?

(A) The speaker's replacement

(B) The speaker's contact number

(C) The speaker's current position

(D) The speaker's future work place

這則宣布中沒有提供什麼訊息？

(A) 說話者的接替者

(B) 說話者的聯絡號碼

(C) 說話者的現在職位

(D) 說話者的未來工作地點

【解析】說話者表示自己將調到Nanjing headquarters（南京總公司），提到了未來工作地點；說話者也表示Jennifer將接替自己擔任Director of HR Department一職，說明了自己的現職即為「人事部主任」，也同時提到了「接替職位的人」，可知選項(A)(C)(D)都有在宣布中告知。唯一沒有在這則宣布中提到的就是說話者的聯絡電話號碼，故正解為(B)。

【類型】提問細節題型

【詞彙】

replacement 接替者

【正解】(B)

97 What most likely is the reason the speaker's leaving her current position?

(A) She got laid off.

(B) She is retiring.

(C) She is job-hopping to another company.

(D) She has been promoted.

說話者離開現職的原因最有可能是什麼？

(A) 她被解僱了。

(B) 她要退休了。

(C) 她要跳槽到另一間公司。

(D) 她被升職了。

【解析】由說話者表示自己是要調任到南京總公司，並提到自己自大學畢業就在這間分公司工作，可知說話者還是在同一間公司上班，並沒有job-hop（跳槽）；當然也沒有got laid off（被解僱）或是retire（退休），因此最有可能的職務調動原因就是他被升職了，故(D)為正解。

【類型】提問細節題型

【詞彙】

lay off 解僱／job-hop 跳槽

【正解】(D)

男　嗨，Amanda，我是John。我剛收到你跟Brian二十週年結婚紀念慶祝的邀請。非常謝謝你邀請我。我真的很希望可以參加這個慶祝會，但我的行程表可能無法讓我如願，因為Cindy和我那天晚上有計劃了。我們希望能跟你們在其他時間聚會。事實上，Cindy想知道你們這個星期五能不能來我們家吃晚餐。再打給我吧。

Questions 98-100 refer to the following message.

M　Hi, Amanda, this is John. I've just received the invitation to you and Brian's twentieth wedding anniversary. Thank you so much for including me. I really wish I could join the celebration, but my schedule probably won't allow me to do so because Cindy and I already have plans for the evening. We'd love to get together with you at another time. In fact, Cindy wants to know if you can come over to our place for dinner this Friday. Call me back.

男子為何要打電話？
(A) 婉拒一個邀請
(B) 要求產品樣本
(C) 重新安排會議
(D) 取消採購訂單

【類型】內容主題題型

【詞彙】
turn down 拒絕

【正解】(A)

98 Why is the man calling?
　　(A) To turn down an invitation
　　(B) To request a product sample
　　(C) To reschedule a meeting
　　(D) To cancel a purchase order

【解析】由留言內容可知男子獲得邀請，但是他表示my schedule probably won't allow me to do so（我的行程可能不能讓我參加），可知他是來電婉拒這個邀請，故正解為(A)。

99 Why can't the man join the celebration?
(A) He is hospitalized.
(B) He is on a vacation.
(C) He has a prior arrangement.
(D) He has to work overtime.

男子為何不能參加慶祝會？
(A) 他住院了。
(B) 他正在度假。
(C) 他有事先安排活動了。
(D) 他必須加班工作。

【解析】本題要問的是婉拒邀請的「原因」。男子表示I already have plans for the evening（我那晚已有計劃），可知他無法接受邀請是因為已經有事先安排事情，故正解為(C)。

【類型】提問細節題型

【詞彙】
hospitalize 使住院／
prior 先前的

【正解】(C)

---

100 What does the man offer at the end of his message?
(A) A special discount
(B) A dinner invitation
(C) A business proposal
(D) An apprenticeship

男子在留言最後提出了什麼？
(A) 一項特別優惠
(B) 一個晚餐邀請
(C) 一宗合作提案
(D) 一個實習機會

【解析】男子拒絕邀請後，提出想要另找時間跟對方聚會的想法，並表示if you can come over to our place for dinner（你們可否來我們家吃晚餐），具體提出邀請，可知正確答案為(B)。

【類型】提問細節題型

【詞彙】
apprenticeship 實習工作

【正解】(B)

(A) 男孩正在騎單車。
(B) 女子是個理髮師。
(C) 這裡是個菜市場。
(D) 男子是個眼科醫生。

【類型】多人照片題型

【詞彙】
barber 理髮師／
eye doctor 眼科醫師

【正解】(D)

01 (A) The boy is riding a bike.
　　(B) The woman is a barber.
　　(C) It is a food market.
　　(D) The man is an eye doctor.

【解析】由照片中的背景場景及儀器，可看出男孩正在接受眼睛檢查，旁邊的女子協助男孩保持正確姿勢，而穿白袍的男子則正透過儀器檢查男孩的眼睛。因此選項(A)(B)(C)所述皆與照片內容不符，只有選項(D)是最符合照片的敘述，故為正解。

(A) 女子是個單親媽媽。
(B) 男嬰在推車裡面。
(C) 女子正在遛狗。
(D) 他們正在玩捉迷藏。

【類型】人物景色題型

【詞彙】
single mother 單親媽媽／
trolley 推車／
hide and seek 捉迷藏

【正解】(B)

02 (A) The woman is a single mother.
　　(B) The baby boy is in the trolley.
　　(C) The woman is walking a dog.
　　(D) They are playing hide and seek.

【解析】照片中為一個女子扶著一輛嬰兒推車，而推車中躺著一名嬰孩。單由照片並無法得知照片中女子的身份，既無從知道她是否為嬰孩的母親，更遑論她是否是個單親媽媽，故選項(A)可直接刪除不選。照片中沒有狗，而且照片中的人物並未出現玩捉迷藏的動作，因此選項(C)(D)所述亦不符合照片內容。正解為(B)。

(A) 人們正在等他們的行李。
(B) 一場會議即將開始。
(C) 櫃檯前有一條隊伍。
(D) 自動販賣機都故障了。

【類型】多人照片題型

【正解】(C)

03 (A) People are waiting for their luggage.
　　(B) A meeting is about to start.
　　(C) There's queue in front of the counter.
　　(D) The vending machines are out of order.

【解析】這是一張多人出現的照片，觀其背景，判斷照片地點並非會議室，此外也沒有出現行李轉檯或自動販賣機，因此選項(A)(B)(D)所述皆與照片內容不符。從照片中可以看到一個長櫃檯，後面有數位結帳人員，櫃檯前有一個等著結帳的隊伍，可知選項(C)所述符合照片內容，故為正解。

(A) 男子剛洗過手。
(B) 男子是三個孩子的爸。
(C) 男子是個清潔工。
(D) 男子愛吃甜食。

【類型】單人照片題

【詞彙】
sweet tooth 愛吃甜品者

【正解】(C)

04 (A) The man just washed his hands.
　　(B) The man is a father of three.
　　(C) The man is a cleaner.
　　(D) The man has a sweet tooth.

【解析】無論是什麼樣的照片題，從照片無法得到的訊息就不是正確或適當的描述。由這張單人照片題中的人物，手持掃把畚箕正在做出掃地動作，我們只能得到「他正在掃地」或是「他可能是個清潔人員」等訊息，選項中只有(C)符合我們所知道的訊息，故為最適當的答案。其他選項所述皆無法從照片得知，故不選。

(A) 這是個健身房。
(B) 這是個公園。
(C) 有一個湖泊。
(D) 他們在跳舞。

【類型】人物景物題型

【正解】(B)

05 (A) It's a gym.
(B) It's a park.
(C) There's a lake.
(D) They are dancing.

【解析】由照片的人物互動情況及背景景物看來，可知這裡並不是一個健身房，而且看不到湖泊，照片中的兩個人一個正在腳踏車上，另一個正在走路，彼此沒有互動，因此選項(A)(C)(D)皆為錯誤描述。由背景的花草樹木及硬體擺設看來，推測這裡應該是一個公園，正解為(B)。

(A) 這天風很大。
(B) 這天暴風雨
(C) 這天是晴天。
(D) 這天下雪。

【類型】人物景物題型

【正解】(C)

06 (A) It's windy.
(B) It's stormy.
(C) It's sunny.
(D) It's snowy.

【解析】出現這種單人照片題時，雖然重點常會放在人物的舉止行動上，但也別忘了注意背景環境所透露的訊息。如本題，四個選項的描述重點完全不在人物上，反而是在照片的背景天氣。由照片中地面出現的扶疏映影，可知這天的天氣應該是出太陽的晴朗天氣，既看不出有颶風也無落雨跡象，故正解為(C)。

▶ PART 2

Directions: You will hear a question or statement and three responses spoken in English. They will not be printed in your test book and will be spoken only one time. Select the best response to the question or statement and mark the letter (A), (B) or (C) on your answer sheet.

Example
You will hear:
Did you have dinner at the restaurant yesterday?
You will also hear:
(A) Yes, it lasted all day.
(B) No, I went to a movie with my girlfriend.
(C) Yes, the client was nice.

The best response to the question "Did you have dinner at the restaurant yesterday?" is choice (B), "No, I went to a movie with my girlfriend," so (B) is the best answer. You should mark answer (B) on your answer sheet.

07 I'm nervous about speaking in front of a group of people.
(A) Please be on time.
(B) You'll get used to it.
(C) I have no idea.

【解析】本題是在表示自己「要在一群人面前講話很緊張」的陳述，選項(B)以You'll get used to it.（你會習慣的），暗示「多講幾次就會習慣了」作為安撫，是最適當的回應，故為正確答案。

我對於要在一群人面前講話感到好緊張。
(A) 請準時。
(B) 你會習慣的。
(C) 我不知道。

【類型】陳述句題型

【正解】(B)

你難道沒看到我留在你桌上的字條嗎？
(A) 什麼字條？
(B) 為什麼？
(C) 去哪兒？

【類型】否定疑問句題型

【正解】(A)

08 Didn't you see the note I left on your desk?
    (A) What note?
    (B) How come?
    (C) Where to?

【解析】本題以否定助動詞Didn't為句首，意在詢問對方「難道沒有看到我留在你桌上的字條？」選項(A)反問What note?（什麼字條？）表示自己根本沒有注意到有字條在桌上，是最合情理的反應，故為正解。how come為「怎麼會？」、「為什麼會如此？」的口語化用法；where to則是「去哪裡？」的口語化表示法，均不適合用來回應此問句，故不選。

你今天晚上要做什麼？
(A) 跟朋友出去。
(B) 大約二十分鐘。
(C) 我們盡快把它完成吧。

【類型】未來式疑問句題型

【正解】(A)

09 What will you be doing this evening?
    (A) Hanging out with friends.
    (B) About twenty minutes.
    (C) Let's finish it as soon as possible.

【解析】未來進行式will be doing... 常用來表示「未來某個時間點將會進行的事情」，有「已經確定那時候會做某件事」的含義。本題疑問句以未來進行式詢問「今晚會做什麼」，選項(A)回答「跟朋友出去玩」，是最適當的回應，故為正解。hang out這個片語動詞在此表示「出去玩」。

在忙嗎？
(A) 對，我在看這本書。
(B) 那不是我的意思。
(C) 請填寫這張表格。

【類型】片語疑問句題型

【詞彙】
in the middle of... 在中間

【正解】(A)

10 In the middle of something?
    (A) Yeah, I'm reading this book.
    (B) That's not what I meant.
    (C) Please fill out this form.

【解析】以in the middle of sth. 這個片語來表示「位置」時，是「在……中間」的意思，除此之外也可以抽象地表示「某事進行到一半」，本題問句省略了主詞與be動詞，詢問對方(Are you) in the middle of something?（你在忙嗎？）選項(A)回答「正在看書」，是最適當的回應，故為正解。選項(B)(C)答非所問。

11 Have you seen Mike recently?
(A) It's nice to meet you too.
(B) She's on leave today.
(C) No. I lost contact with him.

【解析】現在完成式是用在表示「從過去到現在為止的這段時間所發生的事件或動作」，本題疑問句以現在完成式的時態，詢問對方「最近有沒有見到Mike？」選項(A)(B)的回答皆與Mike無關，答非所問故不選。選項(C)以過去式表示「已經跟他失去聯絡」，也就是「在過去某一時間點，失聯的狀態就已經確定了」，是最適當的回應，故為正解。contact表「聯繫」，lose contact with sb.意指「與某人失去聯繫」。

你最近有看到Mike嗎？
(A) 我也很高興認識你。
(B) 她今天休假。
(C) 不，我跟他失聯了。

【類型】完成式疑問句題型

【詞彙】
lose contact with sb. 與某人失去聯絡

【正解】(C)

---

12 The food at this restaurant is not as good as I expected.
(A) I'm glad you like it.
(B) Right. It's too greasy.
(C) I need another five minutes.

【解析】本題是一個否定直述句，以not as good as I expected（不如我所期待的好）來陳述「這家餐廳食物不好吃」。選項(B)附和這個說法，表示「對，太油膩了」，是最合情理的回應，故為正解。

這間餐廳的食物沒有我所期待的好吃。
(A) 很高興你喜歡。
(B) 對。太油膩了。
(C) 我需要再五分鐘。

【類型】陳述句題型

【詞彙】
greasy 油膩的

【正解】(B)

---

13 I'm sorry that I didn't bring the book.
(A) It's all right.
(B) You shouldn't have.
(C) It was yesterday.

【解析】sorry可以有兩種意思，一種表達「抱歉」，一種表達「遺憾」，由本題後半句I didn't bring the book（我沒帶書），可知這一句是在為「沒有帶書」而「致歉」，選項(A)回答It's all right.，也就是「沒關係」的意思，是最適當的回應，故為正解。

很抱歉我沒帶那本書。
(A) 沒關係。
(B) 你不該這麼做的。
(C) 那是昨天的事。

【類型】表達歉意題型

【正解】(A)

如果我需要一些辦公用品，要找誰呢？

(A) 我們的班機現在在33號登機們登機。

(B) 我們的新辦公室助理Stephanie。

(C) 你不能穿那件衣服去參加派對。

【類型】who疑問句題型

【正解】(B)

---

14 Who should I talk to if I need some office supplies?
 (A) Our flight is boarding at gate 33.
 (B) Stephanie, our new office assistant.
 (C) You can't wear that to the party.

【解析】以疑問詞who為句首的疑問句要問的是「人」，本題想知道「如果需要辦公室用品需要跟誰說」，選項(B)回答Stephanie，並以同位語解釋Stephanie的身份是「我們的新辦公室助理」，是正確答案。

你會去參加Jimmy的派對，對不對？

(A) 不，他不在這裡。

(B) 我很遺憾我錯過了。

(C) 對，我會準時到的。

【類型】附加問句題型

【正解】(C)

---

15 You will go to Jimmy's party, won't you?
 (A) No, he's not here.
 (B) I'm sorry I missed it.
 (C) Yes, I'll be there on time.

【解析】附加問句通常是用來「向對方確定自己的想法正確」，因此本題先表示「你會去Jimmy的派對」，接著以附加問句won't you? 來向對方確認「對嗎？」選項(C)肯定回答，並表示自己會準時到，是最適當的回應，故為正解。

地圖在手冊的最後一頁。

(A) 噢，謝謝。

(B) 三點吧，我想。

(C) 一點也不。

【類型】陳述句題型

【詞彙】
brochure 小冊子

【正解】(A)

---

16 The map is on the last page of the brochure.
 (A) Oh, thanks.
 (B) Three o'clock, I think.
 (C) Not at all.

【解析】本題以陳述句告訴對方「地圖在手冊最後一頁」，選項(A)回答「謝謝」，意在感謝對方告訴自己地圖在哪裡，是為正解。

17 Hurry up! We're going to be late!
    (A) The restaurant is full now.
    (B) Take it easy. No need to rush!
    (C) Please keep it nice and neat.

【解析】本題用祈使句Hurry up! 來催促對方「動作快一點！」選項(B)回答Take it easy. 意指「放輕鬆」，別那麼緊張，並省略there is表示No need to rush（沒必要趕），是選項中最合情理的回應，是為正解。

快點！我們要遲到了！
(A) 餐廳現在客滿。
(B) 放輕鬆！不用趕啦。
(C) 請保持乾淨整齊。

【類型】祈使句題型

【正解】(B)

18 How many copies do we need?
    (A) Fifteen, I guess.
    (B) That's not true.
    (C) I don't have it.

【解析】how many意在詢問「幾個」，因此答案通常會包含具體的「數字」。本題問「我們需要幾份副本」，選項(A)回答「十五份」，是為正解。

我們需要幾份副本？
(A) 十五份吧，我猜。
(B) 那不是真的。
(C) 我沒有那個東西。

【類型】how many題型

【正解】(A)

19 How come you didn't show up last night?
    (A) It will arrive later.
    (B) I had to work overtime.
    (C) She didn't do that.

【解析】疑問詞how come意在詢問「為什麼」、「怎麼會」，本題問的是「你昨晚怎麼沒有出現？」想知道對方「昨晚沒出現的原因」，選項(B)表示「我得加班」，為自己沒有出現提供了合理的理由，故為正解。

為什麼你昨天沒出現？
(A) 它晚點就會送來。
(B) 我得加班。
(C) 她沒有做那件事。

【類型】詢問原因題型

【詞彙】
show up 出現

【正解】(B)

你現在覺得怎麼樣？
(A) 我已經遲到了。
(B) 我目前待業中。
(C) 還是很想吐。

【類型】詢問感覺題型

【詞彙】
between jobs 待業中／
nauseous 想吐的

【正解】(C)

---

20 How do you feel right now?
　　(A) I'm already late.
　　(B) I'm between jobs.
　　(C) Still nauseous.

【解析】聽到問句中出現feel，即知這題要問的是「感覺如何」，選項(A)(B)的回答均與「感覺」無關，只有選項(C)的nauseous能表示「想吐的」，故(C)為最適當的答案。

有可能在這星期排個時間跟Laymen先生開個會嗎？
(A) 我問問他的助理。
(B) 電話忙線中。
(C) 它三點出發。

【類型】詢問可能性題型

【詞彙】
schedule 安排時間

【正解】(A)

---

21 Would it be possible to schedule a meeting with Mr. Laymen this week?
　　(A) I'll ask his assistant.
　　(B) The line is busy.
　　(C) It departs at three.

【解析】Would it be possible to... 為非常禮貌客氣地詢問「是否有可能……」的問句句型。本題意在詢問「有沒有可能在這星期跟Laymen先生安排一個會議時間」，選項(A)表示「要問他的助理」才會知道，是最合情理的回應，故為正解。選項(B)的line指「電話線路」，the line is busy意指「電話忙線中」。

誰將要致歡迎詞？
(A) 在影印室隔壁。
(B) Layla Josh。
(C) 她還沒準備好。

【類型】who疑問句題型

【詞彙】
welcome speech 歡迎詞／
copy room 影印室

【正解】(B)

---

22 Who is going to give the welcome speech?
　　(A) Next to the copy room.
　　(B) Layla Josh
　　(C) She's not ready yet.

【解析】疑問詞who要問的是「誰」。本題詢問「誰」將致歡迎詞，選項(B)回答人名Layla Josh，是最適當的回答，故為正解。選項(B)是用來回答「地點或位置」，選項(C)也是答非所問，故不考慮。

23 Do you have any siblings?
(A) I'm the only child.
(B) It's my first day at work.
(C) Much better.

【解析】sibling意指「手足」，也就是「兄弟姐妹」。本題問「有任何兄弟姐妹嗎」，選項(A)表示I'm the only child（我是獨生子），only child顧名思義為「唯一的孩子」，也就是「沒有兄弟姐妹的意思」，是最適當的回答，故為正解。

你有任何兄弟姐妹嗎？
(A) 我是獨子。
(B) 這是我第一天上班。
(C) 好多了。

【類型】助動詞疑問句題型

【詞彙】
sibling 兄弟姐妹
【正解】(A)

---

24 When would be a convenient time for me to contact you?
(A) Probably in my office.
(B) That's not an option.
(C) Tomorrow morning.

【解析】本題為以when為句首的疑問句，要問的是方便與對方聯絡的「時間」，選項(A)回答的是「地點」，選項(B)回答與問句無關，選項(C)回答「明天上午」，是一個有具體範圍的時間，為最適合的回答，故(C)為正解。

我什麼時候方便跟您聯絡呢？
(A) 可能在我辦公室。
(B) 那不是個選項。
(C) 明天早上。

【類型】when疑問句題型
【正解】(C)

---

25 I can't find the yellow folder.
(A) Isn't it in the conference room?
(B) We haven't ordered yet.
(C) Shanghai and Beijing.

【解析】本題為表示「找不到文件夾」的陳述句。選項(A)反問「它不是在會議室嗎？」暗示文件夾應該是在會議室裡，是最適當的回答，故為正解。

我找不到那個黃色文件夾。
(A) 它不是在會議室嗎？
(B) 我們還沒有點餐。
(C) 上海和北京。

【類型】陳述句題型
【詞彙】
folder 文件夾
【正解】(A)

---

26 You know tomorrow is the deadline, don't you?
(A) This is on me. I insist.
(B) You know I'm right.
(C) Don't worry. I will turn it in on time.

【解析】本題以附加問句向對方確認「你知道明天是截止期限」這件事，有擔心對方不知道，而想再次確認的含義，選項(C)表示「別擔心，我會準時交」，間接表示自己確實知道明天是最後期限，故為正解。

你知道明天就是最後一天了，對吧？
(A) 這頓我請客。我堅持。
(B) 你知道我是對的。
(C) 別擔心。我會準時交的。

【類型】附加問句題型
【詞彙】
inisit 堅持／turn in 交
【正解】(C)

晚宴何時舉行？
(A) 以前的一個客戶。
(B) 七點鐘。
(C) 搭計程車。

【類型】when疑問句題型

【正解】(B)

27 When will the dinner party take place?
    (A) A former client.
    (B) At seven o'clock.
    (C) By taxi.

【解析】when 疑問句問的是「時間」，本題意在詢問dinner party舉行的時間，選項(B)回答seven o'clock是最適當的回應，故為正解。選項(A)是用來回答「對象是誰」，而選項(C)是用來回答「交通方式」。

我要多久才能拿到退稅？
(A) 六到八週。
(B) 如果現在出發就不會。
(C) 謝謝提醒。

【類型】how long疑問句題型

【詞彙】
tax return 退稅

【正解】(A)

28 How long does it take to get my tax return?
    (A) Six to eight months.
    (B) Not if we leave now.
    (C) Thanks for the reminder.

【解析】疑問詞how long問的是「多長時間」，本題要問「拿到退稅要多久時間」，選項(A)回答「六到八週」，提供了一個時間範圍，是最適當的回答，故為正解。

你覺得Peter的行銷計劃怎麼樣？
(A) 我比較喜歡咖啡。
(B) 我覺得蠻可行的。
(C) 我不這麼認為。

【類型】詢問意見題型

【詞彙】
workable 可行的

【正解】(B)

29 What do you think about Peter's marketing plan?
    (A) I prefer coffee.
    (B) I think it's workable.
    (C) I don't think so.

【解析】what do you think about sth. 是用來詢問「對某事有何看法」的疑問句型，本題意在詢問對方「對Peter的行銷計劃有什麼看法」，選項(B)表示「我認為（他的計劃）是可行的」，為最適當的回應，故為正解。選項(A)是用來回答「自己的偏好」，而選項(C)是用來表示「相反意見」，皆答非所問。

30 Aren't you joining us for lunch?
   (A) It's working very well.
   (B) It's quite near.
   (C) No, not today.

你不跟我們一起去吃午餐嗎？
(A) 它運作得很順利。
(B) 它蠻近的。
(C) 不，今天不了。

【解析】本題以否定疑問句的方式詢問「要不要跟我們一起吃午餐」，選項(A)(B)均為正面回答問題，故不選。選項(C)回答「今天不要」，是最適當的回應，故為正解。

【類型】否定疑問句題型

【正解】(C)

---

31 I noticed some errors in the new catalogue.
   (A) Can I do it after lunch?
   (B) It's newly designed.
   (C) Can you point them out?

我發現新型錄裡有些錯誤。
(A) 我可以午餐後再做嗎？
(B) 這是新設計的。
(C) 可以請你指出來嗎？

【解析】本題為表示「新型錄有錯誤」的陳述句，選項(C)以希望對方「將（錯誤）指出來」作為回應，是最適當的回答，故為正解。

【類型】陳述句題型

【詞彙】
catalogue 型錄

【正解】(C)

男A Alice什麼時候會回來上班？

男B 不確定。我昨晚打給她，她仍然很不舒服。

女 不知道她明天能不能來開會。

男A 如果她明天不能來上班，誰要代替她主持會議？

男B 我來做這件事。我是她不在時的代理人。

女 很好。如果有任何我可以幫忙的地方，就跟我說一下。

【詞彙】
stand in 代替／
deputy 代理人

Directions: You will hear some conversations between two people. You will be asked to answer three questions about what the speakers say in each conversation. Select the best response to each question and mark the letter (A), (B), (C) or (D) on your answer sheet. The conversations will not be printed in your test book and will be spoken only one time.

Questions 32-34 refer to the following conversation.

Man A   When will Alice return to work?

Man B   Not sure. I called her last night. She was still unwell.

Woman   I'm wondering if she could make it to the meeting tomorrow.

Man A   If she still can't come to work tomorrow, who's gonna stand in to host the meeting?

Man B   I'm doing it. I'm her deputy while she's away.

Woman   Good. Let me know if there's anything I can do to help.

說話者在談論什麼？
(A) 一個名人的婚姻生活
(B) 一場上週末舉行的派對
(C) 一個沒來上班的同事
(D) 一個上個月上市的新產品

【類型】內容主題題型

【詞彙】
celebrity 名人／
marriage life 婚姻生活

【正解】(C)

32 What are the speakers talking about?
(A) A celebrity's marriage life
(B) A party held last weekend
(C) A colleague absent from work
(D) A new product launched last month

【解析】由說話者在對話中談論「Alice因為身體不舒服沒來上班，明天可能要代替她主持會議」，可知選項(C)是最符合對話內容的描述，故(C)為正解。

33 According to the conversation, what do you know about Alice?
(A) She is in the meeting.
(B) She is under the weather.
(C) She is the speakers' supervisor.
(D) She's on business trip.

根據對話內容，我們對Alice有何認識？
(A) 她正在度假。
(B) 她身體不舒服。
(C) 她是說話者的主管。
(D) 她在出差。

【解析】由對話中詢問Alice目前的狀況：She was still unwell.（她仍不舒服），符合選項(B) She's under the weather（她身體不舒服）的描述，可知(B)為正確答案。選項(A)(D)所述與對話內容不符，而由對話內容也無從知道Alice的職位是什麼，故(C)亦不是適當的答案。

【類型】提問細節題型

【詞彙】
under the weather 不舒服／
supervisor 主管

【正解】(B)

---

34 What's Alice's role in the meeting tomorrow?
(A) The chairperson
(B) The minute taker
(C) The interpreter
(D) The photographer

Alice在明天會議中的角色為何？
(A) 主席
(B) 會議記錄
(C) 口譯
(D) 攝影師

【解析】由對話中說話者詢問誰將代替Alice主持會議，可推測Alice在會議中的角色應為會議主席，正解為(A)。

【類型】提問細節題型

【詞彙】
chairperson 主席／
minute taker 會議記錄／
interpreter 口譯員

【正解】(A)

Questions 35-37 refer to the following conversation.

Woman   Shall we arrange a meeting to move ahead on this?

Man A   I agree. Can we schedule it sometime this week?

Man B   I can do Wednesday morning or Thursday afternoon.

Woman   Wednesday morning is out. I'm meeting a client in town. Thursday afternoon works for me, though.

女　我們是不是應該安排一個會議繼續討論這個議題？

男A　我贊成。我們可以把會議安排在這個星期嗎？

男B　我星期三上午或星期四下午可以。

女　星期三早上不行。我要跟一個客戶在市中心碰面。但是星期四下午我可以。

男A 我星期四下午沒事。兩點可以嗎？	Man A My Thursday afternoon's wide open. How does two o'clock sound?
男B 可以。我來訂會議室。	Man B Great. I'll book a meeting room.
女 我會把相關文件準備好。	Woman I'll get related documents ready.

說話者正在做什麼？
(A) 針對行銷計劃做辯論
(B) 安排會議的時間
(C) 聊他們老闆的八卦
(D) 為週末做計劃

【類型】內容主題題型

【詞彙】
debate 辯論／
gossip 聊八卦

【正解】(B)

35 What are the speakers doing?
  (A) Debating on the marketing plan
  (B) Setting up a time to meet
  (C) Gossiping about their boss
  (D) Planning for their weekend

【解析】由說話者在對話中協商一個彼此都方便的時間來開會，可知他們正在安排會議時間，正解為(B)。

女子為何星期三不行？
(A) 她將飛去東京開會。
(B) 她將休一天假。
(C) 她有事先安排好的事。
(D) 她將要去採買雜貨。

【類型】提問細節題型

【詞彙】
prior 先前的／
arrangement 安排／
grocery 雜貨

【正解】(C)

36 Why doesn't Wednesday work for the woman?
  (A) She will fly to Tokyo for a meeting.
  (B) She's going to take a day off.
  (C) She has a prior arrangement.
  (D) She is going grocery shopping.

【解析】由女子在對話中表示I'm meeting a client in town.（我要跟一個客戶在市中心碰面），可知女子在此之前已經跟那位客戶約好見面時間了，也就是已經事先作了安排，故正解為(C)。

37 What does the woman volunteer to do?
(A) Send the meeting invitation
(B) Make document copies
(C) Book the meeting room
(D) Prepare related documents

【解析】由女子在對話中表示I'll get related documents ready.（我會把相關文件準備好），可知正解為(D)。

女子自願做什麼？
(A) 發會議通知
(B) 影印文件
(C) 訂會議室
(D) 準備相關文件

【類型】提問細節題型

【詞彙】
volunteer 自願

【正解】(D)

Questions 38-40 refer to the following conversation and table.

M Hi, Ms. Sullivan, what would you like to do with your hair this time?

W I haven't thought about what I want, but my hair looks really flat. Maybe I should get a perm?

M How about big curls? I'm sure you'll look good with big curls.

W Sounds good.

M You can also try some highlights this time. That would brighten your looks.

W I'd like that. But is that gonna be very expensive?

M Not today. We offer various Mother's Day deals this month. Let's get your hair washed first.

★

Mother's Day Deals		
Deal 1	Shampoo + Haircut + Treatment	$1,200
Deal 2	Shampoo + Haircut + Perm	$3,200
Deal 3	Shampoo + Haircut + Highlights	$3,500
Deal 4	Shampoo + Perm + Highlights	$5,000

男　嗨，Sullivan小姐，妳這次想怎麼弄妳的頭髮？

女　我還沒有想過我想要什麼樣子的頭髮，但我頭髮看起來很塌。也許我該燙一下？

男　要不要燙大捲？我相信妳燙大捲會很好看。

女　聽起來不錯。

男　妳這次也可以嘗試挑染。那會讓妳看起來亮一點。

女　我喜歡。不過那會很貴嗎？

男　今天不會。我們這個月有提供各種母親節優惠。我們先來洗頭吧。

★

母親節優惠		
優惠1	洗髮＋剪髮＋護髮	$1,200
優惠2	洗髮＋剪髮＋燙髮	$3,200
優惠3	洗髮＋剪髮＋挑染	$3,500
優惠4	洗髮＋燙髮＋挑染	$5,000

說話者位在何處？
(A) 警察局
(B) 美容院
(C) 市政府
(D) 大賣場

【類型】對話背景題型

【詞彙】
beauty parlor 美容院／
hypermarket 大賣場

【正解】(B)

女子正在跟誰說話？
(A) 她的私人助理
(B) 便利商店店員
(C) 髮型設計師
(D) 室內設計師

【類型】說話者身份題型

【詞彙】
stylist 造型師／
interior designer 室內設計師

【正解】(C)

請看表格。女子將花費多少錢處理頭髮？
(A) $1,200
(B) $3,200
(C) $3,500
(D) $5,000

【類型】圖表對照題型

【正解】(D)

---

38 Where are the speakers?
(A) The police station
(B) A beauty parlor
(C) The City Hall
(D) A hypermarket

【解析】由對話中男子詢問女子想要怎麼弄頭髮，以及對話中的關鍵字get a perm（燙個頭髮）、highlights（挑染）與get your hair washed（幫你洗個頭），可推測這個地方應該是可以處理女子髮型的地方，選項中以(B)的Beauty parlor（美容院）為最有可能的答案，故(B)為正解。

---

39 Who's the woman talking to?
(A) Her personal assistant
(B) A convenience store clerk
(C) A hair stylist
(D) An interior designer

【解析】對話中，女子跟對方討論應該如何處理自己的髮型，可推測對方的身份最有可能與髮型設計或造型有關，選項中以(C)為最有可能的答案，故為正解。

---

40 Look at the table. How much money is the woman going to spend on her hair?
(A) $1,200
(B) $3,200
(C) $3,500
(D) $5,000

【解析】由對話內容可知女子將進行get your hair washed（洗頭）＋get a perm（燙頭髮）＋try some highlights（試試挑染）這三種組合，對照圖表中的優惠方案，這三種組合適用「優惠4」，價格為$5,000，故答案為(D)。

Questions 41-43 refer to the following conversation.

W Hello, Ben. This is Olivia. I'm calling to tell you that we haven't received your payment so far.

M Sorry about that, but I don't remember receiving any invoice from you.

W What? ... Oh, no! I can't believe I forgot to send you the invoice. It's right here in my drawer!

M Well, you know I need the invoice to request for reimbursement.

W I'll send you the invoice by express courier as soon as possible.

M OK, but you'll have to wait until the tenth of the next month to receive the payment.

女　哈囉，Ben。我是Olivia。我是打來跟你說我們到現在還沒有收到你們的帳款。

男　真是抱歉，不過我不記得我有收到妳的請款單耶。

女　什麼？……噢，不！我真不敢相信我居然忘記把請款單寄給你了。它就在我的抽屜裡！

男　這樣啊，妳知道我需要請款單才能報帳的。

女　我會盡快將請款單用快遞寄給你。

男　好，不過妳得等到下個月十號才能收到帳款囉。

【詞彙】
invoice 請款單／drawer 抽屜／
reimbursement 銷帳／
express courier 快遞

---

41 Why is the woman making this call?
(A) To request for reimbursement
(B) To apologize for not making the payment
(C) To remind the man to settle their account
(D) To request for an invoice

【解析】由女子在對話一開始便表示來電的目的是「告訴你我們到現在還沒收到你們的帳款」，可知女子打這通電話是為了要提醒男子要付帳款，正解為(C)。

女子為何要打這通電話？
(A) 為了請款報帳
(B) 為了未支付帳款致歉
(C) 為了提醒男子付清帳款
(D) 為了要求請款單

【類型】內容主題題型

【詞彙】
settle one's account 付清帳款

【正解】(C)

男子為何沒有支付帳款？
(A) 他忘記報帳請款。
(B) 他沒有收到請款單。
(C) 他的公司有財務問題。
(D) 請款單上有錯誤。

【類型】提問細節題型

【正解】(B)

女子最早何時可以收到帳款？
(A) 七天內
(B) 這個月內
(C) 下個月十日
(D) 十天後

【類型】提問細節題型

【詞彙】

at the earliest 最快

【正解】(C)

男A　Rodman先生剛打來請我們
　　　將他的訂單提前交貨。

女　　他希望他的訂單多早可以
　　　交貨？

男A　他想知道我們能不能把交貨
　　　日期提前到七月十五日。

男B　那是不可能的。完成整個
　　　生產流程至少需要十五個
　　　工作天。

男A　我們可以請工廠加速生產嗎？

女　　我不覺得可以。那只會影
　　　響我們最後產品的品質。

男B　我同意。我們不能拿我們
　　　的信譽冒險。

【詞彙】

move up 向前挪動／
hasten 加速；催促／
reputation 信譽

42 Why didn't the man make the payment?
(A) He forgot to request for reimbursement.
(B) He didn't receive the invoice.
(C) His company has financial problems.
(D) There was an error on the invoice.

【解析】由男子在對話中表示I don't remember receiving any invoice from you.（我不記得有收到你們的請款單），可知男子沒有支付帳款是因為「沒有收到請款單」，正解為(B)。

---

43 When will the woman receive the payment at the earliest?
(A) Within seven days
(B) Within this month
(C) The tenth of the next month
(D) Ten days later

【解析】由男子在對話最後表示you'll have to wait until the tenth of the next month to receive the payment（你得等到下個月十號才能收到帳款了），可知女子最快也要到下個月十日才能收到帳款，答案為(C)。

Questions 44-46 refer to the following conversation.

Man A　Mr. Rodman just called and requested an earlier delivery of his order.

Woman　How early does he want his order to be delivered?

Man A　He wanted to know if we could move up the delivery date to July 15.

Man B　That's not possible. It takes at least fifteen working days to complete the entire production.

Man A　Could we ask the factory to hasten the production?

Woman　I don't think so. That would only impact the quality of our final products.

Man B　I agree. We can't risk our reputation.

44 What are the speakers discussing?
(A) The budget of the project
(B) A client's request
(C) The company's dress code
(D) The meeting agenda

說話者在討論什麼？
(A) 專案預算
(B) 一個客戶的要求
(C) 公司的服裝規定
(D) 會議議程

【解析】由整篇對話以「Rodman先生提出提前交貨的請求」為主軸，可知對話者主要是在討論這位客戶所提出的要求，故選項(B)為正確答案。

【類型】內容主題題型

【正解】(B)

45 What request did they receive?
(A) To advance the delivery date
(B) To work overtime on the weekend
(C) To make a further discount
(D) To issue an invoice

他們收到什麼請求？
(A) 提前交貨日期
(B) 週末加班工作
(C) 提供更多折扣
(D) 開立請款單

【解析】由說話者表示Rodman先生希望能move up the delivery date（將交貨日期提前），可知他們收到的請求即「提前交貨日期」，正解為(A)；片語動詞move up在此做「向前挪動」解，與advance同義。

【類型】主題內容題型

【詞彙】
advance 提前／
issue 開立

【正解】(A)

46 What is the speakers' conclusion?
(A) To hasten the production
(B) To breach the contract
(C) To turn down the request
(D) To follow the instruction

說話者的結論是什麼？
(A) 加快生產速度
(B) 違反合約
(C) 拒絕請求
(D) 聽從指令

【解析】說話者在對話中討論了向工廠催促生產速度的可能性，女子考慮到加速生產將會影響到產品品質，而以I don't think so（我不這麼認為）表示不同意，另一位說話者也附和女子的說法，認為這麼做將危及公司信譽，因此可推測他們對「提前交貨」這個情求的討論結果，應該會予以拒絕，最有可能的答案為(C)。

【類型】提問細節題型

【詞彙】
breach 違反；破壞

【正解】(C)

男　早安。這是我的護照。

女　謝謝你，先生。有要託運的行李嗎？

男　有的。

女　可以請你幫我把它放在秤台上嗎？

男　當然。它有在限重之內嗎？

女　呃……有的，但你的行李恐怕過大囉。每件託運行李包含提把及輪子的最大尺寸是320公分。

男　好吧。超大行李費用是多少？

女　四千元。

★

地區	過大行李費
美國及加拿大	$ 4,800
歐洲	$ 4,500
亞洲	$ 4,200
澳洲及紐西蘭	$ 4,000

【詞彙】
maximum 最大的／
excess luggage fee 過大行李費

Questions 47-49 refer to the following conversation and table.

M　Good morning. Here's my passport.

W　Thank you, sir. Any luggage to check in?

M　Yes.

W　Would you please place it on the scale for me?

M　Sure. Is it under the limit?

W　Uh,... it is, but I'm afraid your luggage is oversized. The maximum size for every piece of checked luggage is 320 centimeters including handles and wheels.

M　Alright. How much is the excess luggage fee?

W　NT$4,000.

★

Region	Oversize Luggage Fees
U.S. & Canada	$ 4,800
Europe	$ 4,500
Asia	$ 4,200
Australia & New Zealand	$ 4,000

這段對話發生在何處？
(A) 登機門
(B) 飯店報到櫃檯
(C) 機場報到櫃檯
(D) 超市結帳櫃檯

【類型】對話背景題型

【詞彙】
boarding gate 登機門

【正解】(C)

47 Where is this conversation taking place?
(A) At the boarding gate
(B) At the hotel check-in counter
(C) At the airport check-in counter
(D) At the supermarket check-out counter

【解析】由對話內容與check in luggage（託運行李）有關，由於行李一般是在報到櫃檯辦理託運手續，因此推測對話發生地點最有可能是機場的報到櫃檯，正解為(C)。

48 What does the man need to pay for?
(A) His overweight luggage
(B) His oversize luggage
(B) His extra luggage
(D) His carry-on luggage

男子需要為了什麼付錢？
(A) 他的超重行李
(B) 他的過大行李
(C) 他的超件行李
(D) 他的隨身行李

【解析】由對話內容可知男子的行李雖然under the limit（在重量限制以下）沒有超重，但是卻oversized（尺寸過大），超過航空公司的尺寸規定，因此男子需要為他過大的行李付費，正解為(B)。

【類型】提問細節題型

【詞彙】
carry-on 隨身的

【正解】(B)

49 Look at the table. Where most likely is the man traveling to?
(A) New Zealand
(B) South Korea
(C) Canada
(D) Germany

請看表格。男子最有可能要到何處旅行？
(A) 紐西蘭
(B) 南韓
(C) 加拿大
(D) 德國

【解析】圖表為過大行李收費表，航行至不同地區有不同的收費標準，由對話中女子表示男子需支付4000元的過大行李費用，對照圖表內容即可知道男子是要旅行到Australia（澳洲）或New Zealand（紐西蘭），選項中符合這個收費標準的地區即選項(A)的紐西蘭，故(A)為正解。

【類型】圖表對照題型

【正解】(A)

男A 我們要不要把會議室的乾擦白板換成智慧白板？

男B 我也有想過用智慧白板來提高會議效率及生產力。

女 就我所知，一個智慧白板可不便宜。對我們這種小公司來說是個很大的開銷。

男B 沒錯。但是如果我們能將它發揮最大效用，就會是個值得的投資。

女 我們不能沒有先試用過就做出任何採購決定。

男A 你說的對。我來聯絡供應商，請他們送一個產品樣本來讓我們試用。

【詞彙】
dry erase board 乾擦式白板／
Smart Board 智慧白板／
efficiency 效率／
productivity 生產力／
worthwhile 值得的／
investment 投資／
test out 充分檢驗／try out 試用

Questions 50-52 refer to the following conversation.

Man A   Shall we replace the dry erase board in our conference room with a Smart Board?

Man B   I've thought about using a Smart Board to improve meeting efficiency and productivity, too.

Woman   As far as I know, a Smart Board is not cheap. It's gonna be a big expense for a small company like ours.

Man B   True. But it will be a worthwhile investment if we can make the best use of it.

Woman   We can't make any purchase without testing it out first.

Man A   You're right. I'll approach a supplier about sending a sample product for us to try out.

說話者主要在討論什麼？
(A) 是否要贈送免費試用品
(B) 如何促銷他們的新產品
(C) 是否要購買一個智慧白板
(D) 乾擦白板的缺點

【類型】主題內容題型

【詞彙】
give out 發送／
sample 樣品；試用品／
shortcoming 缺點

【正解】(C)

50 What are the speakers mainly discussing?
(A) Whether to give out free samples
(B) How to promote their new product
(C) Whether to purchase a Smart Board
(D) The shortcomings of a dry erase board

【解析】其中一位說話者提出「以智慧白板取代乾擦式白板」的建議，接下來的對話便以是否該決定購買為主軸來發展，選項(C)所述符合對話內容，故為最適當的答案。

51 What is the woman's main concern about a Smart Board?
(A) The size
(B) The brand
(C) The price
(D) The warranty

【解析】女子在對話中對於是否該購買智慧型白板表示a Smart Board is not cheap（一個智慧型白板可不便宜），而且It's gonna be a big expense for a small company like ours（對我們這種小公司來說是一個大開銷），可知女子關心的重點在於「價格」，正解為(C)。

女子對於智慧白板最關心什麼？
(A) 尺寸
(B) 品牌
(C) 價格
(D) 保固

【類型】提問細節題型

【詞彙】
warranty 保固

【正解】(C)

52 What will the speakers do next?
(A) Place a purchase order
(B) Get a sample to try out
(C) Discard the dry erase board
(D) Have a Smart Board installed

【解析】由於對話走向傾向「未經試用不能下任何採購決定」，因此提出提議的男子表示他會聯絡供應商about sending a sample product for us to try out（請他送個試用產品讓我們試用），可知說話者下一步是會找樣品來試用，正解為(B)。

說話者接下來將會做什麼？
(A) 下訂購單
(B) 找個樣品來試用
(C) 丟掉乾擦白板
(D) 將智慧白板安裝好

【類型】提問細節題型

【詞彙】
discard 丟棄／install 安裝

【正解】(B)

男　Jennifer，我可以跟妳討論
那個建設工程專案的事嗎？

女　噢，好啊，但我現在正要去
跟我們的廣告代理商開會
耶。

男　妳最晚什麼時候會回來呢？

女　我不確定這個會要開多久耶。
不過我們可以在明天下午的國
際商務研討會前開個三十分鐘
的會。

男　聽起來不錯。那我明天一點
半左右到妳辦公室開會。

女　好。我得走了。再見。

【詞彙】
advertising agent 廣告代理商

Questions 53-55 refer to the following conversation.

M　Jennifer, can I discuss the construction project with you?

W　Oh, OK, but I'm going to a meeting with our advertising agent right now.

M　When will you be back at the latest?

W　I'm not sure how long the meeting's gonna last. But we can have a thirty-minute meeting before the international business seminar tomorrow afternoon.

M　Sounds good. So I'll meet you at your office around one thirty tomorrow.

W　Great. Gotta go now. See ya.

說話者在做什麼？
(A) 安排會議時間
(B) 討論一個建設工程案
(C) 協議一個折扣
(D) 為簡報做準備

【類型】內容主題題型

【正解】(A)

53 What are the speakers doing?
(A) Scheduling a meeting
(B) Discussing a construction project
(C) Negotiating a discount
(D) Getting ready for the presentation

【解析】由對話內容可知男子想找女子討論一個案子，但女
子現在有事，因此兩人便另外安排時間討論，選項中最符合
對話內容的敘述為(A)，故(A)為正解。

54 What is the woman busy doing?
   (A) She is dressing up for a party.
   (B) She has a meeting to attend.
   (C) She is looking for a new apartment.
   (D) She is looking for a job.

女子正在忙什麼？
(A) 她正在籌備她的婚禮。
(B) 她要出席一個會議。
(C) 她正在找一間新公寓。
(D) 她正在找工作。

【解析】由對話中女子表示I'm going to a meeting with our advertising agent right now（我現在正要去跟我們的廣告代理商碰面），可推測女子可能跟廣告代理商約好時間處理公事，選項中最有可能的敘述為(B)，其他選項皆與對話內容不符。

【類型】提問細節題型

【詞彙】
be up to sth. 從事某事／
press conference 記者會

【正解】(B)

---

55 When will the speakers meet up for the construction project?
   (A) Later today
   (B) Sometime next week
   (C) This weekend
   (D) Before the seminar

說話者何時會為建設案開會？
(A) 今天稍晚
(B) 下週某一時間
(C) 這個週末
(D) 研討會之前

【解析】由兩位說話者做出have a thirty-minute meeting before the international business seminar tomorrow afternoon（明天下午國際商務研討會前開個半小時的會）的結論，可知他們將會在明天研討會之前討論建設案，故正解為(D)。

【類型】提問細節題型

【正解】(D)

女 嗨，我想預約四月廿二日這天的當地旅遊包車。

男 當然。請問您貴姓？

女 我姓Carter，C-a-r-t-e-r。請問包一輛小巴要多少錢？

男 噢，這要看你需要的是多大的車。

女 我們一共有十一個乘客要搭車。

男 那你會需要一輛12人座的小巴。這是我們一日當地旅遊的包車費用。

女 你們所有的服務都有包含一位司機，對吧？

男 沒錯的。我們的司機都是專業的導遊。

★

2018包車費用表	
車輛型式	一日當地旅遊
55人座遊覽車	$ 10,000
32人座遊覽車	$ 7,500
12人座小巴	$ 4,800
9人座小巴	$ 4,000

【詞彙】charter 包車／
surname 姓／tour guide 導遊

Questions 56-58 refer to the following conversation and table.

W Hi, I'd like to make a charter reservation for a local trip on April 22.

M Sure. May I have your surname, please?

W It's Carter. C-a-r-t-e-r. How much does it cost to charter a van?

M Well, it depends on the size of vehicle you need.

W There are eleven passengers travelling together.

M Then you will need a 12-seat van. This is the table of our charter rates for one-day local trips.

W All of your services include a driver, right?

M That's right. Our drivers are all professional tour guides.

Charter Rates 2018	
Vehicle type	one-day local trip
55-seat coach	$ 10,000
32-seat coach	$ 7,500
12-seat van	$ 4,800
9-seat van	$ 4,000

女子需要什麼？
(A) 宅配服務
(B) 包車司機服務
(C) 機場接機服務
(D) 外燴服務

【類型】內容主題題型

【詞彙】
home delivery 宅配／
pickup 接（機）／
catering 外燴

【正解】(B)

---

56 What is the woman reserving?
    (A) Home delivery service
    (B) Car and driver service
    (C) Airport pickup service
    (D) Catering service

【解析】女子在對話一開始便表示他要make a charter reservation（預定包車），如果不知道charter這個字的意思，也可以從對話中的關鍵字van（小貨車、小巴）、driver（司機）等推測女子需要的應該是有司機的包車服務，正解為(B)。

57 According to the conversation, which statement is true?

(A) Charter service is a type of delivery service.

(B) The woman needs a van without a driver.

(C) The woman is traveling alone.

(D) The woman wants to charter a van.

根據對話內容，哪一項敘述正確？

(A) 包車服務是一種貨運服務。

(B) 女子需要一輛不含司機的小巴。

(C) 女子正在單獨旅行。

(D) 女子想要包一輛小巴。

【類型】提問細節題型

【正解】(D)

【解析】由女子在對話中表示她要charter a van（包一輛小巴），並且有eleven passengers traveling together（十一個人要一起搭），可知女子並非單獨旅行，選項(C)可以先刪除不考慮；女子在對話中並未表示自己不需要司機，且女子在表示要預約charter service 時，提到one-day local trip，因此推測charter service並非delivery service（送貨服務），因此選項(B)(C)亦非正確描述。選項(D)是唯一符合對話內容的答案，故為正解。

---

58 Look at the table. How much will the woman spend on charter service?

(A) $4,000

(B) $4,800

(C) $7,500

(D) $10,000

請看表格。女子將會花多少錢在包車服務上？

(A) $4,000

(B) $4,800

(C) $7,500

(D) $10,000

【類型】圖表對照題型

【正解】(B)

【解析】由對話中女子表示有11個人要搭車，於是男子根據搭車人數表示女子必須租12人座的小巴，對照車費表表示一輛12人座小巴費用為$4,800，可知女子將會花$4,800在包車服務上，正解為(B)。

男A	我們明天應該要幾點到會場？
女	開幕典禮上午十一點開始，所以所有人員都一定要在上午九點之前到達。
男B	我們有辦法在兩小時內將會場準備好嗎？
女	我想是可以的。我們的簽約活動規劃公司會在典禮前三小時就到那兒，所以不用擔心。
男B	很好。Freddie，你有為茶會聯絡外燴公司了嗎？
男A	有的，我今天早上才跟餐廳再次確認過。他們會在十一點四十五分開始供應食物及飲料給我們的貴賓。

Questions 59-61 refer to the following conversation.

Man A　When shall we arrive at the venue tomorrow?

Woman　The opening ceremony starts at 11 a.m., so all staff must arrive by 9 a.m.

Man B　Are we able to get the venue ready within two hours?

Woman　I think so. Our contracted event planner will be there three hours ahead of the ceremony, so no worries.

Man B　Good. Have you contacted the catering company for the tea party, Freddie?

Man A　Yes, I reconfirmed with the restaurant this morning. They will start serving food and beverages for our guests from a quarter to twelve.

說話者在討論什麼？
(A) 上次會議記錄
(B) 展場佈置
(C) 即將到來的活動
(D) 新人訓練程序

【類型】內容主題題型

【詞彙】
exhibition 展覽／
layout 陳列規劃／
orientation 新人訓練

【正解】(C)

59 What are the speakers discussing?
(A) Last meeting's minutes
(B) Exhibition layout
(C) An upcoming event
(D) Orientation program

【解析】由對話內容可知說話者在討論明天的開幕典禮及茶會，由於時間就是明天了，因此可知這是一場即將到來的活動，故正解為(C)。

60 Which event will take place following the opening ceremony?
(A) A two-hour orientation course
(B) A tea party
(C) A press conference
(D) A charity bazaar

哪一項活動會接在開幕典禮後舉行？
(A) 一場兩個小時的新訓課程
(B) 一場茶會
(C) 一場記者會
(D) 一場義賣會

【解析】由對話內容可知開幕典禮在11點舉行，而茶會會在11點45分開始供應餐點，可知茶會是緊接在開幕典禮後舉行，正解為(B)。其他選項的活動都未在本對話中提及，故不選。

【類型】提問細節題型

【詞彙】(B)

61 What have the speakers reserved in preparation for the tea party?
(A) Catering service
(B) A whole restaurant
(C) A shuttle bus
(D) A conference room

說話者為了準備茶會預訂了什麼？
(A) 外燴服務
(B) 整間餐廳
(C) 一輛接駁巴士
(D) 一間會議室

【解析】說話者在對話中表示已經為茶會聯絡catering company（外燴公司），並再次確認他們會在十一點四十五分開始供餐，可知他們為準備茶會預約了外燴服務，正解為(A)。

【類型】提問細節題型

【詞彙】
shuttle bus 接駁巴士

【正解】(A)

女　對新的行銷策略有什麼點子嗎？

男A　我們可以提供顧客一個在決定要不要購買我們的產品前，可以試用我們的產品一段時間的機會。

男B　免費嗎？

男A　對啊。這個行銷點子是一家法國家電製造商想出來的。這家公司去年營收增加了百分之225。

男B　聽起來蠻可行的。這可以吸引更多我們的潛在顧客來試用我們的產品。我相信大部份的試用者都會變成付費顧客。

女　你們兩個可以根據這個寫一個行銷提案嗎？我想在這個月的主管會議上提出來。

【詞彙】
originate 源自於／
revenue 營收／
practicable 可行的／
trial user 試用者／
bring up 提起

Questions 62-64 refer to the following conversation.

Woman　Any ideas on new marketing strategies?

Man A　We can provide our customers a chance to try out our products for a period of time before they decide whether they want to make a purchase.

Man B　For free?

Man A　Yeah. This marketing idea originated with a French home appliance manufacturer. The company increased revenue by 225% last year.

Man B　Sounds practicable. This can attract more potential customers to try out our products. I believe most of our trial users will become paying customers.

Woman　Can you two write a marketing proposal based on this? I'd like to bring this up in the monthly managers' meeting.

說話者正在做什麼？
(A) 試著想出行銷點子
(B) 做他們的行銷提案
(C) 應付一個難纏的顧客
(D) 示範操作他們的新產品

【類型】內容主題題型

【詞彙】
come up with sth. 想出／
difficult 難應付的

【正解】(A)

62 What are the speakers doing?
(A) Trying to come up with marketing ideas
(B) Working on their marketing proposal
(C) Dealing with a difficult customer
(D) Demonstrating their new products

【解析】對話由一開始的Any ideas on new marketing strategies?（對新行銷策略有什麼點子嗎？）之後便繞著一個行銷點子發展，可知說話者正在試著想出新的行銷點子，正解為(A)。

63 What do the speakers think may boost the sales?
(A) Letting customers try out products for free.
(B) Giving out free samples on the streets.
(C) Using celebrities in advertising.
(D) Offering early payment discounts

【解析】由說話者在這段對話中所討論的內容,可知他們認為「讓顧客在決定購買前免費試用產品一段時間」對提高銷售量有幫助,選項(A)符合對話內容,故為正解。

說話者認為什麼可以提高銷售量?
(A) 讓顧客免費試用產品
(B) 在路上發放免費試用品
(C) 讓名人出現在廣告宣傳中
(D) 提供預付折扣

【類型】提問細節題型

【詞彙】
celebrity 知名人士/
advertising 廣告宣傳/
early payment 預付

【正解】(A)

---

64 What is the woman's attitude toward the marketing idea?
(A) Opposing
(B) Doubtful
(C) Hesitant
(D) Supportive

【解析】由女子最後要求另外兩位說話者根據這個行銷點子寫一份行銷提案,好讓她能在主管月會上提出來,可知女子應該是對這個點子蠻有信心才會下這樣的指令,故supportive(支持的)最有可能是女子對此行銷點子的態度,故正解為(D)。

女子對於這個行銷點子的態度為何?
(A) 反對的
(B) 懷疑的
(C) 猶豫的
(D) 支持的

【類型】提問細節題型

【詞彙】
opposing 反對的/
doubtful 懷疑的/
hesitant 猶豫的/
supportive 支持的

【正解】(D)

男 我們在上週會議中決定要買一個檔案櫃。你有聯絡Alpha辦公室傢俱行詢價嗎？

女 有的。這是他們的業務代表今天早上送過來給我們的型錄。

男 很好。我們就看商業用標準尺寸的檔案櫃就好。這個如何？

女 看看價錢。這超過我們的預算了。我們負擔不起超過三千元的檔案櫃。

★

商業用標準尺寸	價格（新台幣）
金屬檔案櫃	$ 4,500
木頭檔案櫃	$ 4,250
塑膠檔案櫃	$ 2,980
活動檔案櫃	$ 3,550

Questions 65-67 refer to the following conversation and table.

M We decided to purchase a filing cabinet in last week's meeting. Have you contact Alpha Office Furniture to make an inquiry?

W Yes, I did. This is the catalogue that their sales rep brought over to us this morning.

M Great. Let's just look at the commercial legal size filing cabinets. What about this one?

W Look at the price. It's over our budget. We can't afford anything more than $3,000.

★

Commercial Legal size	Price (NT$)
metal filing cabinet	$ 4,500
wood filing cabinet	$ 4,250
plastic filing cabinet	$ 2,980
mobile filing cabinet	$ 3,550

說話者正在做什麼？
(A) 聯絡辦公室傢俱製造商
(B) 討論要不要買檔案櫃
(C) 決定該買哪個檔案櫃
(D) 向供應商請求報價單

【類型】內容主題題型

【正解】(C)

65 What are the speakers doing?
    (A) Contacting the office furniture manufacturer
    (B) Discussing whether to buy a filing cabinet
    (C) Determining which filing cabinet to buy
    (D) Requesting quotation from their supplier

【解析】由對話內容可知兩位說話者正在看型錄選擇要購買的檔案櫃，故正解為(C)。

66 What kind of filing cabinet are the speakers looking for?
(A) A commercial legal size one
(B) A two-drawer one
(C) A three-drawer one
(D) A customized one

【解析】由男子在對話中表示Let's just look at the commercial legal size filing cabinets（我們只要看商業標準尺寸檔案櫃就好），可知這是尺寸符合他們需求的檔案櫃，正解為(A)。

說話者要找什麼樣的檔案櫃？
(A) 商業標準尺寸的檔案櫃
(B) 兩抽的檔案櫃
(C) 三抽的檔案櫃
(D) 特別訂製的檔案櫃

【類型】提問細節題型

【詞彙】
commercial legal size
商業標準尺寸

【正解】(A)

---

67 Look at the table. Which cabinet will the speakers probably buy?
(A) Metal filing cabinet
(B) Wood filing cabinet
(C) Plastic filing cabinet
(C) Mobile filing cabinet

【解析】由對話內容可知說話者的檔案櫃預算不能超過三千元，由表格上顯示價格看來，只有選項(C)的塑膠檔案櫃價格$2,980，是符合預算的，故正解為(C)。

請看表格。說話者可能會買哪一個櫃子？
(A) 金屬檔案櫃
(B) 木頭檔案櫃
(C) 塑膠檔案櫃
(D) 活動式檔案櫃

【類型】圖表對照題型

【正解】(C)

男A Fiona，妳負責的案子進行的如何了？

女 嗯，事實上，因為我們目前人手不足，進度有點落後了。

男B 你知道董事會對這個案子期望很高，對吧？

女 是，我知道。問題是企劃部的每個人工作量都太大了。如果要趕上期限，我們絕對會需要更多人來支援這個案子。

男A 行銷部可以提供一些支援嗎？

男B 也許，但我必須先詢問Wayne先生。

【詞彙】
behind schedule 進度落後／
understaffed 人手不足的／
overloaded 超過負荷的

Questions 68-70 refer to the following conversation.

Man A   Fiona, how's your project going?

Woman   Well, actually, it's a bit behind schedule as we're currently understaffed.

Man B   You know the board of directors has high expectations for this project, right?

Woman   Yes, I do. The problem is that everyone in the Planning department is heavily overloaded. We absolutely need more people to cover for this project to meet the deadline.

Man A   Can the Marketing Department offer some support?

Man B   Maybe, but I'll have to check with Mr. Wayne first.

說話者對女子的案子持什麼態度？
(A) 關心的
(B) 沒興趣的
(C) 不耐煩的
(D) 事不關己的

【類型】提問細節題型

【詞彙】
concerned 關心的／
indifferent 冷淡的

【正解】(A)

---

68 What's the speakers' attitude toward the woman's project?
(A) Concerned
(B) Uninterested
(C) Impatient
(D) indifferent

【解析】由説話者在對話中主動關心女子的案子，並在女子提出支援請求之後，也想辦法找支援人手，可知説話者對女子案子的態度基本上是關心的，其他選項所描述的態度都與對話內容不符，故選項(A)為最適當的答案。

69 Which statement is true about the woman's project?
(A) It will be completed early.
(B) It has been put on hold.
(C) It's progressing slowly.
(D) It is short of funds.

【解析】由女子在對話中表示it's a bit behind schedule（它進度有點落後），可知這個案子仍在進行中，只是進度不如預期，符合選項(C)所述，故(C)為正解。

關於女子的案子，哪項敘述正確？
(A) 它將提前完成。
(B) 它被中止了。
(C) 它進度緩慢。
(D) 它缺乏資金。

【類型】提問細節題型

【詞彙】
put sth. on hold 中止某事；暫停某事／
be short of sth. 缺乏某物

【正解】(C)

70 What does the woman request?
(A) Financial assistance
(B) Technical assistance
(C) A multifunction printer
(D) Additional manpower

【解析】由女子表示We absolutely need more people to cover for this project（我們絕對需要更多人來支援這個案子）才能夠meet the deadline（趕上期限），可知女子是在提出「增加人力」的請求，故正解為(D)。

女子提出什麼請求？
(A) 財務支援
(B) 技術支援
(C) 多功能印表機
(D) 增加人力

【類型】提問細節題型

【詞彙】
financial 財務的／
technical 技術的／
multifunction 多功能／
manpower 人力

【正解】(D)

Directions: You will hear some talks given by a single speaker. You will be asked to answer three questions about what the speaker says in each talk. Select the best response to each question and mark the letter (A), (B), (C) or (D) on your answer sheet. The talks will not be printed in your test book and will be spoken only one time.

男 這個嘛，Frank，我必須說這一季的銷售結果讓人感到非常失望。我們的目標是三千萬，但是實際的銷售額卻甚至不到一千萬。這遠低於我們的期望！別把它歸咎於疲弱的經濟，因為所有分店的業績分析顯示我們是唯一一間比去年第三季還低的分店。我想知道你對為什麼會發生這種狀況的看法，以及我們應該怎麼做來改進。我要在這星期之前看到報告。

【詞彙】
quarter 季／
ascribe the blame to sb. or sth.
歸咎某人或某事

Questions 71-73 refer to the following talk.

M Well, Frank, I have to say that the result of the sales for this quarter is very disappointing. Our target was 30 million, but the actual sales were not even 10 million. It was far below our expectations! Don't ascribe the blame to the weak economy, because sales analysis for all the branches shows that our branch was the only one that fell below Q3 last year. I want to know your views about why this happened, and what we can do to correct it. I'd like a report by this week.

71 How does the speaker feel about the sales for Q3?
(A) Dissatisfied
(B) Hopeful
(C) Content
(D) Apathetic

【解析】男子在談話中表示the result of the sales... is very disappointing（銷售結果……令人非常失望），關鍵字 disappointing（令人失望的）表示第三季的銷售結果差強人意，故可知說話者感覺很失望，正解為(A)。

說話者對於第三季的銷售額覺得如何？
(A) 不滿意
(B) 有希望
(C) 很滿意
(D) 無動於衷

【類型】提問細節題型

【詞彙】
content 滿意的／
apathetic 無動於衷的

【正解】(A)

---

72 According to the speaker, which is the least possible reason for the drop in sales?
(A) Out-of-date selling techniques
(B) Incompetent marketing alignment
(C) Inadequate training
(D) Weak economy

【解析】說話者表示Don't ascribe the blame to the weak economy（別歸咎於疲弱的經濟），可知weak economy是首先被說話者屏除在外的原因，故正解為(D)。

依說話者所言，哪一個最不可能是業績下降的原因？
(A) 過時的銷售技巧
(B) 不勝任的行銷團隊
(C) 訓練不足
(D) 疲弱的經濟

【類型】提問細節題型

【詞彙】
out-of-date 過時的／
selling technique 銷售技巧／
incompetent 不勝任的／
alignment 團隊組合／
inadequate 不適當的

【正解】(D)

---

73 What does the speaker expect to get by this week?
(A) A review report
(B) A budget proposal
(C) A draft contract
(D) A quotation

【解析】由說話者在談話中表示想知道聽話者對於業績為什麼未達目標有何看法，以及聽話者認為該怎麼改進這種狀況，可知他希望聽話者能對這個狀況進行反省與檢討；說話者並進一步表示I'd like a report（我要一份報告），可知他希望聽話者能在檢討反省後提供一份具體的報告，故正解為(A)。

說話者希望能在這周前拿到什麼？
(A) 一份檢討報告
(B) 一份預算提案
(C) 一份草擬合約
(D) 一份報價單

【類型】提問細節題型

【詞彙】draft 草稿

【正解】(A)

女　嗨，Michael，我是內湖店的Catherine。這是有關熱風造型梳的事。我們完全低估了銷量。這個產品真是暢銷到一個不行。我三天前請南港店調了一些存貨給我們，但是我們現在已經只剩下五個存貨了。我不希望因為存貨短缺而失去業績。我已經跟工廠下了一筆剩餘存貨的緊急訂單。請確定我能在這星期天之前拿到貨，否則我就得開訂貨購買憑證給顧客了。

【詞彙】

hot air styler 熱風造型梳／
underestimate 低估／
fly out of the doors 暢銷／
inventory 存貨／
stock shortage 存貨短缺／
rain check 訂貨購買憑證

Questions 74-76 refer to the following talk.

W　Hi, Michael, this is Catherine from Neihu branch store. It is about the hot air stylers. We totally underestimated the sales. This product is flying out of the doors. I had the Nangang branch store transfer some of their inventory to us just three days ago, but right now we have only five left in stock. I don't want to lose sales because of stock shortage. I've already put a rush order on the remaining stock from the factory. Please make sure I can get them by this Sunday, or I'll have to issue rain checks to customers.

這通電話的目的為何？
(A) 要求快速到貨
(B) 要求增加人力
(C) 召開緊急會議
(D) 制定新品管流程

【類型】內容主題題型

【詞彙】

work out 制定／
quality control 品質管理

【正解】(A)

74 What is the purpose of this call?
(A) To request for a fast delivery
(B) To request for additional manpower
(C) To call an emergency meeting
(D) To work out new quality control procedures

【解析】由這段留言內容，可知留言者急需增加存貨以供快速銷售，並要聽話者確定能在星期天到貨，可知選項(A)所述最符合這通電話的目的，答案為(A)。

75 According to the talk, what is true about the hot air stylers?
(A) They can be bought online.
(B) They are unsalable.
(C) They are selling like hot cakes.
(D) They haven't been launched yet.

【解析】由女子在留言中表示This product is flying out of the doors（這個產品銷售空前），fly out of the doors指東西「賣掉的速度就像飛出店門一樣的快」，也就是「暢銷到不行」的意思，選項(C)的sell like hot cakes也是跟熱蛋糕一樣賣得那麼好，意指這款商品「造成搶購」，與留言內容相符，故為正解。

根據電話內容，關於熱風造型梳何者正確？
(A) 它們可以在線上購得。
(B) 它們是滯銷的。
(C) 它們造成搶購。
(D) 它們還沒上市。

【類型】提問細節題型

【詞彙】
unsalable 賣不出去的／
sell like hot cakes 造成搶購

【正解】(C)

---

76 What will the woman do if the store is out of stock of the hot air stylers?
(A) Purchase from the supermarket
(B) Complain to customer service
(C) Transfer inventory to head office
(D) Issue rain checks to customers

【解析】由留言內容女子表示希望對方能確定星期天前可以到貨，否則I'll have to issue rain check to customers（我只好開訂貨購買憑證給客人），也就是說，如果到時候店裡沒存貨，她就會開立rain check（訂貨購買憑證）給想買的顧客，正解為(D)。

如果店裡熱風造型梳沒貨了，女子將會怎麼做？
(A) 跟超市購買
(B) 向客服人員抱怨
(C) 調存貨到總公司
(D) 發訂貨購買憑證給顧客

【類型】提問細節題型

【詞彙】
transfer inventory 調貨

【正解】(D)

男 各位可以注意一下我這邊嗎？我們一年一度的公司運動會已經訂在今年四月舉行。運動會活動將會從下午一點開始，提供一下午的戶外體育活動，如沙袋競走、湯匙運蛋競賽、拔河以及八百公尺接力賽等等。運動會活動會一直持續到晚上的晚餐野餐。歡迎你們帶家人來共襄盛舉。如果你需要加訂餐盒，請在三月底之前告Sarah，好讓我們事先加訂。

★ 加訂餐盒份數

Michael	3
Jeremy	2
Lauren	2
Benjamin	1

【詞彙】
sack race 沙袋競走／
egg and spoon race
湯匙運蛋競賽／
tug of war 拔河比賽／
relay race 接力賽／
in advance 事先

Questions 77-79 refer to the following announcement and table.

M Can I have everyone's attention please? Our annual Company Sports Day has been scheduled this coming April. The Sports Day events will start from 13:00, providing an afternoon of outdoor sports activities, such as sack race, egg and spoon race, tug of war and 800-meter relay race and so on. The sports day events can continue into the evening with a picnic dinner. You are welcome to bring your family. If you need additional dinner boxes, please let Sarah know by the end of March so we can place an additional order in advance.

★ Additional order for Dinner Boxes

Michael	3
Jeremy	2
Lauren	2
Benjamin	1

這則宣布主要關於什麼？
(A) 公司週年慶
(B) 公司運動會
(C) 年度公司旅遊
(D) 部門月會

【類型】內容主題題型

【正解】(B)

77 What is this announcement mainly about?
(A) The company's anniversary celebration
(B) The company's sports day
(C) The annual company trip
(D) The department's monthly meeting

【解析】由這則宣布以annual Company Sports Day（年度公司運動會）為主軸做延伸，可知這是一則有關公司運動會的宣布，正解為(B)。

78 Which statement about the sports day events is correct?
(A) It's a morning event.
(B) It can continue to the evening.
(C) It's a staff-only activity.
(D) It's a quarterly event.

【解析】這則宣布中提到這個annual company sports day（年度公司運動會）will start from 13:00（下午一點開始），可知這是個一年一度的活動，將在下午進行，而且會一直continue to the evening（持續到晚上）；除此之外歡迎員工帶家人一起同樂。由以上關鍵字詞可知選項中只有(B)所述正確，故(B)為正解。

關於運動會活動哪項敘述正確？
(A) 它是個上午的活動。
(B) 它將持續到晚上。
(C) 它是只有員工能參加的活動。
(D) 它是季度的活動。

【類型】提問細節題型

【正解】(B)

---

79 Look at the table. Who will bring most people to the Sports Day?
(A) Michael
(B) Jeremy
(C) Lauren
(D) Benjamin

【解析】由登記加訂餐盒數量表看來，Michael登記加訂三個餐盒，可推測他將帶三位家人來參加運動會，是表格上看來帶最多人來參加的人，故正解為(A)。

請看表格。誰會帶最多人來參加運動會？
(A) Michael
(B) Jeremy
(C) Lauren
(D) Benjamin

【類型】圖表對照題型

【正解】(A)

女 哈囉，Carter先生。我是向日葵食品批發行的Nikki。我是打來跟您說您訂購的十五公斤米和十公斤黃豆已經在今天早上派送了，如果沒有意外的話，應該明天就會送到您的交貨地址。您可能會接到我們物流送貨司機的電話，向您確認您方便的時間。謝謝您選購我們的產品。希望能很快再為您服務，再見。

【詞彙】
wholesaler 批發商／
dispatch 派送／
logistics delivery driver
物流送貨司機

Questions 80-82 refer to the following message.

W Hello, Mr. Carter. This is Nikki from Sunflower Food Wholesaler. I'm calling to tell you that the 15 kilograms of rice and 10 kilograms of soybeans you ordered were dispatched this morning and should arrive to your delivery address no later than tomorrow if there's no accident. You may receive a phone call from our logistics delivery driver to confirm your convenient time. Thanks for choosing our products. Hope to serve you again soon. Bye.

說話者為什麼要打電話？
(A) 通知買家訂單狀態
(B) 要求產品目錄
(C) 延後一個好的會議
(D) 邀請一位客戶吃晚餐

【類型】內容主題題型

【正解】(A)

80 Why is the speaker calling?
(A) To notify a buyer of his order status
(B) To request a product catalogue
(C) To postpone a scheduled meeting
(D) To invite a client for dinner

【解析】由說話者在留言中告知對方訂購的物品已經完成派送，目前進入交貨狀態，且將於明天送達，可知這是一通通知買家訂單狀態的電話，正確答案為(A)。

81 Who most likely is the speaker?
(A) A bank clerk
(B) A restaurant manager
(C) A food wholesaler
(D) A school teacher

說話者最有可能是誰？
(A) 一位銀行行員
(B) 一家餐廳經理
(C) 一名食物批發商
(D) 一位學校老師

【解析】由說話者一開始便表明身份This is Nikki from Sunflower Food Wholesaler.（我是向日葵食品批發行的Nikki），可知說話者最有可能是一名食物批發商，故正解為(C)。

【類型】留言者身份題型

【正解】(C)

82 What will Mr. Carter get before the delivery arrives?
(A) A visit from the speaker
(B) A call from the delivery driver
(C) A letter from customer service
(D) An invitation to a tea party

Carter先生在貨寄到前會接到什麼？
(A) 說話者的拜訪
(B) 送貨司機的電話
(C) 客服人員的來信
(D) 一場茶會的邀請函

【解析】留言內容提到You may receive a phone call from our logistics delivery driver to confirm your convenient time.（您可能會接到物流司機跟您確認方便的時間的電話），可知Carter先生在收到貨之前可能會先接到物流司機的電話，正解為(B)。

【類型】提問細節題型

【正解】(B)

女　Jeff早，我是Jenny。我是打來確認你知道由於泰勒颱風的關係，所以公司今天不上班。因為這是緊急事件造成的休假，公司將不會扣這一天的薪水，但是我們要在年底之前將工作時數補齊。別忘了打個電話給Williams先生將你們的會議往後延。外面真的狂風暴雨的，所以平安地待在家裡就好。下週一見。

【詞彙】
make up 補上／
put off 延後

Questions 83-85 refer to the following talk.

W Good morning, Jeff, this is Jenny. I'm calling to make sure you know the office is not open for business today due to Typhoon Taylor. Because it's a day off due to emergency circumstances, the company will not take the pay off, but we are supposed to make up for the working hours by the end of this year. Don't forget to give Mr. Williams a call to put off your meeting. It's really stormy out there, so stay safe inside. See you next Monday.

這則留言的目的為何？
(A) 延後會議
(B) 訂外帶餐點
(C) 請求休一天假
(D) 傳遞一則訊息

【類型】內容主題題型

【詞彙】
pass on 傳遞、轉告

【正解】(D)

---

83 What's the purpose of this message?
(A) To put off a meeting
(B) To order takeout
(C) To ask for a day off
(D) To pass on a message

【解析】由留言內容可知說話者是要確認對方知道公司今天不上班的消息，選項(A)(B)(C)所述皆與留言內容不符，只有選項(D)表示「傳遞訊息」，即「傳達不用上班的訊息」是最符合內容的答案，故(D)為正解。

84 Why is the office closed today?
(A) Due to water shortage
(B) Due to a power failure
(C) Due to a typhoon
(D) Due to office renovation

公司今天為何關門？
(A) 由於缺水
(B) 由於停電
(C) 由於颱風
(D) 由於公司整修

【解析】由留言內容提到the office is not open for business today due to Typhoon Taylor（由於泰勒颱風的緣故，公司今天不開放營業），可知公司今天關門是因為颱風的關係，正解為(C)。

【類型】提問細節題型

【詞彙】
water shortage 缺水／
power failure 停電／
renovation 整修

【正解】(C)

---

85 What does the speaker remind the listener to do?
(A) Fill out the leave request form
(B) Put off the meeting with his client
(C) Ask someone to cover his position
(D) Take the laundry to the cleaners

說話者提醒聽話者要做什麼？
(A) 填休假申請單
(B) 延後他跟客戶的會面
(C) 請人幫他代理職務
(D) 把衣服拿去洗衣店

【解析】說話者在留言中提醒Don't forget to give Mr. Williams a call to put off your meeting （別忘了打電話給Williams先生將會議延後），雖然無法從留言中得知Williams先生的身份為何，但選項(B)確實為選項中最有可能的答案，故為正解。

【類型】提問細節題型

【詞彙】
cleaners 洗衣店

【正解】(B)

男　嗨，Ann。我是Gallia燈具行的Matt。謝謝你對我們的產品有興趣，但是很抱歉必須告訴您我們目前沒有可以符合您訂單的足夠存貨。您想要訂購的商品目前缺貨中，而且近期內我們並不會針對這項商品進行補貨。我們店裡還有很多其他的燈具可能適合您的需要。如果您願意的話，我可以親自送一本型錄過去給您。歡迎您在我們上班時間打0912345678這支電話跟我聯絡。

★ 訂單

顧客	電話	商品	數量
Ann Jordan	2123-4567	吸頂燈 ZR24566-GB	20

【詞彙】
in short supply 供貨不足／
replenish 補貨／
ceiling light 吸頂燈

Questions 86-88 refer to the following message and form.

M　Hi, Ann. This is Matt from Gallia Lighting Store. Thank you very much for your interest in our products, but I'm sorry to have to tell you that we don't have enough stock to fulfill your order at the moment. The item you wished to order is currently in short supply and we will not replenish this item any time soon. There are many other lights in our store that may suit your needs. If you'd like, I can send you a catalogue in person. Please feel free to contact me at 0912345678 anytime during our business hours.

★ Order Form

Customer	Phone	Item	Qty
Ann Jordan	2123-4567	Ceiling light ZR24566-GB	20

說話者為什麼要打電話？
(A) 確認一筆購買訂單
(B) 要求產品型錄
(C) 拒絕一筆購買訂單
(D) 取消與客戶的會議

【類型】內容主題題型

【正解】(C)

86 Why is the speaker calling?
　　(A) To confirm a purchase order
　　(B) To request a product catalogue
　　(C) To turn down a purchase order
　　(D) To cancel a meeting with a client

【解析】由留言內容可知說話者接到聽話者的訂單，但是說話者表示we don't have enough stock to fulfill your order（我們現在沒有可以符合您訂單的足夠存貨），可知他打電話的目的是要婉拒聽話者的訂單，正解為(C)。

87 What does the speaker wish to offer?
(A) A special discount
(B) The product catalogue
(C) A helping hand
(D) Free home delivery

【解析】由留言中男子表示If you'd like, I can send you a catalogue in person.（如果你願意的話，我可以親自送一本型錄過去給你），可知說話者希望能夠提供對方型錄，正解為(B)。

說話者希望能提供什麼？
(A) 一個特別折扣
(B) 產品型錄
(C) 協助支援
(D) 免費宅配

【類型】提問細節題型

【詞彙】
helping hand 幫忙、支援

【正解】(B)

---

88 Look at the form. What item is the store running short of?
(A) Wall lights
(B) Ceiling lights
(C) floor lamps
(D) Table lamps

【解析】說話者在留言中表示存貨不足以符合訂單需求，而訂單上訂購的商品為ceiling light（吸頂燈），可知這家店目前供貨不足的商品為吸頂燈，正解為(B)。

請看表格。這家店現在什麼商品供貨不足？
(A) 壁燈
(B) 吸頂燈
(C) 落地燈
(D) 桌燈

【類型】圖表對照題型

【詞彙】
run short of sth. 缺乏某物／
wall light 壁燈／
floor lamp 落地燈／
table lamp 桌燈

【正解】(B)

女 哈囉Jack嗎，我Lily啦。我今天早上太匆忙了，結果忘了把電費帳單帶出來。我昨天收到電力公司的催繳單，說我們一定要在今天前繳費，否則他們就會切斷我們的電。我們可能應該設定自動扣繳，如此一來就可以不用再煩惱紙本帳單的事。但是在那之前，可以請你今天上班路上順便到便利商店去繳個錢嗎？謝啦。

【詞彙】
electricity bill 電費帳單／
reminder notice 催繳單／
electricity company 電力公司／
shut off service 切斷服務／
automatic bill payments
自動扣款

Questions 89-91 refer to the following talk.

W Hello, Jack? Lily. I was in such a hurry this morning that I forgot to bring the electricity bill with me. I got a reminder notice from the electricity company yesterday, saying that we must make the payment by today or they will shut off our service. Maybe we should set up automatic bill payments so we can stop worrying about paper bills. But before that, would you please stop by the convenience store on your way to the office and pay the bill? Thank you.

說話者為何要打電話？
(A) 她忘了鎖門。
(B) 她把帳單留在家裡了。
(C) 她的車無法發動。
(D) 她覺得身體不舒服。

【類型】內容主題題型

【正解】(B)

89 Why is the speaker calling?
(A) She forgot to lock the door.
(B) She left the bills at home.
(C) Her car won't start.
(D) She feels under the weather.

【解析】由女子在電話中表示自己早上太急著出門所以forgot to bring the electricity bill（忘了帶電費帳單），選項(B)符合電話內容，故為正解。

90 What does the speaker ask the listener to do?
(A) Pay the bill
(B) Call the landlord
(C) Call the police
(D) Flush the toilet

【解析】由女子在電話最後表示please... pay the bill（請……繳帳單），可知正解為(A)。

說話者要求聽話者做什麼？
(A) 繳帳單
(B) 打電話給房東
(C) 報警
(D) 沖馬桶

【類型】提問細節題型

【詞彙】
landlord 房東／
flush 沖水

【正解】(A)

91 What does the speaker plan on doing?
(A) Getting an alarm system
(B) Setting up automatic payments
(C) Installing anti-theft security alarm
(D) Applying for leave without pay

【正解】(B)

【解析】由女子在電話中表示Maybe we should set up automatic bill payments...（也許我們應該設定自動扣繳……）可知她有設定自動扣繳功能的打算，答案為(B)。

說話者打算做什麼？
(A) 裝一個警報系統
(B) 設定自動扣款
(C) 安裝防盜安全警鈴
(D) 申請留職停薪

【類型】提問細節題型

【詞彙】
alarm system 警報系統／
anti-theft security alarm
防盜安全警鈴／
leave without pay 留職停薪

女　嘿，Max。我是打來跟你說我我得加班，因此今晚沒辦法回家吃晚餐。你可以加熱冷凍千層麵或是訂中餐外帶當晚餐。對了，我需要你拿垃圾出去丟。垃圾車會在七點半左右來。我們也有一些塑膠瓶和紙箱需要回收，不過我不確定回收車今天是不是會來。請你看一下廚房冰箱上的回收時間表。謝啦。愛你噢！

★

白松街收回收時間表	
星期一	下午七點三十分
星期二	無
星期三	下午四點
星期四	無
星期五	下午七點三十分
星期六與日	無

【詞彙】
lasagna 千層麵／
recycle 回收／
recycling truck 回收車

Questions 92-94 refer to the following message and schedule.

W　Hey, Max. I'm calling to tell you that I have to work overtime and therefore won't make it to dinner tonight. You can either reheat the frozen lasagna or order Chinese takeout for dinner. By the way, I need you to take out the garbage. The garbage truck will come around seven thirty. We also have some plastic bottles and paper boxes that need to be recycled, but I'm not sure whether the recycling truck will come today. Please check the recycling collection schedule on the kitchen fridge. Thanks. Love you.

★

Recycling collection for White Pine Street	
Monday	19:30 p.m.
Tuesday	NA
Wednesday	16:00 p.m.
Thursday	NA
Friday	19:30 p.m.
Saturday & Sunday	NA

*NA=Not Available

根據留言內容，哪一項敘述正確？
(A) 說話者會帶晚餐回家。
(B) 說話者不會回家吃晚餐。
(C) 說話者將會自己做晚餐。
(D) 說話者今天放一天假。

【類型】提問細節題型

【正解】(B)

92 According to the message, which statement is true?
(A) The speaker will bring dinner home.
(B) The speaker won't come home for dinner.
(C) The speaker will cook dinner by herself.
(D) The speaker is having a day off today.

【解析】由說話者表示won't make it to dinner（無法回家吃晚餐）可之選項(B)所述為最符合留言內容的答案，故為正解。由留言內容無法得知說話者將如何解決自己的晚餐，故選項(A)(C)皆不是最適當的選項。說話者表示自己要work overtime（加班），故選項(D)不需考慮。

93 What is the listener asked to do?
(A) Drive the speaker home
(B) Pick up the kids at school
(C) Take out the garbage
(D) Do the dishes

聽話者被要求做什麼事？
(A) 載說話者回家
(B) 接小孩放學
(C) 拿垃圾出去丟
(D) 洗碗

【類型】提問細節題型

【解析】由說話者在留言中表示I need you to take out the garbage（我需要你拿垃圾出去丟），可知她要求聽話者倒垃圾，答案為(C)。

【正解】(C)

94 Look at the schedule. How often does the recycling truck come?
(A) Once a week
(B) Twice a week
(C) Thrice a week
(D) Every other day

請看時間表。回收車多久來一次？
(A) 一星期一次
(B) 一星期兩次
(C) 一星期三次
(D) 兩天一次

【類型】圖表對照題型

【詞彙】
thrice 三次

【解析】由回收時間表顯示一星期中的星期一三五共三天會來收回收，可知回收車一星期會來三次，正解為(C)。thrice= three times（三次）。

【正解】(C)

男　好。我們現在來到市立美術
　　館。如果你不知道要從哪裡
　　開始，可以選擇參加焦點導
　　覽團或重點導覽團。免費的
　　20分鐘焦點導覽團是由志工
　　帶領，將會介紹不同區域的
　　館藏；重點導覽團由受過訓
　　練的導遊帶領，會帶你參觀
　　不同樓層的許多展覽館。這
　　導覽有九十分鐘，且一人要
　　收300元。你也可以在入口
　　處租借一台語音導覽幫你充
　　分利用這次參觀。

★

語音導覽	費用 （每人每天）
一般民眾	$150
12歲以下孩童	$100
二十人以上團體	$60
65歲以上老人	免費

Questions 95-97 refer to the following talk and table.

M OK. Here we are, the City Gallery. If you don't know where to start, you can either choose a spotlight tour or a highlights tour. The free 20-minute spotlight tour, led by volunteers, will introduce different areas of the collection; the highlights tour, led by trained guides, will visit a number of galleries on different floors. The tour will take about 90 minutes and it costs $300 per person. You can also rent an audio guide at the entrance to help you make the most of your visit.

★

Audio guide	fees (per person per day)
Regular	$150
Children under 12	$100
Groups of 20 or more	$60
Seniors over 65	Free

這篇談話的目的是什麼？
(A) 介紹館內不同的導覽團
(B) 請求聽話者捐錢
(C) 為這間美術館做介紹
(D) 要求聽話者遵守規則

【類型】內容主題題型

【詞彙】
donation 捐款

【正解】(A)

95 What is the purpose of this talk?
　　(A) To introduce different tours at the gallery
　　(B) To request the listeners to make a donation
　　(C) To make an introduction of the gallery
　　(D) To ask the listeners to follow the rules

【解析】由談話內容介紹了spotlight tour（焦點導覽）、
highlights tour（重點導覽）以及audio tour（語音導覽），可
知這篇談話的目的是在介紹館內不同的導覽團，正解為(A)。

96 According to the talk, which statement is true?
(A) The highlights tour is free.
(B) The spotlight tour is only 20 minutes.
(C) The audio guide is designed for adults only.
(D) The audio guide is not for rent.

【解析】由談話內容對各種導覽的介紹，可知spotlight tour（焦點導覽）只有20分鐘，且免費參加；highlights tour（重點導覽）有90分鐘但需要300元費用；語音導覽適合各種年齡層，且費用不同。選項中只有(B)所述正確，故為正解。

根據談話內容，哪一項敘述正確？
(A) 重點導覽是免費的。
(B) 焦點導覽只有二十分鐘。
(C) 語音導覽只為成人設計。
(D) 語音導覽是不能租借的。

【類型】提問細節題型

【詞彙】
for rent 供租用的

【正解】(B)

97 Look at the table. Who can use the audio guide for free?
(A) Regular visitors
(B) Children under 12
(C) Groups of 25
(D) Seniors aged 70

【解析】由語音導覽租借費用表看來，只有六十五歲以上的老人是可以免費使用的，故選項(D)為正解。

請看表格。誰可以免費使用語音導覽？
(A) 一般參觀民眾
(B) 十二歲以下孩童
(C) 二十五人的團體
(D) 七十歲的老人

【類型】圖表對照題型

【正解】(D)

男　瑪莉亞颱風之後，島嶼南方的蔬菜價格預計本週會出現飆漲。有些蔬菜的價格比起先前的價格幾乎漲了一倍。農業部表示問題不是出在蔬菜供應，而是出在用來運輸貨物的道路。有關單位表示菜價在道路再度能夠通行之後，便能立刻恢復正常。

★

蔬菜	現在價格 （每公斤）	先前價格 （每公斤）
高麗菜	$140-$150	$70
紅蘿蔔	$180	$100
芹菜	$180	$70
黃瓜	$50	$20

【詞彙】
spike up 上揚／
Department of Agriculture
農業部／authority 有關單位／
passable 可通行的

Questions 98-100 refer to the following talk and form.

M　The prices of vegetables coming from the southern island are expected to spike up this week after Typhoon Maria. Prices of some vegetables almost doubled from its previous price. The Department of Agriculture said the problem is not with the supply but with the roads being used to deliver the goods. The authorities said the prices of vegetables would immediately go back to normal as soon as the roads become passable again.

Vegetables	Current price (per kilo)	previous price (per kilo)
Cabbage	$140-$150	$70
Carrots	$180	$100
Celery	$180	$70
Cucumber	$50	$20

這篇新聞報導是有關什麼？
(A) 油價上漲
(B) 菜價上漲
(C) 房價崩盤
(D) 股市崩盤

【類型】內容主題題型

【詞彙】
price hike 價格上揚／
petro 汽油／
price crash 價格下跌／
stock market 股市

【正解】(B)

98 What is this news report about?
(A) Petrol price hike
(B) Vegetables price hike
(C) House price crash
(D) Stock market crash

【解析】由新聞一開始就表示The prices of vegetables... are expected to spike up（菜價……預計會飆漲），可知這是一則有關菜價上漲的新聞，正解為(B)。

99 According to the report, what is the main cause of the price hike?
(A) The typhoon
(B) The flood
(C) The blizzard
(D) The impassable roads

根據報導，價格飆漲的主要原因是什麼？
(A) 颱風
(B) 水災
(C) 暴風雪
(D) 不能通行的道路

【解析】由新聞報導中提到the problem is ... with the roads being used to deliver the goods（問題是跟用來運送貨品的道路有關），而且一旦the roads become passable again（道路再度可以通行），菜價就會立刻恢復正常，可知菜價飆漲的原因主要是「道路目前無法通行」，故正解為(D)。

【類型】提問細節題型

【詞彙】
flood 水災／blizzard 暴風雪／impassable 不能通行的

【正解】(D)

---

100 Look at the table. Which vegetable is twice as expensive?
(A) Cabbage
(B) Carrots
(C) Celery
(D) Cucumbers

請看表格。哪樣蔬菜貴了兩倍？
(A) 高麗菜
(B) 紅蘿蔔
(C) 芹菜
(D) 黃瓜

【解析】由表格上比較菜價上漲前及上漲後的價格，高麗菜原本每公斤70元，飆漲後變成每公斤140-150元，可知高麗菜菜價貴了兩倍，故正解為(A)。

【類型】圖表對照題型

【詞彙】
twice as expensive 貴兩倍

【正解】(A)

原來如此 系列 **E177**

TOEIC新多益考試金色證書
一擊必殺－聽力全真模擬試題

提前把握新制多益聽力題，正式上場不緊張！

作　　者	李宇凡、蔡文宜◎合著
顧　　問	曾文旭
總 編 輯	王毓芳
編輯統籌	耿文國、黃璽宇
主　　編	吳靜宜
執行編輯	黃筠婷
美術編輯	王桂芳、張嘉容
行銷企劃	姜怡安
法律顧問	北辰著作權事務所　蕭雄淋律師、嚴裕欽律師

初　　版	2018年01月
出　　版	捷徑文化出版事業有限公司
電　　話	（02）2752-5618
傳　　真	（02）2752-5619
地　　址	106 台北市大安區忠孝東路四段250號11樓-1

定　　價	新台幣599元／港幣200元
產品內容	1書+1MP3

總 經 銷	采舍國際有限公司
地　　址	235 新北市中和區中山路二段366巷10號3樓
電　　話	（02）8245-8786
傳　　真	（02）8245-8718

港澳地區總經銷	和平圖書有限公司
地　　址	香港柴灣嘉業街12號百樂門大廈17樓
電　　話	（852）2804-6687
傳　　真	（852）2804-6409

本書圖片由作者、Shutterstock 提供

捷徑 Book站

現在就上臉書（FACEBOOK）「捷徑BOOK站」並按讚加入粉絲團，
就可享每月不定期新書資訊和粉絲專享小禮物喔！

http://www.facebook.com/royalroadbooks
讀者來函：**royalroadbooks@gmail.com**

國家圖書館出版品預行編目資料

TOEIC新多益考試金色證書一擊必殺－聽力全
真模擬試題 / 李宇凡、蔡文宜合著. -- 初版.
-- 臺北市：捷徑文化, 2018.01
　面；　公分（原來如此：E177）

ISBN 978-957-8904-05-7（平裝）

多益測驗

805.1895　　　　　　　　　　　106023627